Eldridge Parker woke up gradually. He was in a chair, in a room with three large, bearlike creatures watching him.

"I am going to tell you where you are, first," said one. "You're on a world roughly similar to your own, but many . . ." he hesitated.

"Light-years," said another of the aliens.

"Many light-years distant from your home. Briefly, there is a race that has three times broken out to overrun this mapped area of our galaxy and dominate other civilized cultures—until some inherent weakness caused the advance to die out. In each case, though the home planet of the race was destroyed, unknown seed communities remained to furnish the material for a new advance thousands of your years later. That race," said the academician, "is your own."

Eldridge watched the other without moving.

"There *must* be something more in you, some genius, some capability above the normal, to account for the fantastic nature of your race's previous successes. But our legends say only—*Danger, Human! Do not touch*—and we find nothing in you to justify the warning."

Another alien spoke. "A joint meeting recommended that we pick up one specimen for intensive observation. You were the one chosen. This will be your home from now on. We will keep you under observation. We hope to influence you to search for the solution yourself."

"And if I find it—what?" cried Eldridge.

"Then," said the commander, "we will deal with you in the kindest manner permitted. It may be even possible to return you to your home world. At the very least, we can see to it that you are quickly and painlessly destroyed. . . ."

THE
HUMAN EDGE

GORDON R. DICKSON
selected by Hank Davis

THE HUMAN EDGE

"Danger—Human," first published in *Astounding Science Fiction*, December 1957, © 1957 by Street & Smith Publications, Inc. "Sleight of Wit," first published in *Analog*, December 1961, © 1961 by Street & Smith Publications, Inc. "In the Bone," first published in *IF: Worlds of Science Fiction*, October 1966, © 1966 by Galaxy Publishing Corporation. "3-Part Puzzle," first published in *Analog*, June 1962, © 1962 by the Condé Nast Publications, Inc. "An Ounce of Emotion," first published in *IF: Worlds of Science Fiction*, October, 1965, © 1965 by Galaxy Publishing Corporation. "Brother Charlie," first published in *The Magazine of Fantasy and Science Fiction*, July 1958, © 1958 by Mercury Press, Inc. "The Game of Five," first published in *The Magazine of Fantasy and Science Fiction*, April 1960, © 1960 by Mercury Press, Inc. "Tiger Green," first published in *IF: Worlds of Science Fiction*, November 1965, © 1965 by Galaxy Publishing Corporation. "The Hard Way," first published in *Analog*, January 1963, © 1963 by the Condé Nast Publications, Inc. "Jackal's Meal," first published in *Analog*, June 1969, © 1969 by the Condé Nast Publications, Inc. "On Messenger Mountain," first published in *Worlds of Tomorrow*, June 1964, © 1964 by Galaxy Publishing Corporation. "The Catch," first published in *Astounding Science Fiction*, April 1959, © 1959 by Street & Smith Publications, Inc.

A Baen Book

Baen Publishing Enterprises
P.O. Box 1403
Riverdale, NY 10471
www.baen.com

ISBN: 0-7434-7174-1

Cover art by David Mattingly

First printing, December 2003

Distributed by Simon & Schuster
1230 Avenue of the Americas
New York, NY 10020

Typeset by Bell Road Press, Sherwood, OR
Produced by Windhaven Press, Auburn, NH
Printed in the United States of America

CONTENTS

Dedicating a collection of another person's work might seem presumptuous, particularly when that person is no longer around to give an opinion. However, Gordon R. Dickson was a strong supporter of space exploration, and I recall when, at a Nebula Awards ceremony in the early 1970s, he stood up to announce the formation of a loose organization of sf writers called, informally, Friends of the Space Program. I think he would approve of this dedication.

For

Michael P. Anderson
Kalpana Chawla
Laurel Clark
Rick D. Husband
William C. McCool
Ilan Ramon

Pioneers on the Star Road

INTRODUCTION:
THE DICKSON EDGE

Wrong!

I know what you're thinking. . . .

(And it's not "Do I feel lucky?" If you're looking at this page, you have a hefty hunk of first-rate science fiction by Gordon R. Dickson in hand, so you *are* lucky, regardless of what you may feel. I wouldn't recommend buying a lottery ticket, however—lucking into a Dickson book may have used up your quota of good fortune for the day. . . .)

You're thinking, *these are twelve stories by the same author, all on the same subject, so there's liable to be a certain similarity from one story to the next. . . .*

Actually you are right about there being a similarity from one story to the next, except that the similarity is that all the stories are well-crafted, ingeniously plotted, show a wide range of tone (sometimes amusing, sometimes grim, sometimes a bit of both), and never fail to entertain.

Or, to put it more succinctly, the certain similarity is that these stories are all by the same grand master: Gordon R. Dickson.

Why should anyone want to listen to Bach's Goldberg Variations, after all? I mean, two sides of an LP—if you remember LPs—or an entire CD taken up by thirty (or thirty-one, if you count the reprise of the aria) variations on one tune, and played on one instrument, either harpsichord or piano . . . how much variety can there be in that, right?

I'm not going to claim that Gordon R. Dickson was in Bach's league (but then, who in at least the last 100 years has been?), but as with Bach, you are dealing with a high order of talent and craftsmanship. And Dickson can ring ingenious and fresh changes on one theme.

The theme: when human meets alien, even a more technologically advanced alien, said alien had better not get too cocky. Humans can be very tricky when they need to be, giving them an edge—the human edge.

James Blish, reviewing a Dickson novel several years ago, commented that while many critics lumped Dickson and another sf master, Poul Anderson, together, there was a notable difference. Anderson's characters might prevail, or they might fail in spite of their valiant struggle, in stories "written from a floor of brave gloom" (as I recall Blish putting it), but Dickson's characters struggled *and* prevailed. Dickson's universe was neither impersonal nor hostile, and the human spirit would win, Blish wrote approvingly.

I recall several Dickson stories (but no novels) with downer endings, so he definitely wasn't writing from the Pollyanna side of the Force. (I also recall quite a few Blish stories that I consider gloomy, so he wasn't, either.) But on the whole, in Dickson's universe, man not only endures, but prevails, to crib a line from Faulkner. (Was *he* in Bach's league? You decide.)

Algis Budrys once stated that a sure-fire recipe for being thought profound was frequently to reiterate that the universe is very big, and insignificant humans are very, very small. After noting that though the instruments do show that the universe *is* very big, that doesn't necessarily say anything about humans. "They are our instruments, after all," he added, "and we somehow managed to build them." He was writing about a writer whom he praised for having "wider horizons" than other writers who were stuck in the big universe/puny humans mode. And while the writer wasn't Gordon R. Dickson, the same description fits his work very well.

So here Dickson is, spinning virtuoso variations on a theme, in stories written years apart, appearing in many different publications, sometimes with humor, sometimes with grim seriousness, and always with wide horizons; not to mention a towering talent for entertaining.

And you definitely *will* be entertained.

I *told* you that you should feel lucky, didn't I?

—Hank Davis

My appreciative thanks to Jim Baen, who had the idea for a Dickson collection on this theme, gave it its title, and suggested the story "Danger: Human" as the opening shot.

For a curtain raiser, this one takes the viewpoint of the extraterrestrials, a sympathetic bunch of regular guys, who capture a strange monster called a "human" and make the mistake of experimenting on him. There may be things that extraterrestrials Were Not Meant to Know. . . .

DANGER—HUMAN

The spaceboat came down in the silence of perfect working order—down through the cool, dark night of a New Hampshire late spring. There was hardly any moon and the path emerging from the clump of conifers and snaking its way across the dim pasture looked like a long strip of pale cloth, carelessly dropped and forgotten there.

The two aliens checked the boat and stopped it, hovering, some fifty feet above the pasture, and all but invisible against the low-lying clouds. Then they set themselves to wait, their woolly, bearlike forms settled on haunches, their uniform belts glinting a little in the shielded light from the instrument panel, talking now and then in desultory murmurs.

"It's not a bad place," said the one of junior rank, looking down at the earth below.

"Why should it be?" answered the senior.

The junior did not answer. He shifted on his haunches.

"The babies are due soon," he said. "I just got a message."

"How many?" asked the senior.

"Three—the doctor thinks. That's not bad for a first birthing."

"My wife only had two."

"I know. You told me."

They fell silent for a few seconds. The spaceboat rocked almost imperceptibly in the waters of night.

"Look—" said the junior, suddenly. "Here it comes, right on schedule."

The senior glanced overside. Down below, a tall, dark form had emerged from the trees and was coming put along the path. A little beam of light shone before him, terminating in a blob of illumination that danced along the path ahead, lighting his way. The senior stiffened.

"Take controls," he said. The casualness had gone out of his voice. It had become crisp, impersonal.

"Controls," answered the other, in the same emotionless voice.

"Take her down."

"Down it is."

The spaceboat dropped groundward. There was an odd sort of soundless, lightless explosion—it was as if concussive wave had passed, robbed of all effects but one. The figure dropped, the light rolling from its grasp and losing its glow in a tangle of short grass. The spaceboat landed and the two aliens got out.

In the dark night they loomed furrily above the still figure. It was that of a lean, dark man in his early thirties, dressed in clean, much-washed corduroy pants and checkered wool lumberjack shirt. He was unconscious, but breathing slowly, deeply and easily.

"I'll take it up by the head, here," said the senior. "You take the other end. Got it? Lift! Now, carry it into the boat."

The junior backed away, up through the spaceboat's open lock, grunting a little with the awkwardness of his burden.

"It feels slimy," he said.

"Nonsense!" said the senior. "That's your imagination."

Eldridge Timothy Parker drifted in that dreamy limbo between awakeness and full sleep. He found himself contemplating his own name.

Eldridge Timothy Parker. Eldridgetimothyparker. Eldridge TIMOTHYparker. ELdrlDGEtiMOthy PARKer——

There was a hardness under his back, the back on which he was lying—and a coolness. His flaccid right hand turned flat, feeling. It felt like steel beneath him. Metal? He tried to sit up and bumped his forehead against a ceiling a few inches overhead. He blinked his eyes in the darkness—

Darkness?

He flung out his hands, searching, feeling terror leap up inside him. His knuckles bruised against walls to right and left. Frantic, his groping fingers felt out, around and about him. He was walled in, he was surrounded, he was enclosed.

Completely.

Like in a coffin.

Buried—

He began to scream. . . .

Much later, when he awoke again, he was in a strange place that seemed to have no walls, but many instruments. He floated in the center of mechanisms that passed and re-passed about him, touching, probing, turning. He felt touches of heat and cold. Strange hums and notes of various pitches came and went. He felt voices questioning him.

Who are you?

"Eldridge Parker—Eldridge Timothy Parker—"

What are you?

"I'm Eldridge Parker—"

Tell about yourself.

"Tell what? What?"

Tell about yourself.

"What? What do you want to know? What—"

Tell about. . . .

"But I—"

Tell. . . .

. . . well, i suppose i was pretty much like any of the kids around our town . . . i was a pretty good shot and i won the fifth grade seventy-five yard dash . . . i played hockey, too . . . pretty cold weather up around our parts, you know, the air used to smell strange it was so cold winter mornings in January when you first stepped out of doors . . . it is good, open country, new england, and there were lots of smells . . . there were pine smells and grass smells and i remember especially the kitchen smells . . . and then, too, there was the way the oak benches in church used to smell on Sunday when you knelt with your nose right next to the back of the pew ahead. . . .

. . . the fishing up our parts is good too . . . i liked to fish but i never wasted time on weekdays . . . we were presbyterians, you know, and my father had the farm, but he also had money invested in land around the country . . . we have never been badly off but i would have liked a motor-scooter. . . .

. . . no i did not never hate the germans, at least i

did not think i ever did, of course though i was over in europe i never really had it bad, combat, i mean . . . i was in a motor pool with the raw smell of gasoline, i like to work with my hands, and it was not like being in the infantry. . . .

. . . i have as good right to speak up to the town council as any man . . . i do not believe in pushing but if they push me i am going to push right back . . . nor it isn't any man's business what i voted last election no more than my bank balance . . . but i have got as good as right to a say in town doings as if i was the biggest landholder among them. . . .

. . . i did not go to college because it was not necessary . . . too much education can make a fool of any man, i told my father, and i know when i have had enough . . . i am a farmer and will always be a farmer and i will do my own studying as things come up without taking out a pure waste of four years to hang a piece of paper on the wall. . . .

. . . of course i know about the atom bomb, but i am no scientist and no need to be one, no more than i need to be a veterinarian . . . i elect the men that hire the men that need to know those things and the men that i elect will hear from me johnny-quick if things do not go to my liking. . . .

. . . as to why i never married, that is none of your business . . . as it happens, i was never at ease with women much, though there were a couple of times, and i still may if jeanie lind. . . .

. . . i believe in god and the united states of america. . . .

He woke up gradually. He was in a room that might have been any office, except the furniture was different. That is, there was a box with doors on it that might have been a filing cabinet and a table that looked like a desk in spite of the single thin rod underneath the center that supported it. However, there were no chairs—only small, flat cushions, on which three large woolly, bearlike creatures were sitting and watching him in silence.

He himself, he found, was in a chair, though.

As soon as they saw his eyes were open, they turned away from him and began to talk among themselves. Eldridge Parker shook his head and blinked his eyes, and would have blinked his ears if that had been possible. For the sounds the creatures were making were like nothing he had ever heard before; and yet he understood everything they were saying. It was an odd sensation, like a double-image earwise, for he heard the strange mouth-noises just as they came out and then something in his head twisted them around and made them into perfectly understandable English.

Nor was that all. For, as he sat listening to the creatures talk, he began to get the same double image in another way. That is, he still saw the bearlike creature behind the desk as the weird sort of animal he was, while out of the sound of his voice, or from something else, there gradually built up in Eldridge's mind a picture of a thin, rather harassed-looking gray-haired man in something resembling a uniform, but at the same time not quite a uniform. It was the sort of effect an army general might get if he wore his stars and a Sam Browne belt over a civilian double-breasted suit. Similarly, the other creature sitting facing the one behind the desk, at the desk's side, was a young and black-haired man with something of the laboratory about him, and the creature further back, seated almost against the wall, was neither soldier nor scientist, but a heavy older man with a sort of book-won wisdom in him.

"You see, commander," the young one with the

black-haired image was saying, "perfectly restored. At least on the physical and mental levels."

"Good, doctor, good," the outlandish syllables from the one behind the desk translated themselves in Eldridge's head. "And you say it . . . he, I should say . . . will be able to understand?"

"Certainly, sir," said the doctor-psychologist—whatever-he-was. "Identification is absolute—"

"But I mean comprehend—encompass—" The creature behind the desk moved one paw slightly. "Follow what we tell him—"

The doctor turned his ursinoid head toward the third member of the group. This one spoke slowly, in a deeper voice.

"The culture allows. Certainly."

The one behind the desk bowed slightly to the oldest one.

"Certainly, Academician, certainly."

They then fell silent, all looking back at Eldridge, who returned their gaze with equivalent interest. There was something unnatural about the whole proceeding. Both sides were regarding the other with the completely blunt and unshielded curiosity given to freaks.

The silence stretched out. It became tinged with a certain embarrassment. Gradually a mutual recognition arose that no one really wanted to be the first to address an alien being directly.

"It . . . he is comfortable?" asked the commander, turning once more to the doctor.

"I should say so," replied the doctor, slowly. "As far as we know. . . ."

Turning back to Eldridge, the commander said, "Eldridge-timothyparker, I suppose you wonder where you are?"

Caution and habit put a clamp on Eldridge's tongue.

He hesitated about answering so long that the commander turned in distress to the doctor, who reassured him with a slight movement of the head.

"Well, speak up," said the commander, "we'll be able to understand you, just as you're able to understand us. Nothing's going to hurt you; and anything you say won't have the slightest effect on your . . . er . . . situation."

He paused again, looking at Eldridge for a comment. Eldridge still held his silence, but one of his hands unconsciously made a short, fumbling motion at his breast pocket.

"My pipe—" said Eldridge.

The three looked at each other. They looked back at Eldridge.

"We have it," said the doctor. "After a while we may give it back to you. For now . . . we cannot allow . . . it would not suit us."

"Smoke bother you?" said Eldridge, with a touch of his native canniness.

"It does not bother us. It is . . . merely . . . distasteful," said the commander. "Let's get on. I'm going to tell you where you are, first. You're on a world roughly similar to your own, but many . . ." he hesitated, looking at the academician.

"Light-years," supplemented the deep voice. " . . . Light-years in terms of what a year means to you," went on the commander, with growing briskness. "Many light-years distant from your home. We didn't bring you here because of any personal . . . dislike . . . or enmity for you; but for. . . ."

"Observation," supplied the doctor. The commander turned and bowed slightly to him, and was bowed back at in return.

" . . . Observation," went on the commander. "Now, do you understand what I've told you so far?"

"I'm listening," said Eldridge.

"Very well," said the commander. "I will go on.
There is something about your people that we are very
anxious to discover. We have been, and intend to
continue, studying you to find it out. So far—I will
admit quite frankly and freely—we have not found it;
and the concensus among our best minds is that you,
yourself, do not know what it is. Accordingly, we have
hopes of . . . causing . . . you to discover it for yourself.
And for us."

"Hey. . . ." breathed Eldridge.

"Oh, you will be well treated. I assure you," said the
commander, hurriedly. "You have been well treated. You
have been . . . but you did not know . . . I mean you did
not feel—"

"Can you remember any discomfort since we picked
you up?" asked the doctor, leaning forward.

"Depends what you mean—"

"And you will feel none." The doctor turned to the
commander. "Perhaps I'm getting ahead of myself?"

"Perhaps," said the commander. He bowed and
turned back to Eldridge. "To explain—we hope you will
discover our answer for it. We're only going to put you
in a position to work on it. Therefore, we've decided
to tell you everything. First—the problem. Academician?"

The oldest one bowed. His deep voice made the
room ring oddly.

"If you will look this way," he said. Eldridge turned
his head. The other raised one paw and the wall beside
him dissolved into a maze of lines and points. "Do you
know what this is?"

"No," said Eldridge.

"It is," rumbled the one called the academician, "a
map of the known universe. You lack the training to
read it in four dimensions, as it should be read. No
matter. You will take my word for it . . . it is a map.

A map covering hundreds of thousands of your light-years and millions of your years."

He looked at Eldridge, who said nothing.

"To go on, then. What we know of your race is based upon two sources of information. History. And Legend. The history is sketchy. It rests on archaeological discoveries for the most part. The legend is even sketchier and—fantastic."

He paused again. Still Eldridge guarded his tongue.

"Briefly, there is a race that has three times broken out to overrun this mapped area of our galaxy and dominate other civilized cultures—until some inherent lack or weakness in the individual caused the component parts of this advance to die out. The periods of these outbreaks has always been disastrous for the dominated cultures and uniformly without benefit to the race I am talking about. In the case of each outbreak, though the home planet was destroyed and all known remnants of the advancing race hunted out, unknown seed communities remained to furnish the material for a new advance some thousands of years later. That race," said the academician, and coughed—or at least made some kind of noise in his throat, "is your own."

Eldridge watched the other carefully and without moving.

"We see your race, therefore," went on the academician, and Eldridge received the mental impression of an elderly man putting the tips of his ringers together judiciously, "as one with great or overwhelming natural talents, but unfortunately also with one great natural flaw. This flaw seems to be a desire—almost a need—to acquire and possess things. To reach out, encompass, and absorb. It is not," shrugged the academician, "a unique trait. Other races have it—

but not to such an extent that it makes them a threat to their co-existing cultures. Yet, this in itself is not the real problem. If it was a simple matter of rapacity, a combination of other races should be able to contain your people. There is a natural inevitable balance of that sort continually at work in the galaxy. No," said the academician and paused, looking at the commander.

"Go on. Go on," said the commander. The academician bowed.

"No, it is not that simple. As a guide to what remains, we have only the legend, made anew and reinforced after each outward sweep of you people. We know that there must be something more than we have found—and we have studied you carefully, both your home world and now you, personally. There *must* be something more in you, some genius, some capability above the normal, to account for the fantastic nature of your race's previous successes. But the legend says only —*Danger, Human! High Explosive. Do not touch*—and we find nothing in you to justify the warning."

He sighed. Or at least Eldridge received a sudden, unexpected intimation of deep weariness.

"Because of a number of factors—too numerous to go into and most of them not understandable to you— it is our race which must deal with this problem for the rest of the galaxy. What can we do? We dare not leave you be until you grow strong and come out once more. And the legend expressly warns us against touching you in any way. So we have chosen to pick one— but I intrude upon your field, doctor."

The two of them exchanged bows. The doctor took up the talk speaking briskly and entirely to Eldridge.

"A joint meeting of those of us best suited to consider the situation recommended that we pick up

one specimen for intensive observation. For reasons
of availability, you were the one chosen. Following
your return under drugs to this planet, you were
thoroughly examined, by the best of medical tech-
niques, both mentally and physically. I will not go
into detail, since we have no wish to depress you
unduly. I merely want to impress on you the fact
that we found nothing. Nothing. No unusual power
or ability of any sort, such as history shows you to
have had and legend hints at. I mention this because
of the further course of action we have decided to
take. Commander?"

The being behind the desk got to his hind feet. The
other two rose.

"You will come with us," said the commander.

Herded by them, Eldridge went out through the
room's door into brilliant sunlight and across a small
stretch of something like concrete to a stubby egg-
shaped craft with ridiculous little wings.

"Inside," said the commander. They got in. The
commander squatted before a bank of instruments,
manipulated a simple sticklike control, and after a
moment the ship took to the air. They flew for perhaps half an hour, with Eldridge wishing he was in a
position to see out one of the high windows, then
landed at a field apparently literally hacked out of a
small forest of mountains.

Crossing this field on foot, Eldridge got a glimpse
of some truly huge ships, as well as a number of
smaller ones such as the one in which he had arrived.
Numbers of the furry aliens moved about, none with
any great air of hurry, but all with purposefulness.
There was a sudden, single, thunderous sound that was
gone almost before the ear could register it; and
Eldridge, who had ducked instinctively, looked up again
to see one of the huge ships falling—there is no other

word for it—skyward with such unbelievable rapidity it was out of sight in seconds.

The four of them came at last to a shallow, open trench in the stuff which made the field surface. It was less than a foot wide and they stepped across it with ease. But once they had crossed it, Eldridge noticed a difference. In the five hundred yard square enclosed by the trench—for it turned at right angles off to his right and to his left—there was an air of tightly-established desertedness, as of some highly restricted area, and the rectangular concrete-looking building that occupied the square's very center glittered unoccupied in the clear light.

They marched to the door of this building and it opened without any of them touching it. Inside was perhaps twenty feet of floor, stretching inward as a run inside the walls. Then a sort of moat—Eldridge could not see its depth—filled with a dark fluid with a faint, sharp odor. This was perhaps another twenty feet wide and enclosed a small, flat island perhaps fifteen feet by fifteen feet, almost wholly taken up by a cage whose walls and ceiling appeared to be made of metal bars as thick as a man's thumb and spaced about six inches apart. Two more of the aliens, wearing a sort of harness and holding a short, black tube apiece, stood on the ledge of the outer rim. A temporary bridge had been laid across the moat, protruding through the open door of the cage.

They all went across the bridge and into the cage. There, standing around rather like a board of directors viewing an addition to the company plant, they faced Eldridge; and the commander spoke.

"This will be your home from now on," he said. He indicated the cot, the human-type chair and the other items furnishing the cage. "It's as comfortable as we can make it."

"Why?" burst out Eldridge, suddenly. "Why're you locking me up here? Why—"

"In our attempt to solve the problem that still exists," interrupted the doctor, smoothly, "we can do nothing more than keep you under observation and hope that time will work with us. Also, we hope to influence you to search for the solution, yourself."

"And if I find it—what?" cried Eldridge.

"Then," said the commander, "we will deal with you in the kindest manner that the solution permits. It may be even possible to return you to your own world. At the very least, once you are no longer needed, we can see to it that you are quickly and painlessly destroyed."

Eldridge felt his insides twist within him.

"Kill me?" he choked. "You think that's going to make me help you? The hope of getting killed?"

They looked at him almost compassionately.

"You may find," said the doctor, "that death may be something you will want very much, only for the purpose of putting a close to a life you've become weary of. Look,"—he gestured around him—"you are locked up beyond any chance of ever escaping. This cage will be illuminated night and day; and you will be locked in it. When we leave, the bridge will be withdrawn, and the only thing crossing that moat— which is filled with acid—will be a mechanical arm which will extend across and through a small opening to bring you food twice a day. Beyond the moat, there will be two armed guards on duty at all times, but even they cannot open the door to this building. That is opened by remote control from outside, only after the operator has checked on his vision screen to make sure all is as it should be inside here."

He gestured through the bars, across the moat and through a window in the outer wall.

"Look out there," he said.

Eldridge looked. Out beyond, and surrounding the building the shallow trench no longer lay still and empty under the sun. It now spouted a vertical wall of flickering, weaving distortion, like a barrier of heat waves.

"That is our final defense, the ultimate in destructiveness that our science provides us—it would literally burn you to nothingness, if you touch it. It will be turned off only for seconds, and with elaborate precautions, to let guards in, or out."

Eldridge looked back in, to see them all watching him.

"We do this," said the doctor, "not only because we may discover you to be more dangerous than you seem, but to impress you with your helplessness so that you may be more ready to help *us*. Here you are, and here you will stay."

"And you think," demanded Eldridge hoarsely, "that this's all going to make me want to help you?"

"Yes," said the doctor, "because there's one thing more that enters into the situation. You were literally taken apart physically, after your capture; and as literally put back together again. We are advanced in the organic field, and certain things are true of all life forms. I supervised the work on you, myself. You will find that you are, for all practical purposes, immortal and irretrievably sane. This will be your home forever, and you will find that neither death nor insanity will provide you a way of escape."

They turned and filed out. From some remote control, the cage door was swung shut. He heard it click and lock. The bridge was withdrawn from the moat. A screen lit up and a woolly face surveyed the building's interior.

The building's door opened. They went out; and the guards took up their patrol, around the rim in opposite directions, keeping their eyes on Eldridge and their weapons ready in their hands. The building's door closed again. Outside, the flickering wall blinked out for a second and then returned again.

The silence of a warm, summer, mountain afternoon descended upon the building. The footsteps of the guards made shuffling noises on their path around the rim. The bars enclosed him.

Eldridge stood still, holding the bars in both hands and looking out.

He could not believe it.

He could not believe it as the days piled up into weeks, and the weeks into months. But as the seasons shifted and the year came around to a new year, the realities of his situation began to soak into him like water into a length of dock piling. For outside, Time could be seen at its visible and regular motion; but in his prison, there was no Time.

Always, the lights burned overhead, always the guards paced about him. Always the barrier burned beyond the building, the meals came swinging in on the end of a long metal arm extended over the moat and through a small hatchway which opened automatically as the arm approached; regularly, twice weekly, the doctor came and checked him over, briefly, impersonally—and went out again with the changing of the guard.

He felt the unbearableness of his situation, like a hand winding tighter and tighter day by day the spring of tension within him. He took to pacing feverishly up and down the cage. He went back and forth, back and forth, until the room swam. He lay awake nights, staring at the endless glow of illumination from the ceiling. He rose to pace again.

The doctor came and examined him. He talked to Eldridge, but Eldridge would not answer. Finally there

came a day when everything split wide open and he
began to howl and bang on the bars. The guards were
frightened and called the doctor. The doctor came, and
with two others, entered the cage and strapped him
down. They did something odd that hurt at the back
of his neck and he passed out.

When he opened his eyes again, the first thing he
saw was the doctor's woolly face, looking down at him—
he had learned to recognize that countenance in the
same way a sheep-herder eventually comes to recognize individual sheep in his flock. Eldridge felt very
weak, but calm.

"You tried hard—" said the doctor. "But you see, you
didn't make it. There's no way out *that* way for you."

Eldridge smiled.

"Stop that!" said the doctor sharply. "You aren't
fooling us. We know you're perfectly rational."

Eldridge continued to smile.

"What do you think you're doing?" demanded the
doctor. Eldridge looked happily up at him.

"I'm going home," he said.

"I'm sorry," said the doctor. "You don't convince me."
He turned and left. Eldridge turned over on his side and
dropped off into the first good sleep he'd had in months.

In spite of himself, however, the doctor was worried. He had the guards doubled, but nothing happened. The days slipped into weeks again and nothing
happened. Eldridge was apparently fully recovered. He
still spent a great deal of time walking up and down
his cage and grasping the bars as if to pull them out
of the way before him—but the frenzy of his earlier
pacing was gone. He had also moved his cot over next
to the small, two-foot square hatch that opened to
admit the mechanical arm bearing his meals, and would
lie there, with his face pressed against it, waiting for

the food to be delivered. The doctor felt uneasy, and spoke to the commander privately about it.

"Well," said the commander, "just what is it you suspect?"

"I don't know," confessed the doctor. "It's just that I see him more frequently than any of us. Perhaps I've become sensitized—but he bothers me."

"Bothers you?"

"Frightens me, perhaps. I wonder if we've taken the right way with him."

"We took the only way." The commander made the little gesture and sound that was his race's equivalent of a sigh. "We must have data. What do you do when you run across a possibly dangerous virus, doctor? You isolate it—for study, until you know. It is not possible, and too risky to try to study his race at close hand, so we study him. That's all we're doing. You lose objectivity, doctor. Would you like to take a short vacation?"

"No," said the doctor, slowly. "No. But he frightens me."

Still, time went on and nothing happened. Eldridge paced his cage and lay on his cot, face pressed to the bars of the hatch, and staring at the outside world. Another year passed; and another. The double guards were withdrawn. The doctor came reluctantly to the conclusion that the human had at last accepted the fact of his confinement and felt growing within him that normal sort of sympathy that feeds on familiarity. He tried to talk to Eldridge on his regularly scheduled visits, but Eldridge showed little interest in conversation. He lay on the cot watching the doctor as the doctor examined him, with something in his eyes as if he looked on from some distant place in which all decisions were already made and finished.

"You're as healthy as ever," said the doctor,

concluding his examination. He regarded Eldridge. "I wish you would, though—" He broke off. "We aren't a cruel people, you know. We don't like the necessity that makes us do this."

He paused. Eldridge considered him without stirring.

"If you'd accept that fact," said the doctor, "I'm sure you'd make it easier on yourself. Possibly our figures of speech have given you a false impression. We said you are immortal. Well, of course, that's not true. Only practically speaking, are you immortal. You are now capable of living a very, very, very long time. That's all."

He paused again. After a moment of waiting, he went on.

"Just the same way, this business isn't really intended to go on for eternity. By its very nature, of course, it can't. Even races have a finite lifetime. But even that would be too long. No, it's just a matter of a long time as you might live it. Eventually, everything must come to a conclusion—that's inevitable."

Eldridge still did not speak. The doctor sighed.

"Is there anything you'd like?" he said. "We'd like to make this as little unpleasant as possible. Anything we can give you?"

Eldridge opened his mouth.

"Give me a boat," he said. "I want a fishing rod. I want a bottle of applejack."

The doctor shook his head sadly. He turned and signaled the guards. The cage door opened. He went out.

"Get me some pumpkin pie," cried Eldridge after him, sitting up on the cot and grasping the bars as the door closed. "Give me some green grass in here."

The doctor crossed the bridge. The bridge was lifted up and the monitor screen lit up. A woolly face looked out and saw that all was well. Slowly the outer door swung open.

"Get me some pine trees!" yelled Eldridge at the doctor's retreating back. "Get me some plowed fields! Get me some earth, some dirt, some plain, earth dirt! *Get me that!*"

The door shut behind the doctor; and Eldridge burst into laughter, clinging to the bars, hanging there with glowing eyes.

"I would like to be relieved of this job," said the doctor to the commander, appearing formally in the latter's office.

"I'm sorry," said the commander. "I'm very sorry. But it was our tactical team that initiated this action; and no one has the experience with the prisoner you have. I'm sorry."

The doctor bowed his head; and went out.

Certain mild but emotion-deadening drugs were also known to the woolly, bearlike race. The doctor went out and began to indulge in them. Meanwhile, Eldridge lay on his cot, occasionally smiling to himself. His position was such that he could see out the window and over the weaving curtain of the barrier that ringed his building, to the landing field. After a while one of the large ships landed and when he saw the three members of its crew disembark from it and move, antlike, off across the field toward the buildings at its far end, he smiled again.

He settled back and closed his eyes. He seemed to doze for a couple of hours and then the sound of the door opening to admit the extra single guard bearing the food for his three o'clock mid-afternoon feeding. He sat up, pushed the cot down a ways, and sat on the end of it, waiting for the meal.

The bridge was not extended—that happened only when someone physically was to enter his cage. The monitor screen lit up and a woolly face watched as the tray of food was loaded on the mechanical arm. It swung out across the acid-filled moat, stretched itself toward the cage, and under the vigilance of the face in the monitor, the two-foot square hatch opened just before it to let it extend into the cage.

Smiling, Eldridge took the tray. The arm withdrew, as it cleared the cage, the hatch swung shut and locked. Outside the cage, guards, food carrier and face in the monitor relaxed. The food carrier turned toward the door, the face in the monitor looked down at some invisible control board before it and the outer door swung open.

In that moment, Eldridge moved.

In one swift second he was on his feet and his hands had closed around the bars of the hatch. There was a single screech of metal, as—incredibly—he tore it loose and threw it aside. Then he was diving through the hatch opening.

He rolled head over heels like a gymnast and came up with his feet standing on the inner edge of the moat. The acrid scent of the acid faintly burnt at his nostrils. He sprang forward in a standing jump, arms outstretched—and his clutching fingers closed on the end of the food arm, now halfway in the process of its leisurely mechanical retraction across the moat.

The metal creaked and bent, dipping downward toward the acid, but Eldridge was already swinging onward under the powerful impetus of his arms from which the sleeves had fallen back to reveal bulging ropes of smooth, powerful muscle. He flew forward through the air, feet first, and his boots took the nearest guard in the face, so that they crashed to the ground together.

For a second they rolled entangled, then the guard flopped and Eldridge came up on one knee, holding the black tube of the guard's weapon. It spat a single tongue of flame and the other guard dropped. Eldridge thrust to his feet, turning to the still-open door.

The door was closing. But the panicked food-carrier, unarmed, had turned to run. A bolt from Eldridge's weapon took him in the back. He fell forward and the door jammed on his body. Leaping after him, Eldridge squeezed through the remaining opening.

Then he was out under the free sky. The sounds of alarm screechers were splitting the air. He began to run—

The doctor was already drugged—but not so badly that he could not make it to the field when the news came. Driven by a strange perversity of spirit, he went first to the prison to inspect the broken hatch and the bent food arm. He traced Eldridge's outward path and it led him to the landing field where he found the commander and the academician by a bare, darkened area of concrete. They acknowledged his presence by little bows.

"He took a ship here?" said the doctor.

"He took a ship here," said the commander.

There was a little silence between them.

"Well," said the academician, "we have been answered."

"Have we?" the commander looked at them almost appealingly. "There's no chance—that it was just chance? No chance that the hatch just happened to fail—and he acted without thinking, and was lucky?"

The doctor shook his head. He felt a little dizzy and unnatural from the drug, but the ordinary processes of his thinking were unimpaired.

"The hinges of the hatch," he said, "were rotten—eaten away by acid."

"Acid?" the commander stared at him. "Where would he get acid?"

"From his own digestive processes—regurgitated and spat directly into the hinges. He secreted hydrochloric acid among other things. Not too powerful—but over a period of time—"

"Still—" said the commander, desperately, "I think it must have been more luck than otherwise."

"Can you believe that?" asked the academician. "Consider the timing of it all, the choosing of a moment when the food arm was in the proper position, the door open at the proper angle, the guard in a vulnerable situation. Consider his unhesitating and sure use of a weapon—which could only be the fruits of hours of observation, his choice of a moment when a fully supplied ship, its drive unit not yet cooled down, was waiting for him on the field. No," he shook his woolly head, "we have been answered. We put him in an escape-proof prison and he escaped."

"But none of this was possible!" cried the commander.

The doctor laughed, a fuzzy, drug-blurred laugh. He opened his mouth but the academician was before him.

"It's not what he did," said the academician, "but the fact that he did it. No member of another culture that we know would have even entertained the possibility in their minds. Don't you see—he disregarded, he *denied* the fact that escape was impossible. *That* is what makes his kind so fearful, so dangerous. The fact that something is impossible presents no barrier to their seeking minds. That, alone, places them above us on a plane we can never reach."

"But it's a false premise!" protested the commander. "They cannot contravene natural laws. They are still bound by the physical order of the universe."

The doctor laughed again. His laugh had a wild quality. The commander looked at him.

"You're drugged," he said.

"Yes," choked the doctor. "And I'll be more drugged. I toast the end of our race, our culture, and our order."

"Hysteria!" said the commander.

"Hysteria?" echoed the doctor. "No—*guilt!* Didn't we do it, we three? The legend told us not to touch them, not to set a spark to the explosive mixture of their kind. And we went ahead and did it, you, and you, and I. And now we've sent forth an enemy—safely into the safe hiding place of space, in a ship that can take him across the galaxy, supplied with food to keep him for years, rebuilt into a body that will not die, with star charts and all the keys to understand our culture and locate his home again, using the ability to learn we have encouraged in him."

"I say," said the commander, doggedly, "he is not that dangerous—yet. So far he has done nothing one of us could not do, had we entertained the notion. He's shown nothing, nothing supernormal."

"Hasn't he?" said the doctor thickly. "What about the defensive screen—our most dangerous most terrible weapon—that could burn him to nothingness if he touched it?"

The commander stared at him.

"But—" said the commander. "The screen was shut off, of course, to let the food carrier out, at the same time the door was opened. I assumed—"

"I checked," said the doctor, his eyes burning on the commander. "They turned it on again before he could get out."

"But he *did* get out! You don't mean . . ." the commander's voice faltered and dropped. The three stood caught in a sudden silence like stone. Slowly, as if drawn by strings controlled by an invisible hand, they turned as one to stare up into the empty sky and space beyond.

"You mean—" the commander's voice tried again, and died.

"Exactly!" whispered the doctor.

Halfway across the galaxy, a child of a sensitive race cried out in its sleep and clutched at its mother. "I had a bad dream," it whimpered.

"Hush," said its mother. "Hush." But she lay still, staring at the ceiling. She, too, had dreamed.

Somewhere, Eldridge was smiling at the stars.

From the serious to the not-so. The rough, tough alien, a very unsympathetic one this time, obviously comes from a planet with no equivalent of poker. This is one of a handful of stories Dickson wrote about the somewhat wacky adventures of Hank Shallo, and the title "Sleight of Wit" could have applied to any and all of them. I wish he had stuck around longer, not only to finish his Childe Cycle, but also because he might have let Mr. Shallo do still more interstellar trouble-shooting. And not just because one seldom runs across a hero named Hank. . . .

SLEIGHT OF WIT

It was a good world. It was a very good world—well worth a Class A bonus. Hank Shallo wiped his lips with the back of one square, hairy, big-knuckled hand, put his coffee cup down, and threw his ship into orbit around the place. The orbit had a slight drift to it because the gyros needed overhauling; but Hank was used to their anomalies, as he was to the fact that the coffee maker had to be set lower on the thermostat than its directions called for. He made automatic course corrections while he looked the planet over for a place to sit down.

Hank was a world scout—an interstellar pioneer far-flung in his fleet one-man spacecraft in search of new homes for humanity. He had been picked to model as such for a government publicity release the last time he had been back to Earth. The picture that resulted, in three-dimensional full-color, showed Hank barrel-chested in a fitted blue uniform, carelessly open at the throat, seated at the gleaming controls of a scout cabin mock-up. Utilitarianly tidy, the little cabin surrounded him, from the folded up Pullman-type bunk to the arms rack with well-oiled weapons gleaming on their hooks. A battered guitar leaned in one corner.

True life showed differences—Hank, barrel-chested in a pair of khaki shorts, seated at the somewhat rubbed-down controls of the *Andnowyoudont*. Utilitarianly untidy, the little cabin surrounded him, from the anchored down and unmade bunk to the former arms rack, with well-oiled spade, ax, posthole digger, wire-clippers, et cetera, hanging from the hooks. (In the ammunition locker were five sticks of non-issue dynamite. Hank, when talking shop on his infrequent trips back home, was capable of waxing lyrical over dynamite. "A tool," he would call it—"a weapon. It'll dig for you, fight for you, run a bluff for you. The only thing it won't do for you is cook the meals and make the bunk.")

A battered guitar leaned in one corner.

On the ninth time around, Hank had complete surface maps of the world below. He ran them back through the ship's library and punched for that spot on one of the world's three continents where landing conditions were optimum. Then he turned everything over to the automatic pilot and took a little nap.

When instinct woke him up, *Andnowyoudont* was just balancing herself in for a landing in a little meadow surrounded by trees and pleasant-looking enough to be parklike. What hint of warning it was that reached him in the midst of his slumber he was never to know; but one moment he was asleep—and the next he was halfway to the control panel.

Then concussion slammed the ship like a giant's hand. He tripped, caught one glimpse of the near wall of the cabin tilting at him, and consciousness dissolved in one of the prettiest displays of shooting stars he had seen in some time.

He woke again—this time to a throbbing headache and a lump on his forehead. He sat up groggily, hoisted himself the rest of the way to his feet and stumped over to the medicine chest, absently noting that the ship was, at least, still upright. The outside screen was on, showing a view of the meadow. Five years before he would have looked out of it immediately. Now he was more interested in aspirin.

When he had the aspirin inside him and had checked to make sure the bump on his head was not bleeding and the guitar had not been damaged he turned at last to the screen, sat down in the pilot chair and swept the outside scanner about the meadow. The meadow turned before him, stopped, and the screen steadied on a tall, gray shape.

At the far end of the meadow was another ship. It was half again as big as the *Andnowyoudont,* it resembled no ship of human manufacture that Hank had ever seen; and it had a sort of metal bubble or turret where its nose should be. From this turret projected a pair of short, blunt wide-mouthed tubes bearing an uncomfortable resemblance to the muzzles of guns. They were pointed directly at the *Andnowyoudont.*

Hank whistled the first three notes of "There'll Be A Hot Time In The Old Town, Tonight"—and broke off rather abruptly. He sat staring out the screen at the alien spaceship.

"Now," he said, after a while to the room around him, "against this—the odds against this happening, both of us here at the same time, in the same place, must be something like ten billion to one."

Which was possibly true. But which also, the saying of it didn't help a bit.

Hank got up rather heavily, went over to the coffee maker, and drew himself a cup of coffee. He sat down in his chair before the controls and examined a bank of tell-tale gauges. Not too much to his surprise, these mechanical watchdogs informed him that the *Andnowyoudont* was being sniffed at by various kinds of radiation. He was careful not to touch anything just yet. The thought of the five sticks of dynamite popped into his head and popped out again. The human race's expansion to the stars had brought them before this into contact with some life forms which might reasonably be called intelligent—but no one before that Hank knew of, in his line of work or out of it, had actually run across what you might call a comparable, *space-going* intelligent race.

"Except now Mrs. Shallo's little boy," said Hank to himself. "Naturally. Of course."

No, it was clearly not a dynamite-solution type problem. The stranger yonder was obviously armed and touchy. The *Andnowyoudont* packed five sticks of dynamite, a lot of useful, peaceful sorts of tools, and Hank. Hank leaned back in his chair, sipped on his coffee and turned the situation over to the one device on the ship that had a tinker's chance of handling it— some fifty ounces of gray matter just abaft his eyebrows and between his ears.

He was working this device rather hard, when the hull of the *Andnowyoudont* began to vibrate at short intervals. The vibration resulted in a series of short hums or buzzes. Hank plugged in to the ship's library and asked it what it thought of this new development.

"The alien ship appears to be trying to communicate with you," the library informed him.

"Well, see if you can make any sense out of its code," Hanks directed. "But don't answer—not yet, anyway."

He went back to his thinking.

One of the less glamorous aspects of Hank's profession—and one that had been hardly mentioned in the publicity release containing the picture he had modeled for, aforesaid—was a heavy schedule for classes, lectures, and briefing sections he was obligated to attend every time he returned to Headquarters, back on Earth. The purpose of these home chores was to keep him, and others like him, abreast of the latest developments and discoveries that might prove useful to him.

It was unfortunate that this would have meant informing him about practically everything that had happened since his last visit, if the intent had been followed literally. Ideally, a world scout should know everything from aardvark psychology to the Zyrian language. Practically, since such overall coverage was impossible, an effort was made to hit hard only the obviously relevant new information and merely survey other areas of new knowledge.

All new information, of course, was incorporated into the memory crystals of the library; but the trick from Hank's point of view was to remember what to ask for and how to ask for it. Covered in one of the surveys when he had been back last trip had been a rather controversial theory by somebody or other to the effect that an alien space-going race interested in the same sort of planets as humans were, would not only look a lot like, but act a lot like, humans. Hank closed his eyes.

"Bandits," he recited to himself. "Bayberry, barberry, burberry, buckle—May Sixteenth, Sinuses, shamuses, cyclical, sops—milk-and-bread . . . Library, Walter M. Breadon's 'Speculations on Alien Responses.' "

There was an almost perceptible delay, and then a screen in front of Hank lit up with a pictured text.

" . . . *Let us amuse ourselves now,* (commenced the pictured text) *with a few speculations about the personality and nature of a space-going alien such as one of you might encounter . . .*"

Hank snorted and settled down to read.

Twenty minutes later he had confirmed his remembrance of the fact that Breadon thought that an alien, such as must be in the ship opposite Hank right now, would react necessarily very similarly to a human. Because, Breadon's theory ran, of necessarily parallel environments and past stages of development.

At this moment, the call bell on Hank's deep-space receiver rang loudly.

"What's up?" he asked the library, keying it in.

"The alien ship has evidently concluded that it can speak to you over normal communication equipment. It is calling the *Andnowyoudont.*"

"Fine," said Hank. "I wonder what the name of Breadon's opposite number is among the aliens."

"I am sorry. I do not have that information."

"Yeah. Well, stand by to translate." Hank keyed in the communicator board. A screen before him lit up with the image of a hairless individual, lacking even eyebrows; with pronounced bony brow ridges, a wide mouth, no chin to speak of, and what appeared to be a turtleneck sweater drawn high on a thick neck.

This individual stared for a long second; and then began to gobble at him. Eventually he ran down and went back to staring again. Hank, his finger still off the send button, turned to the library.

"What'd he say?"

"I will need more referents. Possibly if you speak now, he will perhaps speak again."

"Not on your life." Hank looked at the alien. The alien looked back. The staring match went on for some time. Abruptly the alien started gobbling again. He gobbled for some time, this time. He also waved a fist in the air. It was a rather slim fist considering the thickness of his neck.

"Well?" demanded Hank of the library, after the figure in the screen had fallen silent a second time.

"First message: 'You are under arrest.'"

"That's *all* he said?"

"Agglutination appears to be a prime characteristic of his language."

"All right—" growled Hank. "Go on."

"Second message: 'You have offended the responsible authorities and their immediate representative, in the person of I who address you. You are arrested and helpless. Submit therefore immediately or you will be utterly destroyed.'"

Hank thought for a minute.

"Translate," he said to the library. He pressed the send button. "Tut-tut!" he said to the alien.

"I am unable to translate 'tut-tut,'" said the library.

"Oh?" Hank grinned. His grin widened. He began to laugh. He laughed louder.

"I am unable to translate laughter," said the library.

Hank was rolling around in his seat and hiccuping with helpless merriment. He reached out with one hand and slapped the send button to *off*. The screen went dark before him as the still-blankly staring alien faded from view. Whooping, Hank pulled himself to an upright position. Abruptly he stopped.

"What am I doing?" he muttered. "The set's off now." He wiped a damp forehead with the hairy back of one large hand and got up to totter over to one of the food compartments. He opened it and hauled out a large brown bottle.

Liquor was not a normal part of the supply list on scout ships—for reasons of space, rather than those of sobriety, a drinking world scout being a sort of self-canceling problem. On the other hand, a closed cycle that reprocessed waste matter of an organic nature and started it around again to become food required efficient little manufactories that were quite as capable of turning out ersatz beer as ersatz steak. The result was that world scouts were beer drinkers if they were any sort of drinkers at all.

They were also the despair of waiters, waitresses, and bartenders. A group of world scouts spending a social moment together would order a bottle apiece of cold beer; drain their bottles, when they came, in a couple of seconds; and then sit with the empty bottles before them, refusing to reorder until about forty-five minutes had passed. Then the whole process would be repeated.

A world scout determined to get drunk merely shortened the interval between bottles. One determined to stay cold sober, while appearing to drink, lengthened it. A member of the laity, sitting in with them on these sessions, was normally destroyed—either by drink or frustration.

In this particular case Hank flipped the seal off the top of the bottle in his hand, poured half a liter of beer down his throat, carefully resealed the bottle and put it back in its refrigerator compartment. He then carefully counted the remaining full containers of beer in the compartment and set the beer-producing controls on high.

After this he was almost attacked by another spasm

of laughter, but he fought it down. He went over to the desk of controls and flicked on an outside screen. It lit up with a view of the meadow with the afternoon sun beaming down on the soft grass and the tall gunmetal-colored shape of the alien ship.

"A beautiful day," said Hank aloud, "for a picnic."

"Do you wish me to make a note of that fact?" inquired the library, which had been left on.

"Why not?" said Hank. He went cheerfully about the room, opening lockers and taking things out. A sudden thought occurred to him. He went across to the desk controls to check the readings on certain instruments concerned with the physical environment of the world outside—but these gave the meadow a clean bill of health. He added the full bottles of beer to his pile, enclosing them in a temperature bag, and headed out the air lock of his ship.

Reaching the ground outside, he proceeded to a comfortable spot on the grass and about midway between his ship and that of the alien.

Half an hour later, he had a cheerful small fire going in the center of a small circle of stones, a hammock hung on wooden posts, and small conveniences such as a beer-cooler and an insulated box of assorted snacks within easy reach. He lay in the hammock and strummed his guitar and sang. He also swallowed a half liter of beer approximately every thirty-five minutes.

The beer did nothing to improve his voice. There was a reason Hank Shallo sang while off on his lonely trips of exploration—no civilized community could endure the horrendousness of his vocal cords when these vibrated in song. By a combination of bribery and intimidation he had forced an indigent music instructor once to teach him how to stay in key. So, stay in key he did; but the result was still a sort of bass bray capable of penetrating six-inch walls and rattling windows.

The alien ship showed no sign of life.

As the sun began slowly to drown itself in twilight, however, Hank became aware to his pleasant surprise that the local inhabitants of this world did not seem to join most of the rest of the galaxy in its disdain for his singing. An assortment of small animals of various shapes and sizes had gathered around his camping spot and sat in a circle. He was not unduly surprised, what with the beer he had drunk and all, when after a little while one of the larger creatures—a sort of rabbit-shaped beast sitting up on its hind legs—began to harmonize with him.

If Hank's voice had somewhat the sonority of a cross-cut saw, the beast's had the pure liquidity of an angel's. They were rendering a remarkable performance, albeit four octaves apart—and it had grown rather dark—when a blinding light burst suddenly into being from the top of the alien ship. It washed the meadow in a brilliance like that of an atomic flare; and the native animals took to their heels. Sitting up in the hammock and blinking, Hank saw the alien approaching him on foot. The alien was pushing a black box the size of a suitcase on two wheels. He trundled it up to the campfire, hitched up the floppy, black, bell-bottomed trousers which supplemented the turtle-necked upper garment Hank had remarked on the screen earlier, and gobbled at Hank.

"Sorry, buddy," said Hank. "I haven't got my translator with me."

The alien gobbled some more. Hank idly strummed a few stray chords and regretted the fact that he hadn't gotten the native animal to harmonizing with him on "Love's Old Sweet Song," which would have been ideally suited to their two voices together.

The alien stopped gobbling and jabbed one finger—somewhat angrily, it seemed to Hank, down on a button on top of the black box. There was a moment's hesitation; then he gobbled again and a curiously flat and unaccented English came out of the box.

"You are under arrest," it said.

"Think again," said Hank.

"What do you mean?"

"I mean I refuse to be arrested. Have a drink?"

"If you resist arrest, I will destroy you."

"No, you won't."

"I assure you I will."

"You can't," said Hank.

The alien looked at him with an expression that Hank took to be one of suspicion.

"My ship," said the alien, "is armed and yours is not."

"Oh, you mean those silly little weapons in your ship's nose?" Hank said. "They're no good against me."

"No good?"

"That's right, brother."

"We are not even of the same species. Do not allow your ignorance to lead you into the error of insulting me. To amuse myself, I will ask you why you are under the illusion that the most powerful scientific weapons known have no power against you?"

"I have," said Hank, "a greater weapon."

The alien looked at him suspiciously a second time.

"You are a liar," the box said, after a moment.

"Tut-tut," said Hank.

"What was that last noise you made? My translator does not yet recognize it."

"And it never will."

"This translator will sooner or later recognize every word in your language."

"Not a geepfleish word like *tut-tut*."

"What kind of a word?" It might, thought Hank, be merely false optimism on his part; but he thought the alien was beginning to look a little uncertain.

"Geepfleish—words dealing with the Ultimate Art-Science."

The alien hesitated for a third time.

"To get back to this fantastic claim of yours to having a weapon—what kind of weapon could be greater than a nuclear cannon capable of destroying a mountain?"

"Obviously," said Hank. "The Ultimate Weapon."

"The . . . Ultimate Weapon?"

"Certainly. The weapon evolved on Ultimate Art-Science principles."

"What kind of a weapon," said the alien, "is that?"

"It's quite impossible to explain," said Hank, airily, "to someone having no understanding of the Ultimate Art-Science."

"May I see this weapon?"

"You ain't capable of seeing it, kid," said Hank.

"If you will demonstrate its power to me," said the alien, after a pause, "I will believe your claim."

"The only way to demonstrate it would be to use it on you," said Hank. "It only works on intelligent life forms."

He reached over the edge of his hammock and opened another beer. When he set the half-empty bottle down again the alien was still standing there.

"You are a liar," the alien said.

"A crude individual like you," said Hank, delicately wiping a fleck of foam from his upper lip with the back of one hairy hand, "would naturally think so."

The alien turned abruptly and trundled his translator back toward his ship. A few moments later, the overhead light went out and the meadow was swallowed up in darkness except for the feeble light of the fire.

"Well," said Hank, getting up out of the hammock and yawning, "I guess that's that for today."

He took the guitar and went back to his ship. As he was going back in through the air lock, he thought he felt something about the size of a mouse scurry over his foot; and he caught a glimpse of something small, black and metallic that slipped out of sight under the control desk as he looked at it.

Hank grinned rather foolishly at the room about him and went to bed.

He woke once during the night; and lay there listening. By straining his ears, he could just occasionally make out a faint noise of movements. Satisfied, he went back to sleep again.

Early morning found him out of bed and humming to himself. He flipped the thermostat on the coffee maker up for a quick cup, set up the cabin thermostat and opened both doors of the air lock to let in the fresh morning air. Then he drew his cup of coffee, lowered the thermostat on the coffee maker again and keyed in the automatic broom. The broom scurried about, accumulating a small heap of dust and minor rubble, which it dumped outside the air lock. In the heap, Hank had time to notice, were a number of tiny mobile mechanical devices—like robot ants. Still drinking his coffee, he went over to the drawer that held the operating manual for ships of the class of *Andnowyoudont*. Holding it up by the binding, he shook it. A couple more of the tiny devices fell out; and the automatic broom, buzzing—it seemed to Hank—reproachfully, scurried over to collect them.

Hank was fixing himself breakfast, when the screen announced he was being called from the other ship. He stepped over and answered. The image of the alien lit up on the screen.

"You have had the night to think things over," said the flat voice of the alien's translator. "I will give you twelve point three seven five nine of your minutes more in which to surrender you and your ship to me. If you have not surrendered by the end of that time, I will destroy you."

"You could at least wait until I've had breakfast," said Hank. He yawned, and shut off the set.

He went back to fixing his breakfast, whistling as he did so. But the whistle ran a little flat; and he found he was keeping one eye on the clock. He decided he wasn't hungry after all, and sat down to watch the clock in the control desk as its hands marked off the seconds toward the deadline.

Nothing happened, however. When the deadline was a good several minutes past, he let out a relieved sigh and unclenched his hands, which he found had been maintaining quite a grip on the arms of his chair. He went back and had breakfast after all.

Then he set the coffee maker to turn itself on as soon as he came in, got down some fresh reading material from the top shelf of his bookcase—giving his head a rather painful bang on the fire-control sprinkler overhead, in the process—and stopped to rub his head and swear at the sprinkler. He then comforted himself with the last cup of coffee that was still in the coffee maker, unplugged the emergency automatic controls so that the air-lock doors would stay open while he was out, loaded himself up with beer—but left the reading material roasting on top of the coffee maker—and went out to his hammock.

Forty minutes and a liter and a half of beer later, he was again in a good mood. He took an ax into the nearby woods and began chopping poles for a lean-to. By lunch-time his hammock was swinging comfortably in the shade of the lean-to, his guitar was in tune, and his native audience was gathering again. He sang for about an hour, the small, rabbitlike creature harmonizing with parrotlike faithfulness to the tune, and had lunch. He was just about to take a small nap in the hammock when he saw the alien once more trundling his translator in the direction of the camp.

He reached the fireplace and stopped. Hank sat up with his legs over the edge of the hammock.

"Let us talk," said the alien.

"Fine," said Hank.

"I will be frank.

"Fine."

"And I will expect you to be frank."

"Why not?"

"We are both," said the alien, "intelligent beings of a high level of scientific culture. In spite of the apparent differences between us, we actually have a great deal in common. We must consider first the amazing coincidence that caused us both to land on the same world at the same spot at the same time—"

"Not so much of a coincidence," said Hank.

"What do you mean?" The alien all but glowered at him.

"It stands to reason," Hank leaned back comfortably in the hammock and caught hold of his knee with both hands to balance himself. "Your people and mine have probably been pretty close to bumping into each other all along. They've probably been close to each other a number of times before. But space is pretty big. Your ship and mine could easily zip right by each other a thousand times and never be noticed by one another. The most logical place to bump into each other is on a planet we both want. As for coming down in the same place—I set my equipment to pick out the most likely landing spot. I suppose you did the same?"

"It is not my function," said the alien, "to give you information."

"It isn't necessary for you to, either," grunted Hank. "It's pretty obvious your native star and mine aren't too far apart as galactic distances go—and exploratory ships have been getting closer to the opposing home worlds all the time. Instead of it being such a coincidence, you might say our meeting was close to inevitable." He cocked an eye at the alien. "And I'm sure you've already figured that out for yourself as well as I did."

The alien hesitated for a moment.

"I see," he said at last, "there is no point in my trying to deceive you."

"Oh you can *try* if you like," said Hank, generously.

"No, I will be absolutely frank."

"Suit yourself."

"You obviously have assessed the situation here as fully and correctly as I have myself. Here we stand, facing each other in an armed truce. There can be no question of either of us allowing the other to carry word of the other's civilization back to his own people. We cannot take the chance that the other's people are not inimical and highly dangerous. It becomes, therefore, the duty of each of us to capture the other." He cocked an eye at Hank. "Am I correct?"

"You're doing the talking," said Hank.

"At the present moment, we find ourselves at an impasse. My ship is possessed of a weapon which, by all the laws of science, should be able to destroy your ship utterly. Logically, you are at my mercy. However, illogically, you deny this."

"Yep." said Hank.

"You lay claim to an invisible weapon which you claim is greater than my own, and puts me at your mercy. For my own part I believe you are lying. But for the sake of my people I cannot put the matter to a test as things now stand. If I should do so and it should turn out I was wrong, I would be responsible for calamity."

"Yes, indeed," said Hank.

"However, an area of doubt remains in my mind. If you are so sure of the relative superiority of your weapon, why have you hesitated to make me prisoner in your turn?"

"Why bother?" Hank let go of his knee and leaned forward confidentially with both feet on the ground. "To be frank right back at you—you're harmless. Besides, I'm going to settle down here."

"Settle down? You mean you are going to set up residence here?"

"Certainly. It's my world."

"Your world?"

"Among my people," said Hank, loftily, "when you find a world you like that no one else of our own kind has already staked out, you get to keep it."

The pause the alien made this time was a very long one indeed.

"Now I know you are a liar," he said.

"Well, suit yourself," said Hank, mildly.

The alien stood staring at him.

"You leave me no alternative," said the alien at last. "I offer you a proposition. I will give you proof that I have destroyed my cannon, if you will give me proof that you have destroyed your weapon. Then we can settle matters on the even basis that will result."

"Unfortunately," said Hank, "this weapon of mine can't be destroyed."

"Then," the alien backed off a step and started to turn his translator around back toward the ship. "I must take the chance that you are not a liar and do my best to destroy you after all."

"Hey! Hold on a minute!" said Hank. The alien

paused and turned back. "Don't rush off like that," Hank stood up and flexed his muscles casually. The two were about the same height but it was obvious Hank carried what would have been an Earth-weight advantage of about fifty pounds. "You want to settle this man-to-man, I'm willing. No weapons, no holds barred. There's a sporting proposition for you."

"I am not a savage," retorted the alien. "Or a fool."

"Clubs?" said Hank, hopefully.

"No."

"Knives?"

"Certainly not."

"All right," said Hank, shrugging, "have it your way. Go get yourself destroyed. I did my best to find some way out for you."

The alien stood still as if thinking.

"Let me make you a second proposition," he said at last. "All the alternatives you propose are those which give you the advantage. Let us reverse that. Let me propose that we trade ships, you and I."

"What?" squawked Hank.

"You see? You are not interested in any fair encounter."

"Certainly I am! But trade ships—why don't you just ask me to give up right now?"

"Because you obviously will not do so."

"There's no difference between that and asking me to trade ships!" shouted Hank.

"Who knows?" said the alien. "Possibly you will learn to operate my cannon before I learn to operate your weapon."

"You never could anyway—work mine, that is!" snorted Hank.

"I am willing to take my chances."

"It's ridiculous!"

"Very well." The alien turned away. "I have no alternative but to do my best to destroy you."

"Hold on. Hold on—" said Hank. "Look, all right. I agree. Just let me go back to my ship for a minute and pick up a few personal—"

"No. Neither one of us can take the chance of the other setting up a trap in his own ship. We trade now—without either of us going back to our ships."

"Well, now look—" Hank took a step toward him.

"Stand back," said the alien. "I am connected with my cannon by remote controls at this moment."

"The air-lock doors to my ship are open. Yours aren't."

The alien reached out and touched the black box. Behind him, the air-lock door of the alien ship swung open, revealing an open inner door and a dark interior.

"I will abandon my translator at the entrance to your ship," said the alien. "Is it settled?"

"Settled!" said Hank. He began walking toward the alien ship, looking back over his shoulder. The alien began trundling his black box toward Hank's ship. As the distance between them widened, they began to put on speed. Halfway to the alien ship, Hank found himself running. He came panting up to the entrance of the alien air lock, and looked back just in time to see the alien dragging his black box in through the air lock of Hank's ship.

"Hey!" yelled Hank, outraged. "You promised—"

The slam of the outer air-lock door, on his own ship, cut him off in mid-protest. He leaned against the open door of the alien ship's air lock, getting his breath back. It occurred to him as a stray thought that he was built for power rather than speed.

"I should have walked," he told the alien ship. "It wouldn't have made any difference." He glanced at his wrist watch. "I'll give him three minutes. He sure didn't lose any time finding those air-lock controls."

He watched the second hand of his watch go around. When it passed the two and a half minute point, he began walking back to his own ship. He reached its closed air-lock door and fumbled with his fingers under the doorframe for the outside lock control button. He found and pressed it.

The door swung open. Smoke spurted out, followed instantly—as the door swung wide—by a flood of water. Washed out on the crest of this escaping flood came a very bedraggled looking alien. He stirred feebly, gargled something at Hank, and collapsed. Inside the spaceship a small torrential shower seemed to be in progress.

Hank hooked one big hand into the alien's turtle-neck upper garment and dragged him back into the ship. Groping around in the downpour, he found the controls for the automatic fire sprinkler system and turned them off. The shower ceased. Hank fanned smoke away from in front of his face, stepped across to the coffee maker and turned it off. He punched buttons to start the ventilating system and close the air-lock doors. Then he set about tying the alien to the bunk.

When the alien began to stir, they were already in null-space, on the first point-to-point jump of the three-day trip that would bring them back to Earth. The alien opened his eyes; and Hank, looking up from his job of repairing the coffee maker, saw the other's stare full upon him.

"Oh!" said Hank. He stopped work, went across the room and brought back the black box on wheels to within reach of the alien's bound hands. The alien reached out and touched it. The box spoke, echoing his gobble.

"What did I do wrong?"

Hank nodded at the coffee maker. He sat down and went back to work on it. It was in bad shape, having evidently suffered some kind of an explosion.

"I had that set to turn on when I came back in," he said. "Closing the air-lock doors turned it on. Convenient little connection I installed about a year or so back. Only, it just so happened I'd drawn the last cup out of it before I went out. There was just enough moisture in it to cause a steam explosion."

"But the water? The smoke?"

"The automatic sprinkling system," explained Hank, "It reacts to any spot of dangerously high temperature in the room here. When the coffee maker split open, the heating element was exposed. The sprinkling system began flooding the place."

"But the smoke?"

"Some burnable reading material I had on top of the coffee maker. Now that," said Hank, finishing his repairs on the coffee maker, "was something I was absolutely counting on—that the books would fall down onto the burner. And they did." He slapped the coffee maker affectionately and stood up. He looked down at the alien. "Afraid you're going to be somewhat hungry for the next three days or so. But as soon as we get to Earth, you can tell our nutritionists what you eat and they'll synthesize it for you."

He grinned at the other.

"Don't take it so hard," he said. "You'll find we humans aren't all that tough to take when you get to know us."

The alien closed his eyes. Something like a sigh of defeat came from the black box.

"So you had no weapon," it said.

"What do you mean?" said Hank, dropping into the chair at the control board, indignantly. "Of course I had a weapon."

The eyes of the alien flew wide open.

"Where is it?" he cried. "I sent robots in. They examined this ship of yours right down to the elements that hold it together. They found no weapon. I found no weapon."

"You're my prisoner aren't you?" said Hank.

"Of course I am. What of it? What I'm asking is to see your weapon. I could not find it; but you say you still have it. Show it to me. I tell you, I do not see it!"

Hank shook his head sadly; and reached for the controls of the *Andnowyoudont* to set up the next jump.

"Brother," he said, "I don't know. If you don't see it—after all this—then I pity your people when my people really get to know them. That's all I've got to say!"

This yarn can be considered a companion piece to "Sleight of Wit," taking a similar situation, but this time with deadly seriousness. The intrepid human was out exploring the galaxy, confident that his highly advanced technology could handle anything he ran into. Then he ran into an alien with much *more* advanced technology at its disposal. The alien thought the game was all over, but there was still that ol' human edge. . . .

IN THE BONE

I

Personally, his name was Harry Brennan.

Officially, he was the *John Paul Jones*, which consisted of four billion dollars' worth of irresistible equipment—the latest and best of human science—designed to spread its four thousand components out through some fifteen cubic meters of space under ordinary conditions—designed also to stretch across light-years under extraordinary conditions (such as sending an emergency messenger-component home) or to clump into a single magnetic unit in order to shift through space and explore the galaxy. Both officially and personally—but most of all personally—he represents a case in point.

The case is one having to do with the relative importance of the made thing and its maker.

It was, as we know, the armored horseman who dominated the early wars of the Middle Ages in Europe. But, knowing this, it is still wise to remember that it was not the iron shell that made the combination of man and metal terrible to the enemy—but rather the essentially naked man inside the shell. Later, French knights depending on their armor went down before the clothyard shafts of unarmored footmen with bows, at Crécy and Poitiers.

And what holds true for armor holds true for the latest developments of our science as well. It is not the spacecraft or the laser on which we will find ourselves depending when a time of ultimate decision comes, but the naked men within and behind these things. When that time comes, those who rank the made thing before its maker will die as the French knights died at Crécy and Poitiers. This is a law of nature as wide as the universe, which Harry Brennan, totally unsuspecting, was to discover once more for us, in his personal capacity.

Personally, he was in his mid-twenties, unremarkable except for two years of special training with the *John Paul Jones* and his superb physical condition. He was five eleven, a hundred seventy-two pounds, with a round, cheerful face under his brown crew-cut hair. I was Public Relations Director of the Project that sent him out; and I was there with the rest to slap him on the back the day he left.

"Don't get lost, now," said someone. Harry grinned.

"The way you guys built this thing," he answered, "if I got lost the galaxy would just have to shift itself around to get me back on plot."

There was an unconscious arrogance hidden in that answer, but no one marked it at the time. It was r ot the hour of suspicions.

He climbed into the twelve-foot-tall control-suit that with his separate living tank were the main components of the *John Paul Jones,* and took off. Up in orbit, he spent some thirty-two hours testing to make sure all the several thousand other component parts were responding properly. Then he left the solar system.

He clumped together his components, made his first shift to orbit Procyon—and from there commenced his explorations of the stars. In the next nine weeks, he accumulated literally amazing amounts of new information about the nearby stars and their solar systems. And—this is an even better index of his success—located four new worlds on which men could step with never a spacesuit or even a water canteen to sustain them. Worlds so like Earth in gravity, atmosphere, and even flora and fauna, that they could be colonized tomorrow.

Those were his first four worlds. On the fifth he encountered his fate—a fate for which he was unconsciously ripe.

The fact was the medical men and psychologists had overlooked a factor—a factor having to do with the effect of Harry's official *John Paul Jones* self upon his entirely human personal self. And over nine weeks this effect changed Harry without his ever having suspected it.

You see, nothing seemed barred to him. He could cross light-years by touching a few buttons. He could send a sensing element into the core of the hottest star, into the most poisonous planetary atmospheres or crushing gravities, to look around as if he were down there in person. From orbit, he could crack open a mountain, burn off a forest, or vaporize a section of icecap in search of information just by tapping the energy of a nearby sun. And so, subtly, the unconscious arrogance born during two years of training, that should have been noted in him at take-off from Earth, emerged and took him over—until he felt that there was nothing he could not do; that all things must give way to him; that he was, in effect, master of the universe.

The day may come when a man like Harry Brennan may hold such a belief and be justified. But not yet. On the fifth Earth-like world he discovered—World 1242 in his records—Harry encountered the proof that his belief was unjustified.

II

The world was one which, from orbit, seemed to be the best of all the planets which he had discovered were suitable for human settlement; and he was about to go down to its surface personally in the control-suit, when his instruments picked out something already down there.

It was a squat, metallic pyramid about the size of a four-plex apartment building; and it was radiating on a number of interesting frequencies. Around its base there was mechanical movement and an area of cleared ground. Further out, in the native forest, were treaded vehicles taking samples of the soil, rock, and vegetation.

Harry had been trained for all conceivable situations, including an encounter with other intelligent, space-going life. Automatically, he struck a specific button, and immediately a small torpedo shape leaped away to shift through alternate space and back to Earth with the information so far obtained. And a pale, thin beam reached up and out from the pyramid below. Harry's emergency messenger component ceased to exist.

Shaken, but not yet really worried, Harry struck back instantly with all the power his official self could draw from the G0-type sun, nearby.

The power was funneled by some action below, directly into the pyramid itself; and it vanished there as indifferently as the single glance of a sunbeam upon a leaf.

Harry's mind woke suddenly to some understanding of what he had encountered. He reached for the controls to send the *John Paul Jones* shifting into the alternate universe and away.

His hands never touched the controls. From the pyramid below, a blue lance of light reached up to paralyze him, select the control-suit from among the other components, and send it tumbling to the planetary surface below like a swatted insect.

But the suit had been designed to protect its occupant, whether he himself was operative or not. At fifteen hundred feet, the drag chute broke free, looking like a silver cloth candle-snuffer in the sunlight; and at five hundred feet the retro-rockets cut in. The suit tumbled to earth among some trees two kilometers from the pyramid, with Harry inside bruised, but released from his paralysis.

From the pyramid, a jagged arm of something like white lightning lashed the ground as far as the suit, and the suit's outer surface glowed cherry-red. Inside, the temperature suddenly shot up fifty degrees; instinctively Harry hit the panic button available to him inside the suit.

The suit split down the center like an overcooked frankfurter and spat Harry out; he rolled among the brush and fernlike ground cover, six or seven meters from the suit.

❖   ❖   ❖

From the distant pyramid, the lightning lashed the suit, breaking it up. The headpiece rolled drunkenly aside, turning the dark gape of its interior toward Harry like the hollow of an empty skull. In the dimness of that hollow Harry saw the twinkle of his control buttons.

The lightning vanished. A yellow lightness filled the air about Harry and the dismembered suit. There was a strange quivering to the yellowness; and Harry half-smelled, half-tasted the sudden, flat bite of ozone. In the headpiece a button clicked without being touched; and the suit speaker, still radio-connected with the recording tank in orbit, spoke aloud in Harry's voice.

"Orbit . . ." it said. " . . . into . . . going . . ."

These were, in reverse order, the last three words Harry had recorded before sighting the pyramid. Now, swiftly gaining speed, the speaker began to recite backward, word for word, everything Harry had said into it in nine weeks. Faster it went, and faster until it mounted to a chatter, a gabble, and finally a whine pushing against the upper limits of Harry's auditory register.

Suddenly, it stopped.

The little clearing about Harry was full of silence. Only the odd and distant creaking of something that might have been a rubbing branch or an alien insect came to Harry's ears. Then the speaker spoke once more.

"Animal . . ." it said flatly in Harry's calm, recorded voice and went on to pick further words from the recordings. " . . . best. You . . . were an animal . . . wrapped in . . . made clothing. I have stripped you back to . . . animal again. Live, beast . . ."

Then the yellowness went out of the air and the taste of ozone with it. The headpiece of the dismembered suit grinned, empty as old bones in the sunlight. Harry scrambled to his feet and ran wildly away through the trees and brush. He ran in panic and utter fear, his lungs gasping, his feet pounding the alien earth, until the earth, the trees, the sky itself swam about him from exhaustion; and he fell tumbling to earth and away into the dark haven of unconsciousness.

When he woke, it was night, and he could not quite remember where he was or why. His thoughts seemed numb and unimportant. But he was cold, so he blundered about until he found the standing half-trunk of a lightning-blasted tree and crept into the burned hollow of its interior, raking frill-edged, alien leaves about him out of some half-forgotten instinct, until his own body warmth in the leaves formed a cocoon of comfort about him; and he slept.

From then on began a period in which nothing was very clear. It was as if his mind had huddled itself away somehow like a wounded animal and refused to think. There was no past or future, only the endless now. If now was warm, it had always been warm; if dark—it had always been dark. He learned to smell water from a distance and go to it when he was thirsty. He put small things in his mouth to taste them. If they tasted good he ate them. If he got sick afterward, he did not eat them again.

Gradually, blindly, the world about him began to take on a certain order. He came to know where there were plants with portions he could eat, where there were small creatures he could catch and pull apart and eat, and where there was water.

He did not know how lucky he was in the sheer chance of finding flora and fauna on an alien world that were edible—let alone nourishing. He did not realize that he had come down on a plateau in the tropical highlands, with little variation in day and night temperature and no large native predators which might have attacked him.

None of this he knew. Nor would it have made any difference to him if he had, for the intellectual center of his brain had gone on vacation, so to speak, and refused to be called back. He was, in fact, a victim of severe psychological shock. The shock of someone who had come to feel himself absolute master of a universe and who then, in a few short seconds, had been cast down from that high estate by something or someone inconceivably greater, into the state of a beast of the field.

But still, he could not be a true beast of the field, in spite of the fact his intellectual processes had momentarily abdicated. His perceptive abilities still worked. His eyes could not help noting, even if incuriously, the progressive drying of the vegetation, the day-by-day shifting in the points of setting and rising of the sun. Slowly, instinctively, the eternal moment that held him stretched and lengthened until he began to perceive divisions within it—a difference between *now* and *was,* between *now* and *will be.*

III

The day came at last when he saw himself.

A hundred times he had crouched by the water to drink and, lowering his lips to its surface, seen color and shape rising to meet him. The hundredth and something time, he checked, a few inches above the liquid plane, staring at what he saw.

For several long seconds it made no sense to him. Then, at first slowly, then with a rush like pain flooding back on someone rousing from the anesthesia of unconsciousness, he recognized what he saw.

Those were eyes at which he stared, sunken and dark-circled under a dirty tangle of hair. That was a nose jutting between gaunt and sunken cheeks above a mouth, and there was a chin naked only because once an ultrafine laser had burned out the thousand and one roots of the beard that grew on it. That was a man he saw—*himself*.

He jerked back like someone who has come face-to-face with the devil. But he returned eventually, because he was thirsty, to drink and see himself again. And so, gradually, he got used to the sight of himself.

So it was that memory started to return to him. But it did not come back quickly or all at once. It returned instead by jerks and sudden, partial revelations—until finally the whole memory of what had happened was back in his conscious mind again.

But he was really not a man again.

He was still essentially what the operator of the pyramid had broken him down into. He was still an animal. Only the memory and imaginings of a man had returned to live like a prisoner in a body that went on reacting and surviving in the bestial way it had come to regard as natural.

But his animal peace was broken. For his imprisoned mind worked now. With the control-suit broken up—he had returned to the spot of its destruction many times, to gaze beastlike at the rusting parts— his mind knew he was a prisoner, alone on this alien world until he died. To know that was not so bad, but remembering this much meant remembering also the existence of the someone or something that had made him a prisoner here.

The whoever it was who was in the pyramid.

That the pyramid might have been an automated,

mechanical device never entered his mind for a moment. There had been a personal, directed, living viciousness behind the announcement that had condemned him to live as a beast. No, in that blank-walled, metallic structure, whose treaded mechanical servants still prospected through the woods, there was something alive—something that could treat the awesome power of a solar tap as a human treated the attack of a mosquito—but something *living*. Some being. Some Other, who lived in the pyramid, moving, breathing, eating, and gloating—or worse yet, entirely forgetful of what he had done to Harry Brennan.

And now that he knew that the Other was there, Harry began to dream of him nightly. At first, in his dreams, Harry whimpered with fear each time the dark shape he pursued seemed about to turn and show its face. But slowly, hatred came to grow inside and then outside his fear. Unbearable that Harry should never know the face of his destroyer. Lying curled in the nest of leaves under the moonless, star-brilliant sky, he snarled, thinking of his deprivation.

Then hate came to strengthen him in the daylight also. From the beginning he had avoided the pyramid, as a wild coyote avoids the farmyard where he was once shot by the farmer. But now, day after day, Harry circled closer to the alien shape. From the beginning he had run and hidden from the treaded prospecting machines. But now, slowly, he grew bolder, standing close enough at last to touch them as they passed. And he found that they paid no attention to him. No attention at all.

He came to ignore them in turn, and day by day he ventured closer to the pyramid. Until the morning came when he lay, silently snarling, behind a bush, looking out across the tread-trampled space that separated him from the nearest copper-colored face of the pyramid.

The space was roughly circular, thirty yards across, broken only by a small stream which had been diverted to loop inward toward the pyramid before returning to its original channel. In the bight of the loop a machine like a stork straddled the artificial four-foot-wide channel, dipping a pair of long necks with tentacle-clustered heads into the water at intervals. Sometimes Harry could see nothing in the tentacles when they came up. Occasionally they carried some small water creature which they deposited in a tank.

Making a perfect circle about the tramped area, so that the storklike machine was guarded within them, was an open fence of slender wands set upright in the earth, far enough apart for any of the machines that came and went to the forest to pass between any two of them. There seemed to be nothing connecting the wands, and nothing happened to the prospecting machines as they passed through—but the very purposelessness of the wands filled Harry with uneasiness.

It was not until after several days of watching that he had a chance to see a small native animal, frightened by something in the woods behind it, attempt to bolt across a corner of the clearing.

As it passed between two of the wands there was a waveriness in the air between them. The small animal leaped high, came down, and lay still. It did not move after that, and later in the day, Harry saw the indifferent treads of one of the prospecting machines bury it in the trampled earth in passing.

That evening, Harry brought several captive, small animals bound with grass up to the wand line and thrust them through, one by one at different spots. All died.

The next night he tried pushing a captive through

a small trench scooped out so that the creature passed the killing line below ground level. But this one died also. For several days he was baffled. Then he tried running behind a slow-moving machine as it returned and tying a small animal to it with grass.

For a moment as the front of the machine passed through, he thought the little animal would live. But then, as the back of the machine passed the line, it, too, died.

Snarling, Harry paced around outside the circle in the brush until the sun set and stars filled the moonless sky.

In the days that followed, he probed every gap in the wand-fence, but found no safe way through it. Finally, he came to concentrate on the two points at which the diverted stream entered and left the circle to flow beneath the storklike machine.

He studied this without really knowing what he was seeking. He did not even put his studying into words. Vaguely, he knew that the water went in and the water came out again unchanged; and he also wished to enter and come out safely. Then, one day, studying the stream and the machine, he noticed that a small creature plucked from the water by the storklike neck's mass of tentacles was still wriggling

That evening, at twilight, while there was still light to see, he waded up the two-foot depth of the stream to the point where the killing line cut across its watery surface and pushed some more of his little animals toward the line underwater.

Two of the three surfaced immediately, twitched, and floated on limply, to be plucked from the water and cast aside on the ground by the storklike machine. But the third swam on several strokes before surfacing and came up living to scramble ashore, race for the forest, and be killed by wands further around the circle.

Harry investigated the channel below the killing line. There was water there up to his midthigh, plenty to cover him completely. He crouched down in the water and took a deep breath.

Ducking below the surface, he pulled himself along with his fingertips, holding himself close to the bottom. He moved in as far as the tentacled ends. These grabbed at him, but could not reach far enough back to touch him. He saw that they came within a few inches of the gravel bottom.

He began to need air. He backed carefully out and rose above the water, gasping. After a while his hard breathing stopped, and he sat staring at the water for a long while. When it was dark, he left.

The next day he came and crept underwater to the grabbing area of the storklike machine again. He scooped out several handfuls of the gravel from under the place where the arms grabbed, before he felt a desperate need for air and had to withdraw. But that day began his labors.

IV

Four days later the bottom under the grasping tentacles was scooped out to an additional two feet of depth. And the fifth twilight after that, he pulled himself, dripping and triumphant, up out of the bend of the diverted stream inside the circle of the killing wands.

He rested and then went to the pyramid, approaching it cautiously and sidelong like a suspicious animal. There was a door in the side he approached through which he had seen the prospecting machines trundle in and out. In the dimness he could not see it; and when he touched the metallic side of the structure, his fingers, grimed and toughened from scrabbling in the dirt, told him little. But his nose, beast-sensitive now, located and traced the outline of the almost invisible crack around the door panel by its reek of earth and lubricant.

He settled down to wait. An hour later, one of the machines came back. He jumped up, ready to follow it in; but the door opened just before it and closed the minute it was inside—nor was there any room to squeeze in beside it. He hunkered down, disappointed, snarling a little to himself.

He stayed until dawn and watched several more machines enter and leave. But there was no room to squeeze inside, even with the smallest of them.

During the next week or so he watched the machines enter and leave nightly. He tied one of his small animals to an entering machine and saw it pass through the entrance alive and scamper out again with the next machine that left. And every flight his rage increased. Then, wordlessly, one daytime after he had seen a machine deep in the woods lurch and tilt as its tread passed over a rock, inspiration took him.

That night he carried through the water with him several cantaloupe-sized stones. When the first machine came back to the pyramid, in the moment in which the door opened before it, he pushed one of the rocks before the right-hand tread. The machine, unable to stop, mounted the rock with its right tread, tilted to the left, and struck against that side of the entrance.

It checked, backed off, and put out an arm with the grasping end to remove the rock. Then it entered the opening. But Harry was already before it, having slipped through while the door was still up and the machine busy pulling the stone aside.

He plunged into a corridor of darkness, full of clankings and smells. A little light from the opening behind him showed him a further, larger chamber where other machines stood parked. He ran toward them.

Long before he reached them, the door closed behind him, and he was in pitch darkness. But the clanking of the incoming machine was close behind him, and the adrenalinized memory of a wild beast did not fail him. He ran, hands outstretched, directly into the side of the parked machine at which he had aimed and clambered up on it. The machine entering behind him clanked harmlessly past him and stopped moving.

He climbed cautiously down in the impenetrable darkness. He could see nothing; but the new, animal sensitivity of his nose offered a substitute for vision. He moved like a hunting dog around the chamber, sniffing and touching; and slowly a clear picture of it and its treaded occupants built up in his mind.

He was still at this when suddenly a door he had not seen opened almost in his face. He had just time to leap backward as a smaller machine with a boxlike body and a number of upward-thrusting arms entered, trundled to the machine that had just come back, and began to relieve the prospecting machine of its sample box, replacing it with the one it carried itself.

This much, in the dim light from the open door, Harry was able to see. But then, the small machine turned back toward the doorway; and Harry, waking to his opportunity, ducked through ahead of it.

He found himself in a corridor dimly lit by a luminescent strip down the center of the ceiling. The corridor was wide enough for the box-collecting machine to pass him; and, in fact, it rolled out around him as he shrank back against one metal wall. It went on down the corridor, and he followed it into a larger room with a number of machines, some mobile, some not, under a ceiling lit as the corridor had been with a crossing of luminescent strip.

In this area all the machines avoided each other—and him. They were busy with each other and at other incomprehensible duties. Hunched and tense, hair erect on the back of his neck and nostrils spread wide, Harry moved through them to explore other rooms and corridors that opened off this one. It took him some little time; but he discovered that they were all on a level, and there was nothing but machines in any of them. He found two more doors with shallow steps leading up to them, but these would not open for him; and though he watched by one for some time, no machine went up the steps and through it.

He began to be conscious of thirst and hunger. He made his way back to the door leading to the chamber where the prospecting machines were parked. To his surprise, it opened as he approached it. He slipped through into darkness.

Immediately, the door closed behind him; and sudden panic grabbed him, when he found he could not open it from this side. Then, self-possession returned to him.

By touch, smell, and memory, he made his way among the parked machines and down the corridor to the outside door. To his gratification, this also opened when he came close. He slipped through into cool, fresh outer air and a sky already graying with dawn. A few moments later, wet but free, he was back in the woods again.

From then on, each night he returned. He found it was not necessary to do more than put any sizable object before the returning machine. It would stop to clear the path, and he could enter ahead of it. Then, shortly after he was inside, a box-collecting machine would open the inner door.

Gradually, his fear of the machines faded. He came to hold them in a certain contempt. They always did the same thing in the same situation, and it was easy to trick or outmaneuver them.

But the two inner doors of the machine area with the steps would not open to him; and he knew the upper parts of the pyramid were still unexplored by him. He sniffed at the cracks of these doors, and a scent came through—not of lubricating medium and metal alone, but of a different, musky odor that raised the hairs on the back of his neck again. He snarled at the doors.

He went back to exploring minutely the machine level. The sample boxes from the prospecting machines, he found, were put on conveyor-beltlike strips that floated up on thin air through openings in the ceiling— but the openings were too small for him to pass through. But he discovered something else. One day he came upon one of the machines taking a grille off the face of one of the immobile devices. It carried the grille away, and he explored the opening that had been revealed. It was the entrance to a tunnel or duct leading upward; and it was large enough to let him enter it. Air blew silently from it; and the air was heavy with the musky odor he had smelled around the doors that did not open.

The duct tempted him, but fear held him back. The machine came back and replaced the grille; and he noticed that it fitted into place with a little pressure from the outside, top and bottom. After the machine had left he pressed, and the grille fell out into his hands.

After a long wait, he ventured timorously into the tube—but a sudden sound like heavy breathing mixed with a wave of a strong, musky odor came at him. He backed out in panic, fled the pyramid, and did not come back for two days.

When he came back, the grille was again neatly in place. He removed it and sat a long time getting his courage up. Finally, he put the grille up high out of reach of the machine which had originally removed it and crawled into the duct.

He crept up the tube at an angle into darkness. His eyes were useless, but the musky odor came strongly at him. Soon, he heard sounds.

There was an occasional ticking, then a thumping or shuffling sound. Finally, after he had crawled a long way up through the tube, there was a sound like a heavy puffing or hoarse breathing. It was the sound that had accompanied the strengthening of the musky odor once before; and this time the scent came strong again.

He lay, almost paralyzed with terror in the tube, as the odor grew in his nostrils. He could not move until sound and scent had retreated. As soon as they had, he wormed his way backward down to the lower level and freedom, replaced the grille, and fled for the outside air, once again.

But once more, in time he came back. Eventually he returned to explore the whole network of tubes to which the one he had entered connected. Many of the branching tubes were too small for him to enter, and the biggest tube he could find led to another grille from which the musky-smelling air was blasted with force.

Clearly it was the prime mover for the circulation of air through the exhaust half of the pyramid's ventilating system. Harry did not reason it out to himself in those intellectual terms, but he grasped the concept wordlessly and went back to exploring those smaller tubes that he could crawl into.

These, he found, terminated in grilles set in their floors through which he could look down and catch a glimpse of some chamber or other. What he saw was mainly incomprehensible. There were a number of corridors, a number of what could be rooms containing fixed or movable objects of various sizes and shapes. Some of them could be the equivalent of chairs or beds—but if so, they were scaled for a being plainly larger than himself. The lighting was invariably the low-key illumination he had encountered in the lower, machine level of the pyramid, supplied by the single luminescent strip running across the ceiling.

Occasionally, from one grille or another, he heard in the distance the heavy sound of breathing, among other sounds, and smelled more strongly the musky odor. But for more than a week of surreptitious visits to the pyramid, he watched through various grilles without seeing anything living.

V

However, a day finally came when he was crouched, staring down into a circular room containing what might be a bed shape, several chair shapes, and a number of other fixed shapes with variously spaced and depthed indentations in their surfaces. In a far edge of the circular room was a narrow alcove, the walls of which were filled with ranked indentations, among which several lights of different colors winked and glowed.

Suddenly, the dim illumination of the room began to brighten. The illumination increased rapidly, so that

Harry cringed back from the grille, lifting a palm to protect his dimness-accustomed eyes. At the same moment, he heard approaching the sound of heavy breathing and sniffed a sudden increase in the musky odor.

He froze. Motionless above the grille, he stopped even his breathing. He would have stopped his heart if he could, but it raced, shaking his whole body and sounding its rapid beat in his ears until he felt the noise of it must be booming through the pyramid like a drum. But there was no sign from below that this was so.

Then, sliding into sight below him, came a massive figure on a small platform that seemed to drift without support into the room.

The aperture of the grille was small. Harry's viewpoint was cramped and limited, looking down directly from overhead. He found himself looking down onto thick, hairless brown-skinned shoulders, a thick neck with the skin creased at the back, and a forward sloping, hairless brown head, egg-shaped in outline from above, with the point forward.

Foreshortened below the head and shoulders was a bulging chinline with something like a tusk showing; it had a squat, heavy, hairless brown body and thick short forearms with stubby claws at the end of four-fingered hands. There was something walruslike about the tusks and the hunching; and the musky odor rose sickeningly into Harry's human nostrils.

The platform slid level with the alcove, which was too narrow for it to enter. Breathing hoarsely, the heavy figure on it heaved itself suddenly off the platform into the alcove, and the stubby hands moved over the pattern of indentations. Then, it turned and heaved itself out of the alcove, onto the flat, bed surface adjoining. Just as Harry's gaze began to get a full-length picture of it, the illumination below went out.

Harry was left, staring dazzled into darkness, while the heavy breathing and the sound of the figure readjusting itself on the bed surface came up to his ears. After a while, there was no noise but the breathing. But Harry did not dare move. For a long time he held his cramped posture, hardly breathing himself. Finally, cautiously, inch by inch, he retreated down the tube, which was too small to let him turn around. When he reached the larger tubes, he fled for the outside and the safety of the forest.

The next day, he did not go near the pyramid. Or the next. Every time he thought of the heavy brown figure entering the room below the grille, he became soaked with the clammy sweat of a deep, emotional terror. He could understand how the Other had not heard him or seen him up behind the grille. But he could not understand how the alien had not *smelled* him.

Slowly, however, he came to accept the fact that the Other had not. Possibly the Other did not have a sense of smell. Possibly . . . there was no end to the possibilities. The fact was that the Other had not smelled Harry—or heard him—or seen him. Harry was like a rat in the walls—unknown because he was unsuspected.

At the end of the week, Harry was once more prowling around back by the pyramid. He had not intended to come back, but his hatred drew him like the need of a drug addict for the drug of his addiction. He had to see the Other again, to feed his hate more surely. He had to look at the Other, while hating the alien, and feel the wild black current of his emotions running toward the brown and hairless shape. At night, buried in his nest of leaves, Harry tossed and snarled in his sleep, dreaming of the small stream backing up to flood the interior of the pyramid, and the Other drowning—of lightning striking the pyramid and fire racing through it—of the Other burning. His dreams became so full of rage and so terrible that he woke, twisting, and with the few rags of clothing that still managed to cling unnoticed to him soaked with sweat.

In the end, he went back into the pyramid.

Daily he went back. And gradually, it came to the point where he was no longer fearful of seeing the Other. Instead, he could barely endure the search and the waiting at the grilles until the Other came into sight. Meanwhile, outside the pyramid in the forest, the frill-edged leaves began to dry and wither and drop. The little stream sank in its bed—only a few inches, but enough so that Harry had to dig out the bottom of the streambed under the killing barrier in order to pass safely underwater into the pyramid area.

One day he noticed that there were hardly any of the treaded machines out taking samples in the woods any more.

He was on his way to the pyramid through the woods, when the realization struck him. He stopped dead, freezing in mid-stride like a hunting dog. Immediately, there flooded into his mind the memory of how the parking chamber for the treaded machines, inside the base of the pyramid, had been full of unmoving vehicles during his last few visits.

Immediately, also, he realized the significance of the drying leaves, the dropping of the water level of the stream. And something with the urgency of a great gong began to ring and ring inside him like the pealing of an alarm over a drowning city.

Time had been, when there had been no pyramid here. Time was now, with the year fading and the work of the collecting machines almost done. Time would be, when the pyramid might leave.

Taking with it the Other.

He began to run, instinctively, toward the pyramid. But, when he came within sight of it, he stopped. For a moment he was torn with indecision, an emotional maelstrom of fear and hatred all whirling together. Then, he went on.

He emerged a moment later, dripping, a fist-sized rock in each hand, to stand before the closed door that gave the machines entrance to the pyramid. He stood staring at it, in broad daylight. He had never come here before in full daylight, but his head now was full of madness. Fury seethed in him, but there was no machine to open the door for him. It was then that the fury and madness in him might have driven him to pound wildly on the door with his stones or to wrench off one of the necks of the storklike machine at the stream and try to pry the door open. Any of these insane things he might have done and so have attracted discovery and the awesome power of the machinery and killing weapons at the command of the Other. Any such thing he might have done if he was simply a man out of his head with rage—but he was no longer a man.

He was what the Other had made him, an animal, although with a man locked inside him. And like an animal, he did not rave or rant, any more than does the cat at the mousehole, or the wolf waiting for the shepherd to turn in for the night. Instead, without further question, the human beast that had been Harry Brennan—that still called himself Harry Brennan, in a little, locked-away, back corner of its mind—dropped on his haunches beside the door and hunkered there, panting lightly in the sunlight, and waiting.

Four hours later, as the sun was dropping close to the treetops, a single machine came trundling out of the woods. Harry tricked it with one of his stones and, still carrying the other, ran into the pyramid.

He waited patiently for the small collecting machine to come and empty out the machine returned from outside, then dodged ahead of it, when it came, into the interior, lower level of the pyramid. He made his way calmly to the grille that gave him entrance to the ventilating system, took out the grille, and entered the tube. Once in the system, he crawled through the maze of ductwork, until he came at last to the grille overlooking the room with the alcove and the rows of indentations on the alcove walls.

When he looked down through the grille, it was completely dark below. He could hear the hoarse breathing and smell the musky odor of the Other, resting or perhaps asleep, on the bed surface. Harry lay there for a number of slow minutes, smelling and listening. Then he lifted the second rock and banged with it upon the grille.

For a second there was nothing but the echoing clang of the beaten metal in the darkness. Then the room suddenly blazed with light, and Harry, blinking his blinded eyes against the glare, finally made out the figure of the Other rising upright upon the bed surface. Great, round, yellow eyes in a puglike face with a thick upper lip wrinkled over two tusks stared up through the grille at Harry.

The lip lifted, and a bubbling roar burst from the heavy fat-looking shape of the Other. He heaved his round body off the bed surface and rolled, waddling across the floor to just below the grille.

Reaching up with one blunt-clawed hand, he touched the grille, and it fell to the floor at his feet. Left unguarded in the darkness of the ductwork, Harry shrank back. But the Other straightened up to his full near six-and-a-half feet of height and reached up into the ductwork. His blunt-clawed hand fastened on Harry and jerked. Off balance, Harry came tumbling to the floor of the chamber.

A completely human man probably would have stiffened up and broken both arms, if not his neck, in such a fall. Harry, animallike, attempted to cling to the shape of the Other as he fell, and so broke the impact of his landing. On the floor, he let go of the Other and huddled away from the heavy shape, whimpering.

The Other looked down, and his round, yellow eyes focused on the stone Harry had clung to even through his fall. The Other reached down and grasped it, and Harry gave it up like a child releasing something he has been told many times not to handle. The Other made another, lower-toned, bubbling roar deep in his chest, examining the rock. Then he laid it carefully aside on a low table surface and turned back to stare down at Harry.

Harry cringed away from the alien stare and huddled into himself, as the blunt fingers reached down to feel some of the rags of a shirt that still clung about his shoulders.

The Other rumbled interrogatively at Harry. Harry hid his head. When he looked up again, the Other had moved over to a wall at the right of the alcove and was feeling about in some indentations there. He bubbled at the wall, and a second later Harry's voice sounded eerily in the room.

"You . . . You are . . . the one I . . . made a beast . . ."

Harry whimpered, hiding his head again.

"You can't . . . ." said Harry's voice, " . . . even speak now. Is . . . that so . . ."

Harry ventured to peek upward out of his folded arms, but ducked his head again at the sight of the cold, yellow eyes staring down at him.

" . . . I thought . . . you would be . . . dead by now,"
said the disembodied voice of Harry, hanging in the air
of the chamber. " . . . Amazing . . . survival completely
without . . . equipment. Must keep you now . . ." The
eyes, yellow as topaz, considered Harry, huddled abjectly
on the floor. " . . . cage . . . collector's item . . ."

The alien revolved back to the indentation of the
wall a little way from the alcove. The broad, fleshy
back turned contemptuously on Harry, who stared up
at it.

The pitiful expression of fear on Harry's face faded
suddenly into a soundless snarl. Silently, he uncoiled,
snatched up the rock the Other had so easily taken
from him, and sprang with it onto the broad back.

As he caught and clung there, one arm wrapped
around a thick neck, the stone striking down on the
hairless skull, his silent snarl burst out at last into the
sound of a scream of triumph.

The Other screamed too—a bubbling roar—as he
clumsily turned, trying to reach around himself with
his thick short arms and pluck Harry loose. His claws
raked Harry's throat-encircling arm, and blood streamed
from the arm; but it might have been so much stage
makeup for the effect it had in loosening Harry's hold.
Screaming, Harry continued to pound crushingly on the
Other's skull. With a furious spasm, the alien tore Harry
loose, and they both fell on the floor.

The Other was first up; and for a second he loomed
like a giant over Harry, as Harry was scrambling to his
own feet and retrieving the fallen rock. But instead of
attacking, the Other flung away, lunging for the alcove
and the control indentations there.

Harry reached the alcove entrance before him. The
alien dodged away from the striking rock. Roaring and
bubbling, he fled waddling from his human pursuer,
trying to circle around the room and get back to the

alcove. Half a head taller than Harry and twice Harry's weight, he was refusing personal battle and putting all his efforts into reaching the alcove with its rows of indented controls. Twice Harry headed him off; and then by sheer mass and desperation, the Other turned and burst past into the alcove, thick hands outstretched and grasping at its walls. Harry leaped in pursuit, landing and clinging to the broad, fleshy back.

The Other stumbled under the added weight, and fell, face down. Triumphantly yelling, Harry rode the heavy body to the floor, striking at the hairless head . . . and striking . . . and striking . . .

VI

Sometime later, Harry came wearily to his senses and dropped a rock he no longer had the strength to lift. He blinked around himself like a man waking from a dream, becoming aware of a brilliantly lit room full of strange shapes—and of a small alcove, the walls of which were covered with rows of indentations, in which something large and dead lay with its head smashed into ruin. A deep, clawing thirst rose to take Harry by the throat, and he staggered to his feet.

He looked longingly up at the dark opening of the ventilator over his head; but he was too exhausted to jump up, cling to its edge, and pull himself back into the ductwork, from which he could return to the stream outside the pyramid and to the flowing water there. He turned and stumbled from the chamber into unfamiliar rooms and corridors.

A brilliant light illuminated everything around him as he went. He sniffed and thought he scented, through the musky reek that filled the air about him, the clear odor of water. Gradually, the scent grew stronger and led him at last to a room where a bright stream leaped from a wall into a basin where it pooled brightly before draining away. He drank deeply and rested.

Finally, satiated, he turned away from the basin and came face-to-face with a wall that was an all-reflecting surface; and he stopped dead, staring at himself, like Adam before the Fall.

It was only then, with the upwelling of his returning humanness, that he realized his condition. And words spoken aloud for the first time in months broke harshly and rustily from his lips like the sounds of a machine unused for years.

"My God!" he said croakingly. "I've got no clothes left!"

And he began to laugh. Cackling, cackling rasping more unnaturally even than his speech, his laughter lifted and echoed hideously through the silent, alien rooms. But it was laughter all the same—the one sound that distinguishes man from the animal.

He was six months after that learning to be a complete human being again and finding out how to control the pyramid. If it had not been for the highly sophisticated safety devices built into the alien machine, he would never have lived to complete that bit of self-education.

But finally he mastered the controls and got the pyramid into orbit, where he collected the rest of his official self and shifted back through the alternate universe to Earth.

He messaged ahead before he landed; and everybody who could be there was on hand to meet him as he landed the pyramid. Some of the hands that had slapped his back on leaving were raised to slap him again when at last he stepped forth among them.

But, not very surprisingly, when his gaunt figure in a spare coverall now too big for it, with shoulder-length hair and burning eyes, stepped into their midst, not one hand finished its gesture. No one in his right senses slaps an unchained wolf on the back; and no one, after one look, wished to risk slapping the man who seemed to have taken the place of Harry.

Of course, he was still the same man they had sent out—of *course* he was. But at the same time he was also the man who had returned from a world numbered 1242 and from a duel to the death there with a representative of a race a hundred times more advanced than his own. And in the process he had been pared down to something very basic in his human blood and bone, something dating back to before the first crude wheel or chipped flint knife.

And what was that? Go down into the valley of the shades and demand your answer of a dead alien with his head crushed in, who once treated the utmost powers of modern human science as a man treats the annoyance of a buzzing mosquito.

Or, if that once-mighty traveler in spacegoing pyramids is disinclined to talk, turn and inquire of other ghosts you will find there—those of the aurochs, the great cave bear, and the woolly mammoth.

They, too, can testify to the effectiveness of naked men.

Here's another story from the viewpoint of the aliens, but this time they are a less sympathetic lot. The galactic overlords had neatly divided the intelligent species of the galaxy into three categories, and when the humans showed up, they were obviously victims just begging to be conquered. And when that didn't work, the overlords decided that instead, those humans obviously belonged in the conqueror category. But did they?

3-PART PUZZLE

The Mologhese ship twinkled across the light years separating the human-conquered planets of the Bahrin system from Mologh. Aboard her, the Mologh Envoy sat deep in study. For he was a thinker as well as a warrior, the Envoy, and his duties had gone far beyond obtaining the capsule propped on the Mologhese version of a desk before him—a sealed message capsule containing the diplomatic response of the human authorities to the proposal he had brought from Mologh. His object of study at the moment, however, was not the capsule, but a translation of something human he had painfully resolved into Mologhese terms.

His furry brow wrinkled and his bulldog-shaped jaw clamped as he worked his way through it. He had been over it a number of times, but he still could not conceive of a reason for a reaction he had observed among human young to its message. It was, he had been reliably informed, one of a group of such stories for the human young.—What he was looking at in translation was approximately this:—

THE THREE (Name) (Domestic animals) (Name)

Once upon a time there was a (horrendous, carnivorous, mythical creature) who lived under a bridge and one day he became very hungry. He was sitting there thinking of good things to eat when he heard the sounds of someone crossing the bridge over his head. (Sharp hoof-sound)—(sharp hoof-sound) went the sounds on the bridge overhead.

"Who's there?" cried the (horrendous, carnivorous, mythical creature).

"It's only I, the smallest (Name) (Domestic animal) (Name)" came back the answer.

"Well, I am the (horrendous, carnivorous, mythical creature) who lives under the bridge," replied the (horrendous, carnivorous, mythical creature) "and I'm coming up to eat you all up."

"Oh, don't do that, please!" cried the smallest (Name) (Domestic animal) (Name). "I wouldn't even make you a good meal. My (relative), the (middle-sized? next-oldest?) (Name) (Domestic animal) (Name) will be along in a minute. Let me go. He's much bigger than I. You'll get a much better meal out of him. Let me go and eat him instead."

"Very well," said the (horrendous, carnivorous, mythical creature); and (hoof-sound)—(hoof-sound) the (Name) (Domestic animal) (Name) hurried across the bridge to safety.

After a while the (horrendous, carnivorous, mythical

creature) heard (heavier hoof-sound)—(heavier hoof-sound) on the bridge overhead.

"Who's there?" he cried.

"It is I, the (middle-sized?) (Name) (Domestic animal) (Name)," replied a (deeper?) voice.

"Then I am coming up to eat you up," said the (horrendous, carnivorous, mythical creature). "Your smaller (relative?) the smallest (Name) (Domestic animal) (Name) told me you were coming and I let him go by so I could have a bigger meal by eating you. So here I come."

"Oh, you are, are you?" said the (middle-sized) (Name) (Domestic animal) (Name). "Well, suit yourself; but our oldest (relative?), the big (Name) (Domestic animal) (Name) will be along in just a moment If you want to wait for him, you'll really have a meal to remember."

"Is that so?" said the (horrendous, carnivorous, mythical creature), who was very (greedy? Avaricious? Gluttonous?). "All right, go ahead." And the (middle-sized) (Name) (Domestic animal) (Name) went (heavier hoof-sound)—(heavier hoof-sound) across the bridge to safety.

It was not long before the (horrendous, carnivorous, mythical creature) heard (thunderous hoof-sound)—(thunderous hoof-sound) shaking the bridge overhead.

"Who's there?" cried the (horrendous, carnivorous, mythical creature).

"It is I!" rumbled an (earth-shaking?) deep (bass?) voice. "The biggest (Name) (Domestic animal) (Name). Who calls?"

"I do!" cried the (horrendous, carnivorous, mythical creature). "And I'm coming up to eat you all up!" And he sprang up on the bridge. But the big (Name) (Domestic animal) (Name) merely took one look at him, and lowered (his?) head and came charging forward, with his (horns?) down. And he butted that (horrendous, carnivorous, mythical creature) over the hills and so far away he could never find his way back to bother anyone ever again.

The Mologhese Envoy put the translation aside and blinked his red-brown eyes wearily. It was ridiculous, he thought, to let such a small conundrum bother him this way. The story was perfectly simple and obvious; it related how an organization of three individuals delayed conflict with a dangerous enemy until their strongest member arrived to deal with the situation. Perfectly usual and good Conqueror indoctrination literature for Conqueror young.

But still, there was something—a difference about it he could not quite put his finger on. The human children he had observed having it told to them at that school he had visited had greeted the ending with an entirely disproportionate glee. Why? Even to a student of tactics like himself the lesson was a simple and rather boring one. It was as if a set of young students were suddenly to become jubilant on being informed that two plus two equaled four. Was there some hidden value in the lesson that he failed to discover? Or merely some freakish twist to the human character that caused the emotional response to be disproportionate?

If there was, the Envoy would be everlastingly destroyed if he could not lay the finger of his perception on what it was. Perhaps, thought the Envoy, leaning back in the piece of furniture in which he sat, this problem was merely part and parcel of that larger and more widespread anomaly he had remarked during the several weeks, local time, he had been the guest of the human HQ on Bahrin II. . . .

✦   ✦   ✦

The humans had emerged on to the galactic scene rather suddenly, but not too suddenly to escape notice by potentially interested parties. They had fanned out from their home system; doing it at first the hard way by taking over and attempting to pioneer uninhabited planets of nearby systems. Eventually they had bumped into the nearest Conqueror civilization—which was that of the Bahrin, a ursinoid type established over four small but respectable systems and having three Submissive types in bondage, one of which was a degraded Conqueror strain.

Like most primitive races, the humans did not at first seem to realize what they were up against. They attempted at first to establish friendly relations with the Bahrin without attempting any proof of their own Conqueror instincts. The Bahrin, of course, recognized Conqueror elements potential in the form of the human civilization; and for that reason struck all the harder, to take advantage of their own age and experience. They managed to destroy nearly all the major planetary installations of the humans, and over twenty per cent of the population at first strike. However, the humans rebounded with surprising ferocity and speed, to drop guerrilla land troops on the Bahrin planets while they gathered power for a strikeback. The strikeback was an overwhelming success, the Bahrin power being enfeebled by the unexpected fierceness of the human guerrillas and the fact that these seemed to have the unusual ability to enlist the sympathy of the Submissives under the Bahrin rule. The Bahrin were utterly broken; and the humans had for some little time been occupying the Bahrin worlds.

Meanwhile, the ponderous mills of the Galactic social order had been grinding up the information all this had provided. It was known that human exploration ships had stumbled across their first contact with one of the Shielded Worlds; and immediately made eager overtures of friendship to the people upon it. It was reported that when the Shielded peoples went on about their apparently meaningless business under that transparent protective element which no known Conqueror had ever been able to breach; (and the human overtures were ignored, as all Conqueror attempts at contact had always been), that a storm of emotion swept over the humans—a storm involving the whole spectrum of emotions. It was as if the rejection had had the equivalent of a calculated insult from an equivalent, Conqueror, race.

In that particular neighborhood of the galaxy the Mologhese currently held the balance of power among the Conqueror races. They sent an Envoy with a proposal to the human authorities.

—And that, thought the Envoy, aboard the returning spaceship as he put aside the problem of the translation to examine the larger question, was the beginning of an educative process on both sides.

His job had been to point out politely but firmly that there were many races in the galaxy; but that they had all evolved on the same type of world, and they all fell into one of three temperamental categories. They were by nature Conquerors, Submissives, or Invulnerables. The Invulnerables were, of course, the people of the Shielded Worlds; who went their own pacific, non-technologic ways. And if these could not be dominated behind the protections of their strange abilities, they did not seem interested in dominating themselves, or interfering with the Conquerors. So the situation worked out to equalities and they could be safely ignored.

The Submissive races, of course, were there for any Conqueror race's taking. That disposed of them. But there were certain elements entering into inter-

Conqueror relationships, that were important for the humans to know.

No Conqueror race could, naturally, be denied its birthright, which was to take as much as it could from Submissives and its fellow-Conquerors. On the other hand, there were advantages to be gamed by semi-peaceful existence even within the laws of a society of Conqueror races. Obvious advantages dealing with trade, travel, and a reciprocal recognition of rights and customs. To be entitled to these, the one prime requirement upon any Conqueror race was that it should not rock the boat. It might take on one or more of its neighbors, or make an attempt to move up a notch in the pecking order in this neck of the galactic woods; but it must not become a bother to the local community of Conquerors as a whole by such things as general piracy, et cetera.

"In short," had replied the Envoy's opposite number—a tall, rather thin and elderly human with a sad smile, "a gentleman's agreement?"

"Please?" said the Envoy. The Opposite Number explained.

"Essentially, yes," said the Envoy, feeling pleased. He was pleased enough, in fact, to take time out for a little dissertation on this as an example of the striking cultural similarities between Conqueror races that often produced parallel terms in completely different languages, and out of completely different backgrounds.

" . . . In fact," he wound up, "let me say that personally, I find you people very much akin. That is one of the things that makes me so certain that you will eventually be very pleased that you have agreed to this proposal I brought. Essentially, all it asks is that you subscribe to the principles of a Conqueror intersociety—which is, after all, your own kind of society—and recognize its limitations as well as its privileges by pledging to maintain the principles which are the hard facts of its existence."

"Well," said his Opposite Number, whose name was Harrigan or Hargan, or some such, "that is something to be decided on in executive committee. Meanwhile, suppose I show you around here; and you can tell me more about the galaxy."

There followed several weeks in which the Envoy found himself being convoyed around the planet which had originally been the seat of the former Bahrin ruling group. It was quite obviously a tactic to observe him over a period of time and under various conditions; and he did not try to resist it He had his own observations to make, and this gave him an excellent opportunity to do so.

For one thing, he noted down as his opinion that they were an exceedingly touchy people where slights were concerned. Here they had just finished their war with the Bahrin in the last decade and were facing entrance into an interstellar society of races as violent as themselves; and yet the first questions on the tips of the tongues of nearly all those he met were concerned with the Shielded Worlds. Even Harrigan, or whatever his name was, confessed to an interest in the people on the Invulnerable planets.

"How long have they been like that?" Harrigan asked.

The Envoy could not shrug. His pause before answering fulfilled the same function.

"There is no way of telling," he said. "Things on Shielded Worlds are as the people there make them. Take away the signs of a technical civilization from a planet—turn it all into parkland—and how do you tell how long the people there have been as they are? All we ever knew is that they are older than any of *our* histories."

"Older?" said Harrigan. "There must be some legend, at least, about how they came to be?"

"No," said the Envoy. "Oh, once in a great while some worthless planet without a population will suddenly develop a shield and become fertile, forested and populated—but this is pretty clearly a case of colonization. The Invulnerables seem to be able to move from point to point in space by some nonphysical means. That's all."

"All?" said Harrigan.

"All," said the Envoy. "Except for an old Submissive superstition that the Shielded Peoples are a mixed race sprung from an interbreeding between a Conqueror and a Submissive type—something we know, of course, to be a genetic impossibility."

"I see," said Harrigan.

Harrigan took the Envoy around to most of the major cities of the planet. They did not visit any military installations (the Envoy had not expected that they would) but they viewed a lot of new construction taking the place of Bahrin buildings that had been obliterated by the angry scars of the war. It was going up with surprising swiftness—or perhaps not so surprising, noted the Envoy thoughtfully, since the humans seemed to have been able to enlist the enthusiastic cooperation of the Submissives they had taken over. The humans appeared to have a knack for making conquered peoples willing to work with them. Even the Bahrin, what there were left of them, were behaving most unlike a recently crushed race of Conquerors, in the extent of their cooperation. Certainly the humans seemed to be allowing their former enemies a great deal of freedom, and even responsibility in the new era. The Envoy sought for an opportunity, and eventually found the chance to talk to one of the Bahrin alone.

This particular Bahrin was an assistant architect on a school that was being erected on the outskirts of one city. (The humans seemed slightly crazy on the subject of schools; and only slightly less crazy on the subjects of hospitals, libraries, museums, and recreation areas. Large numbers of these were going up all over the planet.) This particular Bahrin, however, was a male who had been through the recent war. He was middle-aged and had lost an arm in the previous conflict. The Envoy found him free to talk, not particularly bitter, but considerably impressed emotionally by his new overlords.

" . . . May your courage be with you," he told the Envoy. "You will have to face them sooner or later; and they are demons."

"What kind of demons?" said the Envoy, skeptically.

"A new kind," said the Bahrin. He rested his heavy, furry, bear-like forearm upon the desk in front of him and stared out a window at a changing landscape. "Demons full of fear and strange notions. Who understands them? Half their history is made up of efforts to understand themselves—and they still don't." He glanced significantly at the Envoy. "Did you know the Submissives are already starting to call them the Mixed People?"

The Envoy wrinkled his furry brow.

"What's that supposed to mean?" he said.

"The Submissives think the humans are really Submissives who have learned how to fight."

The Envoy snorted.

"That's ridiculous."

"Of course," said the Bahrin; and sighed heavily. "But what isn't, these days?" He turned back to his work. "Anyway, don't ask me about them. The more I see of them, the less I understand."

❖   ❖   ❖

They parted on that note—and the Envoy's private conviction that the loss of the Bahrin's arm had driven him slightly insane.

Nonetheless, during the following days as he was escorted around from spot to spot, the essence of that anomaly over which he was later to puzzle during his trip home, emerged. For one thing, there were the schools. The humans, evidently, in addition to being education crazy themselves, believed in wholesale education for their cattle as well. One of the schools he was taken to was an education center for young Bahrin pupils; and—evidently due to a shortage of Bahrin instructors following the war—a good share of the teachers were human.

" . . . I just *love* my class!" one female human teacher told the Envoy, as they stood together watching young Bahrin at play during their relaxation period.

"Please?" said the Envoy, astounded.

"They're so quick and eager to learn," said the teacher. One of the young Bahrin at play dashed up to her, was overcome with shyness at seeing the Envoy, and hung back. She reached out and patted him on the head. A peculiar shiver ran down the Envoy's back; but the young Bahrin nestled up to her.

"They *respond* so," said the teacher. "Don't you think so?"

"They were a quite worthy race at one time," replied the Envoy, with mingled diplomatic confusion and caution.

"Oh, yes!" said the teacher enthusiastically; and proceeded to overwhelm him with facts he already knew about the history of the Bahrin, until the Envoy found himself rescued by Harrigan. The Envoy went off wondering a little to himself whether the humans had indeed conquered the Bahrin or whether, perhaps, it had not been the other way around.

Food for that same wonderment seemed to be supplied by just about everything else that Harrigan let him see. The humans, having just about wiped the Bahrin out of existence, seemed absolutely determined to repair the damage they had done, but improve upon the former situation by way of interest. Why? What kept the Bahrin from seething with plans for revolt at this very minute? The young ones of course—like that pupil with the teacher—might not know any better; but the older ones . . . ? The Envoy thought of the one-armed Bahrin architect he had talked to, and felt further doubt. If they were all like that one—but then what kind of magic had the humans worked to produce such an intellectual and emotional victory? The Envoy went back to his quarters and took a nap to quiet the febrillations of his thinking process.

When he woke up, he set about getting hold of what history he could on the war just past. Accounts both human and Bahrin were available; and, plowing through them, reading them for statistics rather than reports, he was reluctantly forced to the conclusion that the one-armed Bahrin had been right. The humans were demons. —Or at least, they had fought like demons against the Bahrin. A memory of the shiver that had run down his back as he watched the female human teacher patting the young Bahrin on head, troubled the Envoy again. Would this same female be perfectly capable of mowing down adult Bahrin by the automatic hand-weapon clipful? Apparently her exact counterparts had. If so, which was the normal characteristic of the human nature—the head-patting, or the trigger-pulling?

It was almost a relief when the human authorities gave him a sealed answer to the proposal he had brought, and sent him on his way home a few days later. He carried that last question of his away with him.

❖   ❖   ❖

The only conclusion I can come to," said the Envoy to the chief authority among the Mologhese, a week and a half later as they both sat in the Chief's office, "is that there is some kind of racial insanity that sets in in times of peace. In other words, they're Conquerors in the true sense only when engaged in Conquest."

The Chief frowned at the proposal answer, still sealed on the desk before him. He had asked for the Envoy's report before opening it; and now he wondered if this traditional procedure had been the wisest move under the circumstances. He rather suspected the Envoy's wits of having gone somewhat astray during his mission.

"You don't expect me to believe something like that," said the Chief. "No culture that was insane half the time could survive. And if they tried to maintain sanity by continual Conquest, they would bleed to death in two generations."

The Envoy said nothing. His Chief's arguments were logically unassailable.

"The sensible way to look at it," said the Chief, "is to recognize them as simply another Conqueror strain with somewhat more marked individual peculiarities than most. This is—let us say—their form of recreation, of amusement, between conquests. Perhaps they enjoy playing with the danger of cultivating strength in their conquered races."

"Of course, there is that," admitted the Envoy. "You may be right."

"I think," said the Chief, "that it's the only sensible all-around explanation."

"On the other hand—" the Envoy hesitated, remembering. "There was the business of that female human patting the small Bahrin on the head."

"What about it?"

The Envoy looked at his Chief.

"Have *you* ever been patted on the head?" he asked. The Chief stiffened.

"Of course not!" He relaxed slowly, staring at the Envoy. "Why? What makes you ask that?"

"Well, I never have either, of course—especially by anyone of another race. But that little Bahrin liked it. And seeing it gave me—" the Envoy stopped to shiver again.

"Gave you what?" said the Chief.

"A . . . a sort of horrible, affectionate feeling—" The Envoy stopped speaking in helplessness.

"You've been overworking," said the Chief, coldly. "Is there anything more to report?"

"No," said the Envoy. "No. But aside from all this, there's no doubt they'd be a tough nut to crack, those humans. My recommendation is that we wait for optimum conditions before we choose to move against them."

"Your recommendation will go into the record, of course," said the Chief. He picked up the human message capsule. "And now I think it's time I listened to this. They didn't play it for you?"

The Envoy shook his head.

The Chief picked up the capsule (it was one the Envoy had taken along for the humans to use in replying), broke its seal and put it into the speaker unit of his desk. The speaker unit began to murmur a message tight-beamed toward the Chiefs ear alone. The Envoy sat, nursing the faint hope that the Chief would see fit to let him hear, later. The Envoy was very curious as to the contents of that message. He watched his Chief closely, and saw the other's face slowly gather in a frown that deepened as the message purred on.

Abruptly it stopped. The Chief looked up; and his eyes met the Envoy's.

"It just may be," said the Chief slowly, "that I owe you an apology."

"An apology?" said the Envoy.

"Listen to this—" The Chief adjusted a volume control and pressed a button. A human voice speaking translated Mologhese filled the room.

"The Committee of Control for the human race wishes to express its appreciation for—"

"No, no—" said the Chief. "Not this diplomatic slush. Farther on—" He did things with his controls, the voice speeded up to a gabble, a whine, then slowed toward understandability again. "Ah, listen to this."

" . . . Association," said the voice, "but without endorsement of what the Mologhese Authority is pleased to term the Conqueror temperament. While our two races have a great deal in common, the human race has as its ultimate aims not the exercises of war and oppression, plundering, general destruction and the establishment of a tyranny in a community of tyrants; but rather the establishment of an environment of peace for all races. The human race believes in the ultimate establishment of universal freedom, justice, and the inviolable rights of the individual whoever he may be. We believe that our destiny lies neither within the pattern of conquest nor submission, but with the enlightened maturity of independence characterized by what are known as the Shielded Worlds; and, while not ceasing to defend our people and our borders from all attacks foreign and domestic, we intend to emulate these older, protected peoples in hope that they may eventually find us worthy of association. In this hope—"

The Chief clicked off the set and looked grimly at the Envoy. The Envoy stared back at him in shock.

"Insane," said the Envoy. "I was right—quite insane."

He sank back in his seat "At any rate, you too were correct. They're too irrational, too unrealistic to survive. We needn't worry about them."

"On the contrary," said his Chief. "And I'm to blame for not spotting it sooner. There were indications of this in some of the preliminary reports we had on them. They are very dangerous."

The Envoy shook his head.

"I don't see—" he began.

"But I do!" said the Chief. "And I don't hold down this position among our people for nothing. Think for a moment, Envoy! Don't you see it? These people are *causal!*"

"Causal?"

"Exactly," replied the Chief. "They don't act or react to practical or realistic stimuli. They react to emotional or philosophic conclusions of their own."

"I don't see what's so dangerous about that?" said the Envoy, wrinkling his forehead.

"It wouldn't be dangerous if they were a different sort of race," said the Chief. "But these people seem to be able to rationalize their emotional and philosophic conclusions in terms of hard logic and harder science.—You don't believe me? Do you remember that story for the human young you told me about, about the three hoofed and horned creatures crossing a bridge?"

"Of course," said the Envoy.

"All right. It puzzled you that the human young should react so strongly to what was merely a lesson in elementary tactics. But—it wasn't the lesson they were reacting to. It was the emotional message overlaying the lesson. The notion of some sort of abstract right and wrong, so that when the somehow *wrong* mythical creature under the bridge gets what the humans might describe as his just deserts at the horns of the triumphing biggest *right* creature—the humans are tremendously stimulated."

"But I still don't see the danger—"

"The danger," said the Chief, "lies in the fact that while such a story has its existence apparently—to humans—only for its moral and emotional values, the tactical lesson which we so obviously recognize is not lost, either. To us, this story shows a way of conquering. To the humans it shows not only a way but a reason, a justification. A race whose motives are founded upon such justifications is tremendously dangerous to us."

"You must excuse me," said the Envoy, bewilderedly. "Why—"

"Because we—and I mean all the Conqueror races, and all the Submissive races—" said the Chief, strongly, "have no defenses in the emotional and philosophic areas. Look at what you told me about the Bahrin, and the Submissives the humans took over from the Bahrin. Having no strong emotional and philosophic persuasions of their own, they have become immediately infected by the human ones. They are like people unacquainted with a new disease who fall prey to an epidemic. The humans, being self-convinced of such things as justice and love, in spite of their own arbitrariness and violence, convince all of us who lack convictions having never needed them before. Do you remember how you said you felt when you saw the little Bahrin being patted on the head? *That's* how vulnerable we are!"

The Envoy shivered again, remembering.

"Now I see," he said.

"I thought you would," said the Chief, grimly. "The situation to my mind is serious, enough so to call for the greatest emergency measures possible. We mustn't make the mistake of the creature under the bridge in the story. We were prepared to let the humans get by our community strength because we thought of them as embryo Conquerors, and we hoped for better entertainment later. Now they come along again, this time as something we can recognize as Conqueror-plus. And this time we can't let them get by. I'm going to call a meeting of our neighboring Conqueror executive Chiefs; and get an agreement to hit the humans now with a coalition big enough to wipe them out to the last one."

He reached for a button below a screen on his desk. But before he could touch it, it came alight with the figure of his own attaché.

"Sir—" began this officer; and then words failed him.

"Well?" barked the Chief.

"Sir—" the officer swallowed. "From the Shielded Worlds—a message." The Chief stared long and hard.

"From the Shielded Worlds?" said the Chief. "How? From the Shielded Worlds? When?"

"I know it's fantastic, sir. But one of our ships was passing not too far from one of the Shielded Worlds and it found itself caught—"

"And you just now got the message?" The Chief cut him short.

"Just this second, sir. I was just—"

"Let me have it. And keep your channel open," said the Chief. "I've got some messages to send."

The officer made a movement on the screen and something like a message cylinder popped out of a slot in the Chiefs' desk. The Chief reached for it, and hesitated. Looking up, he found the eyes of the Envoy upon him.

"Never—" said the Envoy, softly. "Never in known history have they communicated with any of us. . . ."

"It's addressed to me," said the Chief, looking at the outside of the cylinder. "If they can read our minds, as we suspect, then they know what I've just discovered about the humans and what I plan to do about it." He gave the cylinder a twist to open it "Let's see what they have to say."

The cylinder opened up like a flower. A single white sheet unrolled within it to lie flat on the desk; and the message upon it in the common galactic code looked up at the Chief. The message consisted of just one word. The word was:—

NO.

Back to human viewpoint—with a reminder of just how alien one human can be to another. This story shows Dickson's skill, as he takes two human characters, making neither one sympathetic or easy to identify with, and still creates an engrossing story where these Kilkenny Cats flummox the belligerent aliens. But don't pick a side to root for too soon. You have been warned!

AN OUNCE OF EMOTION

I

"Well? Are the ships joined—or not?" demanded Arthur Mial.

"Look for yourself!" said Tyrone Ross.

Mial turned and went on out of the room. All right, thought Ty savagely, call it a personality conflict. Putting a tag on it is one thing, doing something about it another. And I have to do something—it could just be the fuse to this nitrojelly situation he, I, and Annie are all sitting on. There must be some way I can break down this feeling between us.

Ty glanced for a moment across the spaceliner stateroom at the statistical analysis instrument, called Annie, now sitting silent and unimpressive as a black steamer trunk against a far wall.

It was Annie who held the hope of peace for thousands of cubic light years of interstellar space in every direction. Annie—with the help of Ty. And the dubious help of Mial. The instrument, thought Ty grimly, deserved better than the two particular human companions the Laburti had permitted, to bring her to them.

He turned back to the vision screen he had been watching earlier.

On it, pictured from the viewpoint of one of the tractor mechs now maneuvering the ship, this leviathan of a Laburti spaceliner he was on was being laid alongside and only fifty yards from an equally huge Chedal vessel. Even Ty's untrained eye could see the hair-trigger risks in bringing those hundreds of thousands of tons of mass so close together. But with the two Great Races, so-called, poised on the verge of conflict, the Chedal Observer of the Annie Demonstration five days from now could not be simply ferried from his ship to this like any ordinary passenger.

The two ships must be faced, main airlock to main airlock, and a passageway fitted between the locks. So that the Chedal and his staff could stroll aboard with all due protocol. Better damage either or both of the giant craft than chance any suspicion of a slight by one of the Great Races to a representative of the other.

For the Laburti and the Chedal were at a sparking point. A sparking point of war that—but of course neither race of aliens was concerned about that—could see small Earth drafted into the armed camp of its huge Laburti neighbor; and destroyed by the Chedal horde, if the interstellar conflict swept past Alpha Centauri.

It was merely, if murderously, ironic in this situation that Ty and Mial who came bearing the slim hope of peace that was Annie, should be themselves at a sparking point. A sparking point willed by neither—but to which they had both been born.

Ty's thoughts came back from the vision screen to their original preoccupation.

It happened sometimes, he thought. It just—happened. Sometimes, for no discernable reason, suddenly and without warning, two men meeting for the first time felt the ancient furies buried deep in their forebrains leap abruptly and redly to life. It was rapport between individuals turned inside out—anti-rapport. Under it, the animal instinct in each man instantly snarled and bristled, recognizing a mortal enemy—an enemy not in act or attitude, but simply in *being*.

So it had happened with Ty—and Mial. Back on Earth, thought Ty now, while there was still a chance to do something about the situation, they had each been too civilized to speak up about it. Now it was too late. The mistake was made.

And mistake it had been. For, practical engineer and reasonable man that Ty was, reasonable man and practical politician that Mial was, to the rest of mankind—to each other they were tigers. And common sense dictated that you did not pen two tigers alone together for two weeks; for a delicate mission on which the future existence of the human race might depend. Already, after nine days out—

"We'll have to go meet the Chedal." It was Mial, reentering the room. Ty turned reflexively to face him.

The other man was scarcely a dozen years older than Ty; and in many ways they were nearly alike. There could not be half an inch or five pounds of weight difference between them, thought Ty. Like Ty, Mial was square-shouldered and leanly built. But his hair was dark where Ty's was blond: and that dark hair had

started to recede. The face below it was handsome,
rather than big-boned and open like Ty's. Mial, at
thirty-six, was something of a wonder boy in politics
back on Earth. Barely old enough for the senatorial
seat he held, he had the respect of almost everyone.
But he had been legal counsel for some unsavory
groups in the beginning of his career. He would know
how, thought Ty watching him now, to fight dirty if he
had to. And the two of them were off with none but
aliens to witness.

"I know," said Ty now, harshly. He turned to follow Mial as the other man started out of the room.
"What about Annie?"

Mial looked back over his shoulder.

"She's safe enough. What good's a machine to them
if no one but a human can run her?" Mial's voice was
almost taunting. "You can't go up with the big boys,
Ross, and act scared."

Ty's face flushed with internal heat—but it was true,
what Mial had said. A midget trying to make peace with
giants did well not to act doubtful or afraid. Mial had
courage to see it. Ty felt an unwilling touch of admiration for the man. I could almost like him for that,
he thought—if I didn't hate his guts.

By the time they got to the airlock, the slim, dog-
faced, and darkly-robed Laburti were in their receiv-
ing line, and the first of the squat, yellow-furred Chedal
forms were coming through. First came the guards;
then the Observer himself, distinguishable to a human
eye only by the sky-blue harness he wore. The tall, thin
form of the robed Laburti Captain glided forward to
welcome him aboard first; and then the Observer
moved down the line, to confront Mial.

A high-pitched chattering came from the Chedal's
lipless slit of a mouth, almost instantly overridden by

the artificial, translated human speech from the black translator collar around the alien's thick, yellow-furred neck. Shortly, Mial was replying in kind, his own black translator collar turning his human words into Chedal chitterings. Ty stood listening, half-self conscious, half-bored.

"—and my Demonstration Operator." Ty woke suddenly to the fact that Mial was introducing him to the Chedal.

"Honored," said Ty, and heard his collar translating.

"May I invite you both to my suite now, immediately, for the purpose of improving our acquaintance . . ." The invitation extended itself, became flowery, and ended with a flourish.

"It's an honor to accept . . ." Mial was answering. Ty braced himself for at least another hour of this before they could get back to their own suite.

Then his breath caught in his throat.

" . . . for myself, that is," Mial was completing his answer. "Unfortunately, I earlier ordered my Operator to return immediately to his device, once these greetings were over. And I make it a practice never to change an order. I'm sure you understand."

"Of course. Some other time I will host your Operator. Shall we two go?" The Chedal turned and led off. Mial was turning with him, when Ty stepped in front of him.

"Hold on—" Ty remembered to turn off his translator collar. "What's this about your *ordering* me—"

Mial flicked off his own translator collar.

"You heard me," he said. He stepped around Ty and walked off. Ty stood, staring after him. Then, conscious of the gazing Laburti all about him, he turned and headed back toward their own suite.

Once back there, and with the door to the ship's corridor safely closed behind him, he swore and turned

to checking out Annie, to make sure there had been
no investigation or tampering with her innards while
he was absent. Taking off the side panel of her case,
he pinched his finger between the panel and the case
and swore again. Then he sat down suddenly, ignor-
ing Annie and began to think.

II

With the jab of pain from the pinched finger, an
incredible suspicion had sprung, full-armed into his
brain. For the first time he found himself wondering
if Mial's lie to the Chedal about an 'order' to Ty had
been part of some plan by the other man against Ty.
A plan that required Mial's talking with the Chedal
Observer alone, before Ty did.

It was, Ty had to admit, the kind of suspicion that
only someone who felt as he did about Mial could have
dreamed up. And yet . . .

The orders putting the Annie Demonstration Mission—
which meant Annie and Ty—under the authority of Mial
had been merely a polite fiction. A matter of matching
the high rank and authority of the Laburti and Chedal
officials who would be watching the Demonstration as
Observers. Ty had been clearly given to understand that
by his own Department chief, back on Earth.

In other words, Mial had just now stopped playing
according to the unwritten rules of the Mission. That
might bode ill for Ty. And, thought Ty now, suddenly,
it might bode even worse for the success of the Mission. But it was unthinkable that Mial would go so far
as to risk that.

For, it was one thing to stand here with Annie and
know she represented something possessed by neither

the Laburti nor the Chedal technologies. It was all right
to remind oneself that human science was growing like
the human population; and that population was multiplying at close to three per cent per year—as opposed
to a fraction of a per cent for the older Chedal and
Laburti populations.

But there were present actualities that still had to
be faced—like the size of this ship, and that of the
Chedal ship now parting from it. Also, like the twenty-
odd teeming worlds apiece, the thousands of years each
of post-atomic civilization, the armed might either
sprawling alien empire could boast.

Mial could not—would not—be playing some personal game in the face of all this. Ty shook his head
angrily at the thought. No man could be such a fool,
no matter what basic emotional factor was driving him.

When Mial returned to their stateroom suite a
couple of hours later, Ty made an effort to speak
pleasantly to him.

"Well?" said Ty, "how'd it go? And when am I to
meet him?"

Mial looked at him coldly.

"You'll be told," he said, and went on into his bedroom.

But, in the four days left of the trip to the Laburti
World, where the Demonstration was to be given
before a joint audience of Laburti and Chedal Observers, it became increasingly apparent Ty was not to meet
the Chedal. Meanwhile, Mial was increasingly in conference with the alien representative.

Ty gritted his teeth. At least, at their destination the
Mission would be moving directly to the Human
Consulate. And the Consul in charge was not a human,
but a Laburti citizen who had contracted for the job
of representing the Earth race. Mial could hardly hold

secret conferences with the Chedal under a Laburti nose.

Ty was still reminding himself of this as the spaceliner finally settled toward their destination—a fantastic metropolis, with eight and ten thousand foot tall buildings rising out of what Ty had been informed was a quarter-mile depth of open ocean. Ty had just finished getting Annie rigged for handling when Mial came into the room.

"Ready?" demanded Mial.

"Ready," said Ty.

"You go ahead with Annie and the baggage—" The sudden, soft hooting of the landing horn interrupted Mial, and there was a faint tremor all through the huge ship as it came to rest in its landing cradle of magnetic forces; the main door to the suite from the corridor swung open. A freight-handling mech slid into the room and approached Annie.

"I'll meet you outside in the taxi area," concluded Mial.

Ty felt abrupt and unreasonable suspicion.

"Why?" he asked sharply.

Mial had already turned toward the open door through which the mech had just entered. He paused and turned back to face Ty; a smile, razor blade thin and cruel altered his handsome face.

"Because that's what I'm going to do," he said softly, and turned again toward the door.

Ty stared after him for a moment, jarred and irresolute at the sudden, fresh outbreak of hostilities, and Mial went out through the door.

"Wait a minute!" snapped Ty, heading after him. But the other man was already gone, and the mech, carrying Annie and following close behind him, had blocked Ty's path. Cold with anger, Ty swung back to check their personal baggage, including their food supplies, as another mech entered to carry these to the outside of the ship.

When he finally got outside to the disembarkation area, and got the baggage, as well as Annie, loaded on to one of the flying cargo platforms that did taxi service among the Laburti, he looked around for Mial. He discovered the other man a short distance away in the disembarkation area, talking again with a blue-harnessed, yellow-furred form.

Grimly, Ty turned on his translator collar and gave the cargo platform the address of the human Consulate. Then, he lifted a section of the transparent cover of the platform and stepped aboard, to sit down on the luggage and wait for Mial. After a while, he saw Mial break off his conversation and approach the cargo platform. The statesman spoke briefly to the cargo platform, something Ty could not hear from under the transparent cover, then came aboard and sat down next to Ty.

The platform lifted into the air and headed in between the blue and gray metal of the towers with their gossamer connecting bridges.

"I already told it where to take us," said Ty.

Mial turned to look at him briefly and almost contemptuously, then turned away again without answering.

The platform slid amongst the looming towers and finally flew them in through a wide window opening, into a room set up with human-style furniture. They got off, and Ty looked around as the platform began to unload the baggage. There was no sign of the Laburti individual who filled the role of human Consul. Sudden suspicion blossomed again in Ty.

"Wait a minute—" He wheeled about—but the

platform, already unloaded, was lifting out through the window opening again. Ty turned on Mial. "This isn't the Consulate!"

"That's right," Mial almost drawled the words. "It's a hotel—the way they have them here. The Chedal Observer recommended it to me."

"Recommended—?" Ty stared. "We're supposed to go to the Consulate. You can't—"

"Can't I?" Mial's eyes were beginning to blaze. The throttled fury in him was yammering to be released, evidently, as much as its counterpart in Ty. "I don't trust that Consulate, with its Laburti playing human Consul. Here, if the Chedal wants to drop by—"

"He's not supposed to drop by!" Ty snarled. "We're here to demonstrate Annie, not gabble with the Observers. What'll the Laburti think if they find you and the Chedal glued together half of the time?" He got himself under control and said in a lower voice. "We're going back to the Consulate, now—"

"Are we?" Mial almost hissed. "Are you forgetting that the orders show *me* in charge of this Demonstration—and that the aliens'll believe those orders? Besides, you don't know your way around here. And, after talking to the Chedal—I do!"

He turned abruptly and strode over to an apparently blank wall. He rapped on it, and flicked on his translator collar and spoke to the wall.

"Open up!" The wall slid open to reveal what was evidently an elevator tube. He stepped into it and turned to smile mockingly at Ty, drifting down out of sight. The wall closed behind him.

"Open up!" raged Ty, striding to the wall and rapping on it. He flicked on his translator collar. "Open up. Do you hear me? Open up!"

But the wall did not open. Ty, his knuckles getting sore, at last gave up and turned back to Annie.

III

Whatever else might be going on, his responsibility to her and the Demonstration tomorrow, remained unchanged. He got her handling rigging off, and ran a sample problem through her. When he was done, he checked the resultant figures against the answers to the problem already established by multiple statistics back on Earth. He was within a fraction of a per cent all the way down the line.

Ty glowed, in spite of himself. Operating Annie successfully was not so much a skill, as an art. In any problem, there were from fourteen to twenty factors whose values had to be adjusted according to the instincts and creativity of the Operator. It was this fact that was the human ace in the hole in this situation. Aliens could not run Annie—they had tried on Annie's prototypes and failed. Only a few specially trained and talented humans could run her successfully . . . and of these, Ty Ross was the master Operator. That was why he was here.

Now, tomorrow he would have to prove his right to that title. Under his hands Annie could show that a hundred and twenty-five Earth years after the Laburti and Chedal went to war, the winner would have a Gross Racial Product only eight per cent increased over today—so severe would the conflict have been. But in a hundred and twenty-five years of peaceful co-existence and cooperation, both races would have doubled their G.R.P.s in spite of having made only fractional increases in population. And machines like Annie, with operators like Ty, stood ready to monitor and guide the G.R.P. increases. No sane race could go to war in the face of that.

Meanwhile, Mial had not returned. Outside the weather shield of the wide window, the local sun, a G5 star, was taking its large, orange-yellow shape below the watery horizon. Ty made himself something to eat, read a while, and then took himself to bed in one of the adjoining bedrooms. But disquieting memories kept him from sleeping.

He remembered now that there had been an argument back on Earth, about the proper way to make use of Annie. He had known of this for a long time. Mial's recent actions came forcing it back into the forefront of his sleepless mind.

The political people back home had wanted Annie to be used as a tool, and a bargaining point, rather than a solution to the Laburti-Chedal confrontation, in herself. It was true. Ty reminded himself in the darkness. Mial had not been one of those so arguing. But he was of the same breed and occupation as they, reminded the little red devils of suspicion, coming out to dance on Ty's brain. With a sullen effort Ty shoved them out of his mind and forced himself to think of something else—anything else.

And, after a while, he slept.

He woke suddenly, feeling himself being shaken back to consciousness. The lights were on in the room and Mial was shaking him.

"What?" Ty sat up, knocking the other man's hand aside.

"The Chedal Observer's here with me." said Mial. "He wants a preview demonstration of the analyzer."

"A preview!" Ty burst up out of bed to stand facing the other man. "Why should he get to see Annie before the official Demonstration?"

"Because I said he could." Underneath, Mial's eyes were stained by dark half-circles of fatigue.

"Well, I say he can wait until tomorrow like the Laburti!" snapped Ty. He added, "—And don't try to pull your paper rank on me. If I don't run Annie for him, who's to do it? You?"

Mial's weary face paled with anger.

"The Chedal asked for the preview," he said, in a tight, low voice. "I didn't think I had the right to refuse him, important as this Mission is. Do you want to take the responsibility of doing it? Annie'll come up with the same answers now as seven hours from now."

"Almost the same—" muttered Ty. "They're never exact, I told you that." He swayed on his feet, caught between sleep and resentment.

"As you say," said Mial, "I can't make you do it."

Ty hesitated a second more. But his brain seemed numb.

"All right," he snapped. "I'll have to get dressed. Five minutes!"

Mial turned and went out. When Ty followed, some five minutes later, he found both the other man and the alien in the sitting room. The Chedal came toward Ty, and for a moment they were closer than they had been even in the spaceliner airlock. For the first time, Ty smelled a faint, sickening odor from the alien, a scent like overripe bananas.

The Chedal handed him a roll of paper-like material. Gibberish raved from his lipless mouth and was translated by the translator collar.

"Here is the data you will need."

"Thank you," said Ty, with bare civility. He took the roll over to Annie and examined it. It contained all the necessary statistics on both the Laburti and Chedal races, from the Gross Racial Products down to statistical particulars. He went to work, feeding the data into Annie.

Time flowed by, catching him up in the rhythm of his work as it went.

His job with Annie required just this sort of concentration and involvement, and for a little while he forgot the two watching him. He looked up at last to see the window aperture flushed with yellow-pink dawn, and guessed that perhaps an hour had gone by.

He tore loose the tape he had been handling, and walked with it to the Chedal.

"Here," he said, putting the tape into the blunt, three-fingered hands, and pointing to the first figures. "There's your G.R.P. half a standard year after agreement to co-exist with Laburti.—Up three thousandths of one per cent already. And here it is at the end of a full year—"

"And the Laburti?" demanded the translated chittering of the alien.

"Down here. You see . . ." Ty talked on. The Chedal watched, his perfectly round, black eyes emotionless as the button-eyes of a child's toy. When Ty was finished, the alien, still holding the tape, swung on Mial, turning his back to Ty.

"We will check this, of course," the Chedal said to Mial. "But your price is high." He turned and went out.

Ty stood staring after him.

"What price?" he asked, huskily. His throat was suddenly dry. He swung on Mial. "What price is it that's too high?"

"The price of cooperation with the Laburti!" snarled Mial. "They and the Chedal hate each other—or haven't you noticed?" He turned and stalked off into the opposite bedroom, slamming the door behind him.

Ty stood staring at the closed surface. He made a step toward it. Mial had evidently been up all night. This, combined with the emotional situation between them, would make it pointless for Ty to try to question him.

Besides, thought Ty, hollowly and coldly, there was no need. He turned back across the room to the pile of their supplies and got out the coffeemaker. It was a little self-contained unit that could brew up a fresh cup in something like thirty seconds; for those thirty seconds, Ty kept his mind averted from the problem. Then, with the cup of hot, black coffee in his hands, he sat down to decide what to do.

Mial's answer to his question about the Chedal's mention of price had been thoughtless and transparent—the answer of a man scourged by dislike and mind-numbed by fatigue. Clearly, it could not be anything so simple as the general price of cooperation with a disliked other race, to which the Chedal Observer had been referring. No—it had to have been a specific price. And a specific price that was part of specific, personal negotiations held in secret between the alien and Mial.

Such personal negotiations were no part of the Demonstration plans as Ty knew them. Therefore, Mial was not following those plans. Clearly, he was following some other course of action.

And this, to Ty, could only be the course laid down by those political minds back on Earth who had wanted to use Annie as a pawn to their maneuvering, instead of presenting the statistical analysis instrument plainly and honestly by itself to the Laburti and the Chedal Observers.

If this was the case, the whole hope of the Demonstration hung in the balance. Mial, sparked by instinctive hatred for Ty, was opposing himself not merely to Ty but to everything Ty stood for—including the straightforward presentation of Annie's capabilities.

Instead, he must be dickering with the Chedal for some agreement that would league humanity with the Chedal and against the Laburti—a wild, unrealistic action when the solar system lay wholly within the powerful Laburti stellar sphere of influence.

A moment's annoyance on the part of the Laburti— a moment's belief that the humans had been trying to trick them and play games with their Chedal enemy— and the Laburti forces could turn Earth to a drifting cinder of a world with as little effort as a giant stepping on an ant.

If this was what Mial was doing—and by now Ty was convinced of it—the other man must be stopped, at any cost.

But how?

Ty shivered suddenly and uncontrollably. The room seemed abruptly as icy as a polar tundra.

There was only one way to stop Mial, who could not be reasoned with—by Ty, at least—either on the emotional or the intellectual level; and who held the paper proofs of authority over Ty and Annie. Mial would have to be physically removed from the Demonstration. If necessary—rather than risk the life on Earth and the whole human race—he would have to be killed.

And it would have to look like an accident. Anything else would cause the aliens to halt the Demonstration.

The shiver went away without warning—leaving only a momentary flicker of doubt in Ty, a second's wonder if perhaps his own emotional reaction to Mial was not hurrying him to take a step that might not be justified. Then, that flicker went out. With the Demonstration only hours away, Ty could not stop to examine his motives. He had to act and hope he was right.

He looked across the room at Annie. The statistical analysis instrument housed her own electrical power source and it was powerful enough to give a lethal jolt to a human heart. Her instruments and controls were insulated from the metal case, but the case itself . . .

Ty put down his coffee cup and walked over to the instrument. He got busy. It was not difficult. Half an hour later, as the sun of this world was rising out of the sea, he finished, and went back to his room for a few hours' sleep. He fell instantly into slumber and slept heavily.

IV

He jerked awake. The loon-like hooting in his ears; and standing over his bed was the darkly robed figure of a Laburti.

Ty scrambled to his feet, reaching for a bathrobe. "What . . . ?" he blurted.

Hairless, gray-skinned and dog-faced, narrow-shouldered in the heavy, dark robes he wore, the Laburti looked back at him expressionlessly.

"Where is Demonstration Chief Arthur Mial?" The words came seemingly without emotion from the translator collar, over the sudden deep, harsh-voiced yammering from the face above it.

"I—in the bedroom."

"He is not there."

"But . . ." Ty, belting the bathrobe, strode around the alien, out of his bedroom, across the intervening room and looked into the room into which Mial had disappeared only a few hours before. The bed there was rumpled, but empty. Ty turned back into the center room where Annie stood. Behind her black metal case, the alien sun was approaching the zenith position of noon.

"You will come with me," said the Laburti.

Ty turned to protest. But two more Laburti had come into the suite, carrying the silver-tipped devices which, Ty had been briefed back on Earth, were weapons. Following them came mechs which gathered up the baggage and Annie. Ty cut off the protest before it could reach his lips. There was no point in arguing. But where was Mial?

They crossed a distance of the alien city by flying platform and came at last into another tower, and a large suite of rooms. The Laburti who had woken Ty led him into an interior room where yet another Laburti stood, robed and impassive.

"These," said the Laburti who had brought Ty there, "are the quarters belonging to me. I am the Consul for your human race on this world. This—" the alien nodded at the other robed figure, "is the Observer of our Laburti race, who was to view your device today."

The word was, with all the implications of its past tense, sent a chill creeping through Ty.

"Where is Demonstration Chief Arthur Mial?" demanded the Laburti Observer.

"I don't know!"

The two Laburti stood still. The silence went on in the room, and on until it began to seem to roar in Ty's ears. He swayed a little on his feet, longing to sit down, but knowing enough of protocol not to do so while the Laburti Observer was still standing. Then, finally, the Observer spoke again.

"You have been demonstrating your instrument to the Chedal," he said, "previous to the scheduled Demonstration and without consulting us."

Ty opened his mouth, then closed it again. There was nothing he could say.

The Observer turned and spoke to the Consul with his translator switched off. The Consul produced a roll of paper-like material almost identical with that the Chedal had handed Ty earlier, and passed it into Ty's hands.

"Now," said the Laburti Observer, tonelessly, "you will give a previous Demonstration to me . . ."

The Demonstration was just ending, when a distant hooting called the Laburti Consul out of the room. He returned a minute later—and with him was Mial.

"A Demonstration?" asked Mial, speaking first and looking at the Laburti Observer.

"You were not to be found," replied the alien. "And I am informed of a Demonstration you gave the Chedal Observer some hours past."

"Yes," said Mial. His eyes were still dark from lack of sleep, but his gaze seemed sharp enough. That gaze slid over to fasten on Ty, now. "Perhaps we'd better discuss that, before the official Demonstration. There's less than an hour left."

"You intend still to hold the original Demonstration?"

"Yes," said Mial. "Perhaps we'd better discuss that, too—alone."

"Perhaps we had better," said the Laburti. He nodded to the Consul who started out of the room. Ty stood still.

"Get going," said Mial icily to him, without bothering to turn off his translator collar. "And have the machine ready to go."

Ty turned off his own translator collar, but stood where he was. "What're you up to?" he demanded. "This isn't the way we were supposed to do things. You're running some scheme of your own. Admit it!"

Mial turned his collar off.

"All right," he said, coldly and calmly. "I've had to. There were factors you don't know anything about."

"Such as?"

"There's no time to explain now."

"I won't go until I know what kind of a deal you've been cooking up with the Chedal Observer!"

"You fool!" hissed Mial. "Can't you see this alien's listening and watching every change your face makes? I can't tell you now, and I won't tell you. But I'll tell you this—you're going to get your chance to demonstrate Annie just the way you expected to, to Chedal and Laburti together, if you go along with me. But fight me—and that chance is lost. Now, *will you go?*"

Ty hesitated a moment longer, then he turned and followed the Laburti Consul out. The alien led him to the room where Annie and their baggage had been placed, and shut him in there.

Once alone, he began to pace the floor, fury and worry boiling together inside him. Mial's last words just now had been an open ultimatum. *You're too late to stop me now,* had been the unspoken message behind those words. *Go along with me now, or else lose everything.*

Mial had been clever. He had managed to keep Ty completely in the dark. Puzzle as he would now, Ty could not figure out what it was, specifically, that Mial had set out secretly to do to the Annie Mission.

Or how much of that Mial might already have accomplished. How could Ty fight, completely ignorant of what was going on?

No, Mial was right. Ty could not refuse, blind, to do what he had been sent out to do. That way there would be no hope at all. By going along with Mial he kept alive the faint hope, that things might yet, somehow, turn out as planned back on Earth. Even if—Ty paused in his pacing to smile grimly—Mial's plan included some arrangement not to Ty's personal benefit. For the sake of the original purpose of the Mission, Ty had to go through with the Demonstration, even now, just as if he was Mial's willing accomplice.

But—Ty began to pace again. There was something else to think about. It was possible to attack the problem from the other end. The accomplishment of the Mission was more important than the survival of Ty. Well, then, it was also more important than the survival of Mial—And if Mial should die, whatever commitments he had secretly made to the Chedal against the Laburti, or vice-versa, would die with him.

What would be left would be only what had been intended in the first place. The overwhelming commonsense practicality of peace in preference to war, demonstrated to both the Laburti and the Chedal.

Ty, pausing once more in his pacing to make a final decision, found his decision already made. Annie was already prepared as a lethal weapon. All he needed was to put her to use to stop Mial.

Twenty minutes later, the Laburti Consul for the human race came to collect both Ty and Annie, and bring them back to the room from which Ty had been removed, at Mial's suggestion earlier. Now, Ty saw the room held not only Mial and the Laburti Observer, but one other Laburti in addition. While across the room's width from these, were the Chedal Observer in blue harness with two other Chedals. They were all, with the exception of Mial, aliens, and their expressions were almost unreadable therefore. But, as Ty stepped into the room, he felt the animosity, like a living force, between the two groups of aliens in spite of the full moon's width of distance between them.

It was in the rigidity with which both Chedal and Laburti figures stood. It was in the unwinking gaze they kept on each other. For the first time, Ty realized the need behind the emphasis on protocol and careful procedure between these two races. Here was merely a situation to which protocol was new, with a weaker race standing between representatives of the two Great Ones. But these robed, or yellow-furred, diplomats seemed ready to fly physically at each other's throats.

V

"Get it working—" it was the voice of Mial with his translator turned off, and it betrayed a sense of the same tension in the air that Ty had recognized between the two alien groups. Ty reached for his own collar and then remembered that it was still turned off from before.

"I'll need your help," he said tonelessly. "Annie's been jarred a bit, bringing her here."

"All right," said Mial. He came quickly across the room to join Ty, now standing beside the statistical analysis instrument.

"Stand here, behind Annie," said Ty, "so you don't block my view of the front instrument panel. Reach over the case to the data sorting key here, and hold it down for me."

"This key—all right." From behind Annie, Mial's long right arm reached easily over the top of the case, but—as Ty had planned—not without requiring the other man to lean forward and brace himself with a hand upon the top of the metal case of the instrument. A touch now by Ty on the tape control key would send upwards of thirteen thousand volts suddenly through Mial's body.

He ducked his head down and hastily began to key

in data from the statistic roll lying waiting for him on a nearby table.

The work kept his face hidden, but could not halt the trembling beginning to grow inside him. His reaction against the other man was no less, but now—faced with the moment of pressing the tape control key—he found all his history and environmental training against what he was about to do. *Murder*—screamed his conscious mind—*it'll be murder!*

His throat ached and was dry as some seared and cindered landscape of Earth might one day be after the lashing of a Chedal space-based weapon. His chest muscles had tensed and it seemed hard to get his breath. With an internal gasp of panic, he realized that the longer he hesitated, the harder it would be. His finger touched and trembled against the smooth, cold surface of the tape control key, even as the fingers of his other hand continued to key in data.

"How much longer?" hissed Mial in his ear.

Ty refused to look up. He kept his face hidden. One look at that face would be enough to warn Mial.

What if you're wrong?—screamed his mind. It was a thought he could not afford to have, not with the future of the Earth and all its people riding on this moment. He swallowed, closed his eyes, and jammed sideways on the tape key with his finger. He felt it move under his touch.

He opened his eyes. There had been no sound.

He lifted his gaze and saw Mial's face only inches away staring down at him.

"What's the matter?" whispered Mial, tearingly.

Nothing had happened. Somehow Mial was still alive. Ty swallowed and got his inner trembling under control.

"Nothing . . ." he said.

"What is the cause of this conversation?" broke in the deep, yammering, translated voice of one of the Laburti. "Is there a difficulty with the device?"

"Is there?" hissed Mial.

"No . . ." Ty pulled himself together. "I'll handle it now. You can go back to them."

"All right," said Mial, abruptly straightening up and letting go of the case.

He turned and went back to join the Laburti Observer.

Ty turned back to his work and went on to produce his tape of statistical forecasts for both races. Standing in the center of the room to explain it, while the two alien groups held copies of the tape, he found his voice growing harsher as he talked.

But he made no attempt to moderate it. He had failed to stop Mial. Nothing mattered now.

These were Annie's results, he thought, and they were correct and undeniable. The two alien races could ignore them only at the cost of cutting off their noses to spite their faces. Whatever else would come from Mial's scheming and actions here—this much from Annie was unarguable. No sane race could ignore it.

When he finished, he dropped the tape brusquely on top of Annie's case and looked directly at Mial. The dark-haired man's eyes met his, unreadably.

"You'll go back and wait," said Mial, barely moving his lips. The Laburti Consul glided toward Ty. Together they left and returned to the room with the baggage, where Ty had been kept earlier.

"Your device will be here in a moment," said the Laburti, leaving him. And, in fact, a moment later a mech moved into the room, deposited Annie on the floor and withdrew. Like a man staring out of a daze, Ty fell feverishly upon the side panel of the metal case and began unscrewing the wing nuts securing it.

❖   ❖   ❖

The panel fell away in his hands and he laid it aside. He stared into the inner workings before him, tracing the connections to the power supply, the data control key, and the case that he had made earlier. There were the wires, exactly as he had fitted them in; and there had been no lack of power evident in Annie's regular working. Now, with his forefinger half an inch above the insulation of the wires, he traced them from the data control key back to the negative power lead connection, and from the case toward its connection, with the positive power lead.

He checked, motionless, with pointing finger. The connection was made to the metal case, all right; but the other end of the wire lay limply along other connections, unattached to the power lead. He had evidently, simply forgotten to make that one, final, and vital connection.

Forgotten . . . ? His finger began to tremble. He dropped down limply on the seat-surface facing Annie.

He had not forgotten. Not just . . . forgotten. A man did not forget something like that. It was a lifetime's moral training against murder that had tripped him up. And his squeamishness would, in the long run, probably cost the lives of everyone alive on Earth at this moment.

He was sitting—staring at his hands, when the sound of the door opening brought him to his feet. He whirled about to see Mial.

It was not yet too late. The thought raced through his brain as all his muscles tensed. He could still try to kill the other man with his bare hands—and that was a job where his civilized upbringing could not trip him up. He shifted his weight on to his forward foot preparatory to hurling himself at Mial's throat. But before he could act, Mial spoke.

"Well," said the dark-haired man, harshly, "we did it."

Ty froze—checked by the single small word, *we*.

"We?" He stared at Mial, "did what?"

"What do you think? The Chedal and the Laburti are going to agree—they'll sign a pact for the equivalent of a hundred and twenty-five years of peaceful cooperation, provided matters develop according to the instrument's estimates. They've got to check with their respective governments, of course, but that's only a formality—" he broke off, his face tightening suspiciously. "What's wrong with you?" His gaze went past Ty to the open side of Annie.

"What's wrong with the instrument?"

"Nothing," said Ty. His head was whirling and he felt an insane urge to break out laughing. "—Annie just didn't kill you, that's all."

"Kill me?" Mial's face paled, then darkened. "You were going to kill me—with that?" He pointed at Annie.

"I was going to send thirteen thousand volts through you while you were helping me with the Demonstration," said Ty, still light-headed, "—if I hadn't crossed myself up. But you tell me it's all right, anyway. You say the aliens're going to agree."

"You thought they wouldn't?" said Mial, staring at him.

"I thought you were playing some game of your own. You said you were."

"That's right," said Mial. Some of the dark color faded from his face. "I was. I had to. You couldn't be trusted."

"*I* couldn't be trusted?" Ty burst out.

"Not you—or any of your bunch!" Mial laughed, harshly. "Babes in the woods, all of you. You build a machine that proves peace pays better than war, and think that settles the problem. What would have happened without someone like me along—"

"You! How they let someone like you weasel your way in—"

"Why, you don't think I was assigned to this mission through any kind of accident, do you?" Mial laughed in Ty's face. "They combed the world to find someone like me."

"Combed the world? Why?"

"Because you *had* to come, and the Laburti would only allow two of us with the analyzer to make the trip," said Mial. "You were the best Operator. But you were no politician—and no actor. And there was no time to teach you the facts of life. The only way to make it plain to the aliens that you were at cross purposes with me was to pick someone to head this Mission whom you couldn't help fighting."

"Couldn't help fighting?" Ty stood torn with fury and disbelief. "Why should I have someone along I couldn't help fighting—"

"So the aliens would believe me when I told them your faction back on Earth was strong enough so that I had to carry on the real negotiations behind your back."

"What—real negotiations?"

"Negotiations," said Mial, "to decide whose side we with our Annie-machines and their Operators would be on, during the hundred and twenty-five years of peace between the Great Races." Mial smiled sardonically at Ty.

"Side?" Ty stood staring at the other man. "Why should we be on anyone's side?"

"Why, because by manipulating the data fed to the analyzers, we can control the pattern of growth; so that the Chedal can gain three times as fast as the Laburti in a given period, or the Laburti gain at the same rate over the Chedal. Of course," said Mial, dryly, "I didn't ever exactly promise we could do that in so many words, but they got the idea. Of course, it was the Laburti we had to close with—but I dickered with the Chedal first to get the Laburti price up."

"What price?"

"Better relationships, more travel between the races."

"But—" Ty stammered. "It's not true! That about manipulating the data."

"Of course it's not true!" snapped Mial. "And they never would have believed it if they hadn't seen you— the neutralist—fighting me like a Kilkenny cat." Mial stared at him. "Neither alien bunch ever thought seriously about not going to war anyway. They each just considered putting it off until they could go into it with a greater advantage over the other."

"But—they can't *prefer* war to peace!"

Mial made a disgusted noise in his throat.

"You amateur statesmen!" he said. "You build a better mousetrap and you think that's all there is to it. Just because something's better for individuals, or races, doesn't mean they'll automatically go for it. The Chedal and Laburti have a reason for going to war that can't be figured on your Annie-machine."

"What?" Ty was stung.

"It's called the emotional factor," said Mial, grimly. "The climate of feeling that exists between the Chedal and the Laburti races—like the climate between you and me."

Ty found his gaze locked with the other man's. He opened his mouth to speak—then closed it again. A cold, electric shock of knowledge seemed to flow through him. Of course, if the Laburti felt about the Chedal as he felt about Mial . . .

All at once, things fell together for him, and he saw

the true picture with painfully clear eyes. But the sudden knowledge was a tough pill to get down. He hesitated.

"But you've just put off war a hundred and twenty-five years!" he said. "And both alien races'll be twice as strong, then!"

"And we'll be forty times as strong as we are now," said Mial, dryly. "What do you think a nearly three percent growth advantage amounts to, compounded over a hundred and twenty-five years? By that time we'll be strong enough to hold the balance of power between them and force peace, if we want it. They'd like to cut each other's throats, all right, but not at the cost of cutting their own, for sure. Besides," he went on, more slowly, "if your peace can prove itself in that length of time—now's its chance to do it."

He fell silent. Ty stood, feeling betrayed and ridiculed. All the time he had been suspecting Mial, the other man had been working clear-eyed toward the goal. For if the Laburti and the Chedal felt as did he and Mial, the unemotional calm sense of Annie's forecast never would have convinced the aliens to make peace.

Ty saw Mial watching him now with a sardonic smile. He thinks I haven't got the guts to congratulate him, thought Ty.

"All right," he said, out loud. "You did a fine job—in spite of me. Good for you."

"Thanks," said Mial grimly. They looked at each other.

"But—" said Ty, after a minute, between his teeth, the instinctive venom in him against the other man rushing up behind his words, "I still hate your guts! Once I thought there was a way out of that, but you've convinced me different, as far as people like us are concerned. Once this is over, I hope to heaven I never set eyes on you again!"

Their glances met nakedly.

"Amen," said Mial softly. "Because next time *I'll* kill *you*."

"Unless I beat you to it," said Ty.

Mial looked at him a second longer, then turned and quit the room. From then on, and all the way back to Earth they avoided each other's company and did not speak again. For there was no need of any more talk.

They understood each other very well.

Once again, a story that makes a companion piece with the previous story. This time, it's two aliens at each other's throats (though at least one may not have a throat, quite), with a human caught in the middle, and stuck on an untamed planet with very hungry predators. What an awful fix for the human to be in. *Please* don't throw me in that briar patch. . . .

BROTHER CHARLIE

I

The mutter of her standby burners trembled through the APC9 like the grumbling of an imminent and not entirely unominous storm. In the cramped, lightly grease-smelling cockpit, Chuck Wagnall sat running through the customary preflight check on his instruments and controls. There were a great many to check out—almost too many for the small cockpit space to hold; but then old number 9, like all of her breed, was equipped to operate almost anywhere but underwater. She could even have operated there as well, but she would have needed a little time to prepare herself, before immersion.

On his left-hand field screen the Tomah envoy escort was to be seen in the process of moving the Tomah envoy aboard. The Lugh, Binichi, was already in his bin. Chuck wasted neither time nor attention on these—but when his ship range screen lit up directly before him, he glanced at it immediately.

"Hold Seventy-nine," he said automatically to himself, and pressed the acknowledge button.

The light cleared to reveal the face of Roy Marlie, Advance Unit Supervisor. Roy's brown hair was neatly combed in place, his uniform closure pressed tight, and his blue eyes casual and relaxed—and at these top danger signals, Chuck felt his own spine stiffen.

"Yo, how's it going, Chuck?" Roy asked.

"Lift in about five minutes."

"Any trouble picking up Binichi?"

"A snap," said Chuck. "He was waiting for me right on the surface of the bay. For two cents' worth of protocol he could have boarded her here with the Tomah." Chuck studied the face of his superior in the screen. He wanted very badly to ask Roy what was up; but when and if the supervisor wanted to get to the point of his call, he would do so on his own initiative.

"Let's see your flight plan," said Roy.

Chuck played the fingers of his left hand over the keys of a charter to his right. There appeared superimposed on the face of the screen between himself and Roy an outline of the two continents of this planet that the Tomah called Mant and the Lugh called Vanyinni. A red line that was his projected course crept across a great circle arc from the dot of his present position, over the ocean gap to the dot well inside the coastline of the southern continent. The dot was the human Base camp position.

"You could take a coastal route," said Roy, studying it.

"This one doesn't put us more than eight hundred nautical miles from land at the midpoint between the continents."

"Well, it's your neck," said Roy, with a lightheartedness as ominous as the noise of the standby burners. "Oh, by the way, guess who we've got here? Just landed. Your uncle, Member Wagnall."

Aha! said Chuck. But he said it to himself.

"Tommy?" he said aloud. "Is he handy, there?"

"Right here," answered Roy, and backed out of the screen to allow a heavy, graying-haired man with a kind, broad face to take his place.

"Chuck, boy, how are you?" said the man.

"Never better, Tommy," said Chuck. "How's politicking?"

"The appropriations committee's got me out on a one-man junket to check up on you lads," said Earth District Member 439 Thomas L. Wagnall. "I promised your mother I'd say hello to you if I got to this Base. What's all this about having this project named after you?"

"Oh, not after me," said Chuck. "Its full name isn't Project Charlie, it's Project Big Brother Charlie. With us humans as Big Brother."

"I don't seem to know the reference."

"Didn't you ever hear that story?" said Chuck. "About three brothers—the youngest were twins and fought all the time. The only thing that stopped them was their big brother Charlie coming on the scene."

"I see," said Tommy. "With the Tomah and the Lugh as the two twins. Very apt. Let's just hope Big Brother can be as successful in this instance."

"Amen," said Chuck. "They're a couple of touchy peoples."

"Well," said Tommy. "I was going to run out where

you are now and surprise you, but I understand you've got the only atmosphere pot of the outfit."

"You see?" said Chuck. "That proves we need more funds and equipment. Talk it up for us when you get back, Tommy. Those little airfoils you saw on the field when you came in have no range at all."

"Well, we'll see," said Tommy. "When do you expect to get here?"

"I'll be taking off in a few minutes. Say four hours."

"Good. I'll buy you a drink of diplomatic scotch when you get in."

Chuck grinned.

"Bless the governmental special supply. And you. See you, Tommy."

"I'll be waiting," said the Member. "You want to talk to your chief, again?"

He looked away outside the screen range. "He says nothing more. So long, Chuck."

"So long."

They cut connections. Chuck drew a deep breath. "Hold Seventy-nine," he murmured to his memory, and went back to check that item on his list.

He had barely completed his full check when a roll of drums from outside the ship, penetrating even over the sound of the burners, announced that the Tomah envoy was entering the ship. Chuck got up and went back through the door that separated the cockpit from the passenger and freight sections.

The envoy had just entered through the lock and was standing with his great claw almost in salute. He most nearly resembled, like all the Tomah, a very large ant with the front pair of legs developed into arms with six fingers each and double-opposed thumbs. In addition, however, a large, lobsterlike claw was hinged just behind and above the waist. When standing erect, as now, he measured about four feet from mandibles to the point where his rear pair of legs rested on the ground, although the great claw, fully extended, could have lifted something off a shelf a good foot or more above Chuck's head—and Chuck was over six feet in height. Completely unadorned as he was, this Tomah weighed possibly ninety to a hundred and ten Earth-pounds.

Chuck supplied him with a small throat-mike translator.

"Bright seasons," said the Tomah, as soon as this was adjusted. The translator supplied him with a measured, if uninflected, voice.

"Bright seasons," responded Chuck. "And welcome aboard, as we humans say. Now, if you'll just come over here—"

He went about the process of assisting the envoy into the bin across the aisle from the Lugh, Binichi. The Tomah had completely ignored the other; and all through the process of strapping in the envoy, Binichi neither stirred, nor spoke.

"There you are," said Chuck, when he was finished, looking down at the reclining form of the envoy. "Comfortable?"

"Pardon me," said the envoy. "Your throat-talker did not express itself."

"I said, comfortable?"

"You will excuse me," said the envoy. "You appear to be saying something I don't understand."

"Are you suffering any pain, no matter how slight, from the harness and bin I put you in?"

"Thank you," said the envoy. "My health is perfect."

He saluted Chuck from the reclining position. Chuck saluted back and turned to his other passenger. The similarity here was the throat-translator, that little miracle of engineering, which the Lugh, in common with the envoy and Chuck, wore as close as possible to his larynx.

"How about you?" said Chuck. "Still comfortable?"

"Like sleeping on a ground-swell," said Binichi. He grinned up at Chuck. Or perhaps he did not grin—like that of the dolphin he so much resembled, the mouth of the Lugh had a built-in upward twist at the corners. He lay. Extended at length in the bin he measured a few inches over five feet and weighed most undoubtedly over two hundred pounds. His wide-spreading tail was folded up like a fan into something resembling a club and his four short limbs were tucked in close to the short snowy fur of his belly. "I would like to see what the ocean looks like from high up."

"I can manage that for you," said Chuck. He went up front, unplugged one of the extra screens and brought it back. "When you look into this," he said, plugging it in above the bin, "it'll be like looking down through a hole in the ship's bottom."

"I will feel upside down," said Binichi. "That should be something new, too." He bubbled in his throat, an odd sound that the throat-box made no attempt to translate. Human sociologists had tried to equate this Lugh noise with laughter, but without much success. The difficulty lay in understanding what might be funny and what might not, to a different race. "You've got my opposite number tied down over there?"

"He's in harness," said Chuck.

"Good." Binichi bubbled again. "No point in putting temptation in my way."

He closed his eyes. Chuck went back to the cockpit, closed the door behind him, and sat down at the controls. The field had been cleared. He fired up and took off.

When the pot was safely airborne, he set the course on autopilot and leaned back to light a cigarette. For the first time he felt the tension in his neck and shoulder blades and stretched, to break its grip. Now was no time to be tightening up. But what had Binichi meant by this last remark? He certainly wouldn't be fool enough to attack the Tomah on dry footing?

Chuck shook off the ridiculous notion. Not that it was entirely ridiculous—the Lugh were individualists from the first moment of birth, and liable to do anything. But in this case both sides had given the humans their words (Binichi his personal word and the nameless Tomah their collective word) that there would be no trouble between the representatives of the two races. The envoy, Chuck was sure, would not violate the word of his people, if only for the reason that he would weigh his own life as nothing in comparison to the breaking of a promise. Binichi, on the other hand . . .

The Lugh were impeccably honest. The strange and difficult thing was, however, that they were much harder to understand than the Tomah, in spite of the fact that being warm-blooded and practically mammalian they appeared much more like the human race than the chitinous land-dwellers. Subtle shades and differences of meaning crept into every contact with the Lugh. They were a proud, strong, free, and oddly artistic people; in contradistinction to the intricately organized, highly logical Tomah, who took their pleasure in spectacle and group action.

But there was no sharp dividing line that placed some talents all on the Tomah side, and other all on the Lugh. Each people had musical instruments, each performed group dances, each had a culture and a science and a history. And, in spite of the fantastic surface sociological differences, each made the family unit a basic one, each was monogamous, each entertained the concept of a single deity, and each had very sensitive personal feelings.

The only trouble was, they had no use for each

other—and a rapidly expanding human culture needed them both.

It so happened that this particular world was the only humanly habitable planet out of six circling a sun which was an ideal jumping-off spot for further spatial expansion. To use this world as a space depot of the size required, however, necessitated a local civilization of a certain type and level to support it. From a practical point of view this could be supplied only by a native culture both agreeable and sufficiently advanced to do so.

Both the Tomah and the Lugh were agreeable, as far as the humans were concerned. They were not advanced enough, and could not be, as long as they remained at odds.

It was not possible to advance one small segment of a civilization. It had to be upgraded as a whole. That meant cooperation, which was not now in effect. The Tomah had a science, but no trade. They were isolated on a few of the large land-masses by the seas that covered nine-tenths of their globe. Ironically, on a world which had great amounts of settleable land and vast untapped natural resources, they were cramped for living room and starved for raw materials. All this because to venture out on the Lugh-owned seas was sheer suicide. Their civilization was still in the candlelit, domestic-beast-powered stage, although they were further advanced in theory.

The Lugh, on the other hand, with the overwhelming resources of the oceans at their disposal, had by their watery environment been prohibited from developing a chemistry. The sea-girt islands and the uninhabited land masses were open to them; but, being already on the favorable end of the current status quo, they had had no great need or urge to develop further. What science they had come up with had been mainly for the purpose of keeping the Tomah in their place.

The human sociologists had given their opinion that the conflicts between the two races were no longer based on valid needs. They were, in fact, hangovers from competition in more primitive times when both peoples sought to control the seashores and marginal lands. To the Tomah in those days (and still), access to the seas had meant a chance to tap a badly needed source of food, and to the Lugh (no longer), access to the shore had meant possession of necessary breeding grounds. In the past the Tomah had attempted to clear the Lugh from their path by exterminating their helpless land-based young. And the Lugh had tried to starve the Tomah out, by way of retaliation.

The problem was to bury these ancient hatreds and prove cooperation was both practical and profitable. The latest step in this direction was to invite representatives of both races to a conference at the human Base on the uninhabited southern continent of this particular hemisphere. The humans would act as mediator, since both sides were friendly toward them. Which was what caused Chuck to be at the controls now, with his two markedly dissimilar passengers in the bins behind him.

Unfortunately, the sudden appearance of Member Thomas Wagnall meant they were getting impatient back home. In fact, he could not have come at a worse time. Human prestige with the two races was all humanity had to work with; and it was a delicate thing. And now had arisen this suddenly new question in Chuck's mind as to whether Binichi had regarded his promise to start no trouble with the Tomah as an ironclad guaranty, or a mere casual agreement contingent upon a number of unknown factors.

The question acquired its full importance a couple of hours later, and forty thousand feet above nothing but ocean, when the main burners abruptly cut out.

II

Chuck wiped blood from his nose and shook his head to clear it. Underneath him, the life raft was rocking in soothing fashion upon the wide swell of the empty ocean; but, in spite of the fact that he knew better, he was having trouble accepting the reality of his present position.

Everything had happened a little too fast. His training for emergency situations of this sort had been semi-hypnotic. He remembered now a blur of action in which he had jabbed the distress button to send out an automatic signal on his position and predicament. Just at that moment the standby burners had cut in automatically—which was where he had acquired the bloody nose, when the unexpected thrust slammed him against the controls. Then he had cut some forty-two various switches, got back to the main compartment, unharnessed his passengers, herded them into the escape hatch, blown them all clear, hit the water, inflated the life raft, and got them aboard it just as the escape hatch itself sank gracefully out of sight. The pot, of course, had gone down like so much pig iron when it hit.

And here they were.

Chuck wiped his nose again and looked at the far end of the rectangular life raft. Binichi, the closer of the two, was half-lolling, half-sitting on the curved muscle of his tail. His curved mouth was half-open as if he might be laughing at them. And indeed, thought Chuck, he very well might. Chuck and the envoy, adrift on this watery waste, in this small raft, were castaways in a situation that threatened their very lives. Binichi the Lugh was merely and comfortably back at home.

"Binichi," said Chuck. "Do you know where we are?"

The curved jaw gaped slightly wider. The Lugh head turned this way and that on the almost nonexistent neck; then, twisting, he leaned over the edge of the raft and plunged his whole head briefly under water like a duck searching for food. He pulled his head out again, now slick with moisture.

"Yes," said Binichi.

"How far are we from the coast of the south continent?"

"A day's swim," said Binichi. "And most of a night."

He gave his information as a simple statement of fact. But Chuck knew the Lugh was reckoning in his own terms of speed and distance, which were roughly twelve nautical miles an hour as a steady pace. Undoubtedly it could be done in better time if a Lugh had wished to push himself. The human Base had clocked some of this race at up to eighty miles an hour through the water for short bursts of speed.

Chuck calculated. With the small outboard thrust unit provided for the raft, they would be able to make about four miles an hour if no currents went against them. Increase Binichi's estimate then by a factor of three—three days and nights with a slight possibility of its being less and a very great probability of its taking more. Thought of the thrust unit reminded him. He went to work unfolding it from its waterproof seal and attaching it in running position. Binichi watched him with interest, his head cocked a little on one side like an inquisitive bird's; but as soon as the unit began to propel the raft through the waves at its maximum cruising speed of four miles an hour, his attention disappeared.

With the raft running smoothly, Chuck had another question.

"Which way?"

Binichi indicated with a short thick-muscled forearm, and Chuck swung the raft in nearly a full turn. A slight shiver ran down his spine as he did so. He had been heading away from land out into nearly three thousand miles of open ocean.

"Now," said Chuck, locking the tiller, and looking at both of them. "It'll take us three days and nights to make the coast. And another three or four days to make it overland from there to the Base. The accident happened so quickly I didn't have time to bring along anything with which I could talk to my friends there." He paused, then added: "I apologize for causing you this inconvenience."

"There is no inconvenience," said Binichi, and bubbled in his throat. The envoy neither moved nor answered.

"This raft," said Chuck, "has food aboard it for me, but nothing, I think, that either one of you could use. There's water, of course. Otherwise, I imagine Binichi can make out with the sea all around him, the way it is; and I'm afraid there's not much to be done for you, Envoy, until we reach land. Then you'll be in Binichi's position of being able to forage for yourself."

The envoy still did not answer. There was no way of knowing what he was thinking. Sitting facing the two of them, Chuck tried to imagine what it must be like for the Tomah, forced into a position inches away from his most deadly traditional enemy. And with the private preserves of that enemy, the deep-gulfed sea, source of all his culture's legends and terrors, surrounding him. True, the envoy was the pick of his people, a learned and intelligent being—but possibly there could be such a situation here that would try his self-control too far.

Chuck had no illusion about his ability to cope, barehanded, with either one of his fellow passengers—let alone come between them if they decided on combat. At the same time he knew that if it came to that, he would have to try. There could be no other choice; for the sake of humanity's future here on this world, all three races would hold him responsible.

The raft plodded on toward the horizon. Neither the Tomah nor Binichi had moved. They seemed to be waiting.

They traveled all through the afternoon, and the night that followed. When the sun came up the following morning they seemed not to have moved at all. The sea was all around them as before and unchanging. Binichi now lay half-curled upon the yielding bottom of the raft, his eyes all but closed. The envoy appeared not to have moved an inch. He stood tensely in his corner, claw at half-cock, like a statue carved from his native rock.

With the rising sun, the wind began to freshen. The gray rolling furrows of the sea's eternal surface deepened and widened. The raft tilted, sliding up one heavy slope and down another.

"Binichi!" said Chuck.

The Lugh opened his near eye lazily.

"Is it going to storm?"

"There will be wind," said Binichi.

"Much wind?" asked Chuck—and then realized that his question was too general. "How high will the waves be?"

"About my height," said Binichi. "It will be calmer in the afternoon."

It began to grow dark rapidly after that. By ten o'clock on Chuck's chronometer it was as murky as twilight. Then the rain came suddenly, and a solid sheet of water blotted out the rest of the raft from his eyes.

Chuck clung to the thrust unit for something to hang onto. In the obscurity, the motion of the storm was eerie. The raft seemed to plunge forward, mounting a slope that stretched endlessly, until with a sudden twist and dip, it adopted a down-slant to forward—and then it seemed to fly backward in that position with increasing rapidity until its angle was as suddenly reversed again. It was like being on a monstrous see-saw that, even as it went up and down, was sliding back and forth on greased rollers.

At some indeterminate time later, Chuck began to worry about their being washed out of the raft. There were lines in the locker attached midway to the left-hand side of the raft. He crawled forward on hands and knees and found the box. It opened to his cold fingers, and he clawed out the coiled lines.

It struck him then, for the first time, that on this small, circumscribed raft, he should have bumped into Binichi or the envoy in making his way to the box. He lifted his face to the wind and the rain and darkness, but it told him nothing. And then he felt something nudge his elbow.

"He is gone," said the voice of the envoy's translator, in Chuck's ear.

"Gone?" yelled Chuck above the storm.

"He went over the side a little while ago."

Chuck clung to the box as the raft suddenly reversed its angle.

"How do you know?"

"I saw him," said the envoy.

"You—" Chuck yelled, "you can see in this?"

There was a slight pause.

"Of course," said the envoy. "Can't you?"

"No." Chuck unwound the lines. "We better tie our-selves into the raft," he shouted. "Keep from being washed overboard."

The envoy did not answer. Taking silence for assent, Chuck reached for him in the obscurity and passed one of the lines about the chitinous body. He secured the line tightly to the ring-handgrips fastened to the inner side of the raft's edge. Then he tied himself securely with a line around his waist to a handgrip further back by the thrust unit.

They continued to ride the pitching ocean. After some time, the brutal beating of the rain slackened off; and a little light began to filter through. The storm cleared then, as suddenly as it had commenced. Within minutes the raft heaved upon a metal-gray sea under thinning clouds in a sky from which the rain had ceased falling.

Teeth chattering, Chuck crawled forward to his single remaining passenger and untied the rope around him. The envoy was crouched down in his corner, his great claw hugging his back, as if he huddled for warmth. When Chuck untied him, he remained so motionless that Chuck was struck with the sudden throat-tightening fear that he was dead.

"Are you all right?" asked Chuck.

"Thank you," said the envoy; "I am in perfect health."

Chuck turned away to contemplate the otherwise empty raft. He was, he told himself, doing marvelously. Already, one of his charges had taken off . . . and then, before he could complete the thought, the raft rocked suddenly and the Lugh slithered aboard over one high side.

He and Chuck looked at each other. Binichi bubbled comfortably.

"Looks like the storm's over," said Chuck.

"It is blowing to the south of us now," said the Lugh.

"How far are we from land, now?"

"We should come to it," said Binichi, "in the morning."

Chuck blinked a little in surprise. This was better time than he had planned. And then he realized that the wind was blowing at their backs, and had been doing so all through the storm. He looked up at the sky. The sun was past its zenith, and a glance at his watch, which was corrected for local time, showed the hands at ten minutes to three. Chuck turned his attention back to Binichi, revolving the phraseology of his next question in his mind.

"Did you get washed overboard?" he asked, at last.

"Washed overboard?" Binichi bubbled. "I went into the water. It was more pleasant."

"Oh," said Chuck.

They settled down once more to their traveling.

A little over an hour later the raft jarred suddenly and rocked as if, without warning, it had found a rock beneath it, here in the middle of the ocean. For a second Chuck entertained the wild idea that it had. But such a notion was preposterous. There were undersea mountains all through this area, but the closest any came to the surface was a good forty fathoms down. At the same time the envoy's claw suddenly shot up and gaped above him, as he recoiled toward the center of the boat; and, looking overboard, Chuck came into view of the explanation for both occurrences.

A gray back as large around as an oil drum and ten to twelve feet in length was sliding by about a fathom and a half below them. At a little distance off Chuck could make out a couple more. As he watched, they turned slowly and came back toward the raft again.

Chuck recognized these sea-creatures. He had been

briefed on them. They were the local counterpart of the Earthly shark—not as bloodthirsty, but they could be dangerous enough. They had wide catfishlike mouths, equipped with cartilaginous ridges rather than teeth. They were scavengers, rather than predators, generally feeding off the surface. As he watched now, the closest rose slowly to the surface in front of him, and suddenly an enormous jaw gaped a full six feet in width and closed over the high rim of the raft. The plastic material squealed to the rubbing of the horny ridges, giving but not puncturing. Temporarily defeated, the jaws opened again and the huge head sank back under the water.

Chuck's hand went instinctively to his belt for the handgun that was, of course, not there.

The raft jolted and twisted and rocked for several moments as the creatures tried to overturn it. The envoy's claw curved and jerked this way and that above him, like a sensitive antenna, at each new sound or jolt. Binichi rested lazy-eyed on the raft's bottom, apparently concerned only with the warmth of the sun upon his drying body.

After several minutes, the attacks on the raft ceased and the creatures drew off through the water. Chuck could catch a glimpse of them some thirty yards or so off, still following. Chuck looked back at Binichi, but the Lugh had his eyes closed as if he dozed. Chuck drew a deep breath and turned to the envoy.

"Would you like some water?" he asked.

The envoy's claw had relaxed slightly upon his back. He turned his head toward Chuck.

"If you have any you do not desire yourself," he said.

Chuck got out the water, debated offering some to the Lugh out of sheer form and politeness, then took his cue from the fact that Binichi appeared asleep, and confined his attentions to the envoy and himself. It surprised him now to remember that he had not thought of water up until this moment. He wondered if the Tomah had been suffering for it in silence, too polite or otherwise to ask for some.

This latter thought decided him against eating any of the food that the boat was also provided with. If they would reach land inside of another twelve or fourteen hours, he could last until then. It would hardly be kind, not to say politic, to eat in front of the Tomah when nothing was available for that individual. Even the Lugh, if he had eaten at all, had done so when he was out of the raft during the night and storm, when they could not see him.

Chuck and the envoy drank and settled down again. Sundown came quickly; and Chuck, making himself as comfortable as possible, went to sleep.

He woke with a start. For a second he merely lay still on the soft, yielding bottom of the raft without any clear idea as to what had brought him into consciousness. Then a very severe bump from underneath the raft almost literally threw him up into a sitting position.

The planet's small, close moon was pouring its brilliant light across the dark waters, from a cloudless sky. The night was close to being over, for the moon was low and its rays struck nearly level on the wave tops. The sea had calmed, but in its closer depths were great moving streaks and flashes of phosphorescence. For a moment these gleams only baffled and confused his eyes; and then Chuck saw that they were being made by the same huge scavengers that had bothered the raft earlier—only now there were more than a dozen of them, filling the water about and underneath the raft.

The raft rocked again as one of them struck it once more from below.

Chuck grabbed at the nearest ring-handhold and glanced at his fellow passengers. Binichi lay as if asleep, but in the dark shadow of his eye-sockets little reflected glints of light showed where his eyeballs gleamed in the darkness. Beyond him, the envoy was fully awake and up on all four feet, his claw extended high above him, and swaying with every shock like the balancing pole of a tightrope walker. His front pair of handed limbs were also extended on either side as if for balance. Chuck opened his mouth to call to the Tomah to take hold on one of the handgrips.

At that moment, however, there rose from out of the sea at his elbow a pair of the enormous ridged jaws. Like the mouth of a trout closing over a fly, these clamped down, suddenly and without warning, on the small, bright metal box of the thrust unit where it was fastened to the rear end of the raft. And the raft itself was suddenly jerked and swung as the sea-creature tore the thrust unit screeching from its moorings into the sea. The raft was upended by the force of the wrench; and Chuck, holding on for dear life from sliding into the sea, saw the creature that had pulled the unit loose release it disappointedly, as if sensing its inedibility. It glittered down through the dark waters, falling from sight.

The raft slammed back down on the watery surface. And immediately on the heels of this came the sound of a large splash. Jerking his head around, Chuck saw the envoy struggling in the ocean.

His black body glittered among the waves, his thrashing limbs kicking up little dashes and glitters of phosphorescence. Chuck hurled himself to the far end of the raft and stretched out his hand, but the Tomah was already beyond his reach. Chuck turned, and dived back to the box at midraft, pawing through it for the line he had used to tie them in the boat earlier. It came up tangled in his hands. He lunged to the end of the raft nearest the envoy again, trying to unravel the line as he did so.

It came slowly and stubbornly out of its snarl. But when he got it clear at last and threw it, its unweighted end fell little more than halfway of the widening distance between the raft and the Tomah.

Chuck hauled it in, in a frenzy of despair. The raft, sitting high in the water, was being pushed by the night wind farther from the envoy with every second. The envoy himself had in all this time made no sound, only continuing to thrash his limbs in furious effort. His light body seemed in no danger of sinking; but his narrow limbs in uncoordinated effort barely moved him through the water—and now the scavengers were once more beginning to enter the picture.

These, like any fish suddenly disturbed, had scattered at the first splash of the Tomah's body. For a short moment it had seemed that they had been frightened away entirely. But now they were beginning to circle in, moving around the envoy, dodging close, then flirting away again—but always ending up a little closer than before.

Chuck twisted about to face Binichi.

"Can't you do something?" he cried.

Binichi regarded him with his race's usual unreadable expression.

"I?" he said.

"You could swim to him and let him hang on to you and tow him back," said Chuck. "Hurry!"

Binichi continued to look at him.

"You don't want the Tomah eaten?" he said at last.

"Of course not!"

"Then why don't you bring him back yourself to this thing?"

"I can't. I can't swim that well!" said Chuck. "You can."

"You can't?" echoed Binichi slowly. "I can?"

"You know that."

"Still," said the Lugh. "I would have thought you had some way—it's nothing to me if the Tomah is eaten."

"You promised."

"Not to harm him," said Binichi. "I have not. The Tomah have killed many children to get at the sea. Now this one has the sea. Let him drink it. The Tomah have been hungry for fish. This one has fish. Let him eat the fish."

Chuck brought his face close to the grinning dolphin head.

"You promised to sit down with us and talk to that Tomah," he said. "If you let him die, you're dodging that promise."

Binichi stared back at him for a short moment. Then he bubbled abruptly and went over the side of the raft in a soaring leap. He entered the water with his short limbs tucked in close to his body and his wide tail fanning out. Chuck had heard about, but never before seen, the swiftness of the Lugh, swimming. Now he saw it. Binichi seemed to give a single wriggle and then torpedo like a streak of phosphorescent lightning just under the surface of the water toward the struggling envoy.

One of the scavengers was just coming up under the Tomah. The streak of watery fire that was Binichi converged upon him and his heavy shape shot struggling from the surface, the sound of a dull impact heavy in the night. Then the phosphorescence of Binichi's path was among the others, striking right and left as a swordfish strikes on his run among a school of smaller feed fish. The scavengers scattered into darkness, all but the one Binichi had first hit, which was flopping upon the surface of the moonlit sea as if partially paralyzed.

Binichi broke surface himself, plowing back toward

the Tomah. His head butted the envoy and a second
later the envoy was skidding and skittering like a toy
across the water's surface to the raft. A final thrust at
the raft's edge sent him up and over it. He tumbled
on his back on the raft's floor, glittering with wetness;
and, righting himself with one swift thrust of his claw,
he whirled, claw high, to face Binichi as the Lugh came
sailing aboard.

Binichi sprang instantly erect on the curved spring
of his tail; and Chuck, with no time for thought, thrust
himself between the two of them.

For a second Chuck's heart froze. He found himself with his right cheek bare inches from the heavy
double meat-choppers of the Tomah claw, while, almost
touching him on the left, the gaping jaws of the Lugh
glinted with thick, short scimitarlike teeth, and the fishy
breath of the sea-dweller filled his nostrils. In this
momentary, murderous tableau they all hung motionless for a long, breathless second. And then the Tomah
claw sank backward to the shiny back below it and the
Lugh slid backward and down upon his tail. Slowly, the
two members of opposing races retreated each to his
own end of the raft.

Chuck, himself, sat down. And the burst of relieved
breath that expelled itself from his tautened lungs echoed
in the black and moonlit world of the seascape night.

III

Some two hours after sunrise, a line of land began
to make its appearance upon their further horizon. It
mounted slowly, as the onshore wind, and perhaps some
current as well, drove them ahead. It was a barren,
semiarid and tropical coastline, with a rise of what

appeared to be hills—light green with a sparse vegetation—beyond it.

As they drifted closer, the shoreline showed itself in a thin pencil-mark of foam. No outer line of reefs was apparent, but the beaches themselves seemed to be rocky or nonexistent. Chuck turned to the Lugh.

"We need a calm, shallow spot to land in," he said. "Otherwise the raft's liable to upset in the surf, going in."

Binichi looked at him, but did not answer.

"I'm sorry," said Chuck. "I guess I didn't explain myself properly. What I mean is, I'm asking for your help again. If the raft upsets or has a hole torn in it when we're landing, the envoy and I will probably drown. Could you find us a fairly smooth beach somewhere and help us get to it?"

Binichi straightened up a little where he half-sat, half-lay propped against the end of the raft where the thrust unit had been attached.

"I had been told," he said, "that you had oceans upon your own world."

"That's right," said Chuck. "But we had to develop the proper equipment to move about on them. If I had the proper equipment here I wouldn't have to ask you for help. If it hadn't been for our crashing in the ocean none of this would be necessary."

"This 'equipment' of yours seems to have an uncertain nature," said Binichi. He came all the way erect. "I'll help you." He flipped overboard and disappeared.

Left alone in the raft with the envoy, Chuck looked over at him.

"The business of landing will probably turn out to be difficult and dangerous—at least we better assume the worst," he said. "You understand you may have to swim for your life when we go in?"

"I have given my word to accomplish this mission," replied the envoy.

A little while after that, it became evident from the angle at which the raft took the waves that they had changed course. Chuck, looking about for an explanation of this, discovered Binichi at the back of the raft, pushing them.

Within the hour, the Lugh had steered them to a small, rocky inlet. Picked up in the landward surge of the surf, the raft went, as Chuck had predicted, end over end in a smother of water up on the pebbly beach. Staggering to his feet with the solid land at last under him, Chuck smeared water from his eyes and took inventory of a gashed and bleeding knee. Binding the cut as best he could with a strip torn from his now-ragged pants, he looked about for his fellow travelers.

The raft was flung upside down between himself and them. Just beyond it, the envoy lay with his claw arm flung limply out on the sand. Binichi, a little further on, was sitting up like a seal. As Chuck watched, the envoy stirred, pulled his claw back into normal position, and got shakily up on all four legs.

Chuck went over to the raft and, with some effort, managed to turn it back, right side up. He dug into the storage boxes and got out food and water. He was not sure whether it was the polite, or even the sensible thing to do, but he was shaky from hunger, parched from the salt water, dizzy from the pounding in the surf—and his knee hurt. He sat down and made his first ravenous meal since the pot had crashed in the sea, almost two days before.

As he was at it, the Tomah envoy approached. Chuck offered him some of the water, which the Tomah accepted.

"Sorry I haven't anything you could eat," said Chuck, a full belly having improved his manners.

"It doesn't matter," said the envoy. "There will be flora growing farther inland that will stay my hunger. It's good to be back on the land."

"I'll go along with you on that statement," said Chuck. Looking up from the food and water, he saw the Lugh approaching. Binichi came up, walking on his four short limbs, his tail folded into a club over his back for balance, and sat down with them.

"And now?" he said, addressing Chuck.

"Well," said Chuck, stretching his cramped back, "we'll head inland toward the Base." He reached into his right-hand pants pocket and produced a small compass. "That direction"—he pointed toward the hills without looking—"and some five hundred miles. Only we shouldn't have to cover it all on foot. If we can get within four hundred miles of Base, we'll be within the airfoils' cruising range, and one of them should locate us and pick us up."

"Your people will find us, but they can't find us here?" said Binichi.

"That's right." Chuck looked at the Lugh's short limbs. "Are you up to making about a hundred-mile trip overland?"

"As you've reminded me before," said Binichi, "I made a promise. It will help, though, if I can find water to go into from time to time."

Chuck turned to the envoy.

"Can we find bodies of water as we go?"

"I don't know this country," said the Tomah, speaking to Chuck. "But there should be water; and I'll watch for it."

"We two could go ahead," said Chuck, turning back to the Lugh. "And maybe we could work some way of getting a vehicle back here to carry you."

"I've never needed to be carried," said Binichi, and turned away abruptly. "Shall we go?"

They went.

Striking back from the stoniness of the beach, they passed through a belt of shallow land covered with shrub and coarse grass. Chuck, watching the envoy, half-expected him to turn and feed on some of this as they passed, but the Tomah went straight ahead. Beyond the vegetated belt, they came on dunes of coarse sand, where the Lugh—although he did not complain, any more than the envoy had when he fell overboard from the raft—had rough going with his short limbs. This stretched for a good five miles; but when they had come at last to firmer ground, the first swellings of the foothills seemed not so far ahead of them.

They were now in an area of small trees with numbers of roots sprouting from the trunk above ground level, and of sticklike plants resembling cacti. The envoy led them, his four narrow limbs propelling him with a curious smoothness over the uncertain ground as if he might at any moment break into a run. However, he regulated his pace to that of the Lugh, who was the slowest in the party, though he showed no signs as yet of discomfort or of tiring.

This even space was broken with dramatic suddenness as they crossed a sort of narrow earth-bridge or ridge between two of the gullies. Without any warning, the envoy wheeled suddenly and sprinted down the almost perpendicular slope on his left, zigzagging up the gully bed as if chasing something and into a large hole in the dry, crumbling earth of the further bank. A sudden thin screaming came from the hole and the envoy tumbled out into the open with a small furry creature roughly in the shape of a weasel and about the size of a large rabbit. The screaming

continued for a few seconds. Chuck turned his head
away, shaken.

He was aware of Binichi staring at him.

"What's wrong?" asked the Lugh. "You showed no
emotion when I hurt the—" His translator failed on
a word.

"What?" said Chuck. "I didn't understand. When you
hurt what?"

"One of those who would have eaten the Tomah."

"I . . ." Chuck hesitated. He could not say that it was
because this small land creature had had a voice to
express its pain while the sea-dweller had not. "It's our
custom to kill our meat before eating it."

Binichi bubbled.

"This will be too new to the Tomah for ritual," he said.

Reinforcement for this remark came a moment or
two later when the envoy came back up the near wall
of the gully to rejoin them.

"This is a paradise of plenty, this land," he said.
"Only once in my life before was I ever lucky enough
to taste meat." He lifted his head to them. "Shall we
go on?"

"We should try to get to some water soon," said
Chuck, glancing at Binichi.

"I have been searching for it," said the envoy. "Now
I smell it not far off. We should reach it before dark."

They went on; and gradually the gullies thinned out
and they found themselves on darker earth, among more
and larger trees. Just as the sunset was reddening the
sky above the upthrust outline of the near hills, they
entered a small glen where a stream trickled down from
a higher slope and spread out into a small pool. Binichi
trotted past them without a word, and plunged in.

Chuck woke when the morning sun was just beginning to touch the glen. For a moment he lay still under

the mass of small-leaved branches with which he had covered himself the night before, a little bewildered to find himself no longer on the raft. Then memory returned and with it sensation, spreading through the stiff limbs of his body.

For the first time, he realized that his strength was ebbing. He had had first the envoy and then Binichi to worry about, and so he had been able to keep his mind off his own state.

His stomach was hollow with hunger that the last night's meager rations he had packed from the raft had done little to assuage. His muscles were cramped from the unusual exercise and he had the sick, dizzy feeling that comes from general overexposure. Also, right now, his throat was dry and aching for water.

He pulled himself up out of the leaves, stumbled to the edge of the pond and fell to hands and knees on its squashy margin. He drank; and as he raised his head and ran a wrist across his lips after quenching his thirst, the head of Binichi parted the surface almost where his lips had been.

"Time to go?" said the Lugh. He turned to one side and heaved himself up out onto the edge of the bank.

"We'll leave in just a little while," Chuck said. "I'm not fully awake yet." He sat back stiffly and exhaustedly on the ground and stretched his arms out to bring some life back into them. He levered himself to his feet and walked up and down, swinging his arms. After a little while his protesting muscles began to warm a little and loosen. He got one of the high-calorie candy bars from his food pack and chewed on it.

"All right," he said. And the envoy turned to lead the way up, out of the glen.

With the bit of food, the exercise, and the new warmth of the sun, Chuck began to feel better as they proceeded. They were breasting the near slopes of the hills now, and shortly before noon they came over the top of them, and paused to rest.

The land did not drop again, but swelled away in a gently rising plateau, into distance. And on its far horizon, insubstantial as clouds, rose the blue peaks of mountains.

"Base is over those mountains," said Chuck.

"Will we have to cross them?" The envoy's translator produced the words evenly, like a casual and unimportant query.

"No." Chuck turned to the Tomah. "How far in from the coast have we come so far?"

"I would estimate"—the translator hesitated a second over the translation of units—"thirty-two and some fraction of a mile."

"Another sixty miles, then," said Chuck, "and we should be within the range of the airfoils they'll have out looking for us." He looked again at the mountains and they seemed to waver before his eyes. Reaching up in an automatic gesture to brush the waveriness away, the back of his hand touched his forehead; and, startled, he pressed the hand against it. It was burning hot.

Feverish! thought Chuck And his mind somersaulted at the impossibility of the fact.

He could see the two others looking at him with the completely remote and unempathetic curiosity of peoples who had nothing in common with either his life or his death. A small rat's-jaw of fear gnawed at him suddenly. It had never occurred to him since the crash that there could be any danger that *he* would not make it safely back to Base. Now, for the first time, he faced that possibility. If the worst came to the worst, it came home to him suddenly, he could count on no help from either the Tomah, or the Lugh.

"What will they look like, these airfoils?" asked Binichi.

"Like a circle made out of bright material," said Chuck. "A round platform about twelve feet across."

"And there will be others of your people in them?"

"On them. No," said Chuck. "Anyway, I don't think so. We're too short of personnel. They operate on re-mote-beamed power from the ship and flash back pictures of the ground they cover. Once they send back a picture of us, Base'll know where to find us."

He levered himself painfully to his feet.

"Let's travel," he said.

They started out again. The walking was more level and easy now than it had been coming up through the hills. Plodding along, Chuck's eyes were suddenly attracted by a peculiarity of Binichi's back and sides. The Lugh was completely covered by a short close hair, which was snow-white under the belly, but shaded to a gray on the back. It seemed to Chuck, now, however, that this gray back hair had taken on a slight hint of rosiness.

"Hey!" he said, stopping. "You're getting sunburned."

The other two halted also; and Binichi looked up at him, inquiringly. Chuck repeated himself in simpler terms that his translator could handle.

"Let's go on," said Binichi, taking up the march again.

"Wait!" said Chuck, as he and the envoy moved to follow up the Lugh. "Don't you know that can be dangerous? Here—" He fumbled out of his own jacket. "We humans get sunburned, too, but we evidently aren't as susceptible as you. Now, I can tie the arms of this around your neck and you'll have some protection—"

Binichi halted suddenly and wheeled to face the human.

"You're intruding," said Binichi, "on something that is my own concern."

"But—" Chuck looked helplessly at him. "The sun is quite strong in these latitudes. I don't think you understand—" He turned to appeal to the Tomah. "Tell him what the sun's like in a country like this."

"Surely," said the envoy, "this has nothing to do with you or me. If his health becomes imperfect, it will be an indication that he isn't fit to survive. He's only a Lugh; but certainly he has the right, like all living things, to make such a choice for himself."

"But he might be mistaken—"

"If he is mistaken, it will be a sign that he is unfit to survive. I don't agree with Lughs—as you people know. But any creature has the basic right to entertain death if he so wishes. To interfere with him in that would be the highest immorality."

"But don't you want to—" began Chuck, incredulously, turning toward the Lugh.

"Let's go on," said Binichi, turning away.

They went on again.

After a while, the grasslands of the early plateau gave way to more forest.

Chuck was plodding along in the late hours of the afternoon with his eyes on the ground a few feet in front of him and his head singing, when a new sound began to penetrate his consciousness. He listened to it, more idly than otherwise, for some seconds—and then abruptly, it registered.

It was a noise like yelping, back along the trail he had just passed.

He checked and straightened and turned about. Binichi was no longer in sight.

"Binichi!" he called. There was no answer, only the yelping. He began to run clumsily, back the way he had come.

Some eight or so yards back, he traced the yelping to a small clearing in a hollow. Breaking through the brush and trees that grew about its lip, he looked down on the Lugh. Binichi was braced at bay upon his clubbed tail, jaws agape, and turning to face half a dozen weasel-shaped creatures the size of small dogs that yelped and darted in and out at him, tearing and slashing.

The Lugh's sharp, tooth-studded jaws were more than a match for the jaws of any one of his attackers, but—here on land—they had many times his speed. No matter which way he turned, one was always at his back, and harrying him. But, like the envoy when he had been knocked into the sea, Binichi made no sound; and, although his eyes met those of Chuck, standing at the clearing edge, he gave no call for help.

Chuck looked about him desperately for a stick or stone he could use as a club. But the ground was bare of everything but the light wands of the bushes, and the trees overhead had all green, sound limbs firmly attached to their trunks. There was a stir in the bushes beside him.

Chuck turned and saw the envoy. He pushed through to stand beside Chuck, and also looked down at the fight going on in the clearing.

"Come on!" said Chuck, starting down into the clearing. Then he halted, for the envoy had not moved. "What's the matter?"

"Matter?" said the envoy, looking at him. "I don't understand."

"Those things will kill him!"

"You"—the envoy turned his head as if peering at Chuck—"appear to think we should interfere. You people have this strange attitude to the natural occurrences of life that I've noticed before."

"Do *you* people just stand by and watch each other get killed?"

"Of course not. Where another Tomah is concerned, it is of course different."

"He saved *your* life from those fish!" cried Chuck.

"I believe you asked him to. You were perfectly free to ask, just as he was perfectly free to accept or refuse. I'm in no way responsible for anything either of you have done."

"He's an intelligent being!" said Chuck desperately. "Like you. Like me. We're all alike."

"Certainly we aren't," said the envoy, stiffening. "You and I are not at all alike, except that we are both civilized. He's not even that. He's a Lugh."

"I told him he'd promised to sit down at Base and discuss with you," cried Chuck, his tongue loosened by the fever. "I said he was dodging his promise if he let you die. And he went out and saved you. But you won't save him."

The envoy turned his head to look at Binichi, now all but swarmed under by the predators.

"Thank you for correcting me," he said. "I hadn't realized there could be honor in this Lugh."

He went down the slope of the hollow in a sudden, blurring rush that seemingly moved him off at top speed from a standing start. He struck the embattled group like a projectile and emerged coated by the predators. For a split second it seemed to Chuck that he had merely thrown another life into the jaws of the attackers. And then the Tomah claw glittered and flashed, right and left like a black scimitar, lightning-swift out of the ruck—and the clearing was emptied, except for four furry bodies that twitched or lay about the hollow.

The envoy turned to the nearest and began to eat. Without a glance or word directed at his rescuer, Binichi, bleeding from a score of superficial cuts and scratches, turned about and climbed slowly up the slope of the hollow to where Chuck stood.

"Shall we go on?" he said.

Chuck looked past him at the feeding envoy.

"Perhaps we should wait for him," he said.

"Why?" said Binichi. "It's up to him to keep up, if he wants to. The Tomah is no concern of ours."

He headed off in the direction they had been going. Chuck waggled his head despairingly, and plodded after.

IV

The envoy caught up to them a little further on; and shortly after that, as the rays of the setting sun were beginning to level through the trees, giving the whole forest a cathedral look, they came on water, and stopped for the night.

It seemed to Chuck that the sun went down very quickly—quicker than it ever had before; and a sudden chill struck through to his very bones. Teeth chattering, he managed to start a fire and drag enough dead wood to it to keep it going while they slept.

Binichi had gone into the waters of the small lake a few yards off, and was not to be seen. But through the long, fever-ridden night hours that were a patchwork of dizzy wakefulness and dreams and half-dreams, Chuck was aware of the smooth, dark insectlike head of the Tomah watching him across the fire with what seemed to be an absorbing fascination.

Toward morning, he slept. He awoke to find the sun risen and Binichi already out of the lake. Chuck did not feel as bad, now, as he had earlier. He moved in a sort of fuzziness; and, although his body was slow responding, as if it was something operated by his mind from such a remote distance that mental directions to his limbs took a long time to be carried out, it was not so actively uncomfortable.

They led off, Chuck in the middle as before. They were moving out of the forest now, into more open country where the trees were interspersed with meadows. Chuck remembered now that he had not eaten in some time; but when he chewed on his food, the taste was uninteresting and he put it back in his pack.

Nor was he too clear about the country he was traversing. It was there all right, but it seemed more than a little unreal. Sometimes things, particularly things far off, appeared distorted. And he began remarking expressions on the faces of his two companions that he would not have believed physically possible to them. Binichi's mouth, in particular, had become remarkably mobile. It was no longer fixed by physiology into a grin. Watching out of the corner of his eye, Chuck caught glimpses of it twisted into all sorts of shapes; sad, sly, cheerful, frowning. And the Tomah was not much better. As the sun mounted up the clear arch of the sky, Chuck discovered the envoy squinting and winking at him, as if to convey some secret message.

"S'all right—s'all right—" mumbled Chuck. "I won't tell." And he giggled suddenly at the joke that he couldn't tell because he really didn't know what all the winking was about.

"I don't understand," said the envoy, winking away like mad.

"S'all right—s'all right—" said Chuck.

He discovered after a time that the other two were no longer close beside him. Peering around, he finally located them walking together at some distance off from him. Discussing something, no doubt, something confidential. He wandered, taking the pitch and slope of the ground at random, stumbling a little now and then when the angle of his footing changed. He was aware in vague fashion that he had drifted into an area with little rises and unexpected sinkholes, their edges tangled with brush. He caught himself on one of the sinkholes, swayed back to safety, tacked off to his right . . .

Suddenly he landed hard on something. The impact drove all the air out of his lungs, so that he fought to breathe—and in that struggle he lost the cobwebs surrounding him for the first time that day.

He had not been aware of his fall, but now he saw that he lay half on his back, some ten feet down from the edge of one of the holes. He tried to get up, but one leg would not work. Panic cut through him like a knife.

"Help!" he shouted. His voice came out hoarse and strange-sounding. "Help!"

He called again; and after what seemed a very long time, the head of the envoy poked over the edge of the sinkhole and looked down at him.

"Get me out of here!" cried Chuck. "Help me out."

The envoy stared at him.

"Give me a hand!" said Chuck. "I can't climb up by myself. I'm hurt."

"I don't understand," said the envoy.

"I think my leg's broken. What's the matter with you?" Now that he had mentioned it, as if it had been lying there waiting for its cue, the leg that would not work sent a sudden, vicious stab of pain through him. And close behind this came a swelling agony that pricked Chuck to fury. "Don't you hear me? I said, pull me out of here! My leg's broken. I can't stand on it!"

"You are damaged?" said the envoy

"Of course I'm damaged!"

The envoy stared down at Chuck for a long moment.

When he spoke again, his words struck an odd, formalistic note in Chuck's fevered brain.

"It is regrettable," said the envoy, "that you are no longer in perfect health."

And he turned away, and disappeared. Above Chuck's straining eyes, the edges of the hole and the little patch of sky beyond them tilted, spun about like a scene painted on a whirling disk, and shredded away into nothingness.

At some time during succeeding events he woke up again; but nothing was really clear or certain until he found himself looking up into the face of Doc Burgis, who was standing over him, with a finger on his pulse.

"How do you feel?" said Burgis.

"I don't know," said Chuck. "Where am I?"

"Back at Base," said Burgis, letting go of his wrist. "Your leg is knitting nicely and we've knocked out your pneumonia. You've been under sedation. A couple more days' rest and you'll be ready to run again."

"That's nice," said Chuck; and went back to sleep.

V

Three days later he was recovered enough to take a ride in his motorized go-cart over to Roy Marlie's office. He found Roy there, and his uncle.

"Hi, Tommy," said Chuck, wheeling through the door. "Hi, Chief."

"How you doing, son?" asked Member Thomas Wagnall. "How's the leg?"

"Doc says I can start getting around on surgical splints in a day or two," Chuck looked at them both. "Well, isn't anybody going to tell me what happened?"

"Those two natives were carrying you when we finally located the three of you," said Tommy, "and we—"

"They were?" said Chuck.

"Why, yes." Tommy looked closely at him. "Didn't you know that?"

"I—I was unconscious before they started carrying me, I guess, "said Chuck.

"At any rate, we got you all back here in good shape." Tommy went across the room to a built-in cabinet and came back carrying a bottle of scotch, capped with three glasses, and a bowl of ice. "Ready for that drink now?"

"Try me," said Chuck, not quite licking his lips. Tommy made a second trip for charged water and brought it back. He passed the drinks around.

"How," he said, raising his glass. They all drank in appreciative silence.

"Well," said Tommy, setting his glass down on the top of Roy's desk, "I suppose you heard about the conference." Chuck glanced over at Roy, who was evincing a polite interest.

"I heard they had a brief meeting and put everything off for a while," said Chuck.

"Until they had a chance to talk things over *between themselves*, yes," said Tommy. He was watching his nephew somewhat closely. "Rather surprising development. We hardly know where we stand now, do we?"

"Oh, I guess it'll work out all right," said Chuck.

"You do?"

"Why, yes," said Chuck. He slowly sipped at his glass again and held it up to the light of the window. "Good scotch."

"*All right!*" Tommy's thick fist came down with a sudden bang on the desk top. "I'll quit playing around. I may be nothing but a chairside Earth-lubber, but

I'll tell you one thing. There's one thing I've developed in twenty years of politics and that's a nose for smells. And something about this situation smells! I don't know what, but it smells. And I want to find out what it is."

Chuck and Roy looked at each other.

"Why, Member," said Roy. "I don't follow you."

"You follow me all right," said Tommy. He took a gulp from his glass and blew out an angry breath. "All right—off the record. But tell me!"

Roy smiled.

"You tell him, Chuck," he said.

Chuck grinned in his turn.

"Well, I'll put it this way, Tommy," he said. "You remember how I explained the story about Big Brother Charlie that gave us the name for this project?"

"What about it?" said the Member.

"Maybe I didn't go into quite enough detail. You see," said Chuck, "the two youngest brothers were twins who lived right next door to each other in one town. They used to fight regularly until their wives got fed up with it. And when that happened, their wives would invite Big Brother Charlie from the next town to come and visit them."

Tommy was watching him with narrowed eyes.

"What happened, of course," said Chuck, lifting his glass again, "was that after about a week, the twins weren't fighting each other at all." He drank.

"All right. All right," said Tommy. "I'll play straight man. Why weren't they fighting with each other?"

"Because," said Chuck, putting his glass back down again, "they were both too busy fighting with Big Brother Charlie."

Tommy stared for a long moment. Then he grunted and sat back in his chair, as if he had just had the wind knocked out of him.

"You see," said Roy, leaning forward over his desk, "what we were required to do here was something impossible. You just *don't* change centuries-old attitudes of distrust and hatred overnight. Trying to get the Lugh and the Tomah to like each other by any pressures we could bring to bear was like trying to move mountains with toothpicks. Too much mass for too little leverage. But we *could* change the attitudes of both of them toward us."

"And what's that supposed to mean?" demanded Tommy, glaring at him.

"Why, we might—and did—arrange for them to find out that, like the twins, they had more in common with each other than either one of them had with Big Brother Charlie. Not that we wanted them, God forbid, to unite in actively *fighting* Big Brother: We do need this planet as a space depot. But we wanted to make them see that they two form one unit—with us on the outside. They don't like each other any better now, but they've begun to discover a reason for hanging together."

"I'm not sure I follow you," said Tommy dryly.

"What I'm telling you," said Roy, "is that we arranged a demonstration to bring home to them the present situation. They weren't prepared to share this world with each other. But when it came to their both sharing it with a third life form, they began to realize that the closer relative might see more eye-to-eye with them than the distant one. Chuck was under strict orders not to intervene, but to manage things so that each of them would be forced to solve the problems of the other, with no assistance from Earth or its technology."

"Brother," Chuck grunted, "the way it all worked out I didn't have to 'manage' a thing. The 'accident' was more thorough than we'd planned, and I was pretty much without the assistance of our glorious technology myself. Each of them had problems I couldn't have solved if I'd wanted to . . . but the other one could."

"Well," Roy nodded, "they are the natives, after all. We are the aliens. Just *how* alien, it was Chuck's job to demonstrate."

"You mean—" exploded Tommy, "that you threw away a half-million-dollar vehicle—that you made that crash-landing in the ocean—on purpose!"

"Off the record, Tommy," said Chuck, holding up a reminding finger. "As for the pot, it's on an undersea peak in forty fathoms. As soon as you can get us some more equipment it'll be duck soup to salvage it."

"Off the record be hanged!" roared Tommy. "Why, you might have killed them. You might have had one or the other species up in arms! You might—"

"We thought it was worth the risk," said Chuck mildly. "After all, remember I was sticking my own neck into the same dangers."

"You thought!" Tommy turned a seething glance on his nephew. He thrust himself out of his chair and stamped up and down the office in a visible effort to control his temper.

"Progress is not made by rules alone," misquoted Chuck complacently, draining the last scotch out of his glass. "Come back and sit down, Tommy. It's all over now."

The older man came glowering back and wearily plumped in his chair.

"All right," he said. "I said off the record, but I didn't expect this. Do you two realize what it is you've just done? Risked the lives of two vital members of intelligent races necessary to our future! Violated every principle of ordinary diplomacy in a harebrained scheme that had nothing more than a wild notion to back it up! And to top it off, involved *me—me*, a Member of the Government! If this comes out nobody will ever believe I didn't know about it!"

"All right, Tommy," said Chuck. "We hear you. Now, what are you going to do about it?"

Earth District Member 439 Thomas L. Wagnall blew out a furious breath.

"Nothing!" he said, violently. "Nothing."

"That's what I thought," said Chuck. "Pass the scotch."

This may start out like a straightforward adventure yarn (though with a healthy dash of humor) about a reluctant hero who has to make a trek across a considerable expanse of a dangerous planet's landscape against heavy odds . . . and it is all those things, but there's a lot more going on. You'll expect by now that the aliens had better watch their backs, but this time, that's also good advice for some of the humans.

THE GAME OF FIVE

"You can't do this!" The big young man was furious. His blunt, not-too-intelligent looking features were going lumpy with anger. "This is—" He pounded the desk he sat before with one huge fist, stuck for a moment as to just what it could be—"it's illegal!"

"Quite legal. A Matter of Expediency, Mr. Yunce," replied the Consul to Yara, cheerfully, waving a smoke tube negligently in his tapering fingers. The Consul's name was Ivor Ben. He was half the size of Coley Yunce, one third the weight, twice the age, fifteen times the aristocrat—and very much in charge.

"You draft me all the way from Sol Four!" shouted Coley. "I'm a tool designer. You picked me off the available list yourself. You knew my qualifications. You aren't supposed to draft a citizen anyway, except you can't get what you want some other way." His glare threatened to wilt the Consul's boutonniere, but failed to disturb the Counsul. "Damn Government seat-warmers! Can't hire like honest people! Send in for lists of the men you want, and pick out just your boy—never mind he's got business on Arga IV ten weeks from now. And now, when I get here you tell me I'm *not* going to design tools."

"That's right," said the Consul.

"You want me for some back-alley stuff! Well, I won't do it!" roared Coley. "I'll refuse. I'll file a protest back at Sol—" He broke off suddenly, and stared at the Consul. "What makes you so sure I won't?"

The Consul contemplated Coley's thick shoulders, massive frame and a certain wildness about Coley's blue eyes and unruly black hair, all with obvious satisfaction

"Certain reasons," he said, easily. "For one, I understand you grew up in a rather tough neighborhood in old Venus City, back on Sol II."

"So?" growled Coley.

"I believe there was something in your citizen's file about knives—"

"Look here!" exploded Coley. "So I knew how to use a knife when I was a kid. I had to, to stay alive in the spaceport district. So I got into a little trouble with the law—"

"Now, now—" said the Consul, comfortably. "Now, now."

"Using a man's past to blackmail him into a job that's none of his business. '*Would I please adjust to a change in plans, unavoidable but necessary—*' Well, I don't please! I don't please at all."

"I'd recommend you do," interrupted the Consul,

allowing a little metal to creep into his voice. "You people who go shopping around on foreign worlds and getting rich at it have a bad tendency to take the protection of your Humanity for granted. Let me correct this tendency in you, even if several billion others continue to perpetuate the notion. The respect aliens have always given your life and possessions is not, though you may have thought so heretofore, something extended out of the kindness of their hearts. They keep their paws off people because they know we Humans never abandon one of our own. You've been living safe within that system all your life, Mr. Yunce. Now it's time to do your part for someone else. Under my authority as Consul, I'm drafting you to aid me in—"

"What's wrong with the star-marines?" roared Coley.

"The few star-marines I have attached to the Consulate are required here," said the Consul.

"Then flash back to Sol for the X-4 Department. Those Government Troubleshooters—"

"The X-4 Department is a popular fiction," said the Consul, coldly. "We draft people we need, we don't keep a glamorous corps of secret operators. Now, no more complaints Mr. Yunce, or I'll put you under arrest. It's that, or take the job. Which?"

"All right," growled Coley. "What's the deal?"

"I wouldn't use you if I didn't have to," said the Consul. "But there's no one else. There's a Human— one of our young lady tourists who's run off from the compound and ended in a Yaran religious center a little over a hundred miles from here.'

"But if she's run off . . . of her own free will—"

"Ah, but we don't believe it was," said the Consul. "We think the Yarans enticed or coerced her into going." He paused. "Do you know anything about the Yarans?"

Coley shook his head.

"Every race we meet," said the Consul, putting the tips of his fingers together, "has to be approached by Humanity in a different way. In the case of Yara, here we've got a highly humanoid race which has a highly unhuman philosophy. They think life's a game."

"Sounds like fun." said Coley.

"Not the kind of a game you think," said the Consul, undisturbed. "They mean Game with a capital G. Everything's a Game to be played under certain rules. Even their relationship as a race to the human race is a Game to be played. A Game of Five, as life is a game of five parts—the parts being childhood, youth, young adulthood, middle age and old age. Right now, as they see it, their relations with Humanity are in the fourth part—Middle Age. In Childhood they tried passive indifference to our attempt to set up diplomatic relations. In Youth, they rioted against our attempt to set up a space terminal and human compound here. In Young Adulthood they attacked us with professional soldiery and made war against us. In each portion of the game, we won out. Now, in Middle Age, they are trying subtlety against us with this coercion of the girl. Only when we beat them at this and at the Old Age portion will they concede defeat and enter into friendly relations with us."

Coley grunted.

"According to them, Sara Illoy—that's the girl—has decided to become one of them and take up her personal Game of Life at the Young Adulthood stage. In this stage she has certain rights, certain liabilities, certain privileges and obligations. Only if she handles these successfully, will she survive to start in on the next stage. You understand," said the Consul, looking over at Coley, "this is a system of taboo raised to the nth level. Someone like her, not born to the system, has literally no chance of surviving."

"I see," said Coley. And he did.

"And of course," said the Consul, quietly, "if she dies, they will have found a way to kill a member of the human race with impunity. Which will win them the Middle Age portion and lose us the game, since we have to be perfect to win. Which means an end to us on this world; and a bad example set that could fire incidents on other non-human worlds."

Coley nodded.

"What am I supposed to do about it?" he asked.

"As a female Young Adult," said the Consul, "she may be made to return to the compound only by her lover or mate. We want you to play the young lover role and get her. If you ask for her, they must let her go with you. That's one of the rules."

Coley nodded again, this time cautiously.

"They have to let her go with me?" he said.

"They have to," repeated the Consul, leaning back in his chair and putting the tips of his fingers together. He looked out the tall window of the office in which he and Coley had been talking. "Go and bring her back. That's your job. We have transportation waiting to take you to her right now."

"Well, then," growled Coley, getting to his feet. "What're we waiting for? Let's get going and get it over with."

Three hours later, Coley found himself in the native Yaran city of Tannakil, in one of the Why towers of the Center of Meaning.

"Wait here," said the native Yaran who had brought him; and walked off leaving him alone in the heavily-draped room of the hexagonal wooden tower. Coley watched the Yaran leave, uneasiness nibbling at him.

Something was wrong, he told himself. His instincts were warning him. The Yaran that had just left him had been the one who had escorted him from the human compound to the native seacoast town outside it. They had taken a native glider that had gotten its original impulse by a stomach-sickening plunge down a wooden incline and out over a high sea-cliff. Thereafter the pilot with a skill that—Coley had to admit—no human could have come close to matching, had worked them up in altitude, and inland, across a low range of mountains, over a patch of desert and to this foothill town lying at the toes of another and greater range of mountains. Granted the air currents of Yara were more congenial to the art of gliding, granted it was a distance of probably no more than a hundred and fifty miles, still it was a prodigious feat by human standards.

But it was not this that had made Coley uneasy. It was something in the air. It was something in the attitude of the accompanying Yaran, Ansash by name. Coley considered and dismissed the possibility that it was the alienness of Ansash that was disturbing him. The Yarans were not all that different. In fact, the difference was so slight that Coley could not lay his finger upon it. When he had first stepped outside the compound, he had thought he saw what the difference was between Yarans and humans. Now, they all looked as Earth-original as any humans he had ever seen.

No, it was something other than physical—something in their attitudes. Sitting next to Ansash in the glider on the trip here, he had felt a coldness, a repulsion, a loneliness—there was no point in trying to describe it. In plain words he had *felt* that Ansash was not human. He had felt it in his skin and blood and bones:—*this is a thing I'm sitting next to, not a man.* And for the first time he realized how impossible and ridiculous were the sniggering stories they told in bars about interbreeding with the humanoids. These beings, too, were alien; as alien as the seal-like race of the

Dorcan system. From the irrational point of view of the emotions, the fact that they looked exactly like people only made it worse.

Coley took a quick turn about the room. The Yaran had been gone for only a couple of minutes, but already it seemed too long. Of course, thought Coley, going on with his musings, it might be something peculiar to Ansash. The glider pilot had not made Coley bristle so. In fact, except for his straight black hair—the Yarans all had black hair, it was what made them all look so much alike—he looked like any friendly guy on any one of the human worlds, intent on doing his job and not worried about anything else. . . . Was Ansash never coming back with that girl?

There was a stir behind the draperies and Ansash appeared, leading a girl by the hand. She was a blonde as tall as the slighter-boned Yaran who was leading her forward. Her lipstick was too red and her skin almost abnormally pale, so that she looked bleached-out beside Ansash's native swarthiness. Moreover, there was something sleepwalking about her face and the way she moved.

"This is Sara Illoy," said Ansash, in Yaran, dropping her hand as they stopped before Coley. Coley understood him without difficulty. Five minutes with a hypnoteacher had given him full command of the language. But he was staring fascinated at the girl, who looked back at him, but did not speak.

"Pleased to meet you," said Coley. "I'm Coley Yunce, Sol II."

She did not answer.

"Are you all right?" Coley demanded. Still she looked up at him without speaking and without interest. There was nothing in her face at all. She was not even curious. She was merely looking.

"She does not speak," the voice of Ansash broke the

silence. "Perhaps you should beat her. Then she might talk."

Coley looked sharply at him. But there was no expression of slyness or derision on the Yaran's face. "Come on," he growled at the girl, and turned away. He had taken several steps before he realized she was not following. He turned back to take her by the hand—and discovered Ansash had disappeared.

"Come on," he growled again; and led the girl off to where his memory told him he and Ansash had entered through the drapes. He felt about among the cloth and found a parting. He towed the girl through.

His memory had not tricked him. He was standing on the stairs up which he and Ansash had come earlier. He led the girl down them and into the streets of Tannakil.

He paused to get his bearings with his feet on the smoothly fitted blocks of the paving. Tannakil was good-sized as Yaran towns went, but it was not all that big. After a second, he figured out that their way back to the glider field was to their right, and he led the girl off.

This was part of the Yaran attitude, he supposed; to deprive him of a guide on the way back. Well, they might have done worse things. Still, he thought, as he led Sara Illoy along, it was odd. No Yaran they passed looked at them or made any move to show surprise at seeing two obvious humans abroad in their town. Not only that, but none of the Yarans seemed to be speaking to each other. Except for the occasional hoof-noises of the Yaran riding-animal—a reindeer-like creature with a long lower lip—the town was silent.

Coley hurried on through the streets. The afternoon was getting along; and he did not fancy a flight back over those mountains at dusk or in the dark, no matter how skillful the Yaran pilots were. And in time the wooden Yaran buildings began to thin out and the two of them emerged onto the grassy field with its towering wooden slide, like a ski-jump, only much taller, up to which the gliders were winched, and down which they were started.

Coley had actually started to lead the girl toward the slide when the facts of the situation penetrated his mind.

The field was empty.

There were no gliders on its grass, at the top of the slide, or winched partway up it. And there were no Yarans.

Coley whirled around, looking back the way he had come. The street he and the girl had walked was also empty. Tannakil was silent and empty—as a ghost town, as a churchyard.

Coley stood spraddle-legged, filled with sudden rage and fear. Rage was in him because he had not expected to find a joker in this expedition right at the start; and fear—because all t e gutter instinct of his early years cried out against t e danger of his position.

He was alone—in a town full of potential enemies. And night was not far off.

Coley looked all around him again. There was nothing; nothing but the grass and the town, the empty sky, and a road leading off straight as a ruler toward the desert over which he had flown, toward the distant mountains, and the coast beyond.

And then he noticed two of the Yaran riding animals twitching up grass with their long lower lips, beside the road a little way off.

"Come on," he said to the girl, and led the way toward the animals. As he drew near, he could see that they had something upon their backs; and when he reached them he discovered, as he had half-expected, that they were both fitted with the Yaran equivalent

of the saddle. Coley grinned without humor; and looked
back toward the town.

"Thanks for nothing," he told it. And he turned to
boost the girl into one of the saddles. She went up
easily, as someone who had ridden one of the beasts
before. He untethered her animal, passed the single
rein back up into her hand, then unhitched and
mounted the other beast himself. There was a knife
tied to its leather pad of a saddle.

They headed off down the road into the descending sun.

They rode until it became too dark to see the road
before them. Then Coley stopped and tethered the
animals. He helped the girl down and unsaddled the
beasts. The saddles came off—and apart—quite easily. In fact, they were the simplest sort of riding equipment. The equivalent of the saddlecloth was a sort of
great sash of coarse but semi-elastic cloth that went
completely around the barrel of the animal and fastened together underneath with a system of hooks and
eyes. The saddle itself was simply a folded-over flap
of leather that hook-and-eyed to the saddle cloth.
Unfolded, Coley discovered the saddle was large
enough to lie on, as a groundsheet; and the unfolded
saddle cloth made a rough blanket.

He and the girl lay down to sleep until the moon
rose. But Coley, not unsurprisingly, found sleep hard
to come by. He lay on his back, gazing up at the
sprinkling of strange stars overhead, and thinking
hard.

It was not hard to realize he had been suckered into
something. Coley had expected that. It was harder to
figure out what he had been suckered into, and by
whom, and why. The presence of the knife on his
saddle pointed the finger at the Consul; but to suppose

the Consul was in league with the humanoids ran counter to Coley's experience with a half a dozen non-human worlds. He was not inexperienced with aliens—his speciality was designing and adapting human-type tools for the grasping of alien appendages. He was only inexperienced with humanoids. Lying on his back, he narrowed his eyes at the stars and wished he had found out more about the Consul.

Four hours after sunset, by Coley's watch, the moon rose. Coley had expected one sooner, since Yara was supposed to have two of them. But then he remembered hearing that the orbits of both were peculiar so that often neither would be visible over any given spot for several nights hand-running. He roused the girl, who got up without protest. They saddled and rode on.

Coley tried from time to time to get the girl to talk. But, although she would look at him when he spoke to her, she would not say a word.

"Is this something you did to yourself?" he asked her. "Or something they did to you? That's what I'd like to know."

She gazed solemnly at him in the moonlight.

"How about nodding your head for yes, or shaking it for no?" . . . He tried speaking to her in Yaran. When that failed, he tried upper middle English, and what he knew of Arcturan's local canting tongue. On a sudden chilling impulse, Coley urged his beast along-side hers, and, reaching out, pressed on her jaw muscles until she automatically opened her mouth. In the moonlight, he saw she still had her tongue.

"It's not that," he said. He had remembered certain ugly things done around the Spaceport district of Venus City. "So it must be psychological. I'll bet you were all right when you left the compound," He found himself clenching his teeth a little and thinking, for no obvious reason, of Ansash. To get his mind off it, he looked at his watch again.

"Time to stop and rest a bit, again," he said. "I want to get as far as possible across this desert at night, but there's no use killing ourselves right at the start."

He stopped the beasts, helped the girl down and unsaddled.

"A couple of hours nap," he said. "And then we go." He set his watch alarm and fell asleep.

He woke up to broad daylight and hooting voices. Automatically, he leaped to his feet. One ankle tripped him and threw him down again. He lay there, half-propped on one elbow, seeing himself surrounded by a bunch of young Yarans.

His hand slipped quietly to his belt where he had tucked the knife from the saddle. To his astonishment, it was still there. He let his hand fall away from it, and pretending to be dazed, glanced around under half-closed eyelids.

Sara Illoy was not to be seen. Of the young Yarans around him—all of them uniformly dressed in a sort of grey loose robe or dress, tightly belted at the waist—the large majority were male. None of them seemed to be paying any great attention to him. They were all hooting at each other without words and and—well, not dancing so much as engaging in a sort of semi-rhythmic horseplay with each other. Most of the males carried knives themselves, tucked in their belts; and some had tucked in beside the knives a sort of pistol with an exaggeratedly long slim barrel and a bulbous handle.

Farther off, he could occasionally glimpse between the bounding and whirling bodies some of the riding animals, tethered in a line and contentedly twitching up grass. Coley measured the distance between himself and the beasts, speculated on the chance of making a run for it—and gave the notion up.

A thought about the girl occurred to him.

"But right now, kid," he thought silently to himself, "if I had the chance, it'd be everyone for himself and the devil take the hindmost. I wasn't raised to be a shining knight."

At the same time he admitted to himself that he was glad she wasn't around to see him, if he did have a chance to make a break for it—no reason to rub in the fact that she would be being abandoned. Then he went back to worrying about his own skin.

Coley had discovered in the gutters and back alleys of Venus City when he was young that the best cure for being afraid was to get angry. He had learned this so well that it had become almost automatic with him; and he began to feel himself growing hot and prickly under his shirt, now, as he lay still with his eyes half-closed, waiting. There would be a chance to go out fighting—he did have the knife.

Suddenly—so suddenly that he found himself unprepared for it—the roughhousing and hooting stopped and he found himself jerked to his feet. A knife flashed, and the tension of the rope binding his ankle fell away. He found himself standing, loosely surrounded by Yarans; and through the gaps between them he could see the line of riding animals clearly and close.

He almost took the bait. Then, just in time, he recognized what was before him as one of the oldest traps known to civilized beings. He had seen exactly the same trick played back in Venus City. He had played it, himself. The idea was to tempt the victim with the hope of an escape, to tempt him into running; and when he did, to chase and catch him again, cat-and-mouse fashion.

With this sudden realization, confidence came

flooding back into him. The alienness of the situation melted away and he found himself back in familiar territory. He stretched up to his full height, which was half a head taller than the tallest of the Yarans surrounding him; and smiled grimly at them, his eyes skipping from individual to individual as he tried to pick out the one that would be the leader.

He almost fell into the error of picking out the largest of the Yarans around him. Then he thought of a surer index of rank, and his eyes swept over the male Yarans at belt level, until they halted on one whose belt held two pistols, with matching butts. Coley smiled again and strode calmly forward toward the Yaran he had picked out.

With a sudden rush the Yarans spread out into a circle, leaving Coley and the male with two pistols inside. Coley halted within double his arms' length of the other, and hooked his thumbs into his own belt. His eye met that of the Yaran before him sardonically.

Up until now, the Yaran had not moved. But, as the circle reached its full dimension and went still, his right hand flashed to the butt of one of his pistols. In the same instant, Coley dropped to one knee. His knife flashed in his hand and glittered suddenly as it flew through the air.

And the Yaran fell, clutching at the knife in his chest.

A chorus of wild hoots went up; and when Coley glanced up from the male he had just knifed, the others were scrambling for their riding animals. Within seconds, they were mounted and gone, the dust of the desert rolling up behind them to mark their trail. Of the long line of riding animals, only two were left.

And, peering around the farther of these, was the girl.

❖   ❖   ❖

Coley buried the Yaran he had killed, before he and the girl took up their road again.

Coley had expected the desert to be a man-killer by day. It was not—for reasons he did not understand, but guessed to have something to do with its altitude, and also the latitude in which this part of Yara lay. Still, it was hot and uncomfortable enough, and they had neither food or water with them. Luckily, later on in the day they came to a wayside well; the water of which, when Coley tasted it gingerly, proved to be sweet enough. He drank and handed the dipper to the girl.

She drank eagerly as well.

"Now, if we could just happen on something to eat," Coley told her. She showed no sign that she understood him, but, later in the day, when they came to the nearer foothills of the coastal mountain range, she rode off among the first trees they came to. When he followed her, he found her eating a black-skinned fruit about the size of a tangerine.

"Here, what are you doing?" shouted Coley, grabbing the fruit out of her hand. She made no protest, but picked another fruit from the small, wide-branched small tree or bush beside her. Seeing her bite into it without hesitation, Coley felt his alarm dwindle.

"I suppose they fed you some of these while you were there," he growled. He sniffed the fruit, then licked at it where the pulp was exposed. It had a rather sour, meaty taste. He took a tentative bite himself. It went down agreeably. He took another.

"Oh, well—what the hell!" he said. And he and the girl filled themselves up on the fruit.

That night, when they camped on the very knees of the mountains themselves, Coley lay stretched out under his animal-blanket, trying to sort out what had happened to them and make some sense from it.

The situation was the wildest he had ever encountered. If certain elements in it seemed to be doing their best to kill him (and undoubtedly the girl as well) off, other elements seemed just as determined to keep them alive. Tannakil had been a death-trap if they had lingered there after nightfall; he knew this as surely as if he had seen it written in Basic on one of the wooden walls there. But Tamakil had apparently provided the riding animals for their escape.

Those Yaran youngsters back there on the desert had not been fooling either. Yet they had ridden off. And the desert had been no joke; but the well had been just where it needed to be—and how come those fruit trees to be so handy, and how did the girl too recognize them, even some way back from the road?

Unthinkingly, he half-rolled over to ask her. Then it came back to him that she would not be able to answer; and he frowned. There was something about this business of the girl herself that was funny, too. . . .

Thinking about it, he fell asleep.

The next day, they pushed on into the mountains, finding pleasanter country full of shaggy-barked, low green trees, and green ground-covering of tiny, thick-growing ferns. They climbed steadily into cooler air, and the road narrowed until it was hardly more than a trail. The mountain tops ahead, at least, were free from snow, so that whatever happened, they would not have to contend with mountain storms and low temperatures, for which neither of them was dressed or equipped.

Then an abrupt and dramatic change took place. The road suddenly leveled out, and then began to dip downward, as if they had come into a pass. Moreover, it was now wider and more carefully engineered than Coley had ever seen it before. And more than that, after a little while it began to sport a crushed rock topping.

They were walled in on both sides by steep rock, and were descending, apparently, into an interior mountain valley. Suddenly they heard a sharp hooting noise, twice repeated, from up ahead of them; and around the curve of the mountain road came a double line of Yarans mounted on running riding animals. The leading Yaran yelled a command, the riding animals were reined in and skidded to a halt; and one mounted Yaran who was holding a sort of two-handed bellows with a long, ornately carved tube projecting from it, pumped the device once, producing a single additional hoot which at this close range hurt Coley's eardrums.

These mounted Yarans were dressed in short grey kilts with grey, woolly-looking leggings underneath that terminated in a sort of mukluk over each foot, and bulky, thick, green sweater-like upper garments with parka-type hoods which they wore thrown back on their shoulders. They did not hold the single reins of their riding animals in their hands, but had them loosely looped and tied leaving their hands free—the right one to carry what was truly a fantastically long-barreled version of the bulbous-handled pistols Coley had encountered in the desert, the left one to be carried in a fist against the left hip, the elbow stylishly cocked out. They were all riding in this position when Coley first saw them; and the sudden sliding halt did not cause a single fist to slip. There was also both a short and a long knife in each man's green belt.

"Permissions?" snapped the Yaran on the lead animal; and continued without waiting for an answer. "None? You are under arrest. Come with me." He started to turn his animal.

"Wait a minute—" began Coley. The other paused, and Coley noticed suddenly that his belt was not green, like the others, but yellow. "Never mind," said Coley. "We're coming."

The yellow-belted Yaran completed his turn, nodded to the one with the bellows, and an ear-splitting hoot shook the air. One moment later Coley found himself and the girl on their animals in a dead run for the valley below, with mounted Yarans all about them. Forgetting everything else, Coley grabbed for the front edge of his saddle flap and concentrated on hanging on.

They swept around a curve and down a long slope, emerging into a sort of interior plateau area which looked as if it might be a number of miles in extent. Coley was unable to make sure of this—not only because most of his attention was concentrated on staying on his mount, but because almost immediately they were surrounded by circular small buildings of stone, which a little farther on gave way to hexagonal small buildings, which yet further on gave way to five-sided, then square, then triangular edifices of the same size. Beyond the triangular buildings was an open space, and then a large, stone structure of rectangular shape.

The bellows hooted, the troop slid to a stop. The yellow-belted Yaran dismounted, signalled Coley and the girl to get down as well, and led them in through a door in the large, rectangular building. Within were a good number of Yarans standing at tall desks arranged in a spiral shape within a large room. The yellow-belted Yaran went to one of these, apparently at random from all Coley could discover, and held a whispered conversation. Then he returned and led them both off through more doors and down halls, until he ushered them into a room about twenty feet square, furnished only with a pile of grey cushions neatly stacked in one corner, and one of the tall desks such as Coley had seen arranged spirally in the large room behind them. A male Yaran, dressed like all the rest except that he wore a silver belt, turned away from the room's single large window, and came to stand behind the tall desk,

"West Entrance. No permissions, Authority," spoke up the yellow-belted one behind Coley.

"Now, wait a minute—" began Coley. "Let me tell you how we happened to come this way—"

"You—" said the silver-belted Yaran, suddenly interrupting. "You speak the real language."

"Of course," said Coley, "that's part of why we happen to be here—"

"You are not one of the real people."

"No. I—"

"Confine yourself to simple answers, please. You are Human?"

"Yes," said Coley.

"A Human, speaking the real language, and here where you have no permission to be. A spy."

"No," said Coley. "Let me explain. Yesterday, our Consul . . ." He explained.

"That is your story," said the silver-belted Yaran. "There's no reason I should believe it—in view of the suspicious circumstances of your being here, an obvious Human, speaking the real tongue and without permission to be here. This young female will be taken into protective custody. You, as a spy, will be strangled."

"I wouldn't do that, if I were you," said Coley. "The old persons down on the coast have their own ideas about how to deal with Humans. If I were you, I'd at least check up on my story before I stuck my neck out by having a Human strangled."

"This is the Army," retorted the silver-belted Yaran. "The old persons down on the coast have no authority over us. They have nothing whatsoever to say about what we do with spies caught in restricted areas. I want you to understand that clearly." He stared at Coley with motionless black eyes for a long moment.

"On the other hand," he continued, "it is, of course, regular Army routine to check up on the stories of spies before strangling them. As I was just about to say, when you interrupted me. Consequently, you will be allowed the freedom of the commercial area adjoining the military establishment under my command here. I warn you, however, against attempting to spy any further, or trying to leave the area without permission. The female will still be taken into protective custody."

He turned to the one in the yellow belt.

"Take him to the commercial area and turn him loose," he ordered. Numbly, Coley followed the yellow-belted Yaran out, casting a rather helpless glance at the girl as he passed. But the girl seemed as blandly unconcerned about this as she had about almost everything else. The Yaran with the yellow belt led Coley out of the building, had him remount, and rode with him to a far side of the camp where they passed a sort of gate in a stone wall and found themselves among a cluster of wooden buildings like those Coley had seen at Tannakil.

Here, the yellow-belted Yaran turned his animal and scooted back into the military compound on the run, leaving Coley sitting alone, on his beast, in the center of a cobbled street.

It was past noon when Coley was turned loose. For more than a couple of hours of the short Yaran day, he rode around the commercial area. It was actually a small town, its buildings set up as permanently as the ones in the military area. What he saw confirmed his original notion that, much as the human sort of army is the same everywhere, the human sort of civilian population that clings to its skirts is pretty much the same, as well. The town—a sign at its geographic center announced its name to be Tegat—revealed itself to be a collection of establishments for the feeding, drinking, and other pleasuring of off-duty soldiers. So had the spaceport district been, back at Venus City. True, the clients of the district had not exactly been soldiers; but there was much similarity between the uniformed breed and the men who worked the starships

Once more, as he had in that moment back on the desert, Coley began to feel at home.

He considered his wealth, which consisted in Yaran terms of his muscle, his knife, and the animal he was riding, and then he stopped a passing Yaran, a civilian type in an unbelted grey robe.

"Who around here lends money?" asked Coley. "And just how do I go about finding him."

The Yaran looked at him for a long moment without answering, and without any expression on his face that Coley could interpret. Then his thin mouth opened in the swarthy face.

"Two streets back, he said. "Turn right. Twelfth building, second floor. Call for Ynesh."

Coley went back, found the second street and turned right into it. This turned out to be little more than an alley; and Coley, moreover, found he had trouble telling where one building left off and another started, since they were all built firmly into each other. Finally, by counting doorways and making a hopeful guess, he entered what he believed was the twelfth building and, passing a couple of interior doors, strode up a ramp and found himself on a landing one floor up. Here there were three more doors. Coley stopped, perplexed; then he remembered that his instructions had been to *call* for Ynesh.

"Ynesh!" he yelled.

The door on the furthest right flew open as if his voice had actuated some sort of spring release. No one came out, however. Coley waited a moment, then walked face first into a hanging drape. He pushed his way past the drape and found himself in a circular room containing cushions and one tall desk behind which a middle-aged Yaran in an unbelted figured green robe was standing. One tall window illuminated the room.

"Live well," said the Yaran, "I am Ynesh. How much would you like to borrow?"

"Nothing," said Coley—although his empty stomach growled at this denial of the hope of the wherewithal to buy something to put in it. Ynesh did not stir so much as a finger that Coley could see, but suddenly three good-sized Yarans in belted, knee-length robes of blue-grey appeared from the drapes. They all had two knives in their belts.

"Don't misunderstand me," said Coley, hastily, "I wouldn't have come here unless I meant to do some business. How'd you like to make some money?"

Ynesh still stood without moving. But the three with knives disappeared back into the drapery. Coley breathed more easily. He walked forward to the desk and leaned close.

"I suppose," he said to the Yaran, "there's some sort of limit set on how much interest you can charge, and how much you can lend the ordinary soldier."

Ynesh parted his thin lips.

"For every grade an amount of credit commensurate with the pay scale for that grade. The interest rate is one tenth of the principal in the period of one year, proportionately decreased for shorter lengths of time. This rate and amount is set by the military Authority in Chief. Everyone but a Human would know that, Human."

"Call me Coley," said Coley.

"Gzoly," replied the Yaran, agreeably.

"You wouldn't want to risk going above the amounts

or charging a greater interest rate, I take it?" said Coley.

"And lose my license to lend?" said Ynesh. He had not pulled back from Coley. They were talking, Coley suspected, with more cozy intimacy than probably any Human and Yaran had talked to date. It was marvelous what the right sort of topic could do to eradicate awkwardness in communication between the races. "I would hardly be sensible to do that, Gzoly."

"What if somebody else would take the risks for you—say, take your money and lend it without a license, quietly, but for better than the usual rates of interest, in any amount wanted?"

"Now who, Gzoly, would do that?" said Ynesh.

"Perhaps certain soldiers wouldn't object to acting as agents," said Coley. "They borrow the money from you and relend to their fellow soldiers at higher rates? Under the blanket, no questions asked, money in a hurry."

"Ah, but I wouldn't be able to lend each one of them more than his grade-amount of credit, since it would surely be traced back to me," said Ynesh, but in no tone that indicated that he considered the topic closed. "Moreover, where would be the extra profit? I'd have to lend to them at legal rates." He paused, almost imperceptibly. The effect was that of a silent shrug. "A pity. But that is the Game."

"Of course," said Coley. "On the other hand, there are no rules set up for me. I could lend them as much as they wanted, at any rate I wanted. And also since I'm a Human, you could lend me the money originally at a higher-than-legal rate of interest."

"Ah," said Ynesh.

"I thought the idea would meet with your approval," said Coley.

"It might be worth trying in a limited way, Gzoly," said Ynesh. "Yes, I think it might. I will be glad to lend you a small trial sum, at, say, a fifth part in yearly interest."

"I'm afraid," said Coley, straightening up from the desk, "that you happen to be one of those real people who would cut open the insect that spins the golden nest. A fifth in interest would force me to relend at rates that would keep my agents from finding any borrowers, after they had upped their own rates to make their cut. I'm afraid I couldn't do business with you unless I borrowed at no more than a ninth part."

"Ridiculous. I'm laughing," said Ynesh, without cracking a smile or twitching a facial muscle. "If you're one of those people who always like to feel they've beaten a little off the price for form's sake, I'll let you have your first sum at five and a half."

"Goodbye," said Coley.

"Now, wait a minute," said Ynesh. "I might consider . . ." And the classical argument proceeded along its classical lines, terminating in a rate to Coley of eight and three-quarters part of the principal on a yearly basis.

"Now, the only question is," said Ynesh, after the rate had been settled, "Whether I can trust you with such a sum as I had in mind. After all, what proof have I—"

"I imagine you've heard by this time," said Coley, drily. "The military Authority has confined me to this area. If I try any tricks you won't have any trouble finding me."

"True," said Ynesh, as if the thought had just struck him for the first time. . . .

Coley went out with money in his pocket and intrigued the Yaran who sold food in one of the eating and drinking establishments by ordering a large number of different items and sampling them all in gingerly fashion. The search was not a particularly pleasant one for Coley's tastebuds; but he did eventually come up with a sort of a stew and a sort of a pudding that tasted reasonably good—and assuaged a two days hunger. He also tried a number of the Yaran drinks, but ended up gagging on their oily taste and settled for water.

Then, having eaten and drunk, he glanced around the establishment. Not far off across the room a Yaran soldier with the green belt of the lower ranks was seated glumly at a table holding an empty bowl and a stick of incense that had burned itself completely out. Coley got up, went over and plumped down on a stool at the same table.

"Cheer up," he said. "Have a drink on me. And tell me—how'd you like to make some money . . . ?"

It took about a week and a half for Coley's presence in the commercial area and in the military establishment to make itself felt. Early the third day, Coley discovered where the girl was being held—in a sort of watchtower not far from the main gate. However, there was no getting in to her and obviously she could not get out—though from the few glimpses Coley had had of her uninterested face when it occasionally showed itself at the window of the tower when he was watching, it was a good question whether she even wanted to.

Otherwise, however, things had gone well. Every day had become a little more comfortable. For one thing, Coley had discovered that the Yaran meats, in spite of their gamey taste, were quite satisfying if soaked in oil before, during, and after cooking. In addition to this, business was good; Coley having noticed that gambling was under as strict regulations as the lending of money, had thoughtfully started a chain-letter scheme to start the financial picture moving.

A desert takes no more thirstily to one of its infrequent rain showers than the Yaran soldiers took to both of Coley's schemes. The local money situation literally exploded; and ten days after Coley's arrival. he was escorted to the office of the Yaran Authority who had originally passed sentence upon him.

The Authority in his silver belt was as inscrutable as ever. He waited until he and Coley were alone together.

"All my officers are in debt," he said to Coley. "My common soldiers are become a rabble, selling their equipment to illegal buyers for money. The army treasury has been broken into and robbed. Where is all our money?"

"I couldn't tell you," replied Coley, who was being perfectly truthful. He knew only where about a fifth of the area's hard cash was—carefully hidden in his room. As for the rest, Coley suspected other prudent souls had squirreled most of the rest out of the way; and that in any case the sum the Authority had in mind was entirely illusory, resulting from vast quantities of credit multiplying the actual cash reserves of the area.

"I will have you tortured to death—which is illegal," said the Authority. "Then I will commit suicide—which is shameful but convenient."

"Why do all that?" said Coley, enunciating clearly in spite of a slight unavoidable dryness of the mouth—for though he had planned this, he realized the extreme touchiness of the situation at this stage. "Let me and the girl go. Then you can declare a moratorium on all debts and blame it on the fact I absconded with the funds."

The Authority thought a moment.

"A very good suggestion," he said, finally. "However, there's no reason I should actually let you go. I might as well have a little fun out of all this."

"Somebody might find out, if I didn't actually escape with the girl. Then the blame would fall on you."

The Authority considered again.

"Very well. A pity," he said. "Perhaps I shall lay hands on you again, some day, Human.'

"I don't think so," said Coley. "Not if I can help it."

"Yes," said the Authority. He went to the entrance of the room and gave orders. Half an hour later, Coley found himself, his belongings, and the girl hurrying on a pair of first-class riding animals out the far end of the pass, headed down toward the seacoast. The early sunset of Yara was upon them and twilight was closing down.

"Great hero," breathed the girl in Yaran. Coley jerked about and stared at her through the gathering gloom. But her expression was as innocuous as ever, and for all the expression there was on her face, it might have been somebody else entirely who had spoken.

"Say that again," said Coley.

But she was through speaking—at least for the present.

Coley had managed to get away with the money hidden in his room. He wore it in a double fold of heavy cloth—a sort of homemade money belt—wrapped around his waist under his shirt; and a few coins taken from it supplied himself and the girl with a room for the night at a way-station that they came to that night after the second moon rose in the sky. The coins also supplied Coley with food—raw meat which he cooked himself over the brazier filled with soft coal which the way-station help brought in to heat the room. He offered some to the girl, but she would not eat it; and if he had not thought of the notion of ordering in some fruit, she might have gone to sleep without any food at all. The last thing he saw, by the dim glow of the dying coals in the brazier was the girl half-curled, half-sitting in a far corner of the room on some cushions and looking in his direction steadily, but still without expression or a word.

The following morning, they left the way-station early. Coley had been wary that in spite of his decision the military Authority might have sent men after them. But evidently the Yaran mind did not work that way. They saw no signs of any threat or soldiers.

By mid-day, between the clumps of bush-like fern that covered the seaward side of these mountains, they began to catch glimpses of the coast below them, and when they stopped to rest their animals in a spot giving them an open view of the lowlands, it was possible for Coley to make out the glittering spire of the traffic control tower in the Human Compound.

He pointed. "We're almost home," he said, in Basic. The girl looked at him interestedly for a long second.

"Hawmn," she said, finally.

"Well!" said Coley, straightening up in his saddle. "Starting to come to life, are you? Say that again."

She looked at him.

"Say that again," repeated Coley, this time in Yaran.

"Hawmn," she said.

"Wonderful! Marvelous!" said Coley. He applauded. "Now say something else in Basic for the nice man."

"Hawmn," she said.

"No," said Coley. "You've said that. Try something else. Say—say—" He leaned toward her, enunciating the words carefully in Basic. "Friends, Romans, Countrymen—"

She hesitated.

"Frendz, Rawmans, Cundzrememns—" she managed.

"Lend me your ears—"

"Lenz me ur ears—"

"Come on, kid," said Coley, turning his own riding animal's head once more back onto the downtrail, "this is too good to let drop. I come not to bury—"

"I cauzm nodt do burrey—"

They rode on. By the time they reached the first gate of the walled town, as dusk was falling, the girl was reciting in Basic like a veteran. The guard at the gate stared at the strange sounds coming from her mouth.

"What's the matter with her? You can't go in, Human; the gate's already closed for the night. What's your business in Akalede?"

Coley gave the Yaran a handful of coins.

"Does that answer your questions?" he asked.

"Partly—" said the guard, peering at the coins in the falling dusk.

"In that case," said Coley, smoothly, "I suppose I'll just have to wait outside tonight; and perhaps some of my good friends inside the city, tomorrow, can fill out the answer for you. Although," said Coley, "perhaps a fuller answer may not be quite what you—"

"Pass, worthy person," said the gateman, swinging the door wide and standing back deferentially. Coley and the girl rode on into the city of Akalede.

The streets they found themselves in were full of Yarans pushing either homeward, or wherever Yarans went at sundown. From his experience with the commercial area outside the military compound, Coley suspected a majority of the males at least were on their way to get drunk. Or drugged, thought Coley, suddenly remembering he had not been able to drink enough of things Yaran to discover what it was in their potables that addicted the populace to them. He had seen Yarans become stupefied from drinking, but what kind of stupefaction it was, he suddenly realized, he had not the slightest idea. This made him abruptly thoughtful; and he rode on automatically, trying to chase down an elusive conclusion that seemed to skitter through his mind just out of reach.

His riding animal stopped suddenly. Coming to himself with a start, he saw he had ridden full up against a barricade that blocked the street.

"What the—"

His bridle strap was seized and he looked down at a kilted Yaran whose clothes bore the cut, if not the color of the army.

"Human, you're under arrest," said the lean face. "Where do you think you're going?"

"To the Compound,' said Coley. "I and this female Human have to get back—"

"Permissions?"

"Well, you see," said Coley, "We—"

But the Yaran was already leading him off; and other kilted Yarans had fallen in around the mounts of Coley and his companion.

Coley stood, cursing inwardly, but with a bland smile on his face. Behind him, the girl was silent. The heavy drapes of the room in the building to which they had both been brought did not stir. The only thing that stirred was the lips of the rather heavy-set, obviously middle-aged Yaran standing behind a tall desk.

"You have made a mistake," said the middle-aged Yaran.

Coley was fully prepared to admit it. The middle-aged native before him was apparently a local magistrate. As such, he had made it obvious that it was up to him whether Coley and the girl were to be allowed through the barricades into the restricted area of the city that lay between them and the Human Compound.

And Coley, judging by his past experience with these people, had just made the mistake of trying to bribe him.

"I am, you see," went on the magistrate, "one of the real people who actually plays the Game. But perhaps you don't know about the Game, Human?"

Coley rubbed his dry lips in what he hoped was a casual gesture.

"A little about it," he said.

"You could hardly," said the magistrate, leaning on the high desk, "know more than a little. Understanding in its full sense would be beyond you. You see— we real people, all of us, hope to reach Old Age." He paused, his black eyes steady on Coley. "Of course, I am not speaking of a physical old age, an age of the body, which is nothing. I am speaking of true Old Age, that highest level of development that is winnable."

"That's pretty much how I heard it," said Cole.

"Few of us," said the magistrate, going on as if Cole had said nothing, "very few of us make it, and we do it only by playing the Game to perfection."

"Oh. I see," said Coley.

"It does not matter if you do," said the magistrate. "What matters is that I offer you this explanation, leaving it up to you to use, misuse or ignore it as you will. Because, you see, there is one thing required of a player of the Game." He paused, looking at Coley.

"What?" said Coley, filling the gap in the conversation

"Consistency," said the magistrate. "His rules of living—which he chooses for himself—may be anything, good or bad. But having adopted them, he must live by them. He cannot do himself the violence of violating his own principles. A person may adopt selfishness as a principle; but, having adopted it, he may not allow himself the luxury of unselfishness. He must live by the principles chosen in youth—and with them try to survive to years of maturity and wisdom." He paused. "If he falters, or if the world kills or destroys him, he has lost the Game. So far—" he leaned a little closer to Coley—"I have neither faltered nor been destroyed. And one of my principles is absolute honesty. Another is the destruction of the dishonest."

"I see," said Coley. "Well, what I meant was—"

"You," went on the magistrate, inexorably, "are one of the dishonest."

"Now, wait! Wait!" cried Coley. "You can't judge us by your standards. We're Human!"

"You say that as if it entitled you to special privileges," said the magistrate, almost dreamily. "The proof of the fact that the Game encompasses even you is the fact that you are here caught up in it." He reached below the table and came up with a sort of hour-glass, filled not with sand but with some heavy liquid. He turned it over. "This will run out in a few moments," he said. "If before it has run out you come up with a good reason why you should, within the rules of the Game, be allowed on into the Human Compound, I will let you and the female go. Otherwise, I will have you both destroyed."

The liquid from the little transparent pyramid at the top of the timing device began to run, drop by drop, down into the pyramid below. The liquid was clear, with no reddish tint, but to Coley it looked like the blood he could feel similarly draining out of his heart. His mind flung itself suddenly open, as if under the influence of some powerfully stimulating drug, and thoughts flashed through it like small bursts of light. His gutter-bred brain was crying out that there was a gimmick somewhere, that there was a loophole in any law, or something new to get around it—The liquid in the top of the timer had almost run out.

And then he had it.

"How can you be sure," said Coley, "that you're not interrupting a process that greater minds than your own have put in motion?"

The magistrate reached slowly out, took the timer from the top of the desk and put it out of sight behind the desk top.

"I'll have you escorted to the gates of the Human Compound by one of our police persons," he said.

Coley was furious—and that fury of his, according to his way of doing things, hid not a little fear.

"Calm down," said his jailer, one of a squad of star-marines attached to the embassy, unlocking the cell door. "I'll have you out in a minute."

"You'd better, lint-picker," said Coley.

"Let's watch the names," said the star-marine. He was almost as big as Coley. He came inside and stood a few inches from Coley, facing him. "They want you upstairs in the Consul's office. But we got a couple of minutes to spare, if you insist," Coley opened his mouth—then shut it again.

"Forget it," growled Coley. "Shoved into jail—locked up all night with no explanation—you'd be hot, too. I want to see that Consul."

"This way," said the jailer, standing aside. Coley allowed himself to be escorted out of the cell, down a corridor, and up a fall-tube. They went a little way down another corridor and through a light-door into the same office Coley had been in before. Some two weeks before, to be precise. The Consul, Ivor Ben was standing with his back to the hunched, smoke tube in his fingers, and a not pleasant look on his aristocratic face.

"Stand over there," he said; and crossing to his desk,

pushed a button on it. "Bring in the girl," he said. He pushed another button. "Let Ansash in now."

He straightened up behind the desk. A door opened behind Coley; and he turned to see the girl he had escorted from Tannakil. She looked at him with her usual look, advanced a few steps into the office, as the door closed behind her, and then halted—as if the machinery that operated her had just run down.

Only a couple of seconds later, a door at the other end of the room opened, and Ansash came in. He walked slowly into the room, taking in Coley and the girl with his eyes.

"Well, hello there," said Coley. Ansash considered him flatly.

"Hello," he said in Basic, with no inflection whatsoever. He turned to the Consul. "May I have an explanation?"

The Consul swiveled about to look at Coley.

"How about it?"

"How about what?" said Coley.

The Consul stalked out from behind his desk and up to Coley, looking like some small rooster ruffling up to a turkey. He pointed past Coley at the girl.

"This is not the woman I sent you to get!" he said tightly.

"Oh, I know that," said Coley.

The Consul stared at him.

"You *know* it?" he echoed.

"He could hardly avoid knowing," put in the smooth voice of Ansash. "He was left alone with this female briefly, when I went to fetch his beloved. When I returned, he had vanished with this one."

The Consul, who had looked aside at Ansash when the other started speaking, looked back at Coley, bleakly and bitterly.

"That," went on Ansash, "is the first cause of the

complaint I brought you this morning. In addition to stealing this real person, the Human, Coley Yunce, has committed other crimes upon the earth of Yara, up to and including murder."

"Yes," breathed the Consul, still staring at Coley. Coley looked bewildered.

"You mean she's no good?" he asked the Consul.

"No good? She isn't Sara Illoy, is she?" exploded the Consul.

"I mean, won't she do?" said Coley. "I mean—she looks pretty human. And she talks fine Basic—" He stepped over to the girl and put a friendly hand on her shoulder. "Recite for them, Honey. Come on, now—'Friends, Romans—'."

She looked up into his face and something that might almost have been a smile twitched at her expressionless mouth. She opened her lips and began to recite in an atrocious accent.

"Frendz, Rawmans, Cundzrememns, I cauzm nodt do burrey Shaayzar, budt do brayze ymn. Dee eefil dwadt memn dooo—"

"Never mind! Never mind!" cried the Consul, furiously; and the girl shut up. "You must have been out of your head!" he barked, and swung about on Ansash. "Very clever, my friend," he grated. "My compliments to Yara. I suppose you know the real Sara Illoy came back of her own accord, the day after this man left."

"I had heard some mention of it," said Ansash, without inflection.

"Very clever indeed," said the Consul. "So it's a choice between handing this man over to your justice to be strangled, or accepting a situation in which contact between our two races on this planet is permanently frozen in a state of Middle-Age restricted contact and chicanery."

"The choice is yours," said Ansash, as if he might have been remarking on the weather.

"I know. Well, don't worry," said the Consul, turning to fling the last three words at Coley. "You know as well as I do I have no choice. Human life must be preserved at all costs. I'll get you safely off-planet, Yunce; though I wouldn't advise you to go boasting about your part in this little adventure. Not that anyone would do anything but laugh at you, if you did." He turned to look at Ansash. "I'm the real loser as you all know," he added softly. "Yara'll never rate an Ambassador, and I'll never rate a promotion. I'll spend the rest of my professional life here as Consul."

"Or," put in Coley, "in jail."

Three heads jerked around to look at him.

"*What kind of a sucker do you take me for?*" snarled Coley, spinning around upon the girl. His long arm shot out, there was a very humanlike shriek, and the girl staggered backward, leaving her blonde locks in Coley's fist. Released, a mass of chestnut hair tumbled down to frame a face that was suddenly contorted with shock.

"I learned to look for the gimmick in something before I could walk." He threw the blonde wig in the direction of the Consul's desk. "This set-up of yours stunk to high heaven right from the beginning. So the girl's gone! How'd she get out of the Compound in the first place? How come you didn't call in regular help from the authorities back at Sol? You were all just sitting back waiting for a tough boy you could use, weren't you?"

He glared around at the three in the room. None of them answered; but they all had their eyes on him.

"I don't know what kind of racket you've got here," he said. "But whatever it is, you didn't want the Humans to win the Game, did you? You wanted things to stay just the way they are now. Why?"

"You're out of your head," said the Consul, though his face was a little pale.

"Out of my head!" Coley laughed. "I can *feel* the difference between Ansash and you, Consul. You think I wouldn't notice that the girl I was with was a Yaran, almost right off the bat? And who could suppose I would need a knife when I left Tannakil, but the man who knew I could use one? How come I never saw her eat anything but fruit? A native Yaran wouldn't have restricted her diet." He leaned forward. "Want *me* to tell *you* what the deal was?"

"I think," said the Consul, "We've listened to enough of your wild guessing."

"No you haven't. Not on your life," said Coley. "I'm back among Humans, now. You can't shut my mouth and get away with it; and either you listen to me, or I'll go tell it to the star-marines. I don't suppose you own them."

"Go ahead, then," said the Consul.

Coley grinned at him. He walked around the Consul's desk and sat down in the Consul's chair. He put his feet on the table.

"There's a world," he said, examining the rather scuffed toes of his boots with a critical eye. "It seems to be run on the basis of an idea about some sort of Game, which is practically a religion. However, when you look a little closer, you see that this Game thing isn't much more than a set of principles which only a few fanatics obey to the actual letter. Still, these principles are what hold the society together. In fact, it goes along fine until another race comes along and creates a situation where the essential conflict between what everybody professes to believe and what they actually believe will eventually be pushed into the open." Coley glanced over at the Consul. "How'm I doing?"

"Go on," said the Consul, wincing.

"The only thing is, this is a conflict which the race has not yet advanced far enough to take. If it came to the breaking point today, half the race would feel it their duty to go fanatic and start exterminating the other half of the race who felt that it was time to discard the old-fashioned Games Ethic." He paused.

"Go on," said the Consul, tonelessly.

"Now, let's suppose this world has a Consul on it, who sees what's happening. He reports back to Sol that the five stages or the Game consist of (1) trying to rid yourself of your enemy by refusing to acknowledge his existence, as a child ignores what it does not like. (2) By reacting against your enemy thoughtlessly and instinctively, as a youth might do. (3) By organized warfare—young manhood. (4) By trickery and subtlety—middle-age. (5) By teaching him your own superior philosophy of existence and bringing him by intellectual means to acknowledge your superiority—old age.

"The only trouble with this, the Consul reports, is that the Yaran philosophy is actually a more primitive one than the human; and any attempt to conquer by stage five would induce a sort of general Yaran psychosis, because they would at once be forced to admit a philosophical inferiority and be *unable* to admit same."

"All right, Mr. Yunce," said the Consul. "You needn't go on—"

"Let me finish. So Sol answers back that they sympathize, but that they cannot violate their own rigid rules of non-interference, sanctity of a single human life, etc., for any situation that does not directly threaten Humanity itself. And this Consul—a dedicated sort—resolves to do the job himself by rigging a

situation with help from one of the more grown-up
Yarans and a young lady—"

"My aide-de-camp," said the Consul, wearily. Coley
bowed a little in the direction of the girl.

"—a situation where a tough but dumb Human sets
out inside the Rules of the Game, but so tears them
to shreds that the Game-with-Humans is abandoned
and set aside—where it will rot quietly and disappear
as the two races become more and more acquainted,
until it gradually is forgotten altogether. Right?"

Coley looked at him. They looked back at him with
peculiarly set faces. Even the Yaran's face had something of that quality of expression to it. They looked
like people who, having risked everything on one throw
or the dice and won, now find that by gambling they
have incurred a sentence of death.

"Fanatics," said Coley, slowly, running his eyes over
them. "Fanatics. Now me—I'm a business man." He
hoisted himself up out of his chair. "No reason why I
shouldn't get on down to the pad, now, and catch the
first ship out of here. Is there?"

"No, Mr. Yunce," said the Consul, bleakly. The three
of them watched him stalk around the desk and past
them to the door. As he opened the door the Consul
cleared his throat.

"Mr. Yunce—" he said.

Coley stopped and turned, the door half open.

"Yes?" he said.

"What's—" the Consul's voice stuck in his throat.
"Wait a minute," he said. "I'll give you a ride to your
ship."

He came around the desk and went out with Coley.
They went down and out of the Consulate, but all
during the short ride to the Compound's landing pad
for the big interspace ships, the Consul said not
another word.

He was silent until they reached the ramp leading up to the ship then in ready position.

"Anywhere near Arga IV?' Coley asked the officer at the ramphead.

"No, Sirius and back to Sol. Try the second ship down. Deneb, and you can get a double transfer out of Deneb Nine."

Coley and the Consul walked down onto the ramp leading up to the entrance port on the second ship, some twenty feet up the steel sides.

"Farewell," said Coley, grinning at the Consul and starting up the ramp.

"Yunce!" the word tore itself at last from the Consul's lips.

Coley stopped, turned around and looked a few feet down into the older man's pleading eyes.

"What can I do for you?' he said.

"Give me a price," said the Consul.

"A price?" Coley, grinning, spread his hands. "A price for what?

"For not reporting this back on Sol. If you do, they'll have to take action. They won't have any choice. They'll undo everything you did."

"Oh, they wouldn't do that," said Coley. He grinned happily, leaned down and slapped the smaller man on the shoulder. "Cheer up," he said. The Consul stared up at him. Slowly, the older man's eyebrows came together in a searching frown.

"Yunce?" he said. "Who . . . ? Just who are you anyway?"

Coley grinned and winked at him. And then he burst into a loud laugh, swing about and went trotting up the airlock ramp and into the ship, still laughing. At the airlock, he stopped, turned, and threw something white that fluttered and side-slipped through the air until it fell on the concrete pad by the Consul's feet. The consul leaned over and picked it up.

It was a folded sheaf of paper, sealed with a met-clip with no identifying symbol upon it. On one side it was stamped TOP SECRET.

The Consul hesitated, broke it open and looked at it. What stared back up at him was that same report he had written back to the authorities on Sol five years before, concerning the Yaran Game of Five and its possible disastrous conclusion. Clipped to it was a little hand-printed note in rather rakish block capitals.

"WHEN SEARCHING THROUGH GOVERNMENT LISTS
DON'T LOOK A GIFT HORSE IN THE MOUTH."

Scratched in the lower right hand corner of the note, as if in idle afterthought, was a small A4.

There is a type of sf (more often appearing in movies or TV or in stories by writers from outside the genre than in works by real sf writers) which has the highly advanced, highly ethical aliens drop in and threaten to exterminate us evil warlike humans. Such stories make me wonder who died and made those self-righteous aliens God, and why their one and only highly advanced, highly ethical solution is to exterminate intelligent species which don't come up to their standards. My reaction is that those aliens are long overdue for a good, swift pie in the face. As you read this story, you may wonder just what this intro has to do with it. Keep reading. . . .

TIGER GREEN

I

A man with hallucinations he cannot stand, trying to strangle himself in a homemade straitjacket, is not a pretty sight. But after a while, grimly thought Jerry McWhin, the *Star Scout's* navigator, the ugly and terrible seem to backfire in effect, filling you with fury instead of harrowing you further. Men in crowds and packs could be stampeded briefly, but after a while the individual among them would turn, get his back up, and slash back.

At least—the hyperstubborn individual in himself had finally so reacted.

Determinedly, with fingers that fumbled from lack of sleep, he got the strangling man—Wally Blake, an assistant ecologist—untangled and into a position where it would be difficult for him to try to choke out his own life again. Then Jerry went out of the sick-bay storeroom, leaving Wally and the other seven men out of the *Star Scout's* complement of twelve who were in total restraint. He was lightheaded from exhaustion; but a berserk something in him snarled like a cornered tiger and refused to break like Wally and the others.

When all's said and done, he thought half-crazily, there's worse ways to come to the end of it than a last charge, win or lose, alone in the midst of all your enemies.

Going down the corridor, the sight of another figure jolted him a little back toward common sense. Ben Akham, the drive engineer, came trudging back from the air-lock corridor with a flame thrower on his back. Soot etched darkly the lines on his once-round face.

"Get the hull cleared?" asked Jerry. Ben nodded exhaustedly.

"There's more jungle on her every morning," he grunted. "Now those big thistles are starting to drip a corrosive liquid. The hull needs an antiacid washing. I can't do it. I'm worn out."

"We all are," said Jerry. His own five-eleven frame was down to a hundred and thirty-eight pounds. There was plenty of food—it was just that the four men left on their feet had no time to prepare it; and little enough time to eat it, prepared or not.

Exploration Team Five-Twenty-Nine, thought Jerry, had finally bitten off more than it could chew, here on the second planet of Star 83476. It was nobody's fault. It had been a gamble for Milt Johnson, the Team captain, either way—to land or not to land. He had landed; and it had turned out bad.

By such small things was the scale toward tragedy tipped. A communication problem with the natives, a native jungle evidently determined to digest the spaceship, and eight of twelve men down with something like suicidal delirium tremens—any two of these things the Team could probably have handled.

But not all three at once.

Jerry and Ben reached the entrance of the Control Room together and peered in, looking for Milt Johnson.

"Must be ootside, talking to that native again," said Jerry.

"Ootside?—*oot*-side!" exploded Ben, with a sudden snapping of frayed nerves. "Can't you say 'out-side'?— '*out* side,' like everybody else?"

The berserk something in Jerry lunged to be free, but he caught it and hauled it back.

"Get hold of yourself!" he snapped.

"Well . . . I wouldn't mind you sounding like a blasted Scotchman all the time!" growled Ben, getting himself, nevertheless, somewhat under control. "It's just you always do it when I don't expect it!"

"If the Lord wanted us all to sound alike, he'd have propped up the Tower of Babel," said Jerry wickedly. He was not particularly religious himself, but he knew Ben to be a table-thumping atheist. He had the satisfaction now of watching the other man bite his lips and control himself in his turn.

Academically, however, Jerry thought as they both headed out through the ship to find Milt, he could not really blame Ben. For Jerry, like many Scot-Canadians, appeared to speak a very middle-western American sort of English most of the time. But only as long as he avoided such vocabulary items as "house" and "out," which popped off Jerry's tongue as "hoose" and "oot." However, every man aboard had his personal peculiarities. You had to get used to them. That was part of spaceship—in fact, part of human—life.

They emerged from the lock, rounded the nose of the spaceship, and found themselves in the neat little clearing on one side of the ship where the jungle paradoxically refused to grow. In this clearing stood the broad-shouldered figure of Milt Johnson, his whitish-blond hair glinting in the yellow-white sunlight.

Facing Milt was the thin, naked, and saddle-colored humanoid figure of one of the natives from the village, or whatever it was, about twenty minutes away by jungle trail. Between Milt and the native was the glittering metal console of the translator machine.

" . . . Let's try it once more," they heard Milt saying as they came up and stopped behind him.

The native gabbled agreeably.

"Yes, yes. Try it again," translated the voice of the console.

"I am Captain Milton Johnson. I am in authority over the crew of the ship you see before me."

"Gladly would I not see it," replied the console on translation of the native's gabblings. "However—I am Communicator, messenger to you sick ones."

"I will call you Communicator, then," began Milt.

"Of course. What else could you call me?"

"Please," said Milt, wearily. "To get back to it—I also am a Communicator."

"No, no," said the native. "You are not a Communicator. It is the sickness that makes you talk this way."

"But," said Milt, and Jerry saw the big, white-haired captain swallow in an attempt to keep his temper. "You will notice, I am communicating with you."

"No, no."

"I see," said Milt patiently. "You mean, we aren't communicating in the sense that we aren't understanding each other. We're talking, but you don't understand me—"

"No, no. I understand you perfectly."

"Well," said Milt, exhaustedly. "I don't understand you."

"That is because you are sick."

Milt blew out a deep breath and wiped his brow.

"Forget that part of it, then," he said. "Many of my crew are upset by nightmares we all have been having. They are sick. But there are still four of us who are well—"

"No, no. You are all sick," said Communicator earnestly. "But you should love what you call nightmares. All people love them."

"Including you and your people?"

"Of course. Love your nightmares. They will make you well. They will make the little bit of proper life in you grow, and heal you."

Ben snorted beside Jerry. Jerry could sympathize with the other man. The nightmares he had been having during his scant hours of sleep, the past two weeks, came back to his mind, with the indescribably alien, terrifying sensation of drifting in a sort of environmental soup with identifiable things changing shape and identity constantly around him. Even pumped full of tranquilizers, he thought—which reminded Jerry.

He had not taken his tranquilizers lately.

When had he taken some last? Not since he woke up, in any case. Not since . . . yesterday, sometime. Though that was now hard to believe.

"Let's forget that, too, then," Milt was saying. "Now, the jungle is growing all over our ship, in spite of all we can do. You tell me your people can make the jungle do anything you want."

"Yes, yes," said Communicator agreeably.

"Then, will you please stop it from growing all over our spaceship?"

"We understand. It is your sickness, the poison that makes you say this. Do not fear. We will never abandon you." Communicator looked almost ready to pat Milt consolingly on the head. "You are people, who are more important than any cost. Soon you will grow and cast off your poisoned part and come to us."

"But we can come to you right now!" said Milt, between his teeth. "In fact—we've come to your village a dozen times."

"No, no." Communicator sounded distressed. "You approach, but you do not come. You have never come to us."

Milt wiped his forehead with the back of a wide hand. "I will come back to your village now, with you," he said. "Would you like that?" he asked.

"I would be so happy!" said Communicator. "But— you will not come. You say it, but you do not come."

"All right. Wait—" About to take a hand transceiver from the console, Milt saw the other two men. "Jerry," he said, "you go this time. Maybe he'll believe it if it's you who goes to the village with him."

"I've been there before. With you, the second time you went," objected Jerry. "And I've got to feed the men in restraint, pretty soon," he added.

"Try going again. That's all we can do—try things. Ben and I'll feed the men," said Milt. Jerry, about to argue further, felt the pressure of a sudden wordless, exhausted appeal from Milt. Milt's basic berserkedness must be just about ready to break loose, too, he realized.

"All right," said Jerry.

"Good," said Milt, looking grateful. "We have to keep trying. I should have lifted ship while I still had five well men to lift it with. Come on, Ben—you and I better go feed those men now, before we fall asleep on our feet."

II

They went away around the nose of the ship. Jerry unhooked the little black-and-white transceiver that would radio-relay his conversations with Communicator back to the console of the translator for sense-making during the trip.

"Come on," he said to Communicator, and led off down the pleasantly wide jungle trail toward the native village.

They passed from under the little patch of open sky above the clearing and into green-roofed stillness. All about them, massive limbs, branches, ferns, and vines intertwined in a majestic maze of growing things. Small flying creatures, looking half-animal and half-insect, flittered among the branches overhead. Some larger, more animallike creatures sat on the heavier limbs and moaned off-key like abandoned puppies. Jerry's head spun with his weariness, and the green over his head seemed to close down on him like a net flung by some giant, crazy fisherman, to take him captive.

He was suddenly and bitterly reminded of the Team's high hopes, the day they had set down on this world. No other Team or Group had yet to turn up any kind of alien life much more intelligent than an anthropoid ape. Now they, Team 529, had not only uncovered an intelligent, evidently semi-cultured alien people, but an alien people eager to establish relations with the humans and communicate. Here, two weeks later, the natives were still apparently just as eager to communicate, but what they said made no sense.

Nor did it help that, with the greatest of patience and kindness, Communicator and his kind seemed to consider that it was the humans who were irrational and uncommunicative.

Nor that, meanwhile, the jungle seemed to be mounting a specifically directed attack on the human spaceship.

Nor that the nightmare afflicting the humans had already laid low eight of the twelve crew and were grinding the four left on their feet down to a choice between suicidal delirium or collapse from exhaustion.

It was a miracle, thought Jerry, lightheadedly trudging through the jungle, that the four of them had been able to survive as long as they had. A miracle based probably on some individual chance peculiarity of strength that the other eight men in straitjackets lacked. Although, thought Jerry now, that strength that they had so far defied analysis. Dizzily, like a man in a high fever, he considered their four surviving personalities in his mind's eye. They were, he thought, the four men of the team with what you might call the biggest mental crotchets.

—or ornery streaks.

Take the fourth member of the group—the medician, Arthyr Loy, who had barely stuck his nose out of the sick-bay lab in the last forty-eight hours. Not only because he was the closest thing to an M.D. aboard the ship was Art still determined to put the eight restrained men back on their feet again. It just happened, in addition, that Art considered himself the only true professional man aboard, and was not the kind to admit any inability to the lesser mortals about him.

And Milt Johnson—Milt made an excellent captain. He was a tower of strength, a great man for making decisions. The only thing was, that having decided, Milt could hardly be brought to consider the remote possibility that anyone else might have wanted to decide differently.

Ben Akham was another matter. Ben hated religion and loved machinery—and the jungle surrounding was attacking *his* spaceship. In fact, Jerry was willing to bet that by the time he got back, Ben would be washing the hull with an acid-counteractant in spite of what he had told Jerry earlier.

And himself? Jerry? Jerry shook his head woozily. It was hard to be self-analytical after ten days of three and four hours sleep per twenty. He had what his grandmother had once described as the curse of the Gael—black stubbornness and red rages.

All of these traits, in all four of them, had normally been buried safely below the surfaces of their personalities and had only colored them as individuals. But now, the last two weeks had worn those surfaces down to basic personality bedrock. Jerry shoved the thought out of his mind.

"Well," he said, turning to Communicator, "we're almost to your village now. . . . You can't say someone didn't come with you, this time."

Communicator gabbled. The transceiver in Jerry's hand translated.

"Alas," the native said, "but you are not with me."

"Cut it out!" said Jerry wearily. "I'm right here beside you."

"No," said Communicator. "You accompany me, but you are not here. You are back with your dead things."

"You mean the ship, and the rest of it?" asked Jerry.

"There is no ship," said Communicator. "A ship must

have grown and been alive. Your thing has always been dead. But we will save you."

III

They came out of the path at last into a clearing dotted with whitish, pumpkinlike shells some ten feet in height above the brown earth in which they were half-buried. Wide cracks in the out-curving sides gave view of tangled roots and plants inside, among which other natives could be seen moving about, scratching, tasting, and making holes in the vegetable surfaces.

"Well," said Jerry, making an effort to speak cheerfully, "here I am."

"You are not here."

The berserk tigerishness in Jerry leaped up unawares and took him by the inner throat. For a long second he looked at Communicator through a red haze. Communicator gazed back patiently, evidently unaware how close he was to having his neck broken by a pair of human hands.

"Look—" said Jerry, slowly, between his teeth, getting himself under control, "if you will just tell me what to do to join you and your people, here, I will do it."

"That is good!"

"Then," said Jerry, still with both hands on the inner fury that fought to tear loose inside him, "what do I do?"

"But you know—" The enthusiasm that had come into Communicator a moment before wavered visibly. "You must get rid of the dead things, and set yourself free to grow, inside. Then, after you have grown, your unsick self will bring you here to join us!"

Jerry stared back. Patience, he said harshly to himself.

"Grow? How? In what way?"

"But you have a little bit of proper life in you," explained Communicator. "Not much, of course . . . but if you will rid yourself of dead things and concentrate on what you call nightmares, it will grow and force out the poison of the dead life in you. The proper life and the nightmares are the hope for you."

"Wait a minute!" Jerry's exhaustion-fogged brain cleared suddenly and nearly miraculously at the sudden surge of excitement into his bloodstream. "This proper life you talk about—does it have something to do with the nightmares?"

"Of course. How could you have what you call nightmares without a little proper life in you to give them to you? As the proper life grows, you will cease to fight so against the 'nightmares' . . ."

Communicator continued to talk earnestly. But Jerry's spinning brain was flying off on a new tangent. What was it he had been thinking earlier about tranquilizers—that he had not taken any himself for some time? Then, what about the nightmares in his last four hours of sleep?

He must have had them—he remembered now that he *had* had them. But evidently they had not bothered him as much as before—at least, not enough to send him scrambling for tranquilizers to dull the dreams' weird impact on him.

"Communicator!" Jerry grabbed at the thin, leathery-skinned arm of the native. "Have I been chang—growing?"

"I do not know, of course," said the native, courteously. "I profoundly hope so. Have you?"

"Excuse me—" gulped Jerry. "I've got to get oot of here—back to th' ship!"

❖   ❖   ❖

He turned, and raced back up the trail. Some twenty minutes later, he burst into the clearing before the ship to find an ominous silence hanging over everything. Only the faint rustle and hissing from the ever-growing jungle swallowing up the ship sounded on his eardrums.

"Milt—Ben!" he shouted, plunging into the ship. "Art!"

A hail from farther down the main corridor reassured him, and he followed it up to find all three unrestrained members of the crew in the sick bay. But—Jerry brought himself up short, his throat closing on him—there was a figure on the table.

"Who . . ." began Jerry. Milt Johnson turned around to face him. The captain's body mercifully hid most of the silent form on the table.

"Wally Blake," said Milt emptily. "He managed to strangle himself after all. Got twisted up in his restraint jacket. Ben and I heard him thumping around in there, but by the time we got to him, it was too late. Art's doing an autopsy."

"Not exactly an autopsy," came the soft, Virginia voice of the medician from beyond Milt. "Just looking for something I suspected . . . and here it is!"

Milt spun about and Jerry pushed between the big captain and Ben. He found himself looking at the back of a human head from which a portion of the skull had been removed. What he saw before him was a small expanse of whitish, soft inner tissue that was the brainstem; and fastened to it almost like a grape growing there, was a small, purplish mass.

Art indicated the purple shape with the tip of a sharp, surgical instrument.

"There," he said. "And I bet we've each got one."

"What is it?" asked Ben's voice, hushed and a little nauseated.

"I don't know," said Art harshly. "How the devil would I be able to tell? But I found organisms in the bloodstreams of those of us I've taken blood samples from—organisms like spores, that look like this, only smaller, microscopic in size."

"You didn't tell me that!" said Milt, turning quickly to face him.

"What was the point?" Art turned toward the Team captain. Jerry saw that the medician's long face was almost bloodless. "I didn't know what they were. I thought if I kept looking, I might know more. Then I could have something positive to tell you, as well as the bad news. But—it's no use now."

"Why do you say that?" snapped Milt.

"Because it's the truth." Art's face seemed to slide apart, go loose and waxy with defeat. "As long as it was something nonphysical we were fighting, there was some hope we could throw it off. But—you see what's going on inside us. We're being changed physically. That's where the nightmares come from. You can't overcome a physical change with an effort of will!"

"What about the Grotto at Lourdes?" asked Jerry. His head was whirling strangely with a mass of ideas. His own great-grandfather—the family story came back to mind—had been judged by his physician in 1896 to have advanced pulmonary tuberculosis. Going home from the doctor's office, Simon Fraser McWhin had decided that he could not afford to have tuberculosis at this time. That he would not, therefore, have tuberculosis at all. And he had dismissed the matter fully from his mind.

One year later, examined by the same physician, he had no signs of tuberculosis whatsoever.

But in this present moment, Art, curling up in his chair at the end of the table, seemed not to have heard Jerry's question. And Jerry was suddenly reminded of the question that had brought him pelting back from the native village.

"Is it growing—I mean was it growing when Wally strangled himself—that growth on his brain?" he asked.

Art roused himself.

"Growing?" he repeated dully. He climbed to his feet and picked up an instrument. He investigated the purple mass for a moment.

"No," he said, dropping the instrument wearily and falling back into his chair. "Looks like its outer layer has died and started to be reabsorbed—I think." He put his head in his hands. "I'm not qualified to answer such questions. I'm not trained . . ."

"Who is?" demanded Milt, grimly, looming over the table and the rest of them. "And we're reaching the limit of our strength as well as the limits of what we know—"

"We're done for," muttered Ben. His eyes were glazed, looking at the dissected body on the table. "It's not my fault—"

"Catch him! Catch Art!" shouted Jerry, leaping forward.

But he was too late. The medician had been gradually curling up in his chair since he had sat down in it again. Now, he slipped out of it to the floor, rolled in a ball, and lay still.

"Leave him alone." Milt's large hand caught Jerry and held him back. "He may as well lie there as someplace else." He got to his feet. "Ben's right. We're done for."

"Done for?" Jerry stared at the big man. The words he had just heard were words he would never have imagined hearing from Milt.

"Yes," said Milt. He seemed somehow to be speaking from a long distance off.

"Listen—" said Jerry. The tigerishness inside him had woken at Milt's words. It tugged and snarled against the words of defeat from the captain's lips. "We're winning. We aren't losing!"

"Quit it, Jerry," said Ben dully, from the far end of the room.

"Quit it—?" Jerry swung on the engineer. "You lost your temper with me before I went down to the village, about the way I said '*oot*'! How could you lose your temper if you were full of tranquilizers? I haven't been taking any myself, and I feel better because of it. Don't tell me you've been taking yours!—and that means we're getting stronger than the nightmares."

"The tranquilizers've been making me sick, if you must know! That's why I haven't been taking them—" Ben broke off, his face graying. He pointed a shaking finger at the purplish mass. "I'm being changed, that's why they made me sick! I'm changing already!" His voice rose toward a scream. "Don't you see, it's changing me—" He broke off, suddenly screaming and leaping at Milt with clawing fingers. "We're all changing! And it's your fault for bringing the ship down here. You did it—"

Milt's huge fist slammed into the side of the smaller man's jaw, driving him to the floor beside the still shape of the medician, where he lay quivering and sobbing.

Slowly Milt lifted his gaze from the fallen man and faced Jerry. It was the standard seventy-two degrees centigrade in the room, but Jerry saw perspiration standing out on Milt's calm face as if he had just stepped out of a steam bath.

"But he may be right," said Milt emotionlessly. His voice seemed to come from the far end of some lightless tunnel. "We may be changing under the influence of those growths right now—each of us."

"Milt!" said Jerry sharply. But Milt's face never changed. It was large, and calm, and pale—and drenched with sweat. "Now's the last time we ought to give up! We're starting to understand it now. I tell you, the thing is to meet Communicator and the other natives head on! Head to head we can crack them wide open. One of us has to go down to that village."

"No. I'm the captain," said Milt, his voice unchanged. "I'm responsible, and I'll decide. We can't lift ship with less than five men and there's only two of us—you and I—actually left. I can't risk one of us coming under the influence of the growth in him, and going over to the alien side."

"Going over?" Jerry stared at him.

"That's what all this has been for—the jungle, the natives, the nightmare. They want to take us over." Sweat ran down Milt's cheeks and dripped off his chin, while he continued to talk tonelessly and gaze straight ahead. "They'll send us—what's left of us— back against our own people. I can't let that happen. We'll have to destroy ourselves so there's nothing for them to use."

"Milt—" said Jerry.

"No." Milt swayed faintly on his feet like a tall tree under a wind too high to be felt on the ground at its base. "We can't risk leaving ship or crew. We'll blow the ship up with ourselves in it—"

"Blow up my ship!"

It was a wild-animal scream from the floor at their feet; and Ben Akham rose from almost under the table like a demented wildcat, aiming for Milt's jugular vein. So unexpected and powerful was the attack that the big captain tottered and fell. With a noise like worrying dogs, they rolled together under the table.

The chained tiger inside Jerry broke its bonds and flung free.

He turned and ducked through the door into the corridor. It was a heavy pressure door with a wheel lock, activating metal dogs to seal it shut in case of a hull blowout and sudden loss of air. Jerry slammed the door shut, and spun the wheel.

The dogs snicked home. Snatching down the portable fire extinguisher hanging on the wall alongside, Jerry dropped the foam container on the floor and jammed the metal nozzle of its hose between a spoke of the locking wheel and the unlocking stop on the door beneath it.

He paused. There was silence inside the sick-bay lab. Then the wheel jerked against the nozzle and the door tried to open.

"What's going on?" demanded the voice of Milt. There was a pause. "Jerry, what's going on out there? Open up!"

A wild, crazy impulse to hysterical laughter rose inside Jerry without warning. It took all his willpower to choke it back.

"You're locked in, Milt," he said.

"Jerry!" The wheel spoke clicked against the jamming metal nozzle, in a futile effort to turn. "Open up! That's an order!"

"Sorry, Milt," said Jerry softly and lightheadedly. "I'm not ready yet to burn the hoose about my ears. This business of you wanting to blow up the ship's the same sort of impulse to suicide that got Wally and the rest. I'm off to face the natives now and let them have their way with me. I'll be back later, to let you oot."

"Jerry!"

Jerry heard Milt's voice behind him as he went off down the corridor.

"*Jerry!*" There was a fusillade of pounding fists against the door, growing fainter as Jerry moved away. "Don't you see?—that growth in you is finally getting you! Jerry, come back! Don't let them take over one of us! Jerry . . ."

Jerry left the noise and the ship together behind

him as he stepped out of the air lock. The jungle, he saw, was covering the ship's hull again, already hiding it for the most part. He went on out to the translator console and began taking off his clothes. When he was completely undressed, he unhooked the transceiver he had brought back from the native village, slung it on a loop of his belt, and hung the belt around his neck.

He headed off down the trail toward the village, wincing a little as the soles of his shoeless feet came into contact with pebbles along the way.

When he got to the village clearing, a naked shape he recognized as that of Communicator tossed up its arms in joy and came running to him.

"Well," said Jerry. "I've grown. I've got rid of the poison of dead things and the sickness. Here I am to join you!"

"At last!" gabbled Communicator. Other natives were running up. "Throw away the dead thing around your neck!"

"I still need it to understand you," said Jerry. "I guess I need a little help to join you all the way."

"Help? We will help!" cried Communicator. "But you must throw that away. You have rid yourself of the dead things that you kept wrapped around your limbs and body," gabbled Communicator. "Now rid yourself of the dead thing hanging about your neck."

"But I tell you, if I do that," objected Jerry, "I won't be able to understand you when you talk, or make you understand me!"

"Throw it away. It is poisoning you! Throw it away!" said Communicator. By this time three or four more natives had come up and others were headed for the gathering. "Shortly you will understand all, and all will understand you. Throw it away!"

"Throw it away!" chorused the other natives.

"Well . . ." said Jerry. Reluctantly, he took off the belt with the transceiver, and dropped it. Communicator gabbled unintelligibly.

" . . . come with me . . ." translated the transceiver like a faint and tinny echo from the ground where it landed.

Communicator took hold of Jerry's hand and drew him toward the nearest whitish structure. Jerry swallowed unobtrusively. It was one thing to make up his mind to do this; it was something else again to actually do it. But he let himself be led to and in through a crack in the structure.

Inside, the place smelled rather like a mixture of a root cellar and a hayloft—earthy and fragrant at the same time. Communicator drew him in among the waist-high tangle of roots rising and reentering the packed earth floor. The other natives swarmed after them. Close to the center of the floor they reached a point where the roots were too thick to allow them to pick their way any further. The roots rose and tangled into a mat, the irregular surface of which was about three feet off the ground. Communicator patted the root surface and gabbled agreeably.

"You want me to get up there?" Jerry swallowed again, then gritted his teeth as the chained fury in him turned suddenly upon himself. There was nothing worse, he snarled at himself, than a man who was long on planning a course of action, but short on carrying it out.

Awkwardly, he clambered up onto the matted surface of the roots. They gave irregularly under him and their rough surfaces scraped his knees and hands. The natives gabbled, and he felt leathery hands urging him to stretch out and lie down on his back.

He did so. The root scored and poked the tender skin of his back. It was exquisitely uncomfortable.

"Now what—?" he gasped. He turned his head to look at the natives and saw that green tendrils, growing rapidly from the root mass, were winding about and garlanding the arms and legs of Communicator and several other of the natives standing by. A sudden pricking at his left wrist made him look down.

Green garlands were twining around his own wrists and ankles, sending wire-thin tendrils into his skin. In unconscious reflex of panic he tried to heave upward, but the green bonds held him fast.

"*Gabble-gabble-gabble . . .*" warbled Communicator reassuringly.

With sudden alarm, Jerry realized that the green tendrils were growing right into the arms and legs of the natives as well. He was abruptly conscious of further prickings in his own arms and legs.

"What's going on—" he started to say, but found his tongue had gone unnaturally thick and unmanageable. A wave of dizziness swept over him as if a powerful general anesthetic was taking hold. The interior of the structure seemed to darken; and he felt as if he was swooping away toward its ceiling on the long swing of some monster pendulum . . .

It swung him on into darkness. And nightmare.

It was the same old nightmare, but more so. It was nightmare experienced *awake* instead of asleep; and the difference was that he had no doubt about the fact that he was experiencing what he was experiencing, nor any tucked-away certainty that waking would bring him out of it.

Once more he floated through a changing soup of uncertainty, himself a changing part of it. It was not painful, it was not even terrifying. But it was hideous— it was an affront to nature. He was not himself. He was a thing, a part of the whole—and he must reconcile himself to being so. He must accept it.

Reconcile himself to it—no! It was not possible for the unbending, solitary, individualistic part that was *him* to do so. But accept it—maybe.

Jerry set a jaw that was no longer a jaw and felt the determination in him to blast through, to comprehend this incomprehensible thing, become hard and undeniable as a sword-point of tungsten steel. He drove through—

And abruptly the soup fell into order. It slid into focus like a blurred scene before the gaze of a badly myopic man who finally gets his spectacles before his eyes. Suddenly, Jerry was aware that what he observed was a scene not just before his eyes, but before his total awareness. And it was not the interior of the structure where he lay on a bed of roots, but the whole planet.

It was a landscape of factories. Countless factories, interconnected, intersupplying, integrated. It lacked only that he find his own working place among them.

Now, said this scene. *This is the sane universe, the way it really is. Reconcile yourself to it.*

The hell I will!

It was the furious, unbending, solitary, individualistic part that was essentially *him* speaking again. Not just speaking. Roaring—snarling its defiance, like a tiger on a hillside.

And the scene went—pop.

Jerry opened his eyes. He sat up. The green shoots around and in his wrists and ankles pulled prickingly at him. But they were already dying and not able to hold him. He swung his legs over the edge of the mat of roots and stood down. Communicator and the others who were standing there, backed fearfully away from him, gabbling.

❖　　　❖　　　❖

He understood their gabbling no better than before, but now he could read the emotional overtones in it. And those overtones were now of horror and disgust, overlying a wild, atavistic panic and terror. He walked forward. They scuttled away before him, gabbling, and he walked through the nearest crack in the wall of the structure and out into the sunlight, toward the transceiver and the belt where he had dropped them.

"Monster!" screamed the transceiver tinnily, faithfully translating the gabbling of the Communicator, who was following a few steps behind like a small dog barking behind a larger. "Brute! Savage! Unclean . . ." It kept up a steady denunciation.

Jerry turned to face Communicator, and the native tensed for flight.

"You know what I'm waiting for," said Jerry, almost smiling, hearing the transceiver translate his words into gabbling—though it was not necessary. As he had said, Communicator knew what he was waiting for.

Communicator cursed a little longer in his own tongue, then went off into one of the structures, and returned with a handful of what looked like lengths of green vine. He dropped them on the ground before Jerry and backed away, cautiously, gabbling.

"Now will you go? And never come back! Never . . ."

"We'll see," said Jerry. He picked up the lengths of green vine and turned away up the path to the ship.

The natives he passed on his way out of the clearing huddled away from him and gabbled as he went.

When he stepped back into the clearing before the ship, he saw that most of the vegetation touching or close to the ship was already brown and dying. He went on into the ship, carefully avoiding the locked sick-bay door, and wound lengths of the green vine around the wrists of each of the men in restraints.

Then he sat down to await results. He had never

been so tired in his life. The minute he touched the chair, his eyes started to close. He struggled to his feet and forced himself to pace the floor until the green vines, which had already sent hair-thin tendrils into the ulnar arteries of the arms around which they were wrapped, pumped certain inhibitory chemicals into the bloodstreams of the seven men.

When the men started to blink their eyes and look about sensibly, he went to work to unfasten the home-made straitjackets that had held them prisoner. When he had released the last one, he managed to get out his final message before collapsing.

"Take the ship up," croaked Jerry. "Then, let yourself into the sick bay and wrap a vine piece around the wrists of Milt, and Art, and Ben. Ship up first—then when you're safely in space, take care of them, in the sick bay. Do it the other way and you'll never see Earth again."

They crowded around him with questions. He waved them off, slumping into one of the abandoned bunks.

"Ship up—" he croaked. "Then release and fix the others. Ask me later. Later—"

. . . And that was all he remembered, then.

IV

At some indefinite time later, not quite sure whether he had woken by himself, or whether someone else had wakened him, Jerry swam back up to consciousness. He was vaguely aware that he had been sleeping a long time; and his body felt sane again, but weak as the body of a man after a long illness.

He blinked and saw the large face of Milt Johnson, partly obscured by a cup of something. Milt was seated in a chair by the side of the bunk Jerry lay in, and the Team captain was offering the cup of steaming black liquid to Jerry. Slowly, Jerry understood that this was coffee and he struggled up on one elbow to take the cup.

He drank from it slowly for a little while, while Milt watched and waited.

"Do you realize," said Milt at last, when Jerry finally put down the three-quarters-empty cup on the nightstand by the bunk, "that what you did in locking me in the sick bay was mutiny?"

Jerry swallowed. Even his vocal cords seemed drained of strength and limp.

"You realize," he croaked, "what would have happened if I hadn't?"

"You took a chance. You followed a wild hunch—"

"No hunch," said Jerry. He cleared his throat. "Art found that growth on Wally's brain had quit growing before Wally killed himself. And I'd been getting along without tranquilizers—handling the nightmares better than I had with them."

"It could have been the growth in your own brain," said Milt, "taking over and running you—working better on you than it had on Wally."

"Working better—talk sense!" said Jerry weakly, too pared down by the past two weeks to care whether school kept or not, in the matter of service courtesy to a superior. "The nightmares had broken Wally down to where we had to wrap him in a straitjacket. They hadn't even knocked me off my feet. If Wally's physiological processes had fought the alien invasion to a standstill, then I, you, Art, and Ben—all of us—had to be doing even better. Besides—I'd figured out what the aliens were after."

"What were they after?" Milt looked strangely at him.

"Curing us—of something we didn't have when we landed, but they thought we had."

"And what was that?"

"Insanity," said Jerry grimly.

Milt's blond eyebrows went up. He opened his mouth as if to say something disbelieving—then closed it again. When he did speak, it was quite calmly and humbly.

"They thought," he asked, "Communicator's people thought that we were insane, and they could cure us?"

Jerry laughed; not cheerfully, but grimly.

"You saw that jungle around us back there?" he asked. "That was a factory complex—an infinitely complex factory complex. You saw their village with those tangles of roots inside the big whitish shells?— that was a highly diversified laboratory."

Milt's blue eyes slowly widened, as Jerry watched.

"You don't mean that—seriously?" said Milt, at last.

"That's right." Jerry drained the cup and set it aside. "Their technology is based on organic chemistry, the way ours is on the physical sciences. By our standards, they're chemical wizards. How'd you like to try changing the mind of an alien organism by managing to grow an extra part on to his brain—the way they tried to do to us humans? To them, it was the simplest way of convincing us."

Milt stared again. Finally, he shook his head.

"Why?" he said. "Why would they want to change our minds?"

"Because their philosophy, their picture of life and the universe around them grew out of a chemically oriented science," answered Jerry. "The result is, they see all life as part of a closed, intra-acting chemical circuit with no loose ends; with every living thing, intelligent or not, a part of the whole. Well, you saw it for yourself in your nightmare. That's the cosmos as they see it—and to them it's beautiful."

"But why did they want us to see it the way they did?"

"Out of sheer kindness," said Jerry and laughed barkingly. "According to their cosmology, there's no such thing as an alien. Therefore we weren't alien—just sick in the head. Poisoned by the lumps of metal like the ship and the translator we claimed were so important. And our clothes and everything else we had. The kind thing was to cure and rescue us."

"Now, wait a minute," said Milt. "They saw those things of ours *work*—"

"What's the fact they worked got to do with it? What you don't understand, Milt," said Jerry, lying back gratefully on the bunk, "is that Communicator's peoples' minds were *closed*. Not just unconvinced, not just refusing to see—but *closed*! Sealed, and welded shut from prehistoric beginnings right down to the present. The fact our translator worked meant nothing to them. According to their cosmology, it shouldn't work, so it didn't. Any stray phenomena tending to prove it did were simply the product of diseased minds."

Jerry paused to emphasize the statement and his eyes drifted shut. The next thing he knew Milt was shaking him.

" . . . Wake up!" Milt was shouting at him. "You can dope off after you've explained. I'm not going to have any crew back in straitjackets again, just because you were too sleepy to warn me they'd revert!"

" . . . Won't revert," said Jerry thickly. He roused himself. "Those lengths of vine released chemicals into their bloodstreams to destroy what was left of the growths. I wouldn't leave until I got them from Communicator." Jerry struggled up on one elbow again. "And after a short walk in a human brain—mine—he and his people couldn't get us out of sight and forgotten fast enough."

"Why?" Milt shook him again as Jerry's eyelids sagged. "Why should getting their minds hooked in with yours shake them up so?"

" . . . Bust—bust their cosmology open. Quit shaking . . . I'm awake."

"*Why* did it bust them wide open?"

"Remember—how it was for you with the nightmares?" said Jerry. "The other way around? Think back, about when you slept. There you were, a lone atom of humanity, caught up in a nightmare like one piece of stew meat in a vat stewing all life together—just one single chemical bit with no independent existence, and no existence at all except as part of the whole. Remember?"

He saw Milt shiver slightly.

"It was like being swallowed up by a soft machine," said the Team captain in a small voice. "I remember."

"All right," said Jerry. "That's how it was for you in Communicator's cosmos. But remember something about that cosmos? It was warm, and safe. It was all-embracing, all-settling, like a great, big, soft, woolly comforter."

"It was too much like a woolly comforter," said Milt, shuddering. "It was unbearable."

"To you. Right," said Jerry. "But to Communicator, it was ideal. And if that was ideal, think what it was like when he had to step into a human mind—mine."

Milt stared at him.

"Why?" Milt asked.

"Because," said Jerry, "he found himself *alone* there!"

Milt's eyes widened.

"Think about it, Milt," said Jerry. "From the time

we're born, we're individuals. From the moment we open our eyes on the world, inside we're alone in the universe. All the emotional and intellectual resources that Communicator draws from his identity with the stewing vat of his cosmos, each one of us has to dig up for and out of himself!"

Jerry stopped to give Milt a chance to say something. But Milt was evidently not in possession of something to say at the moment.

"That's why Communicator and the others couldn't take it, when they hooked into my human mind," Jerry went on. "And that's why, when they found out what we were like inside, they couldn't wait to get rid of us. So they gave me the vines and kicked us out. That's the whole story." He lay back on the bunk.

Milt cleared his throat.

"All right," he said.

Jerry's heavy eyes closed. Then the other man's voice spoke, still close by his ear.

"But," said Milt, "I still think you took a chance, going down to butt heads with the natives that way. What if Communicator and the rest had been able to stand exposure to your mind. You'd locked me in and the other men were in restraint. Our whole team would have been part of that stewing vat."

"Not a chance," said Jerry.

"You can't be sure of that."

"Yes I can." Jerry heard his own voice sounding harshly beyond the darkness of his closed eyelids. "It wasn't just that I knew my cosmological view was too tough for them. It was the fact that their minds were closed—in the vat they had no freedom to change and adapt themselves to anything new."

"What's that got to do with it?" demanded the voice of Milt.

"Everything," said Jerry. "Their point of view only

made us more uncomfortable—but our point of view, being individually adaptable, and open, threatened to destroy the very laws of existence as they saw them. An open mind can always stand a closed one, if it has to—by making room for it in the general picture. But a closed mind can't stand it near an open one without risking immediate and complete destruction in its own terms. In a closed mind, there's no more room."

He stopped speaking and slowly exhaled a weary breath.

"Now," he said, without opening his eyes, "will you finally get oot of here and let me sleep?"

For a long second more, there was silence. Then, he heard a chair scrape softly, and the muted steps of Milt tiptoeing away.

With another sigh, at last Jerry relaxed and let consciousness slip from him.

He slept.

—as sleep the boar upon the plain, the hawk upon the crag, and the tiger on the hill . . .

Once again, the story is told from the alien viewpoint, and Dickson excels at building up the alien society, and the viewpoint character's motivations. Said character is not at all safe to be around, even in the case of members of his own species, yet the reader is liable to have a sneaking urge to root for such a clever alien anti-hero to succeed, even though his success would be very bad news for the Earth and its inhabitants. Of course, the trouble with being clever and having a cunning plan that cannot fail is that someone even more clever just may have incorporated your cunning plan into *their* cunning plan. . . .

THE HARD WAY

Kator Secondcousin, cruising in the neighborhood of a Cepheid variable down on his charts as 47391L, but otherwise known to the race he was shortly to discover as *A Ursae Min.*—or Polaris, the pole star—suddenly found himself smiled upon by a Random Factor. Immediately—for although he was merely a Secondcousin, it was of the family of Brutogas—he grasped the opportunity thus offered and locked the controls while he set about planning his Kingdom. Meanwhile, he took no chances. He fastened a tractor beam on the artifact embodying the Random Factor. It was a beautiful artifact, even in its fragmentary condition, fully five times as large as the two-man scout in which he and Aton Maternaluncle—of the family Ochadi—had been making a routine sampling sweep of debris in the galactic drift. Kator locked it exactly in the center of his viewing screen and leaned back in his pilot's chair. A polished bulkhead to the left of the screen threw back his own image, and he twisted the catlike whiskers of his round face thoughtfully and with satisfaction, as he reviewed the situation with all sensible speed.

The situation could hardly have been more ideal. Aton Maternaluncle was not even a connection by marriage with the family Brutogas. True, he, like the Brutogasi, was of the Hook persuasion politically, rather than Rod. But on the other hand the odds against the appearance of such a Random Factor as this to two men on scientific survey were astronomical. It canceled out Ordinary Duties and Conventions almost automatically. Aton Maternaluncle—had he been merely a disinterested observer rather than the other half of the scout crew—would certainly consider Kator a fool not to take advantage of the situation by integrating the Random Factor positively with Kator's own life pattern. *Besides*, thought Kator, watching his own reflection in the bulkhead and stroking his whiskers, *I am young and life is before me.*

He got up from the chair, loosened a tube on the internal ship's recorder, and extended the three-inch claws on his stubby fingers. He went back to the sleeping quarters behind the pilot room. Back home the door to it would never have been unlocked—but out here in deep space, who would take precautions against such a farfetched situation as this the Random Factor had introduced?

Skillfully, Kator drove his claws into the spinal cord

at the base of Aton's round skull, killing the sleeping man instantly. He then disposed of the body out the air lock, replaced the tube in working position in the recorder, and wrote up the fact that Aton had attacked him in a fit of sudden insanity, damaging the recorder as he did so. Finding Kator ready to defend himself, the insane Aton had then leaped into the air lock, and committed suicide by discharging himself into space.

After all, reflected Kator, as he finished writing up the account in the logbook, *While Others Still Think We Act* had always been the motto of the Brutogasi. He stroked his whiskers in satisfaction.

A period of time roughly corresponding to a half hour later—in the time system of that undiscovered race to whom the artifact had originally belonged—Kator had got a close-line magnetically hooked to the blasted hull of the artifact and was hand-over-hand hauling his spacesuited body along the line toward it. He reached it with little difficulty and set about exploring his find by the headlight of his suit.

It had evidently been a ship operated by people very much like Kator's own human kind. The doors were the right size, the sitting devices were sittable-in. Unfortunately it had evidently been destroyed by a pressure-warp explosion in a drive system very much like that aboard the scout. Everything not bolted down in it had been expelled into space. No, not everything. A sort of hand carrying-case was wedged between the legs of one of the sitting devices. Kator unwedged it and took it back to the scout with him.

After making the routine safety tests on it, Kator got it open. And a magnificent find it turned out to be. Several items of what appeared to be something like cloth, and could well be garments, and what were clearly ornaments or perhaps badges of rank, and a sort of coloring-stick of soft red wax. But these were nothing to the real find.

Enclosed in a clear wrapping material formed in bagshape, were a pair of what could only be foot-protectors with soil still adhering to them. And among the loose soil in the bottom of the bag, was the tiny dried form of an organic creature.

A dirt-worm, practically indistinguishable from the dirt-worms at home.

Kator lifted it tenderly from the dirt with a pair of specimen tweezers and sealed it into a small cube of clear plastic. This, he thought, slipping it into his belt pouch, was his. There was plenty in the wreckage of the ship and in the carrying-case for the examiners to work on back home in discovering the location of the race that had built them all. This corpse—the first of his future subjects—was his. A harbinger of the future, if he played his knuckle-dice right. An earnest of what the Random Factor had brought.

Kator logged his position and the direction of drift the artifact had been taking when he had first sighted it. He headed himself and the artifact toward Homeworld, and turned in for a well-earned rest.

As he drifted off to sleep, he began remembering some of the sweeps he and Aton had made together before this, and tears ran down inside his nose. They had never been related, it was true, even by the marriage of distant connection. But Kator had grown to have a deep friendship for the older Ruml, and Kator was not the sort that made friends easily.

Only, when a Kingdom beckons, what can a man do?

Back on the Ruml Homeworld—capital planet of the seven star-systems where the Ruml were in power—an organization consisting of some of the best minds of the race fell upon the artifact that Kator had brought back, like robber wasps upon the honey-horde of a wild bees hive, where the hollow tree trunk hiding it has been split open by lightning. Unlike the lesser races and perhaps the unknown ones who had created the artifact, there was no large popular excitement over the find, no particular adulation of its discoverer. The artifact could well fail to pan out for a multitude of reasons. Perhaps it was not even of this portion of the galaxy. Perhaps it had been wandering the lightless immensity of space for a million years or more; and the race that had created it was either dead or gone to some strange elsewhere. As for the man who had found it—he was no more than a second cousin of an acceptable, but not great house. And only a few seasons adult, at that.

Only one individual never doubted the promise of reward embodied in the artifact. And that was Kator.

He accepted the reward in wealth that he was given on his return. He took his name off the scout list, and mortgaged every source of income available to him— even down to his emergency right of demand on the family coffers of the Brutogasi. And that was a pledge he would eventually be forced to redeem, or be cut off from the protection of family relationship—which was equivalent to being deprived of the protection of the law among some other races.

He spent his mornings, all morning, in a *salle d'armes,* and his afternoons and evenings either buttonholing or entertaining members of influential families. It was impossible that such activity could remain uninterpreted. The day the examination of the artifact was completed, Kator was summoned to an interview with The Brutogas—head of the family, that individual to whom Kator was second cousin.

Kator put on his best kilt and weapons-harness and made his way at the appointed hour down lofty echoing corridors of white marble to that sunlit office which he had entered, being only a second cousin, only on one previous occasion in his life—his naming day. Behind the desk in the office on a low pedestal squatted The Brutogas, a shrewd, heavy-bodied, middle-aged Ruml. Kator bowed, stopping before the desk.

"We understand," said The Brutogas, "you have ambitions to lead the expedition shortly to be sent to the Home world of the Muffled People."

"Sir?" said Kator, blandly.

"Quite right," said The Brutogas, "don't admit anything. I suppose though you'd like to know what's been extracted in the way of information about them from that artifact you brought home."

"Yes, sir," said Kator, standing straight, "I would."

"Well," said the head of the family, flicking open the lock on a report that lay on the desk before him, "the deduction is that they're about our size, biped, of a comparable level of civilization but probably overloaded with taboos from an earlier and more primitive stage. Classified as violent, intractable, and probably extremely dangerous. You still want to lead that expedition?"

"Sir," said Kator, "if called upon to serve—"

"All right," said The Brutogas, "I respect your desire not to admit your goal. Not that you can seriously believe after all your politicking through the last two seasons that anybody can be left in doubt about what you're after." He breathed out through his nose thoughtfully, stroked his graying cat-whiskers that were nearly twice the length of Kator's, and added, "Of course it would do our family reputation no harm to have a member of our house in charge of such an expedition."

"Thank you, sir."

"Don't mention it. However, the political climate at the moment is not such that I would ordinarily commit the family to attempting to capture the Keysman post in this expedition—or even the post of Captain.

Something perhaps you don't know, for all your conversations lately, is that the selection board will be a seven-man board and it is a practical certainty that the Rods will have four men on it to three of our Hooks."

Kator felt an unhappy sinking sensation in the region of his liver, but he kept his whiskers stiff.

"That makes the selection of someone like me seem pretty difficult, doesn't it, sir?"

"I'd say so, wouldn't you?"

"Yes. sir."

"But you're determined to go ahead with it anyhow?"

"I see no reason to change my present views about the situation, sir."

"I guessed as much." The Brutogas leaned back in his chair. "Every generation or so, one like you crops up in a family. Ninety-nine per cent of them end up familyless men. And only one in a million is remembered in history."

"Yes, sir."

"Well, you might bear in mind then that the family has no concern in this ambition of yours and no intention of officially backing your candidacy for Keysman of the expedition. If by some miracle you should succeed, however, I expect you will give due credit to the wise counsel and guidance of your family elders on an unofficial basis."

"Yes, sir."

"On the other hand, if your attempt should somehow end up with you in a scandalous or unfavorable position, you'd better expect that that mortgage you sold one of the—Chelesi, wasn't it?—on your family rights will probably be immediately called in for payment."

The sinking sensation returned in the region of Kator's liver.

"Yes,. sir."

"Well, that's all. Carry on, Secondcousin. The family blesses you."

"I bless the family," said Kator, automatically, and went out feeling as if his whiskers had been singed.

Five days later, the board to choose officers for the Expedition to the Homeworld of the Muffled People, was convened. The board sent out twelve invitations for Keysman, and the eleventh invitation was sent to Kator.

It could have been worse. He could have been the twelfth invited.

When he was finally summoned in to face the six-man board—from the room in which he had watched the ten previous candidates go for their interviews—he found the men on it exactly as long-whiskered and cold-eyed as he had feared. Only one member looked at him with anything resembling approval—and this was because that member happened to be a Brutogas, himself, Ardof Halfbrother. The other five judges were, in order from Ardof at the extreme right behind the table Kator faced, a Cheles, a Worna (both Hooks, politically, and therefore possible votes at least for Kator), and then four Rods—a Gulbano, a Perth, a Achobka, and The Nelkosan, head of the Nelkosani. The last could hardly be worst. Not only did he outrank everyone else on the board, not only was he a Rod, but it was to the family he headed that Aton Maternaluncle, Kator's dead scoutpartner, had belonged. A board of inquiry had cleared Kator in the matter of Aton's death. But the Nelkosani could hardly have accepted that with good grace, even if they had wanted to, without losing face.

Kator took a deep breath as he halted before the table and saluted briefly with his claws over the central body region of his heart. Now it was make or break.

"The candidate," said The Nelkosan, without pre-amble, "may just as well start out by trying to tell us whatever reasons he may have to justify awarding such a post as Keysman to one so young."

"Honorable Board Members," said Kator, clearly and distinctly, "my record is before you. May I point out, however, that training as a scout, involving work as it does both on a scientific and ship-handling level, as well as associating with one's scoutpartner . . ."

He talked on. He had, like all the candidates, care-fully prepared and rehearsed the speech beforehand. The board listened with the mild boredom of a body which has heard such speeches ten times over already—with the single exception of The Nelkosan, who sat twisting his whiskers maliciously.

When Kator finally concluded the board members turned and looked at each other.

"Well?" said The Nelkosan. "Shall we vote on the candidate?"

Heads nodded down the line. Hands reached for ballot chips—black for acceptance, white for rejection—the four Rods automatically picking up black, the three Hooks reaching for white. Kator licked his whiskers furtively with a dry tongue and opened his mouth before the chips were gathered—

"I appeal!" he said.

Hands checked in midair. The board suddenly woke up as one man. Seven pairs of gray eyes centered suddenly upon Kator. Any candidate might appeal—but to do so was to call the board wrong upon one of its actions, and that meant somebody's honor was due to be called in question. For a candidate without family backing to question the honor of elders such as sat on a board of selection was to put his whole future in jeopardy. The board sat back on its collective haunches and considered Kator.

"On what basis, if the candidate pleases?" inquired The Nelkosan, in far too pleasant a tone of voice.

"Sir, on the basis that I have another reason to urge for my selection than that of past experience," said Kator.

"Interesting," purred The Nelkosan, glancing down the table at the other board members. "Don't you think so, sirs?"

"Sir, I do find it interesting," said Ardof Halfbrother, The Brutogas, in such an even tone that it was impossible to tell whether he was echoing The Nelkosan's hidden sneer, or taking issue with it.

"In that case, candidate," The Nelkosan turned back to Kator, "by all means go ahead. What other reason do you have to urge? I must say"—he glanced down the table again—"I hope it justifies your appeal."

"Sir. I think it will." Kator thrust a hand into his belt pouch, withdrew something small, and stepping forward, put it down on the table before them all. He took his hand away, revealing a cube of clear plastic in which a small figure floated.

"A dirt worm?" said The Nelkosan, raising his whiskers.

"No, sir," said Kator. "The body of a being from the planet of the Muffled People."

"*What?*" Suddenly the room was in an uproar and there was not a board member there who was not upon his feet. For a moment pandemonium reigned and then all the voices died away at once as all eyes turned back to Kator, who was standing once more at attention before them.

"Where did you get this?"

It was The Nelkosan speaking and his voice was like ice.

"Sirs," said Kator, without twitching a whisker, "from the artifact I brought back to Homeworld two seasons ago."

"And you never turned it in to the proper authorities or reported the fact you possessed it?"

"No, sir."

There was a moment's dead silence in the room.

"*You know what this means?*" The words came spaced and distinct from The Nelkosan.

"I realize," said Kator, "what it would mean ordinarily—"

"Ordinarily!"

"Yes, sir. Ordinarily. My case, however," said Kator, as self-possessedly as he could, "is not ordinary. I did not take this organism from the artifact for the mere desire of possessing it."

The Nelkosan sat back and touched his whiskers gently, almost thoughtfully. His eyelids drooped until his eyes were almost hidden.

"You did not?" he murmured softly.

"No, sir," said Kator.

"Why did you take it, if we may ask?"

"Sir," said Kator, "I took it after a great deal of thought for the specific purpose of exhibiting it to this board of selection for Keysman of the Expedition to the planet of the Muffled People."

His words went out and seemed to fall dead in the face of the silence of the watching members of the board. A lengthening pause seemed to ring in his ears as he waited.

"For," said the voice of The Nelkosan, breaking the silence at last, "what reason did you choose to first steal this dead organism, and then plan to show it to us?"

"Sir," said Kator, "I will tell you."

"Please do," murmured The Nelkosan, almost closing his eyes.

Kator took a deep breath.

"Elders of this board," he said, "you, whose responsibility it is to select the Keysman—the man of final

authority, on ship and off—of this expedition, know
better than anyone else how important an expedition
like this is to all our race. In ourselves, we feel confident of our own ability to handle any situation we
may encounter in space. But confidence alone isn't
enough. The Keysman in charge of this expedition
must not merely be confident of his ability to scout
these aliens we have named the Muffled People
because of their habit of wrapping themselves in
cloths. The Keysman you pick must in addition be
able to perform his task, not merely well or
excellently—but *perfectly,* as laid down in the pre-
cepts of The Morahnpa. he who originally founded
a kingdom for our race on the third planet of Star
12A, among the lesser races there."

"Our candidate," interrupted The Nelkosan from
beneath his half-closed eyes, "dreams of founding
himself a kingdom?"

"Sir!" said Kator, standing stiffly. "I think only of our
race."

"You had better convince us of that, candidate?"

"I shall, sir. With my culminating argument and
explanation of why I took the dead alien organism. I
took it, sirs, to show to you. To convince you beyond
doubt of one thing. Confidence is not enough in a
Keysman. Skill is not enough. *Perfection*—fulfillment
of his task without a flaw, as defined by The
Morahnpa—is what is required here. And for perfection a commitment is required beyond the ordinary
duty of a Keysman to his task."

Kator paused. He could tell from none of them
whether he had caught their interest or not.

"I offer you evidence of my own commitment in the
shape of this organism. So highly do I regard the need
for success on this expedition, that I have gambled with
my family, my freedom, and my life to convince you

that I will go to any length to carry it through to the point of perfection. Only someone willing to commit himself to the extent I have demonstrated by taking this organism should be your choice for Keysman on this Expedition!"

He stopped talking. Silence hung in the room. Slowly, The Nelkosan uncurled himself and reaching down the table, gathered in the cube with the worm inside and brought it back to his own place and held it.

"You've made your gesture, candidate," he said, with slitted eyes. "But who can tell whether you meant anything more than a gesture, now that you've given the organism back to us?" He lifted the cube slightly and turned it so that the light caught it. "Tell us, what does it mean to you now, candidate?"

The matter, Kator thought with a cold liverish sense of *fatalism*, was doomed to go all the way. There was no other alternative now. He looked at The Nelkosan.

"I'll kill you to keep it!" he said.

After that, the well-oiled machinery of custom took over. The head of a family, or a member of a selection board, or anyone in authority of course did not have to answer challenges personally. That would be unfair. He could instead name a deputy to answer the challenge for him. The heads of families in particular usually had some rather highly trained fighters to depute for challenges. That this could also bring about an unfair situation was something that occurred only to someone in Kator's position.

The selection board adjourned to the nearest *salle d'armes*. The deputy for The Nelkosan—Horaag Adoptedson—turned out to be a man ten seasons older than Kator, half again as large and possessing both scars and an air of confidence.

"I charge you with insult and threat," he said

formally to Kator as soon as they were met in the center of the floor.

"You must either withdraw that or fight me with the weapons of my choice," said Kator with equal formality.

"I will fight. What weapons?"

Kator licked his whiskers.

"Double-sword," he said. Horaag Adoptedson started to nod—"And shields," added Kator.

Horaag Adoptedson stopped nodding and blinked. The board stared at each other and the match umpire was questioned. The match umpire, a man named Bolf Paternalnephew, checked the books.

"Shields," he announced, "are archaic and generally out of use, but still permissible."

"In that case," said Kator, "I have my own weapons and I'd like to send for them."

The weapons were sent for. While he waited for them, Kator saw his opponent experimenting with the round, target-shaped shield of blank steel that had been found for him. The shield was designed to be held in the left hand while the right hand held the sword. Horaag Adoptedson was trying fencing lunges with his long, twin-bladed sword and trying to decide what to do with the shield which he was required to carry. At arm's length behind him the shield threw him off balance. Held before him, it restricted his movements.

Kator's weapons came. The shield was like the one found for his opponent, but the sword was as archaic as the shield. It was practically hiltless, and its parallel twin blades were several times as wide as the blades of Horaag's sword, and half the length. Kator slid his arm through a wide strap inside the shield and grasped the handle beyond it. He grasped his archaically short sword almost with an underhand grip and took up a stance like a boxer.

The board murmured. Voices commented to the

similarity between Kator's fighting position and that of figures on old carvings depicting ancestral warriors who had used such weapons. Horaag quickly fell into a duplicate of Kator's position—but with some clumsiness evident.

"Go!" said the match umpire. Kator and Horaag moved together and Kator got his shield up just in time to deflect a thrust from Horaag's long sword. Kator ducked down behind his shield and moved in, using his short sword with an underhand stabbing motion. Horaag gave ground. For a few moments swords clanged busily together and on the shields.

Horaag circled suddenly. Kator, turning, tripped and almost went down. Horaag was instantly on top of him. Kator thrust the larger man off with his shield. Horaag, catching on, struck high with his shield, using it as a weapon. Kator slipped underneath, took the full force of the shield blow from the stronger man and was driven to one knee. Horaag struck down with his sword. Kator struck upward from his kneeling position and missed. Horaag shortened his sword for a death-thrust downward and Kator, moving his shorter double blade in a more restricted circle, came up inside the shield and sword-guard of the bigger man and thrust Horaag through the shoulder. Horaag threw his arms around his smaller opponent to break his back and Kator, letting go of his sword handle in these close quarters, reached up and clawed the throat out of his opponent.

They fell together.

When a bloody and breathless Kator was pulled from under the body of Horaag and supported to the table which had been set up for the board, he saw the keys to every room and instrument of the ship which would carry the Expedition to the planet of the Muffled People, lying in full sight, waiting for him.

❖   ❖   ❖

The ship of the Expedition carried fifty-eight men, including Captain and Keysman. Shortly after they lifted from the Ruml Homeworld, just as soon as they were the distance of one shift away from their planetary system, Kator addressed all crew members over the intercommunications system of the ship.

"Expedition members," he said, "you all know that as Keysman, I have taken my pledge to carry this Expedition through to a successful conclusion, and to remain impartial in my concern for its Members, under all conditions. Let me now reinforce that pledge by taking it again before you all. I promise you the order of impartiality which might be expected by strange but equal members of an unknown family; and I commit myself to returning to Homeworld with the order of scouting report on this alien race of Muffled People that only a perfect operation can provide. I direct all your attentions to that word, *perfect,* and a precept laid down by an ancestor of ours, The Morahnpa—*if all things are accomplished to perfection, how can failure attend that operation in which they are accomplished?* I have dedicated myself to the success of this Expedition in discovering how the Muffled People may be understood and conquered. Therefore I have dedicated myself to perfection. I will expect a like dedication from each one of you."

He turned away from the communications board and saw the ship's Captain, standing with arms folded and feet spread a little apart. The Captain's eyes were on him.

"Was that really necessary, Keysman?" said the Captain. He was a middle-aged man, his chest-strap heavy with badges of service. Kator thought that probably now was as good a time as any to establish their relationship.

"Have you any other questions, Captain?" he asked.

"No, sir."

"Then continue with your normal duties."

"Yes, sir."

The Captain inclined his head and turned back to his control board on the other side of the room. His whiskers were noncommittal.

Kator left the control room and went down the narrow corridor to his own quarters. Locking the door behind him—in that allowance of luxury that only the Keysman was permitted—he went across to the small table to which was pinned the ring holding his Keys, his family badge, and the authorization papers of the Expedition.

He rearranged these to make room in the center. Then he took from his belt pouch and put in the place so provided the clear plastic cube containing the alien worm. It glittered in that position under the overhead lights of the room; and the other objects surrounded it, thought Kator, like obsequious servants.

There was only one quarrel on the way requiring the adjudication of the Keysman, and Kator found reason to execute both men involved. The hint was well taken by the rest of the Expedition and there were no more disputes. They backtracked along the direction calculated on their Homeworld to have been the path of the artifact, and found themselves after a couple of nine-day weeks midway between a double star with a faint neighbor, Star Unit 439LC&W—and a single yellow star which was almost the twin of the brighter partner of the double star. Star 440L.

The Ruml investigations of the artifact had indicated the Muffled People's Homeworld to be under a single star. The ship was therefore turned to the yellow sun.

Traces of artificially produced radio emissions were detected well out from the system of the yellow sun.

The ship approached cautiously—but although the Ruml discovered scientific data-collecting devices in orbit as far out as the outer fringes of the planetary system surrounding the yellow sun, they found no warning stations or sentry ships.

Penetrating cautiously further into the system, they discovered stations on the moons of two larger, outer planets, some native ship activity in an asteroid belt, and light settlements of native population on the second and fourth planets. The third planet, on the other hand, was swarming with aliens.

The ship approached under cover of that planet's moon, ducked around to the face turned toward the planet, at nightfall, and quickly sealed itself in, a ship's length under the rock of the moon's airless surface. Tunnels were driven in the rock and extra workrooms hollowed out.

Up until this time the ship's captain had been in some measure in command of the Expedition. But now that they were down, all authority reverted to the Keysman. Kator spent a ship's-day studying the plan of investigation recommended by the Ruml Homeworld authorities, and made what changes he considered necessary in them. Then he came out of his quarters and set the whole force of the expedition to building and sending out collectors.

These were of two types. The primary type were simply lumps of nickel-iron with a monomolecular surface layer sensitized to collect up to three days worth of images, and provided with a tiny internal drive unit that would explode on order from the ship or any attempt to block or interfere with the free movement of the device. Several thousand of these were sent down on to the planet and recovered with a rate of necessary self-destruction less than one tenth of one per cent. Not one of the devices was even perceived, let alone handled, by a native. At the end of five weeks, the Expedition had a complete and detailed map of the world below, its cities and its ocean bottoms. And Kator set up a large chart in the gathering room of the ship, listing Five Phases, numbered in order. Opposite Phase One, he wrote Complete to Perfection.

The next stage was the sending down of the secondary type of collectors—almost identical lumps of nickel iron, but with cargo-carrying space inside them. After nine weeks of this and careful study of the small species of alien life returned to the Expedition Headquarters on the moon, he decided that one small flying blood-sucking insect, one crawling, six-legged pseudo-insect—one of the arthropoda, an arachnid or *spider*, in Muffled People's classification—and a small, sharp-nosed, long-tailed scavenging animal of the Muffled People's cities, should be used as live investigators. He marked Phase Two as Complete to Perfection.

Specimens of the live investigators were collected, controlling mechanisms surgically implanted in them, and they were taken back to the planet's surface. By the use of scanning devices attached to the creatures, Expedition members remote-controlling them from the moon were able to investigate the society of the Muffled People at close hand.

The live investigators were directed by their controller into the libraries, factories, hospitals. The first two phases of the investigation had been cold matters of collecting, collating and filing data. With this third phase, and the on-shift members of the Expedition living vicarious insect and animal lives on the planet below, a spirit of adventure began to permeate the fifty-six men remaining on the moon.

The task before them was almost too great to be imagined. It was necessary that they hunt blindly through the civilization below until chance put them on the trail of the information they were after concerning the character and military strength of the Muffled People. The first six months of this phase produced no evidence at all of military strength on the part of the Muffled People—and in his cabin alone Kator paced the floor, twitching his whiskers. The character of the Muffled People as a race was emerging more clearly every day and it was completely at odds with such a lack of defensive elements. And so was the Muffled People's past history as the Expedition had extracted it from the libraries of the planet below.

He called the Captain in.

"We're overlooking something," he said.

"I'll agree with that, Keysman," said the Captain. "But knowing that doesn't solve our problem. In the limited time we've had with the limited number of men available, we're bound to face blank spots."

"Perfection," Kator said, "admits of no blank spots."

The Captain looked at him with slitted eyes.

"What does the Keysman suggest?" he said.

" . . . Sir."

"For one thing," Kator's eyes were also slitted, "a little more of an attitude of respect."

"Yes, sir."

"And for another thing," said Kator, "I make the suggestion that what we're looking for must be underground. Somewhere the Muffled People must have a source of military strength comparable to our own— their civilization and their past history is too close to our own for there not to be such a source. If it had been on the surface of the planet or in one of the oceans, we would've discovered it by now. So it must be underground."

"I'll have the men check for underground areas."

"You'll do better than that, Captain. You'll take every

man and put them in a hookup with the long-tailed scavenging animals, and run their collectors underground. In all large blank areas."

"Sir."

The Captain went out. The change in assignment was made and two shifts later—by sheer luck or coincidence—the change paid off. One of the long-tailed animal collectors was trapped aboard a large truck transporting food. The truck went out from one of the large cities in the middle of the western continent of the planet below and at about a hundred and fifty of the Muffled People's miles from the city turned into a country route that led to an out-of-operation industrial manufacturing complex. It trundled past a sleepy farm or two, across a bridge over a creek and down a service road into the complex. There it drove into a factory building and unloaded its food onto a still and silent conveyor belt.

Then it left.

The collector, left with the food, suddenly felt the conveyor belt start to move. It carried the food deep into the factory building, through a maze of machinery, and delivered it onto a platform, which dropped without warning into the darkness of a deep shaft.

And it was at this point that the Ruml in contact with the collector, called Kator. Kator did not hesitate.

"Destroy it!" he ordered.

The Ruml touched a button and the collector stiffened suddenly and collapsed. Almost immediately a pinpoint of brilliance appeared in the center of its body and in a second it was nothing but fine gray ash, which blew back up the shaft on the draft around the edges of the descending platform.

While the rest of the men of the Expedition there present in the gathering room watched, Kator walked over to the chart he had put up on the wall. Opposite

Phase Three, with a clear hand he wrote *Complete to Perfection.*

Kator allowed the Expedition a shift in which to celebrate. He did not join the celebration himself or swallow one of the short-lived bacterial cultures that temporarily manufactured ethyl alcohol in the Ruml stomachs from carbohydrates the Expedition Members had eaten. Intoxication was an indulgence he could not at the moment permit himself. He called the Captain into conference in the Keysman's private quarters.

"The next stage," Kator said, "is, of course, to send a man down to examine this underground area."

"Of course, sir," said the Captain. The Captain had swallowed one of the cultures, but because of the necessity of the conference had eaten nothing for the last six hours. He thought of the rest of the Expedition gorging themselves in the gathering room and his own hunger came sharply on him to reinforce the anticipation of intoxication.

"So far," said Kator, "the Expedition has operated without mistakes. Perfection of operation must continue. The man who goes down on to the planet of the Muffled People must be someone whom I can be absolutely sure will carry the work through to success. There's only one individual in this Expedition of whom I'm that sure."

"Sir?" said the Captain, forgetting his hunger suddenly and experiencing an abrupt chilliness in the region of his liver. "You aren't thinking of me, are you, Keysman? My job with the ship, here—"

"I am not thinking of you."

"Oh," said the Captain, breathing freely. "In that case . . . while I would be glad to serve . . ."

"I'm thinking of myself."

"*Keysman!*"

It was almost an explosion from the Captain's lips. His whiskers flattened back against his face.

Kator waited. The Captain's whiskers slowly returned to normal position.

"I beg your pardon, sir," he said. "Of course, you can select whom you wish. It's rather unheard of, but . . . Do you wish me to act as Keysman while you're down there?"

Kator smiled at him.

"No," he said.

The Captain's whiskers twitched slightly, involuntarily, but his face remained impassive.

"Who, then, sir?"

"No one."

This time the Captain did not even explode with the word of Kator's title. He merely stared, almost blindly at Kator.

"No one," repeated Kator, slowly. "You understand me, Captain? I'll be taking the keys of the ship with me."

"But—" the Captain's voice broke and stopped. He took a deep breath. "I must protest officially, Keysman," he said. "It would be extremely difficult to get home safely if the keys were lost and the authority of a Keysman was lacking on the trip back."

"It will be impossible," said Kator, evenly. "Because I intend to lock ship before leaving."

The Captain said nothing.

"Perfection, Captain," remarked Kator in the silence, "can imply no less than utter effort and unanimity— otherwise it isn't perfection. Since to fail of perfection is to fail of our objective here, and to fail of our objective is to render the Expedition worthless—I consider I am only doing my duty in making all Members of the Expedition involved in a successful effort down on the planet's surface."

"Yes, sir," said the Captain woodenly.

"You'd better inform the Expedition of this decision of mine."

"Yes, sir."

"Go ahead then," said Kator. The Captain turned toward the door. "And Captain—" The Captain halted with the door half open, and looked back. Kator was standing in the middle of the room, smiling at him. "Tell them I said for them to enjoy themselves—this shift."

"Yes, sir."

The Captain went out, closing the door behind him and cutting off his sight of Kator's smile. Kator turned and walked over to the table holding his keys, his family badge, his papers and the cube containing the worm. He picked up the cube and for a moment held it almost tenderly.

None of them, he thought, would believe him if he told them that it was not himself he was thinking of, but of something greater. Gently, he replaced the cube among the other precious items on the table. Then he turned and walked across the room to squat at his desk. While the sounds of the celebration in the gathering room came faintly through the locked door of his quarters, he settled down to a long shift of work, planning and figuring the role of every Member of the Expedition in his own single assault upon the secret place of the Muffled People.

The shift after the celebration, Kator set most of the Expedition Members to work constructing mechanical burrowing devices which could dig down to, measure and report on the outside of the underground area he wished to enter. Meanwhile, he himself, with the help of the Captain and two specialists in such things, attacked the problem of making Kator himself into a passable resemblance of one of the Muffled People.

The first and most obvious change was the close-clipping of Kator's catlike whiskers. There was no pain or discomfort involved in this operation, but so deeply involved were the whiskers in the sociological and psychological patterns of the adult male Ruml that having them trimmed down to the point of invisibility was a profound emotional shock. The fact that they would grow again in a matter of months—if not weeks—did not help. Kator suffered more than an adult male of the Muffled People would have suffered if the normal baritone of his voice had suddenly been altered to a musical soprano.

The fact that the whiskers had been clipped at his own order somehow made it worse instead of better.

The depilation that removed the rest of the fur on Kator's head, bad as it was, was by contrast a minor operation. After the shock of losing the whiskers, Kator had been tempted briefly to simply dye the close gray fur covering the skull between his ears like a beanie. But to do so would have been too weak a solution to the fur problem. Even dyed, his natural head-covering bore no relationship to human hair.

Still, dewhiskered and bald, Kator's reflection in a mirror presented him with an unlovely sight. Luckily, he did, now, look like one of the Muffled People after a fashion from the neck up. The effect was that of a pink-skinned oriental with puffy eyelids over unnaturally wide and narrow eyes. But it was undeniably native-like.

The rest of his disguise would have to be taken care of by the mufflings he would be wearing, after the native fashion. These complicated body-coverings, therefore, turned out to be a blessing in disguise, with pun intended. Without them it would have been almost impossible to conceal Kator's body-differences from the natives.

As it was, foot-coverings with built-up undersurfaces helped to disguise the relative shortness of Kator's legs, as the loose hanging skirt of the sleeved outside upper-garment hid the unnatural—by Muffled People physical standards—narrowness of his hips. Not a great deal could be done about the fact that the Ruml spine was so connected to the Ruml pelvis that Kator appeared to walk with his upper body at an angle leaning forward. But heavy padding widened the narrow Ruml shoulders and wide sleeves hid the fact that the Ruml arms, like the Ruml legs, were normally designed to be kept bent at knee and elbow-joint.

When it was done, Kator was a passable imitation of a Muffled Person—but these changes were only the beginning. It was now necessary for him to learn to move about in these hampering garments with some appearance of native naturalness.

The mufflings were hideously uncomfortable—like the clinging but lifeless skin of some loathsome crea-ture. But Kator was as unyielding with himself as he was with the other Expedition Members. Shift after shift, as the rest of the Expedition made their burrow-ing scanners, sent them down and collected them back on the moon to digest the information they had dis-covered, Kator tramped up and down his own quar-ters, muffled and whiskerless—while the Captain and the two specialists compared his actions with tapes of the natives in comparable action, and criticized.

Intelligent life is inconceivably adaptable. There came a shift finally when the three watchers could offer no more criticisms, and Kator himself no longer felt the touch of the mufflings about his body for the unnatural thing it was.

❖ ❖ ❖

Kator announced himself satisfied with himself, and went to the gathering room for a final briefing on the information the burrowing mechanisms had gathered about the Muffled People's secret place. He stood— a weird-looking Ruml figure in his wrappings while he was informed that the mechanisms had charted the underground area and found it to be immense—half a native mile in depth, twenty miles in extent and ten in breadth. Its ceiling was an eighth of a mile below the surface and the whole underground area was walled in by an extremely thick casing of native concrete stiffened by steel rods.

The mechanisms had been unable to scan through the casing and, since Kator had given strict orders that no attempt was to be made to burrow or break through the casing for fear of alarming the natives, nothing was discovered about the interior.

What lay inside, therefore, was still a mystery. If Kator was to invade the secret place, therefore, he would have to do so blind—not knowing what in the way of defenders or defenses he might discover. The only open way in was down the elevator shaft where the food shipments disappeared.

Kator stood in thought, while the other Members of the Expedition waited around him.

"Very well," he said at last "I consider it most likely that this place has been set up to protect against invasion by others of the natives, themselves—rather than by someone like myself. At any rate, we will proceed on that assumption."

And he called them together to give them final orders for the actions they would have to take in his absence.

The face of the planet below them was still in night when Kator breached the moon surface just over the site of the Expedition Headquarters and took off planetward in a small, single-man ship. Behind him, the hole in the dust-covered rock filled itself in as if with a smooth magic.

His small ship lifted from the moon and dropped toward the darkness of the planet below.

He came to the planet's surface, just as the sun was beginning to break over the eastern horizon and the fresh chill of the post-dawn drop of temperature was in the air. He camouflaged his ship, giving it the appearance of some native alder bushes, and stepped from it for the first time onto the alien soil.

The strange, tasteless atmosphere of the planet filled his nostrils. He looked toward the rising sun and saw a line of trees and a ramshackle building blackly outlined against the redness of its half-disk. He turned a quarter-circle and began to walk toward the factory.

Not far from his ship, he hit the dirt road running past the scattered farms to the complex. He continued along it with the sun rising strongly on his left, and after a while he came to the wooden bridge over the creek. On this, as he crossed it, his footcoverings fell with a hollow sound. In the stillness of the dawn these seemed to echo through the whole sleeping world. He hurried to get off the planks back onto dirt road again; and it was with an internal lightening of tension that he stepped finally off the far end of the bridge.

"Up early, aren't you?" said a voice.

Kator checked like a swordsman, just denying in time the impulse that would have whirled him around like a discovered thief. He turned casually. On the grassy bank of the creek just a few feet below this end of the bridge, an adult male native sat.

A container of burning vegetation was in his mouth, and smoke trickled from his lips. He was muffled in blue leg-coverings and his upper body was encased in a worn, sleeved muffling of native leather. He held a long stick in his hands, projecting out over the waters of the creek, and as Kator faced him, his lips twisted upward in the native fashion.

Kator made an effort to copy the gesture. It did not come easily, for a smile did not mean humor among his people as much as triumph, and laughter was almost unknown except in individuals almost at the physical or mental breaking point. But it seemed to satisfy the native.

"Out for a hike?" said the native.

Kator's mind flickered over the meaning of the words. He had drilled himself, to the point of unconscious use, in the native language of this area. But this was the first time he had spoken native to a real native. Strangely, what caught at his throat just then was nothing less than embarrassment. Embarrassment at standing whiskerless before this native—who could know nothing of whiskers, and what they meant to a Ruml.

"Thought I'd tramp around a bit," Kator answered, the alien words sounding awkward in his mouth. "You fishing?"

The native waggled the pole slightly, and a small colored object floating on the water trembled with the vibration sent from the rod down the line attached to it.

"Bass," said the native.

Kator wet his nonexistent whiskers with a flicker of his tongue, and thought fast.

"Bass?" he said. "In a creek?"

"Never know what you'll catch," said the native. "Might as well fish for bass as anything else. You from around here?"

"Not close," said Kator. He felt on firmer ground

now. While he knew something about the fishing habits and jargon of the local natives—the matter of who he was and where from had been rehearsed.

"City?" said the native.

"That's right," said Kator. He thought of the planet-wide city of the Ruml Homeworld.

"Headed where?"

"Oh," said Kator, "just thought I'd cut around the complex up there, see if I can't hit a main road beyond and catch a bus back to town."

"You can do that, all right," said the native. "I'd show you the way, but I've got fish to catch. You can't miss it, anyway. Ahead or back from here both brings you out on the same road."

"That so?" said Kator. He started to move off. "Well, thanks."

"Don't mention it, friend."

"Good luck with your bass."

"Bass or something—never tell what you'll catch."

Kator waved. The native waved and turned back to his contemplation of the creek Kator went on.

Only a little way down the dirt road, around a bend and through some trees, he came on the wide wire gate where the road disappeared into the complex. The gate was closed and locked Kator glanced about him, saw no one and took a small silver cone from his pocket. He touched the point of the cone to the lock. There was a small, upward puff of smoke and the gate sagged open. Kator pushed through, closed the gate behind him and headed for the building which the truck holding the Ruml collector had entered.

The door to the building also was locked. Kator used the cone-shaped object on the lock of a small door set into the big door and slipped inside. He found himself in a small open space, dim-lit by high windows in the building. Beyond the open space was the end of the conveyor belt on which the food boxes had been discharged, and a maze of machinery.

Kator listened, standing in the shadow of the door. He heard nothing. He put away the cone and drew his handgun. Lightly, he leaped up on to the still conveyor belt and began to follow it back into the clutter of machinery.

It was a strange, mechanical jungle through which he found himself traveling. The conveyor belt was not a short one. After he had been on it for some minutes, his listening ears caught sound from up ahead. He stopped and listened.

The sound was that of native voices talking.

He went on, cautiously. Gradually he approached the voices, which did not seem to be on the belt but off it to the right some little distance. Finally, he drew level with them. Kneeling down and peering through the shapes of the machinery he made out a clear area in the building about thirty feet off the belt. Behind the cleared area was a glassed-in cage in which five humans, wearing blue uniforms and weapon harnesses supporting handguns, could be seen—sitting at desks and standing about talking.

Kator lowered his head and crept past like a shadow on the belt. The voices faded a little behind him and in a little distance, he came to the shaft and the elevator platform on to which the conveyor belt discharged its cargo.

Kator examined the platform with an eye already briefed on its probable construction. It was evidently remotely controlled from below, but there should be some kind of controls for operating it from above—if only emergency controls.

Kator searched around the edge of the shaft, and discovered controls set under a plate at the end of the conveyor belt. Using a small magnetic power tool, he removed the plate covering the connections to the switches and spent a moment or two studying the wiring. It was not hard to figure it out from this end—but he had hoped to find some kind of locking device, such as would be standard on a Ruml apparatus of this sort, which would allow him to prevent the elevator being used after he himself had gone down.

But there was no such lock.

He replaced the plate, got on to the platform and looked at the controls. From this point on it was a matter of calculated risk. There was no way of telling what in the way of guards or protective devices waited for him at the bottom of the shaft. He had had his choice of trying to find out with collectors previously and running the risk of alerting the natives—or of taking his chances now. And he had chosen to take his chances now.

He pressed the button. The platform dropped beneath him, and the darkness of the shaft closed over his head.

The platform fell with a rapidity that frightened him. He had a flashing mental picture of it being designed for only nonhuman materials—and then thought of the damageable fruits and vegetables among its food cargo came to mind and reassured him. Sure enough—after what seemed like a much longer drop than the burrowing scanners had reported the shaft to have—the platform slowed quickly but evenly to a gentle halt and emerged into light from an opening in one side of the shaft.

Kator was off the platform the second it emerged, and racing for the nearest cover—behind the door of the small room into which he had been discharged. And no sooner than necessary. A lacework of blue beams lanced across the space where he had been standing a tiny part of a second before.

The beams winked out. The smell of ozone filled the room. For a moment Kator stood frozen and poised, gun in hand. But no living creature showed itself. The beams had evidently been fired automatically from apertures in the wall. And, thought Kator with a cold feeling about his liver, the spot he had chosen to duck into was about the only spot in the room they had not covered.

He came out from behind the door, slipped through the entrance to which it belonged—and checked suddenly, catching his breath.

He stood in an underground area of unbelievable dimensions, suddenly a pygmy. No, less than a pygmy, an ant among giants, dimlit from half a mile overhead.

He was at one end of what was no less than an underground spacefield. Towering away from him, too huge to count, were the brobdingnagian shapes of great spaceships. He had found it—the secret gathering place of the strength of the Muffled People.

From up ahead came the sound of metal on other metal and concrete, sound of feet and voices. Like a hunting animal, Kator slipped from the shadow of one great shape to the next until he came to a spot from which he could see what was going on.

He peered out from behind the roundness of a great, barrel-thick supporting jack and saw that he was at the edge of the field of ships. Beyond stretched immense emptiness, and in a separate corner of this, not fifty feet from where Kator stood, a crew of five natives in green one-piece mufflings were dismounting the governor of a phase-shift drive from one of the ships, which had been taken out of the ship and lowered to the floor here, apparently for servicing. A single native in blue with a weapons harness and handgun stood by them.

As Kator stopped, another native in blue with weapons harness came through the ranked ships from another direction. Kator shrank back behind the supporting jack. The second guard came up to the first.

"Nothing," he said. "May have been a short up in the powerhouse. Anyway, nothing came down the shaft."

"A rat, maybe?" said the first guard.

"No. I looked. The room was empty. It would've got caught by the beams. They're checking upstairs, though."

Kator slipped back among the ships.

The natives were alerted now, even if they did not seriously suspect an intruder like himself. Nonetheless, a great exultation was welling up inside him. He had prepared to break into one of the ships to discover the nature of its internal machinery. Now—thanks to the dismantled unit he had seen being worked on, that was no longer necessary. His high hopes, his long gamble, were about to pay off. His kingdom was before him.

Only two things were still to be done. The first was to make a visual record of the place to take Home, and the other was to get himself safely out of here and back to his small ship.

He took a hand recorder from his weapons belt and adjusted it. This device had been in operation recording his immediate vicinity ever since he had set foot outside his small ship. But adjustments were necessary to allow it to record the vast shapes and spaces about him. Kator made the necessary adjustments and for about half an hour flitted about like an entertainment-maker, taking records not only of the huge ships, and their number, but of everything else about this secret underground field. It was a pity, he thought, that he could not get up to also record the structure of the ceiling lost overhead in the brightness of the half-mile-distant light sources. But it went without saying that the Muffled People would have some means of letting the ships out through the apparently solid ground and buildings overhead.

Finished at last, Kator worked his way back to the room containing the elevator shaft. Almost, in the vast maze of ships and jacks, he had forgotten where it was, but the sense of direction which had been part of his scoutship training paid off. He found it and came at last back to its entrance.

He halted there, peering at the platform sitting innocuously waiting at the shaft bottom. To cross the room to it would undoubtedly fire the automatic mechanism of the blue beams again—which, aside from the danger that posed, would this time fully alert the blue-clad natives with the weapons harnesses.

For a long second Kator stood, thinking with a rapidity he had hardly matched before in his life. Then a farfetched scheme occurred to him. He knew that the area behind the door was safe. From there, two long leaps would carry him to the platform. If he, with his different Ruml muscles, could avoid that single touching of the floor, he might be able to reach the platform without triggering off the defensive mechanism. There was a way but it was a stake-everything sort of proposition. If he missed, there would be no hope of avoiding the beams.

The door opened inward, and it was about six feet in height, three and a half feet in width. From its most inward point of swing it was about twenty-two feet from the platform. Reaching in, Kator swung it at right angles to the entrance, so that it projected into the room. Then he backed up and took off his foot coverings, tucking them into pouches of his mufflings.

He got down on hands and feet and arched his back.

His claws extended themselves from fingers and toes, clicking on the concrete floor. For a moment he felt a wave of despair that the clumsy mufflings hampering him would make the feat impossible. But he resolutely shoved that thought from his mind. He backed up further until he was a good thirty feet from the door.

He thought of his kingdom and launched himself forward.

He was a young adult Ruml in top shape. By the time he had covered the thirty feet he was moving at close to twenty miles an hour. He launched himself from a dozen feet out for the entrance and flew to the inmost top edge of the door.

He seemed barely to touch the door in passing. But four sets of claws clamped on the door, making the all-important change in direction and adding additional impetus to his flying body. Then the platform and the shaft seemed to fly to meet him and he slammed down on the flat surface with an impact that struck the breath from his body.

The beams did not fly. Half-dazed, but mindful of the noise he had made in landing, Kator fumbled around the edge of the shaft for the button he had marked from the doorway, punched it, and felt the platform thrust him upward.

On the ride up he recovered his breath. He made no attempt to replace the clumsy foot-coverings and drew his handgun, keeping it ready in his hand. The second the platform stopped at the top of the shaft he was off it and running noiselessly back along the conveyor belt at a speed which no native would have been able to maintain in the crouched position in which Kator was holding himself.

There were sounds of natives moving all about the factory building in which he was—but for all that he was half-persuaded that he still might make his escape unobserved, when a shout erupted only about a dozen feet away within the maze of machinery off to his left.

"Stop there! You!"

Without hesitation, Kator fired in the direction of the voice and dived off the conveyor belt into a tangle of gears at his right. Behind him came a groan and the sound of a falling body and a blue beam lanced from another direction through the spot where he had stood a second before.

A dozen feet back in the mechanical maze, Kator clung to a piece of ductwork and listened. His first impression had been that there were a large number of the natives searching the building. Now he heard only three voices, converging on the spot where the first voice had hailed him.

"What happened?"

"I thought I saw something——" the voice that had hailed Kator groaned. "I tried to get a clear shot and I slipped down in between the drums, here."

"You jammed in there?"

"I think my leg's broke."

"You say you saw something?"

"I thought I saw something. I don't know. I guess that alarm had me seeing things—there's nothing on the belt now. Help me out of here, will you!"

"Give me a hand, Corry."

"Easy—take it *easy!*"

"All right . . . All right. We'll get you in to the doctor."

Kator clung, listening, as the two who had come up later lifted their hurt companion out of wherever he had fallen, and carried him out of the building. Then there was nothing but silence; and in that silence, Kator drew a deep breath. It was hardly believable; but for this, too, the Morahnpa had had a saying—*Perfection attracts the Random Factor—favorably as well as unfavorably.*

Quietly, Kator began to climb back toward the conveyor belt. Now that he could move with less urgency, he saw a clearer route to it. He clambered along and spotted a straight climb along a sideways-sloping, three-foot-wide strip of metal filling the gap between what seemed to be the high side of a turbine and a narrow strip of darkness a foot wide alongside more ductwork. The strip led straight as a road to the open area where the conveyor belt began, and there was the door where Kator had originally entered.

Perfection attracts the Random Factor. . . . Kator slipped out on the strip of metal and began to scuttle along it. His claws scratched and slipped. It was slicker than he had thought. He felt himself sliding. Grimly, in silence, he tried to hold himself back from the edge of darkness. Still blunting his claws ineffectually on the polished surface, he slid over the edge and fell—

To crashing darkness and oblivion.

When he woke, he could not at first remember where he was. It seemed that he had been unconscious for some time but far above him the light still streamed through the high windows of the building at the same angle, almost, as when he had emerged from the platform on his way out. He was lying in a narrow gap between two vertical surfaces of metal. Voices suddenly struck strongly on his ear—the voices of two natives standing in the open space up ahead between Kator and the door.

"Not possible," one of the voices was saying. "We've looked everywhere."

"But you left the place to carry Rogers to the infirmary?"

"Yes, sir. But I took him in myself. Corry stood guard outside the door there. Then, when I came back we searched the whole place. There's no one here."

"Sort of a funny day," said the second voice. "First, that short or whatever it was, downstairs, and then Rogers thinking he saw someone and breaking his leg." The voice moved off toward the door. "Well, forget it, then. I'll write it up in my report and we'll lock the building behind us until an inspector can look it over."

There was the sound of the small door in the big truck door opening.

"What's anybody going to steal, anyway" said the first voice, following the other through the door. "Put a half million tons of spaceship under one arm and carry it out?"

"Regulations . . ." the second voice faded away into the outdoors as the door closed.

Kator stirred in his darkness.

For a moment he was afraid he had broken a limb himself. But his leg appeared to be bruised, rather than broken. He wriggled his way forward between the two surfaces until some other object blocked his way. He climbed up and over this—more ductwork yet, it seemed—and emerged a second later into the open area.

The local sun was well up in the center of the sky as he slipped out of the building. No one was in sight. At a half-speed, limping run, Kator dodged along in the shade of an adjoining building; and a couple of minutes later he was safely through the gate of the complex and into the safe shelter of the trees paralleling the dirt road—headed back toward his ship.

The native fisherman was no longer beside the creek. No one at all seemed to be in sight in the warm day. Kator made it back to his ship; and, only when he was safely inside its camouflaged entrance, did he allow himself the luxury of a feeling of safety. For—at that—he was not yet completely safe. He simply had a ship in which to make a run for it, if he was discovered now.

He throttled the feeling of safety down. It would be nightfall before he could risk taking off. And that meant that it must be nightfall before he took the final step in securing his kingdom.

He got rid of the loathsome mufflings he had been forced to wear and tended to his wrenched leg. It was painful, but it would be all right in a week at most. And he could use it now for any normal purpose. The recorder he had been carrying was smashed—that must have happened when he had the fall in the building. However, the record of everything he had done up to that moment would be still available within the recording element. No more was needed back Home. Now, if only night would fall!

Kator limped restlessly back and forth in the restricted space of the small ship as the shadows lengthened. At last, the yellow sun touched the horizon and darkness began to flood in long shadows across the land. Kator sat down at the communications board of his small ship and keyed in voice communication alone with the Expedition Headquarters on the moon.

The speaker crackled at him.

"Keysman?"

He said nothing.

"Keysman? This is the Captain. Can you hear us?"

Kator held his silence, a slight smile on his Ruml lips.

"*Keysman!*"

Kator leaned forward to the voice-collector before him. He whispered into it.

"No use—" he husked brokenly, "natives . . . surrounding me here. Captain—"

Kator paused. There was a moment's silence, and then the Captain's voice broke in.

"Keysman! Hold on. We'll get ships down to you and—"

"No time—" husked Kator. "Destroying self and ship. Get Home . . ."

He reached out to his controls and sent the little ship leaping skyward into the dark. As it rose, he fired a cylindrical object back into the ground where it had lain. And, three seconds later, the white, actinic glare of a phase-shift explosion lighted the landscape.

But by that time, Kator was drilling safely upward through the night darkness.

He took upwards of four hours, local time, to return to the Expedition Headquarters. There was no response as he approached the surface above the hidden ship and its connected network of rooms excavated out of the undersurface. He opened the passage that would let his little ship down in, by remote control, and left the small ship for the big one.

There was no one in the corridors or in the outer rooms of the big ship. When Kator got to the gathering room, they were all there, lying silent. As he had expected, they had not followed his orders to return to the Ruml Homeworld. Indeed, with the ship locked and the keys lost with their Keysman, they could not have raised ship except by an extreme butchery of their controls, or navigated her once they had raised her. They had assumed, as Kator had planned, that their Keysman—no doubt wounded and dying on the planet below—had been half-delirious and forgetful of the fact he had locked the ship and taken her keys.

With a choice between a slow death and a fast, they had taken the reasonable choice; and suicided politely, with the lesser ranks first and the Captain last.

Kator smiled, and went to examine the ship's recorder. The Captain had recited a full account of the conversation with Kator, and the Expedition's choice of action. Kator turned back to the waiting bodies. The Expedition's ship had cargo space. He carried the dead bodies into it and set the space at below freezing temperature so that the bodies could be returned to their families—that in itself would be a point in his favor when he returned. Then he unlocked the ship, and checked the controls.

There was no great difference between any of the space-going vessels of the Ruml; and one man could handle the large Expedition ship as well as the smallest scout. Kator set a course for the Ruml Homeworld and broke the ship free of the moon's surface into space.

As soon as he was free of the solar system, he programmed his phase shift mechanism, and left the ship to take itself across immensity. He went back to his own quarters.

There, things were as they had been before he had gone down to the planet of the Muffled People. He opened a service compartment to take out food, and he lifted out also one of the alcohol-producing cultures. But when he had taken this last back with the food to the table that held his papers, badges, and the cube containing the worm, he felt disinclined to swallow the culture.

The situation was too solemn, too great, for drunkenness.

He laid the culture down and took up the cube containing the worm. He held it to the light above the table. In that light the worm seemed almost alive. It seemed to turn and bow to him. He laid the cube back down on the table and walked across to put his smashed recording device in a resolving machine that would project its story onto a life-size cube of the room's atmosphere. Then, as the lights about him dimmed, and the morning he had seen as he emerged from his small ship the morning of that same day, he hunkered down on a seat with a sigh of satisfaction.

It is not every man who is privileged to review a few short hours in which he has gained a Kingdom.

The Expedition ship came back to the Ruml Homeworld, and its single surviving occupant was greeted with the sort of excitement that had not occurred in the lifetime of anyone then living. After several days of due formalities, the moment of real business arrived, and Kator Secondcousin Bruto gas was summoned to report to the heads of the fifty great families of the Homeworld. Now those families would number fifty-one, for The Brutogas would after this day—at which he was only an invited observer—be listed among their number. Fifty-one long-whiskered male Rumls, therefore, took their seats in a half-circle facing a small stage, and out onto that stage came Kator Secondcousin to salute them all with claws over the region of his heart.

"Keysman," said the eldest family head present, "give us your report."

Kator saluted again. His limp was almost gone now but his whiskers were barely grown a few inches. Also, he seemed to have lost weight and aged on the Expedition.

"My written report is before you, sirs," he said. "As you know we set up a headquarters on the moon of the planet of the Muffled People. As you know, my Captain and men, thinking me dead, suicided. As you know, I have returned."

He stopped talking and saluted again. The family heads waited in some surprise. Finally, the eldest broke the silence.

"Is that *all* you have to say, Keysman?"

"No, sirs," said Kator. "But I'd like to show you the recording I made of the secret place of the Muffled People before I say anything further."

"By all means," said the eldest family head. "Go ahead."

Kator saluted again, and put the smashed recorder into a resolving machine at one edge of the stage. He stood beside it while the heads of the great families watched the incidents from Kator's landing to the moment of his fall in the factory building that had smashed the recorder.

"After I fell," said Kator, as he switched the resolving machine off beside him, "I came to hear two natives discussing the fact they had been unable to find anyone prowling about. They left, and I got away, back to my small ship. From then on, it was simple. I waited until darkness ensured that it was safe for me to take off unnoticed. Then I armed the device I had rigged to simulate a small phase-shift explosion, and called Expedition Headquarters. As I'd planned, my voice-message and my imitation explosion with its indication that the ship's keys were lost for good, left the rest of the Expedition no choice but polite suicide. I gave them ample time to do so before I re-entered the Expedition ship and headed her Home."

Kator stopped talking. There was a remarkable silence from the fifty-one faces staring at him for a long moment—and then a rising mutter of question and incredulity. The strong voice of the eldest family head cut across this.

"Are you telling us you *planned* the suicides of your Captain and men?"

Kator's face twisted in a sudden, apparently uncontrollable fashion. Almost as if he had been ready to laugh.

"Yes, sir," he said. "I planned it."

There was another dead silence.

"In the name of . . . *why*?" burst out the eldest. At

one side of the half-circle of faces, the face of The Brutogas looked stricken with paralysis.

Kator's face twisted again.

"Our ancestor, The Morahnpa," he said, "once ensured the conquest of a world and a race by his own individual actions. Because of this, and to encourage others who might do likewise, the principle was laid down that whoever might match The Morahnpa's action, might have, as The Morahnpa did, complete sovereignty over the *natives* of such a conquered world, after the conquest was accomplished. That is—other men might be entitled to take their advantages of the world and race itself. But its true conqueror, during his lifetime, would be the final authority on the planet."

"What's history got to do with this?" It was noticeable that the use of Kator's title of Keysman had begun to be forgotten by the eldest of the family heads. "The Morahnpa not only earned his right to a world, he was in such a position that the world could not be taken without his assistance."

"Or the Muffled People's world without mine," said Kator. "I had intended to return with a situation that was quite clear-cut. I left our base on the moon unhidden when I returned. It would be bound to be discovered within a limited time. During that limited time, I would offer my knowledge of where the place of strength of the Muffled People was—in turn for the planet of the Muffled People being granted to me as my kingdom—as his world was to The Morahnpa."

"In that case," said the eldest, "you made a mistake in showing us your recording."

"No," said Kator. "I've renounced my ambition."

"Renounced?" The fifty-one faces watched Kator without moving as the eldest spoke. "Why?"

Kator's face twitched again.

"Let me show you the rest of the recording."

"The rest—" began the eldest. But Kator was already turning to the resolving machine. He turned it on.

For a second there was nothing to be seen—only the bright flicker of a destroyed recording. Then, this cleared magically and the fifty-one found themselves looking at a native of the Muffled People—the same who had spoken to Kator earlier on the recording.

He took the container of burning vegetation out of his mouth, knocked the vegetation out of it on a rock beside him, overhanging the creek, and put the pipe away. Then he addressed them in perfect Ruml.

"Greetings," he said. "To all, and particularly to those heads of leading families who are viewing this. As you possibly already know, I am a member of that race you Ruml refer to as Muffled People, but which are correctly called humans"—he pronounced the native word carefully for them—"*Heh-eu-manz.* With a little practice you'll find it not hard at all to say."

There was the beginning of a babble from the semi-circle of seats.

"*Quiet!*" barked the eldest head of family.

" . . . We humans," the native was saying, smiling at them, "have quite a warlike history, but we really don't like wars. We prefer to be independent, but on good terms with our neighbors. Accordingly, let me show you some of the means we've developed to obtain our preference."

The scene changed suddenly. The assembled Ruml saw before them one of the small, long-tailed, scavenging animals Kator had used as collectors. This was smaller than Kator's and white-furred. It was nosing its way up and down the corridors of a topless box— here being baffled by a dead end corridor, there finding an entrance through to an adjoining corridor.

"This," said the voice of the native, "is a device called

a 'maze' used to test the intelligence of the experimental animal you see. This device is one of the investi-
gative tools used in our study of a division of knowledge
known as 'psychology'—which corresponds to a certain
extent with the division of knowledge you Ruml refer
to as Family-study."

The scene changed back to the native on the
creekbank.

"Psychology teaches us humans many useful things
about how other organisms must react—this is because
it is founded upon basic and universal desires, such as
the urge of the individual or the race to survive."

He lifted the pole he held.

"This," he said, "though it was used by humans long
before we began to study psychology consciously,
operates upon psychological principle—"

The view slid out along the rod, down the line
attached to its tip, and through the surface of the water.
It continued underwater down the line to a dirt worm
like the one in Kator's cube. Then it moved off to the
side a few inches and picked up the image of a native
underwater creature possessing no limbs, but a fan-
shaped tail and minor fans farther up the body. The
creature swam to the worm and swallowed it. Immediately it began to struggle and a close-up revealed a
barbed metal hook in the worm. The creature, however,
for all its struggling was drawn up out of the water by
the native, who hit it on the head and put it in a woven
box.

"You see," said the native, cheerfully, "that this
device makes use of the subject's—a 'fish' we call
it—desire to survive, on a very primitive level. To
survive the fish must eat. We offer it something to
eat, but in taking it, the fish delivers itself into our
hands, by fastening itself to the hook attached to our
line.

"All intelligent, space-going races we have encountered so far seem to exhibit the universal desire to survive. To survive, most seem to believe that they must dominate any other race they encounter, or risk domination themselves. Our study of psychology shows that this is a false assumption. To maintain its domination over another intelligent race, a race must eventually bankrupt its resources, both physical and non-physical. However—it is entirely practical for one race to maintain its domination long enough to teach another race that domination is impractical.

"The worm on my hook," he said, "is known as 'bait.' The worm you found in the wreckage of the human spaceship was symbolic of the fact that the wreckage itself was bait. We have many such pieces of bait drifting outwards from our area of space here. And as I told Kator Secondcousin Brutogas, you never can tell what you'll catch. The object in catching, of course, is to be able to study what takes the bait. Now, when Kator Secondcousin took the spaceship wreckage in tow, there was a monitor only half a light-year away that notified us of that fact. Kator's path home was charted and we immediately went to work, here.

"When your expeditionary ship came, it was allowed to land on our moon and an extensive study was made not only of it, but of the psychology of the Rumls you sent aboard it. After as much could be learned by that method as possible, we allowed one of your collectors to find our underground launching site and for one of your people to come down and actually enter it.

"We ran a number of maze-level tests on Kator Secondcousin while he was making his entrance to and escaping from the underground launching site. You'll be glad to hear that your Ruml intelligence tests quite highly, although you aren't what we'd call maze-sophisticated. We had little difficulty influencing Kator to leave the conveyor belt and follow a route that would lead him onto a surface too slippery to cross. As he fell we rendered him unconscious—"

There was a collective sound, half-grunt, half-gasp, from the listening Ruml audience.

"And, during the hour that followed, we were able to make complete physical tests and studies of an adult male Ruml. Then Kator was put back where he had fallen and allowed to return to consciousness. Then he was let escape."

The human got up, picked up his rod, picked up his woven basket with the underwater creature inside, and nodded to them.

"We now," he said, "know all about you. And you, with the exception of Kator, know nothing about us. Because of what we have learned about your psychology, we are confident that Kator's knowledge will not be allowed to do you any good." He lifted a finger. "I have one more scene to show you."

He vanished, and they looked instead into the immensity of open space. The constellations were vaguely familiar and those who had had experience recognized the spatial area as not far removed from their own planetary system. Through this star-dimness stretched inconceivable great shape followed by great shape, like dark giant demons waiting.

"Kator," said the voice of the native, "should have asked himself why there was so much empty space in the underground launching area. Come see us on Earth whenever you're ready to talk."

The scene winked out. In the new glare of the lights, the fifty-one proud heads of families stared at Kator Secondcousin, who stared back. Then, as if at some unconscious signal, they rose as one man and swarmed upon him.

"You fools!" cackled Kator with a Ruml's mad laughter, as he saw them coming at him. "Didn't he say you wouldn't have any use of what I know?" He went down under their claws. "Force won't work against these people—that's what he was trying to tell you! Why do you have to take the bait just the way I did—"

But it was no use. He felt himself dying.

"All right!" he choked at them, as a red haze began to blot out the world about him. "Learn the hard way for yourselves. Killing me won't do any good . . ."

And of course he was quite right. It didn't.

You may have noticed by now that you can be reading a Dickson story, thinking you know what's going on, and then suddenly—whoops, you should have watched that last step because it was a lulu! In this one, you're *really* going to have trouble figuring out just what a human is up to. Fortunately, the aliens have the same problem.

JACKAL'S MEAL

I

If there should follow a thousand swords
to carry my bones away—
Belike the price of a jackal's meal were
more than a thief could pay . . .
"The Ballad of East and West,"
by Rudyard Kipling

In the third hour after the docking of the great, personal spaceship of the Morah Jhan—on the planetoid outpost of the 469th Corps which was then stationed just outside the Jhan's spatial frontier—a naked figure in a ragged gray cloak burst from a crate of supplies being unloaded off the huge alien ship. The figure ran around uttering strange cries for a little while, eluding the Morah who had been doing the unloading, until it was captured at last by the human Military Police guarding the smaller, courier vessel, alongside, which had brought Ambassador Alan Dormu here from Earth to talk with the Jhan.

The Jhan himself, and Dormu—along with Marshal Sayers Whin and most of the other ranking officers, Morah and human alike—had already gone inside, to the Headquarters area of the outpost, where an athletic show was being put on for the Jhan's entertainment. But the young captain in charge of the Military Police, on his own initiative, refused the strong demands of the Morah that the fugitive be returned to them. For it, or he, showed signs of being—or of once having been— a man, under his rags and dirt and some surgicallike changes that had been made in him.

One thing was certain. He was deathly afraid of his Morah pursuers; and it was not until he was shut in a room out of sight of them that he quieted down. However, nothing could bring him to say anything humanly understandable. He merely stared at the faces of all those who came close to him, and felt their clothing as someone might fondle the most precious fabric made—and whimpered a little when the questions became too insistent, trying to hide his face in his arms but not succeeding because of the surgery that had been done to him.

The Morah went back to their own ship to contact their chain of command, leading ultimately up to the Jhan; and the young Military Police captain lost no time in getting the fugitive to his Headquarters' Section and the problem, into the hands of his own commanders. From whom, by way of natural military process, it rose through the ranks until it came to the attention of Marshal Sayers Whin.

"Hell's Bells—" exploded Whin, on hearing it. But then he checked himself and lowered his voice. He had been drawn aside by Harold Belman, the one-star general of the Corps who was his aide; and only a thin door separated him from the box where Dormu and the Jhan sat, still watching the athletic show. "Where is the . . . Where is he?"

"Down in my office, sir."

"This has got to be quite a mess!" said Whin. He thought rapidly. He was a tall, lean man from the Alaskan back country and his temper was usually short-lived. "Look, the show in there'll be over in a minute. Go in. My apologies to the Jhan. I've gone ahead to see everything's properly fixed for the meeting at lunch. Got that?"

"Yes, Marshal."

"Stick with the Jhan. Fill in for me."

"What if Dormu—"

"Tell him nothing. Even if he asks, play dumb. I've got to have time to sort this thing out, Harry! You understand?"

"Yes, sir," said his aide.

Whin went out a side door of the small anteroom, catching himself just in time from slamming it behind him. But once out in the corridor, he strode along at a pace that was almost a run.

He had to take a lift tube down eighteen levels to his aide's office. When he stepped in there, he found the fugitive surrounded by the officer of the day and some officers of the Military Police, including General Mack Stigh, Military Police Unit Commandant. Stigh was the ranking officer in the room; and it was to him Whin turned.

"What about it, Mack?"

"Sir, apparently he escaped from the Jhan's ship—"

"Not that. I know that. Did you find out who he is? What he is?" Whin glanced at the fugitive who was chewing hungrily on something grayish-brown that Whin recognized as a Morah product. One of the eatables supplied for the lunch meeting with the Jhan that would be starting any moment now. Whin grimaced.

"We tried him on our own food," said Stigh. "He wouldn't eat it. They may have played games with his digestive system, too. No, sir, we haven't found out anything. There've been a few undercover people sent into Morah territory in the past twenty years. He could be one of them. We've got a records search going on. Of course, chances are his record wouldn't be in our files, anyway."

"Stinking Morah," muttered a voice from among the officers standing around. Whin looked up quickly, and a new silence fell.

"Records search. All right," Whin said, turning back to Stigh, "that's good. What did the Morah say when what's-his-name—that officer on duty down at the docks—wouldn't give him up?"

"Captain—?" Stigh turned and picked out a young officer with his eyes. The young officer stepped forward.

"Captain Gene McKussic, Marshal," he introduced himself.

"You were the one on the docks?" Whin asked.

"Yes, sir."

"What did the Morah say?"

"Just—that he wasn't human, sir," said McKussic. "That he was one of their own experimental pets, made out of one of their own people—just to look human."

"What else?"

"That's all, Marshal."

"And you didn't believe them?"

"Look at him, sir—" McKussic pointed at the fugitive, who by this time had finished his food and was watching them with bright but timid eyes. "He hasn't got a hair on him, except where a man'd have it. Look at his face. And the shape of his head's human. Look at his fingernails, even—"

"Yes—" said Whin slowly, gazing at the fugitive. Then he raised his eyes and looked around at the other officers. "But none of you thought to get a doctor in here to check?"

"Sir," said Stigh, "we thought we should contact you, first—"

"All right. But get a doctor *now!* Get two of them!" said Whin. One of the other officers turned to a desk nearby and spoke into an intercom. "You know what we're up against, don't you—all of you?" Whin's eyes stabbed around the room. "This is just the thing to blow Ambassador Dormu's talk with the Morah Jhan sky high. Now, all of you, except General Stigh, get out of here. Go back to your quarters and stay on tap until you're given other orders. And keep your mouths shut."

"Marshal," it was the young Military Police captain, McKussic, "we aren't going to give him back to the Morah, no matter what, are we, sir . . ."

He trailed off. Whin merely looked at him.

"Get to your quarters, Captain!" said Stigh, roughly.

The room cleared. When they were left alone with the fugitive, Stigh's gaze went slowly to Whin.

"So," said Whin, "you're wondering that too, are you, Mack?"

"No, sir," said Stigh. "But word of this is probably spreading through the men like wildfire, by this time. There'll be no stopping it. And if it comes to the point of our turning back to the Morah a man who's been treated the way this man has—"

"They're soldiers!" said Whin, harshly. "They'll obey orders." He pointed at the fugitive. "That's a soldier."

"Not necessarily, Marshal," said Stigh. "He could have been one of the civilian agents—"

"For my purposes, he's a soldier!" snarled Whin. He took a couple of angry paces up and down the room in each direction, but always wheeling back to confront the fugitive. "Where are those doctors? I've got to get back to the Jhan and Dormu!"

"About Ambassador Dormu," Stigh said. "If he hears something about this and asks us—"

"Tell him nothing!" said Whin. "It's my responsibility! I'm not sure he's got the guts—never mind. The longer it is before the little squirt knows—"

The sound of the office door opening brought both men around.

"The little squirt already knows," said a dry voice from the doorway. Ambassador Alan Dormu came into the room. He was a slight, bent man, of less than average height. His fading blond hair was combed carefully forward over a balding forehead; and his face had deep, narrow lines that testified to even more years than hair and forehead.

"Who told you?" Whin gave him a mechanical grin.

"We diplomats always respect the privacy of our sources," said Dormu. "What difference does it make—as long as I found out? Because you're wrong, you know, Marshal. I'm the one who's responsible. I'm the one who'll have to answer the Jhan when he asks about this at lunch."

"Mack," said Whin, continuing to grin and with his eyes still fixed on Dormu, "see you later."

"Yes, Marshal."

Stigh went toward the door of the office. But before he reached it, it opened and two officers came in; a major and a lieutenant colonel, both wearing the caduceus. Stigh stopped and turned back.

"Here're the doctors, sir."

"Fine. Come here, come here, gentlemen," said Whin. "Take a look at this."

The two medical officers came up to the fugitive, sitting in the chair. They maintained poker faces. One reached for a wrist of the fugitive and felt for a pulse. The other went around back and ran his fingers lightly over the upper back with its misshapen and misplaced shoulder sockets.

"Well?" demanded Whin, after a restless minute. "What about it? Is he a man, all right?"

The two medical officers looked up. Oddly, it was the junior in rank, the major, who answered.

"We'll have to make tests—a good number of tests, sir," he said.

"You've no idea—now?" Whin demanded.

"Now," spoke up the lieutenant colonel, "he could be either Morah or human. The Morah are very, very, good at this sort of thing. The way those arms—We'll need samples of his blood, skin, bone marrow—"

"All right. All right," said Whin. "Take the time you need. But not one second more. We're all on the spot here, gentlemen. Mack—" he turned to Stigh, "I've changed my mind. You stick with the doctors and stand by to keep me informed."

He turned back to Dormu.

"We'd better be getting back upstairs, Mr. Ambassador," he said.

"Yes," answered Dormu, quietly.

They went out, paced down the corridor and entered the lift tube in silence.

"You know, of course, how this complicates things, Marshal," said Dormu, finally, as they began to rise up the tube together. Whin started like a man woken out of deep thought.

"What? You don't have to ask me that," he said. His voice took on an edge. "I suppose you'd expect my men to just stand around and watch, when something like that came running out of a Morah ship?"

"*I* might have," said Dormu. "In their shoes."

"Don't doubt it." Whin gave a single, small grunt of a laugh, without humor.

"I don't think you follow me," said Dormu. "I didn't bring up the subject to assign blame. I was just leading into the fact the damage done is going to have to be repaired, at any cost; and I'm counting on your immediate—note the word, Marshal—*immediate* cooperation, if and when I call for it."

The lift had carried them to the upper floor that was their destination. They got off together. Whin gave another humorless little grunt of laughter.

"You're thinking of handing him back, then?" Whin said.

"Wouldn't you?" asked Dormu.

"Not if he's human. No," said Whin. They walked on down a corridor and into a small room with another door. From beyond that other door came the faint smell of something like incense—it was, in fact, a neutral odor, tolerable to human and Morah alike and designed to hide the differing odors of one race from another. Also, from beyond the door, came the sound of three musical notes, steadily repeated; two notes exactly the same, and then a third, a half-note higher.

Tonk, tonk, TINK! . . .

"It's establishing a solid position for confrontation with the Than that's important right now," said Dormu, as they approached the other door. "He's got us over a barrel on the subject of this talk anyway, even without that business downstairs coming up. So it's the confrontation that counts. Nothing else."

They opened the door and went in.

Within was a rectangular, windowless room. Two tables had been set up. One for Dormu and Whin; and one for the Jhan, placed at right angles to the other table but not quite touching it. Both tables had been furnished and served with food; and the Jhan was already seated at his. To his right and left, each at about five feet of distance from him, flamed two purely symbolic torches in floor standards. Behind him stood three ordinary Morah—two servers, and a musician whose surgically-created, enormous forefinger tapped steadily at the bars of something like a small metal xylophone, hanging vertically on his chest.

The forefinger tapped in time to the three notes Whin and Dormu had heard in the room outside but without really touching the xylophone bars. The three notes actually sounded from a speaker overhead, broadcast throughout the station wherever the Jhan might be, along with the neutral perfume. They were a courtesy of the human hosts.

"Good to see you again, gentlemen," said the Jhan, through the mechanical interpreter at his throat. "I was about to start without you."

He sat, like the other Morah in the room, unclothed to the waist, below which he wore, though hidden now by the table, a simple kilt, or skirt, of dark red, feltlike cloth. The visible skin of his body, arms and face was a reddish brown in color, but there was only a limited amount of it to be seen. His upper chest, back, arms, neck and head—excluding his face—was covered by a mat of closely-trimmed, thick, gray hair, so noticeable in contrast to his hairless areas, that it looked more like a garment—a cowled half-jacket—than any natural growth upon him.

The face that looked out of the cowl-part was humanoid, but with wide jawbones, rounded chin and eyes set far apart over a flat nose. So that, although no one feature suggested it, his face as a whole had a faintly feline look.

"Our apologies," said Dormu, leading the way forward. "The marshal just received an urgent message for me from Earth, in a new code. And only I had the key to it."

"No need to apologize," said the Jhan. "We've had our musician here to entertain us while we waited."

Dormu and Whin sat down at the opposite ends of their table, facing each other and at right angles to the Jhan. The Jhan had already begun to eat. Whin stared deliberately at the foods on the Jhan's table, to make it plain that he was not avoiding looking at them, and then turned back to his own plate. He picked up a roll and buttered it.

"Your young men are remarkable in their agility," the Jhan said to Dormu. "We hope you will convey them our praise—"

They talked of the athletic show; and the meal progressed. As it was drawing to a close, the Jhan came around to the topic that had brought him to this meeting with Dormu.

" . . . It's unfortunate we have to meet under such necessities," he said.

"My own thought," replied Dormu. "You must come to Earth some time on a simple vacation."

"We would like to come to Earth—in peace," said the Jhan.

"We would hope not to welcome you any other way," said Dormu.

"No doubt," said the Than. "That is why it puzzles me, that when you humans can have peace for the asking—by simply refraining from creating problems—you continue to cause incidents, to trouble us and threaten our sovereignty over our own territory of space."

Dormu frowned.

"Incidents?" he echoed. "I don't recall any incidents. Perhaps the Jhan has been misinformed?"

"We are not misinformed," said the Jhan. "I refer to your human settlements on the fourth and fifth worlds of the star you refer to as 27J93; but which we call by a name of our own. Rightfully so because it is in our territory."

Tonk, tonk, TINK . . . went the three notes of the Morah music.

"It seems to me—if my memory is correct," murmured Dormu, "that the Treaty Survey made by our two races jointly, twelve years ago, left Sun 27J93 in unclaimed territory outside both our spatial areas."

"Quite right," said the Jhan. "But the Survey was later amended to include this and several other solar systems in our territory."

"Not by us, I'm afraid," said Dormu. "I'm sorry, but my people can't consider themselves automatically bound by whatever unilateral action you choose to take without consulting us."

"The action was not unilateral," said the Jhan, calmly. "We have since consulted with our brother Emperors—the Morah Selig, the Morah Ben, the Morah Yarra and the Morah Ness. All have concurred in recognizing the solar systems in question as being in our territory."

"But surely the Morah Jhan understands," said Dormu, "that an agreement only between the various political segments of one race can't be considered binding upon a people of another race entirely?"

"We of the Morah," said the Than, "reject your attitude that race is the basis for division between Empires. Territory is the only basis upon which Empires may be differentiated. Distinction between the races refers only to differences in shape or color; and as you know we do not regard any particular shape or color as sacredly, among ourselves, as you do; since we make many individuals over into what shape it pleases us, for our own use, or amusement."

He tilted his head toward the musician with the enormous, steadily jerking, forefinger.

"Nonetheless," said Dormu, "the Morah Jhan will not deny his kinship with the Morah of the other Morah Empires."

"Of course not. But what of it?" said the Jhan calmly. "In our eyes, your empire and those of our brothers, are in all ways similar. In essence you are only another group possessing a territory that is not ours. We make no difference between you and the empires of the other Morah."

"But if it came to an armed dispute between you and us," said Dormu, "would your brother Emperors remain neutral?"

"We hardly expect so," said the Morah Jhan, idly, pushing aside the last container of food that remained on the table before him. A server took it away. "But that would only be because, since right would be on our side, naturally they would rally to assist us."

"I see," said Dormu.

Tonk, tonk, TINK . . . went the sound of the Morah music.

"But why must we talk about such large and problematical issues?" said the Jhan. "Why not listen, instead, to the very simple and generous disposition we suggest for this matter of your settlements under 27J93? You will probably find our solution so agreeable that no more need be said on the subject."

"I'd be happy to hear it," said Dormu.

The Jhan leaned back in his seat at the table.

"In spite of the fact that our territory has been intruded upon," he said, "we ask only that you remove your people from their settlements and promise to avoid that area in future, recognizing these and the other solar systems I mentioned earlier as being in our territory. We will not even ask for ordinary reparations beyond the purely technical matter of your agreement to recognize what we Morah have already recognized, that the division of peoples is by territory, and not by race."

He paused. Dormu opened his mouth to speak.

"Of course," added the Jhan, "there is one additional, trivial concession we insist on. A token reparation— so that no precedent of not asking for reparations be set. That token concession is that you allow us corridors of transit across your spatial territory, through which our ships may pass without inspection between our empire and the empires of our brother Morah."

Dormu's mouth closed. The Jhan sat waiting. After a moment, Dormu spoke.

"I can only say," said Dormu, "that I am stunned and overwhelmed at these demands of the Morah Jhan. I was sent to this meeting only to explain to him that our settlements under Sun number 27J93 were entirely peaceful ones, constituting no human threat to his empire. I have no authority to treat with the conditions and terms just mentioned. I will have to contact my superiors back on Earth for instructions—and that will take several hours."

"Indeed?" said the Morah Jhan. "I'm surprised to hear you were sent all the way here to meet me with no more instructions than that. That represents such a limited authority that I almost begin to doubt the good will of you and your people in agreeing to this meeting."

"On our good will, of course," said Dormu, "the Morah Jhan can always depend."

"Can I?" The wide-spaced eyes narrowed suddenly in the catlike face. "Things seem to conspire to make me doubt it. Just before you gentlemen joined me I was informed of a most curious fact by my officers. It seems some of your Military Police have kidnapped one of my Morah and are holding him prisoner."

"Oh?" said Dormu. His face registered polite astonishment. "I don't see how anything like that could have happened." He turned to Whin. "Marshal, did you hear about anything like that taking place?"

Whin grinned his mechanical grin at the Morah Jhan.

"I heard somebody had been picked up down at the docks," he said. "But I understood he was human. One of our people who'd been missing for some time—a deserter, maybe. A purely routine matter. It's being checked out, now."

"I would suggest that the marshal look more closely into the matter," said the Jhan. His eyes were still slitted. "I promise him he will find the individual is a Morah; and of course, I expect the prisoner's immediate return."

"The Morah Jhan can rest assured," said Whin, "any Morah held by my troops will be returned to him, immediately."

"I will expect that return then," said the Jhan, "by the time Ambassador Dormu has received his instructions from Earth and we meet to talk again."

He rose, abruptly; and without any further word, turned and left the room. The servers and the musician followed him.

❖   ❖   ❖

Dormu got as abruptly to his own feet and led the way back out of the room in the direction from which he and Whin had come.

"Where are you going?" demanded Whin. "We go left for the lifts to the Message Center."

"We're going back to look at our kidnapped prisoner," said Dormu. "I don't need the Message Center."

Whin looked sideways at him.

"So . . . you *were* sent out here with authority to talk on those terms of his, after all, then?" Whin asked.

"We expected them," said Dormu briefly.

"What are you going to do about them?"

"Give in," said Dormu. "On all but the business of giving them corridors through our space. That's a first step to breaking us up into territorial segments."

"Just like that —" said Whin. "You'll give in?"

Dormu looked at him, briefly.

"You'd fight, I suppose?"

"If necessary," said Whin. They got into the lift tube and slipped downward together.

"And you'd lose," said Dormu.

"Against the Morah Jhan?" demanded Whin. "I know within ten ships what his strength is."

"No. Against all the Morah," answered Dormu. "This situation's been carefully set up. Do you think the Jhan would ordinarily be that much concerned about a couple of small settlements of our people, away off beyond his natural frontiers? The Morah—all the Morah—have started to worry about our getting too big for them to handle. They've set up a coalition of all their so-called Empires to contain us before that happens. If we fight the Jhan, we'll find ourselves fighting them all."

The skin of Whin's face grew tight.

"Giving in to a race like the Morah won't help," he said.

"It may gain us time," said Dormu. "We're a single, integrated society. They aren't. In five years, ten years, we can double our fighting strength. Meanwhile their coalition members may even start fighting among themselves. That's why I was sent here to do what I'm doing—give up enough ground so that they'll have no excuse for starting trouble at this time; but not enough ground so that they'll feel safe in trying to push further."

"Why won't they—if they know they can win?"

"Jhan has to count the cost to him personally, if he starts the war," said Dormu, briefly. They got off the lift tube. "Which way's the Medical Section?"

"There"—Whin pointed. They started walking. "What makes you so sure he won't think the cost is worth it?"

"Because," said Dormu, "he has to stop and figure what would happen if, being the one to start the war, he ended up more weakened by it than his brother-emperors were. The others would turn on him like wolves, given the chance; just like he'd turn on any of them. And he knows it."

Whin grunted his little, humorless laugh.

They found the fugitive lying on his back on an examination table in one of the diagnostic rooms of the Medical Section. He was plainly unconscious.

"Well?" Whin demanded bluntly of the medical lieutenant colonel. "Man, or Morah?"

The lieutenant colonel was washing his hands. He hesitated, then rinsed his fingers and took up a towel.

"Out with it!" snapped Whin.

"Marshal," the lieutenant colonel hesitated again, "to be truthful . . . we may never know."

"Never know?" demanded Dormu. General Stigh came into the room, his mouth open as if about to say something to Whin. He checked at the sight of Dormu and the sound of the ambassador's voice.

"There's human RNA involved," said the lieutenant colonel. "But we know that the Morah have access to human bodies from time to time, soon enough after the moment of death so that the RNA might be preserved. But bone and flesh samples indicate Morah, rather than human origin. He could be human and his RNA be the one thing about him the Morah didn't monkey with. Or he could be Morah, treated with human RNA to back up the surgical changes that make him resemble a human. I don't think we can tell, with the facilities we've got here; and in any case—"

"In any case," said Dormu, slowly, "it may not really matter to the Jhan."

Whin raised his eyebrows questioningly; but just then he caught sight of Stigh.

"Mack?" he said. "What is it?"

Stigh produced a folder.

"I think we've found out who he is," the Military Police general said. "Look here—a civilian agent of the Intelligence Service was sent secretly into the spatial territory of the Morah Jhan eight years ago. Name— Paul Edmonds. Description—superficially the same size and build as this man here." He nodded at the still figure on the examining table. "We can check the retinal patterns and fingerprints."

"It won't do you any good," said the lieutenant colonel. "Both fingers and retinas conform to the Morah pattern."

"May I see that?" asked Dormu. Stigh passed over the folder. The little ambassador took it. "Eight years ago, I was the State Department's Liaison Officer with the Intelligence Service."

He ran his eyes over the information on the sheets in the folder.

"There's something I didn't finish telling you," said the lieutenant colonel, appealing to Whin, now that

Dormu's attention was occupied. "I started to say I didn't think we could tell whether he's man or Morah; but in any case—the question's probably academic. He's dying."

"Dying?" said Dormu sharply, looking up from the folder. "What do you mean?"

Without looking, he passed the folder back to Stigh.

"I mean . . . he's dying," said the lieutenant colonel, a little stubbornly. "It's amazing that any organism, human or Morah, was able to survive, in the first place, after being cut up and altered that much. His running around down on the docks was evidently just too much for him. He's bleeding to death internally from a hundred different pinpoint lesions."

"Hm-m-m," said Whin. He looked sharply at Dormu. "Do you think the Jhan would be just as satisfied if he got a body back, instead of a live man?"

"Would you?" retorted Dormu.

"Hm-m-m . . . no. I guess I wouldn't," said Whin. He turned to look grimly at the unconscious figure on the table; and spoke almost to himself. "If he *is* Paul Edmonds—"

"Sir," said Stigh, appealingly.

Whin looked at the general. Stigh hesitated.

"If I could speak to the marshal privately for a moment—" he said.

"Never mind," said Whin. The line of his mouth was tight and straight. "I think I know what you've got to tell me. Let the ambassador hear it, too."

"Yes, sir." But Stigh still looked uncomfortable. He glanced at Dormu, glanced away again, fixed his gaze on Whin. "Sir, word about this man has gotten out all over the Outpost. There's a lot of feeling among the officers and men alike—a lot of feeling against handing him back . . ."

He trailed off.

"You mean to say," said Dormu sharply, "that they won't obey if ordered to return this individual?"

"They'll obey," said Whin, softly. Without turning his head, he spoke to the lieutenant colonel. "Wait outside for us, will you, Doctor?"

The lieutenant colonel went out, and the door closed behind him. Whin turned and looked down at the fugitive on the table. In unconsciousness the face was relaxed, neither human nor Morah, but just a face, out of many possible faces. Whin looked up again and saw Dormu's eyes still on him.

"You don't understand, Mr. Ambassador," Whin said, in the same soft voice. "These men are veterans. You heard the doctor talking about the fact that the Morah have had access to human RNA. This outpost has had little, unreported, border clashes with them every so often. The personnel here have seen the bodies of the men we've recovered. They know what it means to fall into Morah hands. To deliberately deliver anyone back into those hands is something pretty hard for them to take. But they're soldiers. They won't refuse an order."

He stopped talking. For a moment there was silence in the room.

"I see," said Dormu. He went across to the door and opened it. The medical lieutenant colonel was outside, and he turned to face Dormu in the opened door. "Doctor, you said this individual was dying."

"Yes," answered the lieutenant colonel.

"How long?"

"A couple of hours—" the lieutenant colonel shrugged helplessly. "A couple of minutes. I've no way of telling, nothing to go on, by way of comparable experience."

"All right." Dormu turned back to Whin. "Marshal, I'd like to get back to the Jhan as soon as the minimum amount of time's past that could account for a message to Earth and back."

✧   ✧   ✧

An hour and a half later, Whin and Dormu once more entered the room where they had lunched with the Jhan. The tables were removed now; and the servers were gone. The musician was still there; and, joining him now, were two grotesqueries of altered Morah, with tiny, spidery bodies and great, grinning heads. These scuttled and climbed on the heavy, thronelike chair in which the Than sat, grinning around it and their Emperor, at the two humans.

"You're prompt," said the Jhan to Dormu. "That's promising."

"I believe you'll find it so," said Dormu. "I've been authorized to agree completely to your conditions—with the minor exceptions of the matter of recognizing that the division of peoples is by territory and not by race, and the matter of spatial corridors for you through our territory. The first would require a referendum of the total voting population of our people, which would take several years; and the second is beyond the present authority of my superiors to grant. But both matters will be studied."

"This is not satisfactory."

"I'm sorry," said Dormu. "Everything in your proposal that it's possible for us to agree to at this time has been agreed to. The Morah Jhan must give us credit for doing the best we can on short notice to accommodate him."

"Give you credit?" The Jhan's voice thinned; and the two bigheaded monsters playing about his feet froze like startled animals, staring at him. "Where is my kidnapped Morah?"

"I'm sorry," said Dormu, carefully, "that matter has been investigated. As we suspected, the individual you mention turns out not to be a Morah, but a human. We've located his records. A Paul Edmonds."

"What sort of lie is this?" said the Jhan. "He is a Morah. No human. You may let yourself be deluded by the fact he looks like yourselves, but don't try to think you can delude us with looks. As I told you, it's our privilege to play with the shapes of individuals, casting them into the mold we want, to amuse ourselves; and the mold we played with in this case, was like your own. So be more careful in your answers. I would not want to decide you deliberately kidnapped this Morah, as an affront to provoke me."

"The Morah Jhan," said Dormu, colorlessly, "must know how unlikely such an action on our part would be—as unlikely as the possibility that the Morah might have arranged to turn this individual loose, in order to embarrass us in the midst of these talks."

The Jhan's eyes slitted down until their openings showed hardly wider than two heavy pencil lines.

"*You* do not accuse *me*, human!" said the Jhan. "*I* accuse *you*! Affront my dignity; and less than an hour after I lift ship from this planetoid of yours, I can have a fleet here that will reduce it to one large cinder!"

He paused. Dormu said nothing. After a long moment, the slitted eyes relaxed, opening a little.

"But I will be kind," said the Jhan. "Perhaps there is some excuse for your behavior. You have been misled, perhaps—by this business of records, the testimony of those amateur butchers you humans call physicians and surgeons. Let me set your mind at rest. I, the Morah Jhan, assure you that this prisoner of yours is a Morah, one of my own Morah; and no human. Naturally, you will return him now, immediately, in as good shape as when he was taken from us."

"That, in any case, is not possible," said Dormu.

"How?" said the Jhan.

"The man," said Dormu, "is dying."

The Jhan sat without motion or sound for as long as a roan might comfortably hold his breath. Then, he spoke.

"The *Morah*," he said. "I will not warn you again."

"My apologies to the Morah Jhan," said Dormu, tonelessly. "I respect his assurances, but I am required to believe our own records and experienced men. The *man*, I say, is dying."

The Jhan rose suddenly to his feet. The two small Morah scuttled away behind him toward the door.

"I will go to the quarters you've provided me, now," said the Jhan, "and make my retinue ready to leave. In one of your hours, I will reboard my ship. You have until that moment to return my Morah to me."

He turned, went around his chair and out of the room. The door shut behind him.

Dormu turned and headed out the door at their side of the room. Whin followed him. As they opened the door, they saw Stigh, waiting there. Whin opened his mouth to speak, but Dormu beat him to it.

"Dead?" Dormu asked.

"He died just a few minutes ago—almost as soon as you'd both gone in to talk to the Jhan," said Stigh.

Whin slowly closed his mouth. Stigh stood without saying anything further. They both waited, watching Dormu, who did not seem to be aware of their gaze. At Stigh's answer, his face had become tight, his eyes abstract.

"Well," said Whin, after a long moment and Dormu still stood abstracted, "it's a body now."

His eyes were sharp on Dormu. The little man jerked his head up suddenly and turned to face the marshal.

"Yes," said Dormu, a little strangely. "He'll have to

be buried, won't he? You won't object to a burial with full military honors?"

"Hell, no!" said Whin. "He earned it. When?"

"Right away." Dormu puffed out a little sigh like a weary man whose long day is yet far from over. "Before the Jhan leaves. And not quietly. Broadcast it through the Outpost."

Whin swore gently under his breath, with a sort of grim happiness.

"See to it!" he said to Stigh. After Stigh had gone, he added softly to Dormu. "Forgive me. You're a good man once the chips are down, Mr. Ambassador."

"You think so?" said Dormu, wryly. He turned abruptly toward the lift tubes. "We'd better get down to the docking area. The Jhan said an hour—but he may not wait that long."

The Jhan did not wait. He cut his hour short, like someone eager to accomplish his leaving before events should dissuade him. He was at the docking area twenty minutes later; and only the fact that it was Morah protocol that his entourage must board before him, caused him to be still on the dock when the first notes of the Attention Call sounded through the Outpost.

The Jhan stopped, with one foot on the gangway to his vessel. He turned about and saw the dockside Military Police all now at attention, facing the nearest command screen three meters wide by two high, which had just come to life on the side of the main docking warehouse. The Jhan's own eyes went to the image on the screen—to the open grave, the armed soldiers, the chaplain and the bugler.

The chaplain was already reading the last paragraph of the burial service. The religious content of the human words could have no meaning to the Jhan; but his eyes went comprehendingly, directly to Dormu, standing with Whin on the other side of the gangway. The Jhan took a step that brought him within a couple of feet of the little man.

"I see," the Jhan said. "He is dead."

"He died while we were last speaking," answered Dormu, without inflection. "We are giving him an honorable funeral."

"I see—" began the Jhan, again. He was interrupted by the sound of fired volleys as the burial service ended and the blank-faced coffin began to be let down into the pulverized rock of the Outpost. A command sounded from the screen. The soldiers who had just fired went to present arms—along with every soldier in sight in the docking area—as the bugler raised his instrument and taps began to sound.

"Yes." The Jhan looked around at the saluting Military Police, then back at Dormu. "You are a fool," he said, softly. "I had no conception that a human like yourself could be so much a fool. You handled my demands well—but what value is a dead body, to anyone? If you had returned it, I would have taken no action— this time, at least, after your concessions on the settlements. But you not only threw away all you'd gained, you flaunted defiance in my face, by burying the body before I could leave this Outpost. I've no choice now—after an affront like that. I must act."

"No," said Dormu.

"No?" The Jhan stared at him.

"You have no affront to react against," said Dormu. "You erred only through a misunderstanding."

"Misunderstanding?" said the Jhan. "*I* misunderstood? I not only did not misunderstand, I made the greatest effort to see that you did not misunderstand. I cannot let you take a Morah from me, just because he looks like a human. And he *was* a Morah. You did not need your records, or your physicians, to tell you that. My word was enough. But you let your emotions, the counsel of these lesser people, sway you—to your disaster, now. Do you think I didn't know how all these soldiers of yours were feeling? But *I* am the Morah Jhan. Did you think I would lie over anything so insignificant as one stray pet?"

"No," said Dormu.

"Now—" said the Jhan. "Now, you face the fact. But it is too late. You have affronted me. I told you it is our privilege and pleasure to play with the shapes of beings, making them into what we desire. I told you the shape did not mean he was human. I told you he was Morah. You kept him and buried him anyway, thinking he was human—thinking he was that lost spy of yours." He stared down at Dormu. "I told you he was a Morah."

"I believed you," said Dormu.

The Jhan's eyes stared. They widened, flickered, then narrowed down until they were nothing but slits, once more.

"You believed me? You *knew* he was a Morah?"

"I knew," said Dormu. "I was Liaison Officer with the Intelligence Service at the time Edmonds was sent out—and later when his body was recovered. We have no missing agent here."

His voice did not change tone. His face did not change expression. He looked steadily up into the face of the Jhan.

"I explained to the Morah Jhan, just now," said Dormu, almost pedantically, "that through misapprehension, he had erred. We are a reasonable people, who love peace. To soothe the feelings of the Morah Jhan we will abandon our settlements, and make as many other adjustments to his demands as are reasonably possible. But the Jhan must not confuse one thing with another."

"What thing?" demanded the Jhan. "With what thing?"

"Some things we do not permit," said Dormu. Suddenly, astonishingly, to the watching Whin, the little man seemed to grow. His back straightened, his head lifted, his eyes looked almost on a level up into the slit-eyes of the Jhan. His voice sounded hard, suddenly, and loud. "The Morah belong to the Morah Jhan; and you told us it's your privilege to play with their shapes. Play with them then—in all but a single way. Use any shape but one. You played with that shape, and forfeited your right to what we just buried. Remember it, Morah Jhan! *the shape of Man belongs to Men, alone!*"

He stood, facing directly into the slitted gaze of Jhan, as the bugle sounded the last notes of taps and the screen went blank. About the docks, the Military Police lowered their weapons from the present-arms position.

For a long second, the Jhan stared back. Then he spoke.

"I'll be back!" he said; and, turning, the red kilt whipping about his legs, he strode up the gangplank into his ship.

"But he won't," muttered Dormu, with grim satisfaction, gazing at the gangplank, beginning to be sucked up into the ship now, preparatory to departure.

"Won't?" almost stammered Whin, beside him. "What do you mean ... *won't?*"

Dormu turned to the marshal.

"If he were really coming back with all weapons hot, there was no need to tell me." Dormu smiled a little, but still grimly. "He left with a threat because it was the only way he could save face."

"But you ..." Whin was close to stammering again; only this time with anger. "You knew that ... that creation . . . wasn't Edmonds from the start! If the men on this Outpost had known it was a stinking Morah, they'd have been ready to hand him back in a minute. You let us all put our lives on the line here—for something that only *looked* like a man!"

Dormu looked at him.

"Marshal," he said. "I told you it was the confrontation with the Jhan that counted. We've got that. Two hours ago, the Jhan and all the other Morah leaders thought they knew us. Now they—a people who think shape isn't important—suddenly find themselves facing a race who consider their shape sacred. This is a concept they are inherently unable to understand. If that's true of us, what else may not be true? Suddenly, they don't understand us at all. The Morah aren't fools. They'll go back and rethink their plans, now—all their plans."

Whin blinked at him, opened his mouth angrily to speak—closed it again, then opened it once more.

"But you risked . . ." he ran out of words and ended shaking his head, in angry bewilderment. "And you let me bury it—with honors!"

"Marshal," said Dormu, suddenly weary, "it's your job to win wars, after they're started. It's my job to win them before they start. Like you, I do my job in any way I can."

It's hard to pick out a best or favorite story by an author as good and prolific as Gordon R. Dickson, but "On Messenger Mountain" would definitely make my short list. In this one, he adds ingredients from such milestones of sf as Murray Leinster's "First Contact" and John W. Campbell's "Who Goes There?" and comes up with a very different story from either of those classics. Someone once categorized conflict in fiction into three types—man against nature, man against man, and man against himself—and argued that the third type produced the "highest" quality of fiction. Whether or not that is true, this story certainly explores man against nature and man against man (not to mention man against alien and alien against nature), but might seem to ignore man against himself . . . until that very last line (and don't go look at it *now*, dammit—read the *story* first!) that suddenly makes it clear what the story was *really* about.

ON MESSENGER MOUNTAIN

I

It was raw, red war for all of them, from the moment the two ships intercepted each other, one degree off the plane of the ecliptic and three diameters out from the second planet of the star that was down on the charts as K94. K94 was a GO type star; and the yelping battle alarm of the trouble horn tumbled sixteen men to their stations. This was at thirteen hours, twenty-one minutes, four seconds of the ship's day.

Square in the scope of the laser screen, before the Survey Team Leader aboard the *Harrier*, appeared the gray, light-edged silhouette of a ship unknown to the ship's library. And the automatic reflexes of the computer aboard, that takes no account of men not yet into their vacuum suits, took over. The *Harrier* disappeared into no-time.

She came out again at less than a quarter-mile's distance from the stranger ship and released a five-pound weight at a velocity of five miles a second relative to the velocity of the alien ship. Then she had gone back into no-time again—but not before the alien, with computer-driven reflexes of its own, had rolled like the elongated cylinder it resembled, and laid out a soft green-colored beam of radiation which opened up the *Harrier* forward like a hot knife through butter left long on the table. Then it too was gone into no-time. The time aboard the *Harrier* was thirteen hours, twenty-two minutes and eighteen seconds; and on both ships there were dead.

"There are good people in the human race," Cal Hartlett had written only two months before, to his uncle on Earth, *"who feel that it is not right to attack other intelligent beings without warning—to drop five-pound weights at destructive relative velocities on a strange ship simply because you find it at large in space and do not know the race that built it.*

"What these gentle souls forget is that when two strangers encounter in space, nothing at all is known— and everything must be. The fates of both races may hinge on which one is first to kill the other and study the unknown carcass. Once contact is made, there is

*no backing out and no time for consideration. For we
are not out here by chance, neither are they, and we
do not meet by accident."*

Cal Hartlett was Leader of the Mapping Section
aboard the *Harrier,* and one of those who lived
through that first brush with the enemy. He wrote
what he wrote as clearly as if he had been Survey
Leader and in command of the ship. At any moment
up until the final second when it was too late, Joe
Aspinall, the Survey Leader, could have taken the
Harrier into no-time and saved them. He did not; as
no commander of a Survey Ship ever has. In theory,
they could have escaped.

In practice, they had no choice.

When the *Harrier* ducked back into no-time, aboard
her they could hear the slamming of emergency bulkheads. The mapping room, the fore weight-discharge
room and the sleeping quarters all crashed shut as
the atmosphere of the ship whiffed out into space
through the wound the enemy's beam had made. The
men beyond the bulkheads and in the damaged sections would have needed to be in their vacuum suits
to survive. There had not been time for that, so those
men were dead.

The *Harrier* winked back into normal space.

Her computer had brought her out on the far side
of the second planet, which they had not yet surveyed.
It was larger than Earth, with somewhat less gravity
but a deeper atmospheric envelope. The laser screen
picked up the enemy reappearing almost where she had
disappeared, near the edge of that atmosphere.

The *Harrier* winked back all but alongside the other
and laid a second five-pound weight through the center of the cylindrical vessel. The other ship staggered,
disappeared into no-time and appeared again far below,

some five miles above planetary surface in what seemed a desperation attempt to gain breathing time. The *Harrier* winked after her—and came out within five hundred yards, square in the path of the green beam which it seemed was waiting for her. It opened up the drive and control rooms aft like a red-hot poker lays open a cardboard box.

A few miles below, the surface stretched up the peaks of titanic mountains from horizon to horizon.

"Ram!" yelled the voice of Survey Leader Aspinwall, in warning over the intercom.

The *Harrier* flung itself at the enemy. It hit like an elevator falling ten stories to a concrete basement. The cylindrical ship broke in half in midair and bodies erupted from it. Then its broken halves and the ruined *Harrier* were falling separately to the surface below and there was no more time for anyone to look. The clock stood at 13 hrs., 23 minutes and 4 seconds.

The power—except from emergency storage units—was all but gone. As Joe punched for a landing the ship fell angling past the side of a mountain that was a monster among giants, and jarred to a stop. Joe keyed the intercom of the control board before him.

"Report," he said.

In the Mapping Section Cal Hartlett waited for other voices to speak before him. None came. He thumbed his audio.

"The whole front part of the ship's dogged shut, Joe," he said. "No use waiting for anyone up there. So—this is Number Six reporting. I'm all right."

"Number Seven," said another voice over the intercom. "Maury. O.K."

"Number Eight. Sam. O.K."

"Number Nine. John. O.K. . . ."

Reports went on. Numbers Six through Thirteen

reported themselves as not even shaken up. From the rest there was no answer.

In the main Control Section, Joe Aspinwall stared bleakly at his dead control board. Half of his team was dead.

The time was 13 hours, 30 minutes, no seconds.

He shoved that thought from his mind and concentrated on the positive rather than the negative elements of the situation they were in. Cal Hartlett, he thought, was one. Since he could only have eight survivors of his Team, he felt a deep gratitude that Cal should be one of them. He would need Cal in the days to come. And the other survivors of the Team would need him, badly.

Whether they thought so at this moment or not.

"All right," said Joe, when the voices had ended. "We'll meet outside the main airlock, outside the ship. There's no power left to unseal those emergency bulkheads. Cal, Doug, Jeff—you'll probably have to cut your way out through the ship's side. Everybody into respirators and warmsuits. According to pre-survey"—he glanced at the instruments before him—"there's oxygen enough in the local atmosphere for the respirators to extract, so you won't need emergency bottles. But we're at twenty-seven thousand three hundred above local sea-level. So it'll probably be cold—even if the atmosphere's not as thin here as it would be at this altitude on Earth." He paused. "Everybody got that? Report!"

They reported. Joe unharnessed himself and got up from his seat. Turning around, he faced Maury Taller.

Maury, rising and turning from his own communications board on the other side of the Section, saw that the Survey Leader's lean face was set in iron lines of shock and sorrow under his red hair. They were the two oldest members of the Team, whose average age had been in the mid-twenties. They looked at each other without words as they went down the narrow tunnel to the main airlock and, after putting on respirators and warmsuits, out into the alien daylight outside.

The eight of them gathered together outside the arrowhead shape of their *Harrier*, ripped open fore and aft and as still now as any other murdered thing.

Above them was a high, blue-black sky and the peaks of mountains larger than any Earth had ever known. A wind blew about them as they stood on the side of one of the mountains, on a half-mile wide shelf of tilted rock. It narrowed backward and upward like a dry streambed up the side of the mountain in one direction. In the other it broke off abruptly fifty yards away, in a cliff-edge that hung over eye-shuddering depths of a clefted valley, down in which they could just glimpse a touch of something like jungle greenness.

Beyond that narrow clefted depth lifted the great mountains, like carvings of alien devils too huge to be completely seen from one point alone. Several thousand feet above them on their mountain, the white spill of a glacier flung down a slope that was too steep for ice to have clung to in the heavier gravity of Earth. Above the glacier, which was shaped like a hook, red-gray peaks of the mountain rose like short towers stabbing the blue-dark sky. And from these, even as far down as the men were, they could hear the distant trumpeting and screaming of winds whistling in the peaks.

They took it all in in a glance. And that was all they had time to do. Because in the same moment that their eyes took in their surroundings, something no bigger than a man but tiger-striped and moving with a speed that was more than human, came around the near end of the dead *Harrier*, and went through the eight men like a predator through a huddle of goats.

Maury Taller and even Cal, who towered half a head over the rest of the men, all were brushed aside like cardboard cutouts of human figures. Sam Cloate, Cal's assistant in the mapping section, was ripped open by one sweep of a clawed limb as it charged past, and the creature tore out the throat of Mike DeWall with a sideways slash of its jaws. Then it was on Joe Aspinall.

The Survey Team Leader went down under it. Reflex that got metal cuffs on the gloves of his warmsuit up and crossed in front of his throat, his forearms and elbows guarding his belly, before he felt the ferocious weight grinding him into the rock and twisting about on top of him. A snarling, worrying, noise sounded in his ears. He felt teeth shear through the upper part of his thigh and grate on bone.

There was an explosion. He caught just a glimpse of Cal towering oddly above him, a signal pistol fuming in one big hand.

Then the worrying weight pitched itself full upon him and lay still. And unconsciousness claimed him.

II

When Joe came to, his respirator mask was no longer on his face. He was looking out, through the slight waviness of a magnetic bubble field, at ten mounds of small rocks and gravel in a row about twenty feet from the ship. Nine crosses and one six-pointed star. The Star of David would be for Mike DeWall. Joe looked up and saw the unmasked face of Maury Taller looming over him, with the dark outside skin of the ship beyond him.

"How're you feeling, Joe?" Maury asked.

"All right," he answered. Suddenly he lifted his

head in fright. "My leg—I can't feel my leg!" Then he saw the silver anesthetic band that was clamped about his right leg, high on the thigh. He sank back with a sigh.

Maury said, "You'll be all right, Joe."

The words seemed to trip a trigger in his mind. Suddenly the implications of his damaged leg burst on him. He was the Leader!

"Help me!" he gritted, trying to sit up.

"You ought to lie still."

"Help me up, I said!" The leg was a dead weight. Maury's hands took hold and helped raise his body. He got the leg swung off the edge of the surface on which he had been lying, and got into sitting position. He looked around him.

The magnetic bubble had been set up to make a small, air-filled addition of breathable ship's atmosphere around the airlock entrance of the *Harrier*. It enclosed about as much space as a good-sized living room. Its floor was the mountain hillside's rock and gravel. A mattress from one of the ship's bunks had been set up on equipment boxes to make him a bed. At the other end of the bubble-enclosed space something as big as a man was lying zippered up in a gray cargo freeze-sack.

"What's that?" Joe demanded. "Where's everybody?"

"They're checking equipment in the damaged sections," answered Maury. "We shot you full of medical juices. You've been out about twenty hours. That's about three-quarters of a local day-and-night cycle locally, here." He grabbed the wounded man's shoulders suddenly with both hands. "Hold it! What're you trying to do?"

"Have a look in that freeze-sack there," grunted the Team Leader between his teeth. "Let go of me, Maury. I'm still in charge here!"

"Sit still," said Maury. "I'll bring it to you."

He went over to the bag, taking hold of one of the carrying handles he dragged it back. It came easily in the lesser gravity, only a little more than eight-tenths of Earth's. He hauled the thing to the bed and unzipped it.

Joe stared. What was inside was not what he had been expecting.

"Cute, isn't it?" said Maury.

They looked down at the hard-frozen gray body of a biped, with the back of its skull shattered and burnt by the flare of a signal pistol. It lay on its back. The legs were somewhat short for the body and thick, as the arms were thick. But elbow and knee joints were where they should be, and the hands had four stubby gray fingers, each with an opposed thumb. Like the limbs, the body was thick—almost waistless. There were deep creases, as if tucks had been taken in the skin, around the body under the armpits, around the waist and around the legs and arms.

The head, though, was the startling feature. It was heavy and round as a ball, sunk into thick folds of neck and all but featureless. Two long slits ran down each side into the neck and shoulder area. The slits were tight closed. Like the rest of the body, the head had no hair. The eyes were little pock-marks, like raisins sunk into a doughball, and there were no visible brow ridges. The nose was a snout-end set almost flush with the facial surface. The mouth was lipless, a line of skin folded together, through which now glinted barely a glimpse of close-set, large, tridentated teeth.

"What's this?" said Joe. "Where's the thing that attacked us?"

"This is it," said Maury. "One of the aliens from the other ship."

Joe stared at him. In the brighter, harsher light from

the star K94 overhead, he noticed for the first time a sprinkling of gray hairs in the black shock above Maury's spade-shaped face. Maury was no older than Joe himself.

"What're you talking about?" said Joe. "I saw that thing that attacked me. And this isn't it!"

"Look," said Maury and turned to the foot of the bed. From one of the equipment boxes he brought up eight by ten inch density photographs. "Here," he said, handing them to the Survey Team Leader. "The first one is set for bone density."

Joe took them. It showed the skeleton of the being at his feet . . . and it bore only a relative kinship to the shape of the being itself.

Under the flesh and skin that seemed so abnormally thick, the skull was high-forebrained and well developed. Heavy brown ridges showed over deep wells for the eyes. The jaw and teeth were the prognathous equipment of a carnivorous animal.

But that was only the beginning of the oddities. Bony ridges of gill structures were buried under a long fold on either side of the head, neck and shoulders. The rib cage was enormous and the pelvis tiny, buried under eight or nine inches of the gray flesh. The limbs were literally double-jointed. There was a fantastic double structure of ball and socket that seemed wholly unnecessary. Maury saw the Survey Leader staring at one hip joint and leaned over to tap it with the blunt nail of his forefinger.

"Swivel and lock," said Maury. "If the joint's pulled out, it can turn in any direction. Then, if the muscles surrounding it contract, the two ball joints interlace those bony spurs there and lock together so that they operate as a single joint in the direction chosen. That hip joint can act like the hip joint on the hind leg of a quadruped, or the leg of a biped. It can even adapt for jumping and running with maximum efficiency.—Look at the toes and the fingers."

Joe looked. Hidden under flesh, the bones of feet and hands were not stubby and short, but long and powerful. And at the end of finger and toe bones were the curved, conical claws they had seen rip open Sam Cloate with one passing blow.

"Look at these other pictures now," said Maury, taking the first one off the stack Joe held. "These have been set for densities of muscle—that's this one here—and fat. Here. And this one is set for soft internal organs—here." He was down to the last. "And this one was set for the density of the skin. Look at that. See how thick it is, and how great folds of it are literally tucked away underneath in those creases.

"Now," said Maury, "look at this closeup of a muscle. See how it resembles an interlocking arrangement of innumerable tiny muscles? Those small muscles can literally shift to adapt to different skeletal positions. They can take away beef from one area and add it to an adjoining area. Each little muscle actually holds on to its neighbors, and they have little sphincter-sealed tube-systems to hook on to whatever blood-conduit is close. By increased hookup they can increase the blood supply to any particular muscle that's being overworked. There's parallel nerve connections."

Maury stopped and looked at the other man.

"You see?" said Maury. "This alien can literally be four or five different kinds of animal. Even a fish! And no telling how many varieties of each kind. We wondered a little at first why he wasn't wearing any kind of clothing, but we didn't wonder after we got these pictures. Why would he need clothing when he can adapt to any situation—Joe!" said Maury. "You see it, don't you? You see the natural advantage these things have over us all?"

Joe shook his head.

"There's no body hair," he said. "The creature that jumped me was striped like a tiger."

"Pigmentation. In response to emotion, maybe," said Maury. "For camouflage—or for terrifying the victims."

Joe sat staring at the pictures in his hand.

"All right," he said after a bit. "Then tell me how he happened to get here three or four minutes after we fell down here ourselves? And where did he come from? We rammed that other ship a good five miles up."

"There's only one way, the rest of us figured it out," said Maury. "He was one of the ones who were spilled out when we hit them. He must have grabbed our hull and ridden us down."

"That's impossible!"

"Not if he could flatten himself out and develop suckers like a starfish," said Maury. "The skin picture shows he could."

"All right," said Joe. "Then why did he try a suicidal trick like that attack—him alone against the eight of us?"

"Maybe it wasn't so suicidal," said Maury. "Maybe he didn't see Cal's pistol and thought he could take the unarmed eight of us." Maury hesitated. "Maybe he could, too. Or maybe he was just doing his duty—to do as much damage to us as he could before we got him. There's no cover around here that'd have given him a chance to escape from us. He knew that we'd see him the first time he moved."

Joe nodded, looking down at the form in the freeze-sack. For the aliens of the other ship there would be one similarity with the humans—a duty either to get home themselves with the news of contact, at all costs; or failing that, to see their enemy did not get home.

For a moment he found himself thinking of the frozen body before him almost as if it had been human. From what strange home world might this individual now be missed forever? And what thoughts had taken place in that round, gray-skinned skull as it had fallen surfaceward clinging to the ship of its enemies, seeing the certainty of its own death approaching as surely as the rocky mountainside?

"Do we have record films of the battle?" Joe asked.

"I'll get them." Maury went off.

He brought the films. Joe, feeling the weakness of his condition stealing up on him, pushed it aside and set to examining the pictorial record of the battle. Seen in the film viewer, the battle had a remote quality. The alien ship was smaller than Joe had thought, half the size of the *Harrier*. The two dropped weights had made large holes in its midships. It was not surprising that it had broken apart when rammed.

One of the halves of the broken ship had gone up and melted in a sudden flare of green light like their weapons beam, as if some internal explosion had taken place. The other half had fallen parallel to the *Harrier* and almost as slowly—as if the fragment, like the dying *Harrier*, had had yet some powers of flight—and had been lost to sight at last on the opposite side of this mountain, still falling.

Four gray bodies had spilled from the alien ship as it broke apart. Three, at least, had fallen some five miles to their deaths. The record camera had followed their dwindling bodies. And Maury was right; these had been changing even as they fell, flattening and spreading out as if in an instinctive effort to slow their fall. But, slowed or not, a five-mile fall even in this lesser-than-Earth gravity was death.

Joe put the films aside and began to ask Maury questions.

The *Harrier*, Maury told him, would never lift again. Half her drive section was melted down to magnesium alloy slag. She lay here with food supplies adequate for the men who were left for four months. Water was no problem as long as everyone existed still within the ship's recycling system. Oxygen was available in the local atmosphere and respirators would extract it. Storage units gave them housekeeping power for ten years. There was no shortage of medical supplies, the tool shop could fashion ordinary implements, and there was a good stock of usual equipment.

But there was no way of getting off this mountain.

III

The others had come into the bubble while Maury had been speaking. They stood now around the bed. With the single exception of Cal, who showed nothing, they all had a new, taut, skinned-down look about their faces, like men who have been recently exhausted or driven beyond their abilities.

"Look around you," said Jeff Ramsey, taking over from Maury when Maury spoke of the mountain. "Without help we can't leave here."

"Tell him," said Doug Kellas. Like young Jeff, Doug had not shaved recently. But where Jeff's stubble of beard was blond, Doug's was brown-dark and now marked out the hollows under his youthful cheekbones. The two had been the youngest of the Team.

"Well, this is a hanging valley," said Jeff. Jeff was the surface man geologist and meteorologist of the Team. "At one time a glacier used to come down this valley we're lying in, and over that edge there. Then the valley subsided, or the mountain rose or the climate changed. All the slopes below that cliff edge— any way down from here—brings you finally to a sheer cliff."

"How could the land raise that much?" murmured Maury, looking out and down at the green too far below to tell what it represented. Jeff shrugged.

"This is a bigger world than Earth—even if it's lighter," he said. "Possibly more liable to crustal distortion." He nodded at the peaks above them. "These are young mountains. Their height alone reflects the lesser gravity. That glacier up there couldn't have formed on that steep a slope on Earth."

"There's the Messenger," said Cal.

His deeper-toned voice brought them all around. He had been standing behind the rest, looking over their heads. He smiled a little dryly and sadly at the faint unanimous look of hostility on the faces of all but the Survey Leader's. He was unusual in the respect that he was so built as not to need their friendship. But he was a member of the Team as they were and he would have liked to have had that friendship—if it could have been had at any price short of changing his own naturally individualistic character.

"There's no hope of that," said Doug Kellas. "The Messenger was designed for launching from the ship in space. Even in spite of the lower gravity here, it'd never break loose of the planet."

The Messenger was an emergency device every ship carried. It was essentially a miniature ship in itself, with drive unit and controls for one shift through no-time and an attached propulsive unit to kick it well clear of any gravitic field that might inhibit the shift into no-time. It could be set with the location of a ship wishing to send a message back to Earth, and with the location of Earth at the moment of arrival—both figured in terms of angle and distance from the theoretical centerpoint of the galaxy, as determined by ship's observations. It would set off, translate itself through no-time in one jump back to a reception area just outside Earth's critical gravitic field, and there be picked up with the message it contained.

For the *Harrier* team, this message could tell of the aliens and call for rescue. All that was needed was the precise information concerning the *Harrier's* location in relation to Galactic Centerpoint and Earth's location.

In the present instance, this was no problem. The ship's computer log developed the known position and movement of Earth with regard to Centerpoint, with every shift and movement of the ship. And the position of the second planet of star K94 was known to the chartmakers of Earth recorded by last observation aboard the *Harrier.*

Travel in no-time made no difficulty of distance. In no-time all points coincided, and the ship was theoretically touching them all. Distance was not important, but location was. And a precise location was impossible—the very time taken to calculate it would be enough to render it impossibly inaccurate. What ships travelling by no-time operated on were calculations approximately as correct as possible—and *leave a safety factor,* read the rulebook.

Calculate not to the destination, but to a point safely short enough of it, so that the predictable error will not bring the ship out in the center of some solid body. Calculate safely short of the distance remaining . . . and so on by smaller and smaller jumps to a safe conclusion.

But that was with men aboard. With a mechanical unit like the Messenger, a one-jump risk could be taken.

The *Harrier* had the figures to risk it—but a no-time drive could not operate within the critical area of a gravitic field like this planet's. And, as Jeff had said, the propulsive unit of the Messenger was not powerful enough to take off from this mountainside and fight its way to escape from the planet

"That was one of the first things I figured," said Jeff, now. "We're more than four miles above this world's sea-level, but it isn't enough. There's too much atmosphere still above us."

"The Messenger's only two and a half feet long put together," said Maury. "It only weighs fifteen pounds earthside. Can't we send it up on a balloon or something? Did you think of that?"

"Yes," said Jeff. "We can't calculate exactly the time it would take for a balloon to drift to a firing altitude, and we have to know the time to set the destination controls. We can't improvise any sort of a booster propulsion unit for fear of jarring or affecting the destination controls. The Messenger is meant to be handled carefully and used in just the way it's designed to be used, and that's all." He looked around at them. "Remember, the first rule of a Survey Ship is that it never lands anywhere but Earth."

"Still," said Cal, who had been calmly waiting while they talked this out, "we can make the Messenger work."

"How?" challenged Doug, turning on him. "Just how?"

Cal turned and pointed to the wind-piping battlemented peaks of the mountain looming far above.

"I did some calculating myself," he said. "If we climb up there and send the Messenger off from the top, it'll break free and go."

None of the rest of them said anything for a moment. They had all turned and were looking up the steep slope of the mountain, at the cliffs, the glacier where no glacier should be able to hang, and the peaks.

"Any of you had any mountain-climbing experience?" asked Joe.

"There was a rock-climbing club at the University I went to," said Cal. "They used to practice on the rock walls of the bluffs on the St. Croix River—that's about sixty miles west of Minneapolis and St. Paul. I went out with them a few times."

No one else said anything. Now they were looking at Cal.

"And," said Joe, "as our nearest thing to an expert, you think that"—he nodded to the mountain—"can be climbed carrying the Messenger along?"

Cal nodded.

"Yes," he said slowly. "I think it can. I'll carry the Messenger myself. We'll have to make ourselves some equipment in the tool shop, here at the ship. And I'll need help going up the mountain."

"How many?" said Joe.

"Three." Cal looked around at them as he called their names. "Maury, Jeff and Doug. All the able-bodied we've got."

Joe was growing paler with the effort of the conversation.

"What about John?" he asked looking past Doug at John Martin, Number Nine of the Survey Team. John was a short, rugged man with wiry hair—but right now his face was almost as pale as Joe's, and his warmsuit bulged over the chest.

"John got slashed up when he tried to pull the alien off you," said Cal calmly. "Just before I shot. He got it clear across the pectoral muscles at the top of his chest. He's no use to me."

"I'm all right," whispered John. It hurt him even to breathe and he winced in spite of himself at the effort of talking.

"Not all right to climb a mountain," said Cal. "I'll take Maury, Jeff and Doug."

"All right. Get at it then." Joe made a little, awkward

gesture with his hand, and Maury stooped to help pull
the pillows from behind him and help him lie down.
"All of you—get on with it."

"Come with me," said Cal. "I'll show you what we're
going to have to build ourselves in the tool shop."

"I'll be right with you," said Maury. The others went
off. Maury stood looking down at Joe. They had been
friends and teammates for some years.

"Shoot," whispered Joe weakly, staring up at him.
"Get it off your chest, whatever it is, Maury." The
effort of the last few minutes was beginning to tell
on Joe. It seemed to him the bed rocked with a
seasick motion beneath him, and he longed for sleep.

"You want Cal to be in charge?" said Maury, staring down at him.

Joe lifted his head from the pillow. He blinked and
made an effort and the bed stopped moving for a
moment under him.

"You don't think Cal should be?" he said.

Maury simply looked down at him without words.
When men work and sometimes die together as happens with tight units like a Survey Team, there is
generally a closeness amongst them. This closeness, or
the lack of it, is something that is not easily talked
about by the men concerned.

"All right," Joe said. "Here's my reasons for putting
him in charge of this. In the first place he's the only
one who's done any climbing. Secondly, I think the job
is one he deserves." Joe looked squarely back up at the
man who was his best friend on the Team. "Maury, you
and the rest don't understand Cal. I do. I know that
country he was brought up in and I've had access to
his personal record. You all blame him for something
he can't help."

"He's never made any attempt to fit in with the
Team—"

"He's not built to fit himself into things. Maury—" Joe struggled up on one elbow. "He's built to make things fit him. Listen, Maury—he's bright enough, isn't he?"

"I'll give him that," said Maury, grudgingly.

"All right," said Joe. "Now listen. I'm going to violate Department rules and tell you a little bit about what made him what he is. Did you know Cal never saw the inside of a formal school until he was sixteen— and then the school was a university? The uncle and aunt who brought him up in the old voyageur's-trail area of the Minnesota-Canadian border were just brilliant enough and nutty enough to get Cal certified for home education. The result was Cal grew up in the open woods, in a tight little community that was the whole world, as far as he was concerned. And that world was completely indestructible, reasonable and handleable by young Cal Hartlett."

"But—"

"Let me talk, Maury. I'm going to this much trouble," said Joe, with effort, "to convince you of something important. Add that background to Cal's natural intellect and you get a very unusual man. Do you happen to be able to guess what Cal's individual sense of security rates out at on the psych profile?"

"I suppose it's high," said Maury.

"It isn't simply high—it just isn't," Joe said. "He's off the scale. When he showed up at the University of Minnesota at sixteen and whizzed his way through a special ordering of entrance exams, the psychology department there wanted to put him in a cage with the rest of the experimental animals. He couldn't see it. He refused politely, took his bachelor's degree and went into Survey Studies. And here he is." Joe paused. "That's why he's going to be in charge. These aliens we've bumped into could be the one thing the human race can't match. We've got to get word home. And to get word home, we've got to get someone with the Messenger to the top of that mountain."

He stopped talking. Maury stood there.

"You understand me, Maury?" said Joe. "I'm Survey Leader. It's my responsibility. And in my opinion if there's one man who can get the Messenger to the top of the mountain, it's Cal."

The bed seemed to make a slow half-swing under him suddenly. He lost his balance. He toppled back off the support of his elbow, and the sky overhead beyond the bubble began to rotate slowly around him and things blurred.

Desperately he fought to hold on to consciousness. He had to convince Maury, he thought. If he could convince Maury, the others would fall in line. He knew what was wrong with them in their feelings toward Cal as a leader. It was the fact that the mountain was unclimbable. Anyone could see it was unclimbable. But Cal was going to climb it anyway, they all knew that, and in climbing it he would probably require the lives of the men who went with him.

They would not have minded that if he had been one of them. But he had always stood apart, and it was a cold way to give your life—for a man whom you had never understood, or been able to get close to.

"Maury," he choked. "Try to see it from Cal's—try to see it from his—"

The sky spun into a blur. The world blurred and tilted.

"Orders," Joe croaked at Maury. "Cal—command—"

"Yes," said Maury, pressing him back down on the bed as he tried blindly to sit up again. "All right. All right, Joe. Lie still. He'll have the command. He'll be in charge and we'll all follow him. I promise . . ."

IV

During the next two days, the Survey Leader was only intermittently conscious. His fever ran to dangerous levels, and several times he trembled and jerked as if on the verge of going into convulsions. John Martin also, although he was conscious and able to move around and even do simple tasks, was pale, high-fevered and occasionally thick-tongued for no apparent reason. It seemed possible there was an infective agent in the claw and teeth wounds made by the alien, with which the ship's medicines were having trouble coping.

With the morning of the third day when the climbers were about to set out both men showed improvement.

The Survey Leader came suddenly back to clear-headedness as Cal and the three others were standing, all equipped in the bubble, ready to leave. They had been discussing last-minute warnings and advices with a pale but alert John Martin when Joe's voice entered the conversation.

"What?" it said. "Who's alive? What was that?"

They turned and saw him propped up on one elbow on his makeshift bed. They had left him on it since the sleeping quarters section of the ship had been completely destroyed, and the sections left unharmed were too full of equipment to make practical places for the care of a wounded man. Now they saw his eyes taking in their respirator masks, packs, hammers, the home-made pitons and hammers, and other equipment including rope, slung about them.

"What did one of you say?" Joe demanded again. "What was it?"

"Nothing, Joe," said John Martin, coming toward him. "Lie down."

Joe waved him away, frowning. "Something about one being still alive. One what?"

Cal looked down at him. Joe's face had grown lean and fallen in even in these few days but the eyes in the face were sensible.

"He should know," Cal said. His calm, hard, oddly carrying baritone quieted them all. "He's still Survey Leader." He looked around at the rest but no one challenged his decision. He turned and went into the corridor of the ship, down to the main control room, took several photo prints from a drawer and brought them back. When he got back out, he found Joe now propped up on pillows but waiting.

"Here," said Cal, handing Joe the photos. "We sent survey rockets with cameras over the ridge up there for a look at the other side of the mountain. That top picture shows you what they saw."

Joe looked down at the top picture that showed a stony mountainside steeper than the one the *Harrier* lay on. On this rocky slope was what looked like the jagged, broken-off end of a blackened oil drum—with something white spilled out on the rock by the open end of the drum.

"That's what's left of the alien ship," said Cal. "Look at the closeup on the next picture."

Joe discarded the top photo and looked at the one beneath. Enlarged in the second picture he saw that the white something was the body of an alien, lying sprawled out and stiff.

"He's dead, all right," said Cal. "He's been dead a day or two anyway. But take a good look at the whole scene and tell me how it strikes you."

Joe stared at the photo with concentration. For a

long moment he said nothing. Then he shook his head, slowly.

"Something's phony," he said at last, huskily.

"I think so too," said Cal. He sat down on the makeshift bed beside Joe and his weight tilted the wounded man a little toward him. He pointed to the dead alien. "Look at him. He's got nothing in the way of a piece of equipment he was trying to put outside the ship before he died. And that mountainside's as bare as ours. There was no place for him to go outside the ship that made any sense as a destination if he was that close to dying. And if you're dying on a strange world, do you crawl *out* of the one familiar place that's there with you?"

"Not if you're human," said Doug Kellas behind Cal's shoulder. There was the faintly hostile note in Doug's voice still. "There could be a dozen different reasons we don't know anything about. Maybe it's taboo with them to die inside a spaceship. Maybe he was having hallucinations at the end, that home was just beyond the open end of the ship. Anything."

Cal did not bother to turn around.

"It's possible you're right, Doug," he said. "They're about our size physically and their ship was less than half the size of the *Harrier.* Counting this one in the picture and the three that fell with the one that we killed here, accounts for five of them. But just suppose there were six. And the sixth one hauled the body of this one outside in case we came around for a look—just to give us a false sense of security thinking they were all gone."

Joe nodded slowly. He put the photos down on the bed and looked at Cal who stood up.

"You're carrying guns?" said Joe. "You're all armed in case?"

"We're starting out with sidearms," said Cal. "Down

here the weight of them doesn't mean much. But up there . . ." He nodded to the top reaches of the mountain and did not finish. "But you and John better move inside the ship nights and keep your eyes open in the day."

"We will." Joe reached up a hand and Cal shook it. Joe shook hands with the other three who were going. They put their masks on.

"The rest of you ready?" asked Cal, who ' ɣ this time was already across the bubble enclosure, ready to step out. His voice came hollowly through his mask. The others broke away from Joe and went toward Cal, who stepped through the bubble.

"Wait!" said Joe suddenly from the bed. They turned to him. He lay propped up, and his lips moved for a second as if he was hunting for words. "—Good luck!" he said at last.

"Thanks," said Cal for all of them. "To you and John, too. We'll all need it."

He raised a hand in farewell. They turned and went.

They went away from the ship, up the steep slope of the old glacier stream bed that became more steep as they climbed. Cal was in the lead with Maury, then Jeff, then Doug bringing up the rear. The yellow bright rays of K94 struck back at them from the ice-scoured granite surface of the slope, gray with white veinings of quartz. The warmsuits were designed to cool as well as heat their wearers, but they had been designed for observer-wearers, not working wearers. At the bend-spots of arm and leg joints, the soft interior cloth of the warmsuits soon became damp with sweat as the four men toiled upward. And the cooling cycle inside the suits made these damp spots clammy-feeling when they touched the wearer. The respirator masks also became slippery with perspiration where the soft, elastic rims of their transparent faceplates pressed against brow and cheek and chin. And to the equipment-heavy men the *feel* of the angle of the steep rock slope seemed treacherously less than eyes trained to Earth gravity reported it. Like a subtly tilted floor in a fun house at an amusement park.

They climbed upward in silence as the star that was larger than the sun of Earth climbed in the sky at their backs. They moved almost mechanically, wrapped in their own thoughts. What the other three thought were personal, private thoughts having no bearing on the moment. But Cal in the lead, his strong-boned, rectangular face expressionless, was wrapped up in two calculations. Neither of these had anything to do with the angle of the slope or the distance to the top of the mountain.

He was calculating what strains the human material walking behind him would be able to take. He would need more than their-grudging cooperation. And there was something else.

He was thinking about water.

Most of the load carried by each man was taken up with items constructed to be almost miraculously light and compact for the job they would do. One exception was the fifteen Earth pounds of components of the Messenger, which Cal himself carried in addition to his mountain-climbing equipment—the homemade crampons, pitons and ice axe-piton hammer—and his food and the sonic pistol at his belt. Three others were the two-gallon containers of water carried by each of the other three men. Compact rations of solid food they all carried, and in a pinch they could go hungry. But to get to the top of the mountain they would need water.

Above them were ice slopes, and the hook-shaped glacier that they had been able to see from the ship below.

That the ice could be melted to make drinking water was beyond question. Whether that water would be safe to drink was something else. There had been the case of another Survey ship on another world whose melted local ice water had turned out to contain as a deposited impurity a small wind-born organism that came to life in the inner warmth of men's bodies and attacked the walls of their digestive tracts. To play safe here, the glacier ice would have to be distilled.

Again, one of the pieces of compact equipment Cal himself carried was a miniature still. But would he still have it by the time they reached the glacier? They were all ridiculously overloaded now.

Of that overload, only the Messenger itself and the climbing equipment, mask and warmsuit had to be held on to at all costs. The rest could and probably would go. They would probably have to take a chance on the melted glacier ice. If the chance went against them—how much water would be needed to go the rest of the way?

Two men at least would have to be supplied. Only two men helping each other could make it all the way to the top. A single climber would have no chance.

Cal calculated in his head and climbed. They all climbed.

From below, the descending valley stream bed of the former glacier had looked like not too much of a climb. Now that they were on it, they were beginning to appreciate the tricks the eye could have played upon it by sloping distances in a lesser gravity, where everything was constructed to a titanic scale. They were like ants inching up the final stories of the Empire State Building.

Every hour they stopped and rested for ten minutes. And it was nearly seven hours later, with K94 just approaching its noon above them, that they came at last to the narrowed end of the ice-smoothed rock, and saw, only a few hundred yards ahead, the splintered and niched vertical rock wall they would have to climb to the foot of the hook-shaped glacier.

V

They stopped to rest before tackling the distance between them and the foot of the rock wall. They sat in a line on the bare rock, facing downslope, their packloads leaned back against the higher rock. Cal heard the sound of the others breathing heavily in their masks, and the voice of Maury came somewhat hollowly through the diaphragm of his mask.

"Lots of loose rock between us and that cliff," said the older man. "What do you suppose put it there?"

"It's talus," answered Jeff Ramsey's mask-hollowed voice from the far end of the line. "Weathering—heat differences, or maybe even ice from snowstorms during the winter season getting in cracks of that rock face, expanding, and cracking off the sedimentary rock it's constructed of. All that weathering's made the wall full of wide cracks and pockmarks, see?"

Cal glanced over his shoulder.

"Make it easy to climb," he said. And heard the flat sound of his voice thrown back at him inside his mask. "Let's get going. Everybody up!"

They got creakily and protestingly to their feet. Turning, they fell into line and began to follow Cal into the rock debris, which thickened quickly until almost immediately they were walking upon loose rock flakes any size up to that of a garage door, that slipped or slid unexpectedly under their weight and the angle of this slope that would not have permitted such an accumulation under Earth's greater gravity.

"Watch it!" Cal threw back over his shoulder at the others. He had nearly gone down twice when loose rock under his weight threatened to start a miniature avalanche among the surrounding rock. He labored on up the talus slope, hearing the men behind swearing and sliding as they followed.

"Spread out!" he called back. "So you aren't one behind the other—and stay away from the bigger rocks."

These last were a temptation. Often as big as a small platform, they looked like rafts floating on top of the smaller shards of rock, the similarity heightened by the fact that the rock of the cliff-face was evidently planar in structure. Nearly all the rock fragments split off had flat faces. The larger rocks seemed to offer a temptingly clear surface on which to get away from the sliding depth of smaller pieces in which the boots of the men's warmsuits went mid-leg deep with each sliding step. But the big fragments, Cal had already discovered, were generally in precarious balance on the loose rock below them and the angled slope. The lightest step upon them was often enough to make them turn and slide.

He had hardly called the warning before there was a choked-off yell from behind him and the sound of more-than-ordinary roaring and sliding of rock.

He spun around. With the masked figures of Maury on his left and Doug on his right he went scrambling back toward Jeff Ramsey, who was lying on his back, half-buried in rock fragments and all but underneath a ten by six foot slab of rock that now projected reeflike from the smaller rock pieces around it

Jeff did not stir as they came up to him, though he seemed conscious. Cal was first to reach him. He bent over the blond-topped young man and saw through the faceplate of the respirator mask how Jeff's lips were sucked in at the corners and the skin showed white in a circle around his tight mouth.

"My leg's caught." The words came tightly and hollowly through the diaphragm of Jeff's mask. "I think something's wrong with it."

Carefully, Cal and the others dug the smaller rock away. Jeff's right leg was pinned down under an edge of the big rock slab. By extracting the rock underneath it piece by piece, they got the leg loose. But it was bent in a way it should not have been.

"Can you move it?"

Jeff's face stiffened and beaded with sweat behind the mask faceplate.

"No."

"It's broken, all right," said Maury. "One down already," he added bitterly. He had already gone to work, making a splint from two tent poles out of Jeff's pack. He looked up at Cal as he worked, squatting beside Jeff. "What do we do now, Cal? We'll have to carry him back down?"

"No," said Cal. He rose to his feet. Shading his eyes against the sun overhead he looked down the hanging valley to the *Harrier*, tiny below them.

They had already used up nearly an hour floundering over the loose rock, where one step forward often literally had meant two steps sliding backward. His timetable, based on his water supplies, called for them to be at the foot of the ice slope leading to the hook glacier before camping for the night—and it was already noon of the long local day.

"Jeff," he said. "You're going to have to get back down to the *Harrier* by yourself." Maury started to protest, then shut up. Cal could see the other men looking at him.

Jeff nodded. "All right," he said. "I can make it. I can roll most of the way." He managed a grin.

"How's the leg feel?"

"Not bad, Cal." Jeff reached out a warmsuited hand and felt the leg gingerly. "More numb than anything right now."

"Take his load off," said Cal to Doug. "And give him your morphine pack as well as his own. We'll pad that leg and wrap it the best we can, Jeff, but it's going to be giving you a rough time before you get it back to the ship."

"I could go with him to the edge of the loose rock—" began Doug, harshly.

"No. I don't need you. Downhill's going to be easy," said Jeff.

"That's right," said Cal. "But even if he did need you, you couldn't go, Doug. I need you to get to the top of that mountain."

They finished wrapping and padding the broken leg with one of the pup tents and Jeff started off, half-sliding, half dragging himself downslope through the loose rock fragments.

They watched him for a second. Then, at Cal's order, they turned heavily back to covering the weary, strugglesome distance that still separated them from the foot of the rock face.

They reached it at last and passed into the shadow at its base. In the sunlight of the open slope the warmsuits had struggled to cool them. In the shadow, abruptly, the process went the other way. The cliff of the rock face was about two hundred feet in height, leading up to that same ridge over which the weather balloon had been sent to take pictures of the fragment of alien ship on the other side of the mountain. Between the steep rock walls at the end of the glacial valley, the rock face was perhaps fifty yards wide. It was torn and pocked and furrowed vertically by the splitting off of rock from it. It looked like a great chunk of plank standing on end, weathered along the lines of its vertical grain into a decayed roughness of surface.

The rock face actually leaned back a little from the vertical, but, looking up at it from its foot, it seemed not only to go straight up, but—if you looked long enough—to overhang, as if it might come down on the heads of the three men. In the shadowed depths of vertical cracks and holes, dark ice clung.

Cal turned to look back the way they had come. Angling down away behind them, the hanging valley looked like a giant's ski-jump. A small, wounded creature that was the shape of Jeff was dragging itself down the slope, and a child's toy, the shape of the *Harrier*, lay forgotten at the jump's foot.

Cal turned back to the cliff and said to the others, "Rope up."

He had already shown them how this was to be done, and they had practiced it back at the *Harrier.* They tied themselves together with the length of sounding line, the thinness of which Cal had previously padded and thickened so that a man could wrap it around himself to belay another climber without being cut in half. There was no worry about the strength of the sounding line.

"All right," said Cal, when they were tied together—himself in the lead, Maury next, Doug at the end. "Watch where I put my hands and feet as I climb. Put yours in exactly the same places."

"How'll I know when to move?" Doug asked hollowly through his mask.

"Maury'll wave you on, as I'll wave him on," said Cal. Already they were high enough up for the whistling winds up on the mountain peak to interfere with mask-impeded conversations conducted at a distance. "You'll find this cliff is easier than it looks.

Remember what I told you about handling the rope. And don't look down."

"All right."

Cal had picked out a wide rock chimney rising twenty feet to a little ledge of rock. The inner wall of the chimney was studded with projections on which his hands and feet could find purchase. He began to climb.

When he reached the ledge he was pleasantly surprised to find that, in spite of his packload, the lesser gravity had allowed him to make the climb without becoming winded. Maury, he knew, would not be so fortunate. Doug, being the younger man and in better condition, should have less trouble, which was why he had put Doug at the end, so that they would have the weak man between them.

Now Cal stood up on the ledge, braced himself against the rock wall at his back and belayed the rope by passing it over his left shoulder, around his body and under his right arm.

He waved Maury to start climbing. The older man moved to the wall and began to pull himself up as Cal took in the slack of the rope between them.

Maury climbed slowly but well, testing each hand and foothold before he trusted his weight to it. In a little while he was beside Cal on the ledge, and the ascent of Doug began. Doug climbed more swiftly, also without incident. Shortly they were all on the ledge.

Cal had mapped out his climb on this rock face before they had left, studying the cliff with powerful glasses from the *Harrier* below. Accordingly, he now made a traverse, moving horizontally across the rock face to another of the deep, vertical clefts in the rock known as chimneys to climbers. Here he belayed the rope around a projection and, by gesture and shout, coached Maury along the route.

Maury, and then Doug, crossed without trouble.

Cal then led the way up the second chimney, wider than the first and deeper. This took them up another forty-odd feet to a ledge on which all three men could stand or sit together.

Cal was still not winded. But looking at the other two, he saw that Maury was damp-faced behind the faceplate of his mask. The older man's breath was whistling in the respirator. It was time, thought Cal, to lighten loads. He had never expected to get far with some of their equipment in any case, but he had wanted the psychological advantage of starting the others out with everything needful.

"Maury," he said, "I think we'll leave your sidearm here, and some of the other stuff you're carrying."

"I can carry it," said Maury. "I don't need special favors."

"No," said Cal. "You'll leave it. I'm the judge of what's ahead of us, and in my opinion the time to leave it's now." He helped Maury off with most of what he carried, with the exception of a pup tent, his climbing tools and the water container and field rations. Then as soon as Maury was rested, they tackled the first of the two really difficult stretches of the cliff.

This was a ten-foot traverse that any experienced climber would not have found worrisome. To amateurs like themselves it was spine-chilling.

The route to be taken was to the left and up to a large, flat piece of rock wedged in a wide crack running diagonally up the rock face almost to its top. There were plenty of available footrests and handholds along the way. What would bother them was the fact that the path they had to take was around a boss, or protuberance of rock. To get around the boss it was necessary to move out over the empty atmosphere of a clear drop to the talus slope below.

Cal went first.

He made his way slowly but carefully around the outcurve of the rock, driving in one of his homemade pitons and attaching an equally homemade snap-ring to it, at the outermost point in the traverse. Passing the line that connected him to Maury through this, he had a means of holding the other men to the cliff if their holds should slip and they have to depend on the rope on their way around. The snap-ring and piton were also a psychological assurance.

Arrived at the rock slab in the far crack, out of sight of the other two, Cal belayed the rope and gave two tugs. A second later a tug came back. Maury had started crossing the traverse.

He was slow, very slow, about it. After agonizing minutes Cal saw Maury's hand come around the edge of the boss. Slowly he passed the projecting rock to the rock slab. His face was pale and rigid when he got to where Cal stood. His breath came in short, quick pants.

Cal signaled on the rope again. In considerably less time than Maury had taken Doug came around the boss. There was a curious look on his face.

"What is it?" asked Cal.

Doug glanced back the way he had come. "Nothing, I guess," he said. "I just thought I saw something moving back there. Just before I went around the corner. Something I couldn't make out."

Cal stepped to the edge of the rock slab and looked as far back around the boss as he could. But the ledge they had come from was out of sight. He stepped back to the ledge.

"Well," he said to the others, "the next stretch is easier."

VI

It was. The crack up which they climbed now slanted to the right at an almost comfortable angle.

They went up it using hands and feet like climbing a ladder. But if it was easy, it was also long, covering better than a hundred feet of vertical rock face. At the top, where the crack pinched out, there was the second tricky traverse across the rock face, of some eight feet. Then a short climb up a cleft and they stood together on top of the ridge.

Down below, they had been hidden by the mountain walls from the high winds above. Now for the first time, as they emerged onto the ridge they faced and felt them.

The warmsuits cut out the chill of the atmosphere whistling down on them from the mountain peak, but they could feel the pressure of it molding the suits to their bodies. They stood now once more in sunlight. Behind them they could see the hanging valley and the *Harrier.* Ahead was a cwm, a hollow in the steep mountainside that they would have to cross to get to a further ridge leading up to the mountain peak. Beyond and below the further ridge, they could see the far, sloping side of the mountain and, black against it, the tiny, oil-drum-end fragment of alien ship with a dot of white just outside it.

"We'll stay roped," said Cal. He pointed across the steep-sloping hollow they would need to cross to reach the further rocky ridge. The hollow seemed merely a tilted area with occasional large rock chunks perched on it at angles that to Earth eyes seemed to defy gravity. But there was a high shine where the sun's rays struck.

"Is that ice?" said Maury, shading his eyes.

"Patches of it. A thin coating over the rocks," said Cal. "It's time to put on the crampons."

They sat down and attached the metal frameworks to their boots that provided them with spiked footing. They drank sparingly of the water they carried and ate some of their rations. Cal glanced at the descending sun, and the blue-black sky above them. They would have several hours yet to cross the cwm, in daylight. He gave the order to go, and led off.

He moved carefully out across the hollow, cutting or kicking footholds in patches of ice he could not avoid. The slope was like a steep roof. As they approached the deeper center of the cwm, the wind from above seemed to be funnelled at them so that it was like a hand threatening to push them into a fall.

Some of the rock chunks they passed were as large as small houses. It was possible to shelter from the wind in their lees. At the same time, they often hid the other two from Cal's sight, and this bothered him. He would have preferred to be able to watch them in their crossings of the ice patches, so that if one of them started to slide he would be prepared to belay the rope. As it was, in the constant moan and howl of the wind, his first warning would be the sudden strain on the rope itself. And if one of them fell and pulled the other off the mountainside, their double weight could drag Cal loose.

Not for the first time, Cal wished that the respirator masks they wore had been equipped with radio intercom. But these were not and there had been no equipment aboard the *Harrier* to convert them.

They were a little more than halfway across when Cal felt a tugging on the line.

He looked back. Maury was waving him up into a shelter of one of the big rocks. He waved back and turned off from the direct path, crawling up into the ice-free overhang. Behind him, as he turned, he saw Maury coming toward him, and behind Maury, Doug.

"Doug wants to tell you something!" Maury shouted against the wind noise, putting his mask up close to Cal's.

"What is it?" Cal shouted.

"—Saw it again!" came Doug's answer.

"Something moving?" Doug nodded. "Behind us?" Doug's mask rose and fell again in agreement "Was it one of the aliens?"

"I think so!" shouted Doug. "It could be some sort of animal. It was moving awfully fast—I just got a glimpse of it!"

"Was it—" Doug shoved his masked face closer, and Cal raised his voice—"was it wearing any kind of clothing that you could see?"

"No!" Doug's head shook back and forth.

"What kind of life could climb around up here without freezing to death—unless it had some protection?" shouted Maury to them both.

"We don't know!" Cal answered. "Let's not take chances. If it is an alien, he's got all the natural advantages. Don't take chances. You've got your gun, Doug. Shoot anything you see moving!"

Doug grinned and looked harshly at Cal from inside his mask.

"Don't worry about me!" he shouted back. "Maury's the one without a gun."

"We'll both keep an eye on Maury! Let's get going now. There's only about another hour or so before the sun goes behind those other mountains— and we want to be in camp underneath the far ridge before dark!"

He led off again and the other two followed.

As they approached the far ridge, the wind seemed to lessen somewhat. This was what Cal had been hoping for—that the far ridge would give them some protection from the assault of the atmosphere they had been enduring in the open. The dark wall of the ridge, some twenty or thirty feet in sudden height at the edge of the cwm, was now only a hundred yards or so away. It was already in shadow from the descending sun, as were the downslope sides of the big rock chunks. Long shadows stretched toward a far precipice edge where the cwm ended, several thousand feet below. But the open icy spaces were now ruddy and brilliant with the late sunlight. Cal thought wearily of the pup tents and his sleeping bag.

Without warning a frantic tugging on the rope roused him. He jerked around, and saw Maury, less than fifteen feet behind him, gesturing back the way they had come. Behind Maury, the rope to Doug led out of sight around the base of one of the rock chunks.

Then suddenly Doug slid into view.

Automatically Cal's leg muscles spasmed tight, to take the sudden jerk of the rope when Doug's falling body should draw it taut. But the jerk never came.

Sliding, falling, gaining speed as he descended the rooftop-steep slope of the cwm, Doug's body no longer had the rope attached to it. The rope still lay limp on the ground behind Maury. And then Cal saw something he had not seen before. The dark shape of Doug was not falling like a man who finds himself sliding down two thousand feet to eternity. It was making no attempt to stop its slide at all. It fell limply, loosely, like a dead man—and indeed, just at that moment, it slid far upon a small, round boulder in his path which tossed it into the air like a stuffed dummy, arms and legs asprawl, and it came down indifferently upon the slope beyond and continued, gaining speed as it went.

Cal and Maury stood watching. There was nothing else they could do. They saw the dark shape speeding on and on, until finally it was lost for good among the darker shapes of the boulders farther on down the cwm. They were left without knowing whether it came eventually to rest against some rock, or continued on at last to fall from the distant edge of the precipice to the green, unknown depth that was far below them.

After a little while Maury stopped looking. He turned and climbed on until he had caught up with Cal. His eyes were accusing as he pulled in the loose rope to which Doug had been attached. They looked at it together.

The rope's end had been cut as cleanly as any knife could have cut it.

The sun was just touching the further mountains. They turned without speaking and climbed on to the foot of the ridge wall.

Here the rocks were free of ice. They set up a single pup tent and crawled into it with their sleeping bags together, as the sun went down and darkness flooded their barren and howling perch on the mountainside.

VII

They took turns sitting up in their sleeping bags, in the darkness of their tiny tent, with Cal's gun ready in hand.

Lying there in the darkness, staring at the invisible tent roof nine inches above his nose, Cal recognized that in theory the aliens could simply be better than humans—and that was that. But, Cal, being the unique sort of man he was, found that he could not believe such theory.

And so, being the unique sort of man he was, he discarded it. He made a mental note to go on trying to puzzle out the alien's vulnerability tomorrow . . . and closing his eyes, fell into a light doze that was the best to be managed in the way of sleep.

When dawn began to lighten the walls of their tent they managed, with soup powder, a little of their precious water and a chemical thermal unit, to make some hot soup and get it into them. It was amazing what a difference this made, after the long, watchful and practically sleepless night. They put some of their concentrated dry rations into their stomachs on top of the soup and Cal unpacked and set up the small portable still.

He took the gun and his ice-hammer and crawled outside the tent. In the dawnlight and the tearing wind he sought ice which they could melt and then distill to replenish their containers of drinking water. But the only ice to be seen within any reasonable distance of their tent was the thin ice-glaze—*verglas*, mountaineers back on Earth called it—over which they had struggled in crossing the cwm the day before. And Cal dared not take their only gun too far from Maury, in case the alien made a sudden attack on the tent.

There was more than comradeship involved. Alone, Cal knew, there would indeed be no hope of his getting the Messenger to the mountaintop. Not even the alien could do that job alone—and so the alien's strategy must be to frustrate the human party's attempt to send a message.

It could not be doubted that the alien realized what their reason was for trying to climb the mountain. A race whose spaceships made use of the principle of no-time in their drives, who was equipped for war, and who responded to attack with the similarities shown so far, would not have a hard time figuring out why the human party was carrying the equipment on Cal's pack up the side of a mountain.

More, the alien, had he had a companion, would probably have been trying to get message equipment of his own up into favorable dispatching position. Lacking a companion his plan must be to frustrate the human effort. That put the humans at an additional disadvantage. They were the defenders, and could only wait for the attacker to choose the time and place of his attempt against them.

And it would not have to be too successful an attempt, at that. It would not be necessary to kill either Cal or Maury, now that Doug was gone. To cripple one of them enough so that he could not climb and help his companion climb, would be enough. In fact, if one of them were crippled Cal doubted even that they could make it back to the *Harrier.* The alien then could pick them off at leisure.

Engrossed in his thoughts, half-deafened by the ceaseless wind, Cal woke suddenly to the vibration of something thundering down on him.

He jerked his head to stare upslope—and scrambled for his life. It was like a dream, with everything in slow motion—and one large chunk of rock with its small host of lesser rocks roaring down upon him.

Then—somehow—he was clear. The miniature avalanche went crashing by him, growing to a steady roar as it grew in size sweeping down alongside the ridge. Cal found himself at the tent, from which Maury was half-emerged, on hands and knees, staring down at the avalanche.

Cal swore at himself. It was something he had been

told, and had forgotten. Such places as they had camped in last night were natural funnels for avalanches of loose rock. So, he remembered now, were wide cracks like the sloping one in the cliff face they had climbed up yesterday—as, indeed, the cwm itself was on a large scale. And they had crossed the cwm in late afternoon, when the heat of the day would have been most likely to loosen the frost that held precariously balanced rocks in place.

Only fool luck had gotten them this far!

"Load up!" he shouted to Maury. "We've got to get out of here."

Maury had already seen that for himself. They left the pup-tent standing. The tent in Cal's load would do. With that, the Messenger, their climbing equipment, their sleeping bags and their food and water, they began to climb the steeply sloping wall of the ridge below which they had camped. Before they were halfway up it, another large rock with its attendant avalanche of lesser rocks came by below them.

Whether the avalanches were alien-started, or the result of natural causes, made no difference now. They had learned their lesson the hard way. From now on, Cal vowed silently, they would stick to the bare and open ridges unless there was absolutely no alternative to entering avalanche territory. And only after every precaution.

In the beginning Cal had kept a fairly regular check on how Maury was doing behind him. But as the sun rose in the bluish-black of the high altitude sky overhead the weariness of his body seemed to creep into his mind and dull it. He still turned his head at regular intervals to see how Maury was doing. But sometimes he found himself sitting and staring at his companion without any real comprehension of why he should be watching over him.

The blazing furnace of K94 overhead, climbing toward its noontime zenith, contributed to this dullness of the mind. So did the ceaseless roaring of the wind which had long since deafened them beyond any attempt at speech. As the star overhead got higher in the sky this and the wind noise combined to produce something close to hallucinations . . . so that once he looked back and for a moment seemed to see the alien following them, not astraddle the ridge and hunching themselves forward as they were, but walking along the knife-edge of rock like a monkey along a branch, foot over foot, and grasping the rock with toes like fingers, oblivious of the wind and the sun.

Cal blinked and, the illusion—if that was what it was—was gone. But its image lingered in his brain with the glare of the sun and the roar of the wind.

His eyes had fallen into the habit of focusing on the rock only a dozen feet ahead of him. At last he lifted them and saw the ridge broaden, a black shadow lying sharply across it. They had come to the rock walls below the hanging glacier they had named the Hook.

They stopped to rest in the relative wind-break shelter of the first wall, then went on.

Considering the easiness of the climb they made remarkably slow progress. Cal slowly puzzled over this until, like the slow brightening of a candle, the idea grew in him to check the absolute altimeter at his belt

They were now nearly seven thousand feet higher up than they had been at the wreck of the *Harrier.* The mask respirators had been set to extract oxygen for them from the local atmosphere in accordance with the *Harrier* altitude. Pausing on a ledge, Cal adjusted his mask controls.

For a minute there seemed to be no difference at all.

And then he began to come awake. His head cleared. He became sharply conscious, suddenly of where he stood—on a ledge of rock, surrounded by rock walls with, high overhead, the blue-black sky and brilliant sunlight on the higher walls. They were nearly at the foot of the third, and upper, battlement of the rock walls.

He looked over the edge at Maury, intending to signal the man to adjust his mask controls. Maury was not even looking up, a squat, lumpish figure in the warmsuit totally covered, with the black snout of the mask over his face. Cal tugged at the rope and the figure raised its face. Cal with his gloved hands made adjusting motions at the side of his mask. But the other's face below, hidden in the shadow of the faceplate, stared up without apparent comprehension. Cal started to yell down to him—here the wind noise was lessened to the point where a voice might have carried—and then thought better of it.

Instead he tugged on the rope in the signal they had repeated an endless number of times; and the figure below, foreshortened to smallness stood dully for a moment and then began to climb. His eyes sharpened by the fresh increase in the oxygen flow provided by his mask Cal watched that slow climb almost with amazement carefully taking in the rope and belaying it as the other approached.

There was a heaviness, an awkwardness, about the warmsuited limbs, as slowly—but strongly enough—they pulled the climber up toward Cal. There was something abnormal about their movement. As the other drew closer, Cal stared more and more closely until at last the gloves of the climber fastened over the edge of the ledge.

Cal bent to help him. But, head down not looking, the other hoisted himself up alongside Cal and a little turned away.

Then in that last instant the combined flood of instinct and a lifetime of knowledge cried certainty. And Cal knew.

The warmsuited figure beside him was Maury no longer.

VIII

Reflexes have been the saving of many a man's life. In this case, Cal had been all set to turn and climb again, the moment Maury stood beside him on the edge. Now recognizing that somewhere among these rocks, in the past fumbling hours of oxygen starvation, Maury had ceased to live and his place had been taken by the pursuing alien, Cal's reflexes took over.

If the alien had attacked the moment he stood upright on the ledge, different reflexes would have locked Cal in physical combat with the enemy. When the alien did not attack, Cal turned instinctively to the second prepared response of his body and began automatically to climb to the next ledge.

There was no doubt that any other action by Cal, any hesitation, any curiosity about his companion would have forced the alien into an immediate attack. For then there would have been no reason not to attack. As he climbed, Cal felt his human brain beginning to work again after the hours of dullness. He had time to think.

His first thought was to cut the line that bound them together, leaving the alien below. But this would precipitate the attack Cal had already instinctively avoided. Any place Cal could climb at all, the alien could undoubtedly climb with ease. Cal's mind chose and discarded possibilities. Suddenly he remembered the gun that hung innocently at his hip. With that recollection, the situation began to clear and settle in his mind. The gun evened things. The knowledge that it was the alien on the other end of the rope, along with the gun, more than evened things. Armed and prepared, he could afford to risk the present situation for a while. He could play a game of pretense as well as the alien could, he thought.

That amazing emotional center of gravity, Cal's personal sense of security and adequacy that had so startled the psychology department at the university, was once more in command of the situation. Cal felt the impact of the question—why was the alien pretending to be Maury? Why had he adapted himself to man-shape, put on man's clothes and fastened himself to the other end of Cal's climbing rope?

Perhaps the alien desired to study the last human that opposed him before he tried to destroy it. Perhaps he had some hope of rescue by his own people, and wanted all the knowledge for them he could get. If so it was a wish that cut two ways. Cal would not be sorry of the chance to study a living alien in action.

And when the showdown came—there was the gun at Cal's belt to offset the alien's awesome physical natural advantage.

They continued to climb. Cal watched the other figure below him. What he saw was not reassuring.

With each wall climbed, the illusion of humanity grew stronger. The clumsiness Cal had noticed at first—the appearance of heaviness—began to disappear. It began to take on a smoothness and a strength that Maury had never shown in the climbing. It began in fact, to look almost familiar. Now Cal could see manlike hunching and bulgings of the shoulder muscles under the warmsuit's shapelessness, as the alien climbed and a certain trick of throwing the head from right to left to keep a constant watch for a better route up the face of the rock wall.

It was what he did himself, Cal realized suddenly. The alien was watching Cal climb ahead of him and imitating even the smallest mannerisms of the human.

They were almost to the top of the battlements, climbing more and more in sunlight. K94 was already far down the slope of afternoon. Cal began to hear an increase in the wind noise as they drew close to the open area above. Up there was the tumbled rock-strewn ground of a terminal moraine and then the snow slope to the hook glacier.

Cal had planned to camp for the night above the moraine at the edge of the snow slope. Darkness was now only about an hour away and with darkness the showdown must come between himself and the alien. With the gun, Cal felt a fair amount of confidence. With the showdown, he would probably discover the reason for the alien's impersonation of Maury.

Now Cal pulled himself up the last few feet. At the top of the final wall of the battlements the windblast was strong. Cal found himself wondering if the alien recognized the gun as a killing tool. The alien which had attacked them outside the *Harrier* had owned neither weapons nor clothing. Neither had the ones filmed as they fell from the enemy ship, or the one lying dead outside the fragment of that ship on the other side of the mountain. It might be that they were so used to their natural strength and adaptability they did not understand the use of portable weapons. Cal let his hand actually brush against the butt of the sidearm as the alien climbed on to the top of the wall and stood erect, faceplate turned a little from Cal.

But the alien did not attack.

Cal stared at the other for a long second, before

turning and starting to lead the way through the terminal moraine, the rope still binding them together.
The alien moved a little behind him, but enough to
his left so that he was within Cal's range of vision, and
Cal was wholly within his. Threading his way among
the rock rubble of the moraine, Cal cast a glance at
the yellow orb of K94, now just hovering above the
sharp peaks of neighboring mountains around them.

Night was close. The thought of spending the hours
of darkness with the other roped to him cooled the
back of Cal's neck. Was it darkness the alien was
waiting for?

Above them, as they crossed the moraine the setting
sun struck blazing brilliance from the glacier and the
snow slope. In a few more minutes Cal would have to
stop to set up the puptent, if he hoped to have enough
light to do so. For a moment the wild crazy hope of a
notion crossed Cal's mind that the alien had belatedly
chosen life over duty. That at this late hour, he had
changed his mind and was trying to make friends.

Cold logic washed the fantasy from Cal's mind. This
being trudging almost shoulder to shoulder with him was
the same creature than had sent Doug's limp and helpless body skidding and falling down the long ice-slope
to the edge of an abyss. This companion alongside was
the creature that had stalked Maury somewhere among
the rocks of the mountainside and disposed of him, and
stripped his clothing off and taken his place.

Moreover, this other was of the same race and kind
as the alien who had clung to the hull of the falling
Harrier and, instead of trying to save himself and get
away on landing, had made a suicidal attack on the eight
human survivors. The last thing that alien had done,
when there was nothing else to be done, was to try to
take as many humans as possible into death with him.

This member of the same race walking side by side with Cal would certainly do no less.

But why was he waiting so long to do it? Cal frowned hard inside his mask. That question had to be answered. Abruptly he stopped. They were through the big rubble of the moraine, onto a stretch of gravel and small rock. The sun was already partly out of sight behind the mountain peaks. Cal untied the rope and began to unload the pup tent.

Out of the corner of his eyes, he could see the alien imitating his actions. Together they got the tent set up and their sleeping bags inside. Cal crawled in the tiny tent and took off his boots. He felt the skin between his shoulder blades crawl as a second later the masked head of his companion poked itself through the tent opening and the other crept on hands and knees to the other sleeping bag. In the dimness of the tent with the last rays of K94 showing thinly through its walls, the shadow on the far tent wall was a monstrous parody of a man taking off his boots.

The sunlight failed and darkness filled the tent. The wind moaned loudly outside. Cal lay tense, his left hand gripping the gun he had withdrawn from its holster. But there was no movement.

The other had gotten into Maury's sleeping bag and lay with his back to Cal. Facing that back, Cal slowly brought the gun to bear. The only safe thing to do was to shoot the alien now, before sleep put Cal completely at the other's mercy.

Then the muzzle of the gun in Cal's hand sank until it pointed to the fabric of the tent floor. To shoot was the only safe thing—and it was also the only impossible thing.

Ahead of them was the snow-field and the glacier, with its undoubted crevasses and traps hidden under untrustworthy caps of snow. Ahead of them was the final rock climb to the summit. From the beginning, Cal had known no one man could make this final stretch alone. Only two climbers roped together could hope to make it safely to the top.

Sudden understanding burst on Cal's mind. He quietly reholstered the gun. Then, muttering to himself, he sat up suddenly without any attempt to hide the action, drew a storage cell lamp from his pack and lit it. In the sudden illumination that burst on the tent he found his boots and stowed them up alongside his bag.

He shut the light off and lay down again, feeling cool and clear-headed. He had had only a glimpse in turning, but the glimpse was enough. The alien had shoved Maury's pack up into a far corner of the tent as far away from Cal as possible. But the main pockets of that pack now bulked and swelled as they had not since Cal had made Maury lighten his load on the first rock climb.

Cal lay still in the darkness with a grim feeling of humor inside him. Silently, in his own mind he took his hat off to his enemy. From the beginning he had assumed that the only possible aim one of the other race could have would be to frustrate the human attempt to get word back to the human base—so that neither race would know of the two ships' encounter.

Cal had underestimated the other. And he should not have, for technologically they were so similar and equal. The aliens had used a no-time drive. Clearly, they had also had a no-time rescue signalling device like the Messenger, which needed to be operated from the mountaintop.

The alien had planned from the beginning to join the human effort to get up into Messenger-firing position, so as to get his own device up there.

He too, had realized—in spite of his awesome natural advantage over the humans—that no single individual could make the last stage of the climb alone.

Two, roped together, would have a chance. He needed Cal as much as Cal needed him.

In the darkness, Cal almost laughed out loud with the irony of it. He need not be afraid of sleeping. The showdown would come only at the top of the mountain.

Cal patted the butt of the gun at his side and smiling, he fell asleep.

But he did not smile, the next morning when, on waking, he found the holster empty.

IX

When he awoke to sunlight through the tent walls the form beside him seemed not to have stirred, but the gun was gone.

As they broke camp, Cal looked carefully for it. But there was no sign of it either in the tent, or in the immediate vicinity of the camp. He ate some of the concentrated rations he carried and drank some of the water he still carried. He made a point not to look to see if the alien was imitating him. There was a chance, he thought, that the alien was still not sure whether Cal had discovered the replacement.

Cal wondered coldly where on the naked mountainside Maury's body might lie—and whether the other man had recognized the attacker who had killed him, or whether death had taken him unawares.

Almost at once they were on the glacier proper. The glare of ice was nearly blinding. Cal stopped and uncoiled the rope from around him. He tied himself on, and the alien in Maury's warmsuit, without waiting for a signal, tied himself on also.

Cal went first across the ice surface, thrusting

downward with the forearm-length handle of his home-made ice axe. When the handle penetrated only the few niches of top snow and jarred against solidity, he chipped footholds like a series of steps up the steep pitch of the slope. Slowly they worked their way forward.

Beyond the main length of the hook rose a sort of tower of rock that was the main peak. The tower appeared to have a cup-shaped area or depression in its center—an ideal launching spot for the Messenger, Cal had decided, looking at it through a powerful telescopic viewer from the wreck of the *Harrier*. A rare launching spot in this landscape of steeply tilted surfaces.

Without warning a shadow fell across Cal's vision. He started and turned to see the alien towering over him. But, before he could move, the other had begun chipping at the ice higher up. He cut a step and moved up ahead of Cal. He went on, breaking trail, cutting steps for Cal to follow.

A perverse anger began to grow in Cal. He was aware of the superior strength of the other, but there was something contemptuous about the alien's refusal to stop and offer Cal his turn. Cal moved up close behind the other and abruptly began chipping steps in a slightly different direction. As he chipped, he moved up them, and gradually the two of them climbed apart.

When the rope went taut between them they both paused and turned in each other's direction—and without warning the world fell out from underneath Cal.

He felt himself plunging. The cruel and sudden jerk of the rope around his body brought him up short and he dangled, swaying between ice-blue walls.

He craned his head backward and looked up. Fifteen feet above him were two lips of snow, and behind these the blue-black sky. He looked down and saw the narrowing rift below him plunge down into darkness beyond vision.

For a moment his breath caught in his chest

Then there was a jerk on the rope around him, and he saw the wall he was facing drop perhaps eighteen inches. He had been lifted. The jerk came again, and again. Steadily it progressed. A strength greater than that of any human was drawing him up.

Slowly, jerk by jerk, Cal mounted to the edge of the crevasse—to the point where he could reach up and get his gloved hands on the lip of ice and snow, to the point where he could get his forearms out on the slope and help lift his weight from the crevasse.

With the aid of the rope he crawled out at last on the downslope side of the crevasse. Just below him, he saw the alien in Maury's clothing, buried almost to his knees in loose snow, half kneeling, half-crouching on the slope with the rope in his grasp. The alien did not straighten up at once. It was as if even his great strength had been taxed to the utmost

Cal trembling stared at the other's crouched immobility. It made sense. No physical creature was possessed of inexhaustible energy—and the alien had also been climbing a mountain. But, the thought came to chill Cal's sudden hope, if the alien had been weakened, Cal had been weakened also. They stood in the same relationship to each other physically that they had to begin with.

After a couple of minutes, Cal straightened up. The alien straightened up also, and began to move. He stepped out and took the lead off to his left, circling around the crevasse revealed by Cal's fall. He circled wide, testing the surface before him.

They were nearing the bend of the hook—the point at which they could leave the glacier for the short slope of bare rock leading up to the tower of the main peak

and the cup-shaped spot from which Cal had planned
to send off the Messenger. The hook curved to their
left. Its outer bulge reached to the edge of a ridge on
their right running up to the main peak, so that there
was no avoiding a crossing of this final curve of the
glacier. They had been moving closer to the ice-edge
of the right-hand ridge, and now they were close
enough to see how it dropped sheer, a frightening
distance to rocky slopes far below.

The alien, leading the way, had found and circled
a number of suspicious spots in the glacier ice. He was
now a slack thirty feet of line in front of Cal, and some
fifty feet from the ice-edge of the rim.

Suddenly, with almost no noise—as if it had been
a sort of monster conjuring feat—the whole edge of
the ice disappeared.

The alien and Cal both froze in position.

Cal, ice axe automatically dug in to anchor the other,
was still on what seemed to be solid ice-covered rock.
But the alien was revealed to be on an ice-bridge, all
that was left of what must have been a shelf of glacier
overhanging the edge of the rocky ridge. The rock was
visible now—inside the alien's position. The ice-bridge
stretched across a circular gap in the edge of the glacier, to ice-covered rock at the edge of the gap ahead
and behind. It was only a few feet thick and the sun
glinted on it.

Slowly, carefully, the masked and hidden face of the
alien turned to look back at Cal, and the darkness
behind his faceplate looked square into Cal's eyes.

For the first time there was direct communication
between them. The situation was their translator and
there was no doubt between them about the meanings
of their conversation. The alien's ice-bridge might give
way at any second. The jerk of the alien's fall on the

rope would be more than the insecure anchor of Cal's ice-hammer could resist. If the alien fell while Cal was still roped to him, they would both go.

On the other hand, Cal could cut himself loose. Then, if the ice-bridge gave way, Cal would have lost any real chance of making the peak. But he would still be alive.

The alien made no gesture asking for help. He merely looked.

Well, which is it to be? the darkness behind his faceplate asked. If Cal should cut loose, there was only one thing for the alien to do, and that was to try to crawl on across the ice-bridge on his own—an attempt almost certain to be disastrous.

Cal felt a cramping in his jaw muscles. Only then did he realize he was smiling—a tight-lipped, sardonic smile. Careful not to tauten the rope between them, he turned and picked up the ice axe, then drove it into the ice beyond and to his left. Working step by step, from anchor point to anchor point, he made his way carefully around the gap, swinging well inside it, to a point above the upper end of the ice-bridge. Here he hammered and cut deeply into the ice until he stood braced in a two-foot hole with his feet flat against a vertical wall, lying directly back against the pull of the rope leading to the alien.

The alien had followed Cal's movements with his gaze. Now, as he saw Cal bracing himself, the alien moved forward and Cal took up the slack in the rope between them. Slowly, carefully, on hands and knees like a cat stalking in slow motion a resting butterfly, the alien began to move forward across the ice-bridge.

One foot—two feet—and the alien froze suddenly as a section of the bridge broke out behind him.

Now there was no way to go but forward. Squinting over the lower edge of his faceplate and sweating in his warmsuit, Cal saw the other move forward again. There were less than ten feet to go to solid surface. Slowly, the alien crept forward. He had only five feet to go, only four, only three—

The ice-bridge went out from under him.

X

The shock threatened to wrench Cal's arms from their shoulder-sockets—but skittering, clawing forward like a cat in high gear, the alien was snatching at the edge of the solid ice. Cal suddenly gathered in the little slack in the line and threw his weight into the effort of drawing the alien forward.

Suddenly the other was safe, on solid surface. Quickly, without waiting, Cal began to climb.

He did not dare glance down to see what the alien was doing; but from occasional tautenings of the rope around his shoulders and chest, he knew that the other was still tied to him. This was important, for it meant that the moment of their showdown was not yet. Cal was gambling that the other, perhaps secure in the knowledge of his strength and his ability to adapt, had not studied the face of this tower as Cal had studied it through the telescopic viewer from the *Harrier*.

From that study, Cal had realized that it was a face that he himself might be able to climb unaided. And that meant a face that the alien certainly could climb unaided. If the alien should realize this, a simple jerk on the rope that was tied around Cal would settle the problem of the alien as far as human competition went. Cal would be plucked from his meager hand and footholds like a kitten from the back of a chair, and the slope below would dispose of him. He sweated now, climbing, trying to remember the path up the towerside as he had planned it out, from handhold to handhold, gazing through the long-distance viewer.

He drew closer to the top. For some seconds and minutes now, the rope below him had been completely slack. He dared not look down to see what that might mean. Then finally he saw the edge of the cup-shaped depression above him, bulging out a little from the wall.

A second more and his fingers closed on it. Now at last he had a firm handhold. Quickly he pulled himself up and over the edge. For a second perspiration blurred his vision. Then he saw the little, saucer sloping amphitheater not more than eighteen feet wide, and the further walls of the tower enclosing it on three sides.

Into the little depression the light of K94 blazed from the nearly black sky. Unsteadily Cal got to his feet and turned around. He looked down the wall he had just climbed.

The alien still stood at the foot of the wall. He had braced himself there, evidently to belay Cal against a fall that would send him skidding down the rock slope below. Though what use to belay a dead man, Cal could not understand, since the more than thirty feet of fall would undoubtedly have killed him. Now, seeing Cal upright and in solid position, the alien put his hands out toward the tower wall as if he would start to climb.

Cal immediately hauled taut on the line, drew a knife from his belt and, reaching as far down as possible, cut the line.

The rope end fell in coils at the alien's feet. The alien was still staring upward as Cal turned and went as quickly as he could to the center of the cup-shaped depression.

The wind had all but died. In the semi-enclosed rock depression the reflected radiation of the star overhead made it hot. Cal unsnapped his pack and let it drop.

He stripped off the gloves of his warmsuit and, kneeling, began to open up the pack. His ears were alert. He heard nothing from outside the tower, but he knew that he had minutes at most.

He laid out the three sections of the silver-plated Messenger, and began to screw them together. The metal was warm to his touch after being in the sun-warmed backpack, and his fingers, stiff and cramped from gripping at handholds, fumbled. He forced himself to move slowly, methodically, to concentrate on the work at hand and forget the alien now climbing the tower wall with a swiftness no human could have matched.

Cal screwed the computer-message-beacon section of the nose tight to the drive section of the middle. He reached for the propulsive unit that was the third section. It rolled out of his hand. He grabbed it up and began screwing it on to the two connected sections.

The three support legs were still in the pack. He got the first one out and screwed it on. The next stuck for a moment, but he got it connected. His ear seemed to catch a scratching noise from the outside of the tower where the alien would be climbing. He dug in the bag, came out with the third leg and screwed it in. Sweat ran into his eyes inside the mask faceplate, and he blinked to clear his vision.

He set the Messenger upright on its three legs. He bent over on his knees, facemask almost scraping the ground to check the level indicator.

Now he was sure he heard a sound outside on the wall of the tower. The leftmost leg was too long. He shortened it. Now the middle leg was off. He lengthened that. He shortened the leftmost leg again . . . slowly . . . there, the Messenger was leveled.

He glanced at the chronometer on his wrist. He had

set it with the ship's chronometer before leaving. Sixty-six ship's hours thirteen minutes, and . . . the sweep second hand was moving. He fumbled with two fingers in the breast pocket of his warmsuit, felt the small booklet he had made up before leaving and pulled it out. He flipped through the pages of settings, a row of them for each second of time. Here they were . . . sixty-three hours, thirteen minutes—

A gust of wind nipped the tiny booklet from his stiffened fingers. It fluttered across the floor of the cup and into a crack in the rock wall to his right. On hands and knees he scrambled after it, coming up against the rock wall with a bang.

The crack reached all the way through the further wall, narrowing until it was barely wide enough for daylight to enter—or a booklet to exit. The booklet was caught crossways against the unevenness of the rock sides. He reached in at arm's length. His fingers touched it. They shoved it a fraction of an inch further away. Sweat rolled down his face.

He ground the thickness of his upper arm against the aperture of the crack. Gently, gently, he maneuvered two fingers into position over the near edge of the booklet. The fingers closed. He felt it. He pulled back gently. The booklet came.

He pulled it out

He was back at the Messenger in a moment, finding his place in the pages again. Sixteen hours—fourteen minutes—the computer would take four minutes to warm and fire the propulsive unit.

A loud scratching noise just below the lip of the depression distracted him for a second.

He checked his chronometer. Sixty-three hours, sixteen minutes plus . . . moving on toward thirty seconds. Make it sixty-three hours sixteen minutes even.

Setting for sixty-three hours, sixteen minutes plus four minutes—sixty-three hours, twenty minutes.

His fingers made the settings on the computer section as the second hand of his chronometer crawled toward the even minute . . .

There.

His finger activated the computer. The Messenger began to hum faintly, with a soft internal vibration.

The sound of scraping against rock was right at the lip of the depression, but out of sight.

He stood up. Four minutes the Messenger must remain undisturbed. Rapidly, but forcing himself to calmness, he unwound the rest of the rope from about him and unclipped it. He was facing the lip of the depression over which the alien would come, but as yet there was no sign. Cal could not risk the time to step to the depression's edge and make sure.

The alien would not be like a human being, to be dislodged by a push as he crawled over the edge of the lip. He would come adapted and prepared. As quickly as he could without fumbling, Cal fashioned a slipknot in one end of the rope that hung from his waist.

A gray, wide, flat parody of a hand slapped itself over the lip of rock and began to change form even as Cal looked. Cal made a running loop in his rope and looked upward. There was a projection of rock in the ascending walls on the far side of the depression that would do. He tossed his loop up fifteen feet toward the projection. It slipped off—as another hand joined the first on the lip of rock. The knuckles were becoming pale under the pressure of the alien's great weight

Cal tossed the loop again. It caught. He drew it taut.

He backed off across the depression, out of line with the Messenger, and climbed a few feet up the opposite wall. He pulled the rope taut and clung to it with desperate determination.

And a snarling tiger's mask heaved itself into sight over the edge of rock, a tiger body following. Cal gathered his legs under him and pushed off. He swung out and downward, flashing toward the emerging alien, and they slammed together, body against fantastic body.

For a fraction of a second they hung together, toppling over space while the alien's lower extremities snatched and clung to the edge of rock.

Then the alien's hold loosened. And wrapped together, still struggling, they fell out and down toward the rock below accompanied by a cascade of rocks.

XI

"Waking in a hospital," Cal said later, "when you don't expect to wake at all, has certain humbling effects."

It was quite an admission for someone like himself, who had by his very nature omitted much speculation on either humbleness or arrogance before. He went deeper into the subject with Joe Aspinall when the Survey Team Leader visited him in that same hospital back on Earth. Joe by this time, with a cane, was quite ambulatory.

"You see," Cal said, as Joe sat by the hospital bed in which Cal lay, with the friendly and familiar sun of Earth making the white room light about them, "I got to the point of admiring that alien—almost of liking him. After all, he saved my life, and I saved his. That made us close, in a way. Somehow, now that I've been opened up to include creatures like him, I seem to feel closer to the rest of my own human race. You understand me?"

"I don't think so," said Joe.

"I mean, I needed that alien. The fact brings me to

think that I may need the rest of you, after all. I never really believed I did before. It made things lonely."

"I can understand that part of it," said Joe.

"That's why," said Cal, thoughtfully, "I hated to kill him, even if I thought I was killing myself at the same time."

"Who? The alien?" said Joe. "Didn't they tell you? You didn't kill him."

Cal turned his head and stared at his visitor.

"No, you didn't kill him!" said Joe. "When the rescue ship came they found you on top of him and both of you halfway down that rock slope. Evidently landing on top of him saved you. Just his own natural toughness saved him—that and being able to spread himself out like a rug and slow his fall. He got half a dozen broken bones—but he's alive right now."

Cal smiled. "I'll have to go say hello to him when I get out of here."

"I don't think they'll let you do that," said Joe. "They've got him guarded ten deep someplace. Remember, his people still represent a danger to the human race greater than anything we've ever run into."

"Danger?" said Cal. "They're no danger to us."

It was Joe who stared at this. "They've got a definite weakness," said Cal. "I figured they must have. They seemed too good to be true from the start. It was only in trying to beat him out to the top of the mountain and get the Messenger off that I figured out what it had to be, though."

"What weakness? People'll want to hear about this!" said Joe.

"Why, just what you might expect," said Cal. "You don't get something without giving something away. What his race had gotten was the power to adapt to any situation. Their weakness is that same power to adapt."

"What're you talking about?"

"I'm talking about my alien friend on the mountain," said Cal, a little sadly. "How do you suppose I got the Messenger off? He and I both knew we were headed for a showdown when we reached the top of the mountain. And he had the natural advantage of being able to adapt. I was no match for him physically. I had to find some advantage to outweigh that advantage of his. I found an instinctive one."

"Instinctive . . ." said Joe, looking at the big, bandaged man under the covers and wondering whether he ought not to ring for the nurse.

"Of course, instinctive," said Cal thoughtfully, staring at the bed sheet. "His instincts and mine were diametrically opposed. He adapted to fit the situation. I belonged to a people who adapted situations to fit *them*. I couldn't fight a tiger with my bare hands, but I could fight something half-tiger, half something else."

"I think I'll just ring for the nurse," said Joe, leaning forward to the button on the bedside table.

"Leave that alone," said Cal calmly. "It's simple enough. What I had to do was force him into a situation where he would be between adaptations. Remember, he was as exhausted as I was, in his own way; and not prepared to quickly understand the unexpected."

"What unexpected?" Joe gaped at him. "You talk as if you thought you were in control of the situation all the way."

"Most of the way," said Cal. "I knew we were due to have a showdown. I was afraid we'd have it at the foot of the tower—but he was waiting until we were solidly at the top. So I made sure to get up to that flat spot in the tower first, and cut the rope. He had to come up the tower by himself."

"Which he was very able to do."

"Certainly—in one form. He was in one form coming

up," said Cal. "He changed to his fighting form as he came over the edge—and those changes took energy. Physical and nervous, if not emotional energy, when he was pretty exhausted already. Then I swung at him like Tarzan as he was balanced, coming over the edge of the depression in the rock."

"And had the luck to knock him off," said Joe. "Don't tell me with someone as powerful as that it was anything but luck. I was there when Mike and Sam got killed at the *Harrier*, remember."

"Not luck at all," said Cal, quietly. "A foregone conclusion. As I say, I'd figured out the balance sheet for the power of adaptation. It had to be instinctive. That meant that if he was threatened, his adaptation to meet the threat would take place whether consciously he wanted it to or not. He was barely into tiger-shape, barely over the edge of the cliff, when I hit him and threatened to knock him off into thin air. He couldn't help himself. He adapted."

"Adapted!" said Joe, staring.

"Tried to adapt—to a form that would enable him to cling to his perch. That took the strength out of his tiger-fighting form, and I was able to get us both off the cliff together instead of being torn apart the minute I hit him. The minute we started to fall, he instinctively spread out and stopped fighting me altogether."

Joe sat back in his chair. After a moment, he swore.

"And you're just now telling me this?" he said.

Cal smiled a little wryly.

"I'm surprised you're surprised," he said. "I'd thought people back here would have figured all this out by now. This character and his people can't ever pose any real threat to us. For all their strength and slipperiness, their reaction to life is passive. They adapt to it. Ours is active—we adapt it to us. On the instinctive level, we can always choose the battlefield and the weapons, and win every time in a contest."

He stopped speaking and gazed at Joe, who shook his head slowly.

"Cal," said Joe at last, "you don't think like the rest of us."

Cal frowned. A cloud passing beyond the window dimmed the light that had shone upon him.

"I'm afraid you're right," he said quietly. "For just a while, I had hopes it wasn't so."

Time to send the audience out on a light note. Or maybe not so light, after all. Just maybe, there are times when humans might wish that the *aliens* are the ones with the edge.

THE CATCH

"Sure, Mike. Gee!" said the young Tolfian excitedly, and went dashing off from the spaceship in the direction of the temporary camp his local people had set up at a distance of some three hundred yards across the grassy turf of the little valley. Watching him go, Mike Wellsbauer had to admit that in motion he made a pretty sight, scooting along on his hind legs, his sleek black-haired otterlike body leaning into the wind of his passage, and his wide, rather paddle-shaped tail extended behind him to balance the weight of his erected body. All the same . . .

"I don't like it," Mike murmured. "I don't like it one bit."

"First signs of insanity," said a female and very human voice behind him. He turned about.

"All right, Penny," he said. "You can laugh. But this could turn out to be the most unfunny thing that ever happened to the human race. Where is the rest of the crew?"

Peony Matsu sobered, the small gamin grin fading from her pert face, as she gazed up at him.

"Red and Tommy are still trying to make communication contact with home base," she said. "Alvin's out checking the flora—he can't be far." She stared at him curiously. "What's up now?"

"I want to know what they're building."

"Something for us, I'll bet,"

"That's what I'm afraid of. I've just sent for the local squire." Mike peered at the alien camp. Workers were still zipping around it in that typical Tolfian fashion that seemed to dictate that nobody went anywhere except at a run. "This time he's going to give me a straight answer."

"I thought," said Penny, "he had."

"Answers," said Mike, shortly. "Not necessarily straight ones." He heaved a sudden sigh, half of exhaustion, half of exasperation. "That young squirt was talking to me right now in English. In *English!* What can you do?"

Penny bubbled with laughter in spite of herself.

"All right, now hold it!" snapped Mike, glaring at her. "I tell you that whatever this situation is, it's serious. And letting ourselves be conned into making a picnic out of it may be just what they want."

"All right," said Penny, patting him on the arm. "I'm serious. But I don't see that their learning English is any worse than the other parts of it—"

"It's the whole picture," growled Mike, not waiting for her to finish. He stumped about to stand half-turned away from her, facing the Tolfian camp, and she gazed at his short, blocky, red-haired figure with tolerance and a scarce-hidden affection. "The first intelligent race we ever met. They've got science we can't hope to touch for nobody knows how long, they belong to some Interstellar Confederation or other with races as advanced as themselves—and they fall all over themselves learning English and doing every little thing we ask for. 'Sure, Mike!'—that's what he said to me just now . . . 'Sure, Mike!' I tell you, Penny—"

"Here they come now," she said.

A small procession was emerging from the camp. It approached the spaceship at a run, single file, the tallest Tolfian figure in the lead, and the others grading down in size behind until the last was a half-grown alien that was pretty sure to be the one Mike had sent on the errand.

"If we could just get through to home base back on Altair A—" muttered Mike; and then he could mutter no more, because the approaching file was already dashing into hearing distance. The lead Tolfian raced to the very feet of Mike and sat down on his tail. His muzzle was gray with age and authority and the years its color represented had made him almost as tall as Mike.

"Mike!" he said, happily.

The other Tolfians had dispersed themselves in a semicircle and were also sitting on their tails and looking rather like a group of racetrack fans on shooting sticks.

"Hello, Moral," said Mike, in a pleasantly casual tone. "What're you building over there now?"

"A terminal—a transport terminal, I suppose you'd call it in English, Mike," said Moral. "It'll be finished in a few hours. Then you can all go to Barzalac."

"Oh, we can, can we?" said Mike. "And where is Barzalac?"

"I don't know if you know the sun, Mike," said Moral, seriously. "We call it Aimna. It's about a hundred and thirty light-years from ours. Barzalac is the Confederation center—on its sixth planet."

"A hundred and thirty light-years?" said Mike, staring at the Tolfian.

"Isn't that right?" said Moral, confusedly. "Maybe I've got your terms wrong. I haven't been speaking your language since yesterday—"

"You speak it just fine. Just fine," said Mike. "Nice of you all to go to the trouble to learn it."

"Oh, it wasn't any trouble," said Moral. "And for you humans—well," he smiled, "nothing's too good, you know."

He said the last words rather shyly, and ducked his head for a second as if to avoid Mike's eyes.

"That's very nice," said Mike. "Now, would you mind if I asked you again *why* nothing's too good?"

"Oh, didn't I make myself clear before?" said Moral, in distressed tones. "I'm sorry—the thing is, we've met others of your people before."

"I got that, all right," said Mike. "Another race of humans, some thousands or dozens of thousands of years ago. And they aren't around any more?"

"I am very sorry," said Moral, with tears in his eyes. "Very, very sorry—"

"They died off?"

"Our loss—the loss of all the Confederation—was deeply felt. It was like losing our own, and more than our own."

"Yes," said Mike. He locked his hands behind his back and took a step up and down on the springy turf before turning back to the Tolfian squire. "Well, now, Moral, we wouldn't want that to happen to us."

"Oh, no!" cried Moral. "It mustn't happen. Some-how—we must insure its not happening."

"My attitude, exactly," said Mike, a little grimly. "Now, to get back to the matter at hand—why did you people decide to build your transportation center right here by our ship?"

"Oh, it's no trouble, no trouble at all to run one up," said Moral. "We thought you'd want one convenient here."

"Then you have others?"

"Of course," said Moral. "We go back and forth among the Confederation a lot." He hesitated. "I've arranged for them to expect you tomorrow—if it's all right with you."

"Tomorrow? On Barzalac?" cried Mike.

"If it's all right with you."

"Look, how fast is this . . . transportation, or whatever you call it?"

Moral stared at him.

"Why, I don't know, exactly," he said. "I'm just a sort of a rural person, you know. A few millionths of a second, I believe you'd say, in your terms?"

Mike stared. There was a moment's rather uncomfortable silence. Mike drew a deep breath.

"I see," he said.

"I have the honor of being invited to escort you," said Moral, eagerly. "If you want me, that is. I . . . I rather look forward to showing you around the museum in Barzalac. And after all, it was *my* property you landed on."

"Here we go again," said Mike under his breath. Only Penny heard him. "What museum?"

"What museum?" echoed Moral, and looked blank. "Oh, the museum erected in honor of those other humans. It has everything," he went on eagerly, "artifacts, pictures—the whole history of these other people, together with the Confederation. Of course"—he hesitated with shyness again—"there'll be experts around to give you the real details. As I say, I'm only a sort of rural person—"

"All right," said Mike, harshly. "I'll quit beating around the bush. Just why do you want us to go to Barzalac?"

"But the heads of the Confederation," protested Moral. "They'll be expecting you."

"Expecting us?" demanded Mike. "For what?"

"Why to take over the Confederation, of course," said Moral, staring at him as if he thought the human had taken leave of his senses. "You are going to, aren't you?"

Half an hour later, Mike had a council of war going in the lounge of Exploration Ship 29XJ. He paced up and down while Penny, Red Sommers, Tommy Anotu, and Alvin Longhand sat about in their gimballed armchairs, listening.

". . . The point's this," Mike was saying, "we can't get through to base at all because of the distance. Right, Red?"

"The equipment just wasn't designed to carry more than a couple of light-years, Mike," answered Red. "You know that. To get a signal from here to Altair we'd need a power plant nearly big enough to put this ship in its pocket."

"All right," said Mike. "Point one—we're on our own. That leaves it up to me. And my duty as captain of this vessel is to discover anything possible about an intelligent life form like this—particularly since the human race's never bumped into anything much brighter than a horse up until now."

"You're going to go?" asked Penny.

"That's the question. It all depends on what's behind the way these Tolfians are acting. That transporter of theirs could just happen to be a fine little incinerating unit, for all we know. Not that I'm not expendable—we all are. But the deal boils down to whether I'd be playing into alien hands by going along with them, or not."

"You don't think they're telling the truth?" asked

Alvin, his lean face pale against the metal bulkhead behind him.

"I don't know!" said Mike, pounding one fist into the palm of his other hand and continuing to pace. "I just don't know. Of all the fantastic stories—that there are, or have been, other ethnic groups of humans abroad in the galaxy! And that these humans were so good, so wonderful that their memory is revered and this Confederation can't wait to put our own group up on the pedestal the other bunch vacated!"

"What happened to the other humans, Mike?" asked Tommy.

"Moral doesn't know, exactly. He knows they died off, but he's hazy on the why and how. He thinks a small group of them may have just pulled up stakes and moved on—but he thinks maybe that's just a legend. And that's *it*." He pounded his fist into his palm again.

"What's it?" asked Penny.

"The way he talked about it—the way these Tolfians are," said Mike. "They're as bright as we are. Their science—and they know it as well as we do—is miles ahead of us. Look at that transporter, if it's true, that can whisk you light-years in millisecond intervals. Does it make any sense at all that a race that advanced— let alone a bunch of races that advanced—would want to bow down and say 'Master' to *us*?"

Nobody said anything.

"All right," said Mike, more calmly, "you know as well as I do it doesn't. That leaves us right on the spike. Are they telling the truth, or aren't they? If they aren't, then they are obviously setting us up for something. If they are—then there's a catch in it somewhere, because the whole story is just too good to be true. They need us like an idiot uncle, but they claim that now that we've stumbled on to them, they can't think of existing without us. They want us to take over. *Us!*"

Mike threw himself into his own chair and threw his arms wide.

"All right, everybody," he said. "Let's have some opinions."

There was a silence in which everybody looked at everybody else.

"We could pack up and head for home real sudden-like," offered Tommy.

"No," Mike gnawed at his thumb. "If they're this good, they could tell which way we went and maybe track us. Also, we'd be popping off for insufficient reason. So far we've encountered nothing obviously inimical."

"This planet's Earth-like as they come," offered Alvin—and corrected himself, hastily. "I don't mean that perhaps the way it sounded. I mean it's as close to Earth conditions as any of the worlds we've colonized extensively up until now."

"I know," muttered Mike. "Moral says the Confederation worlds are all that close—and *that* I can believe. Now that we know that nearly all suns have planets, and if these people can really hop dozens of light-years in a wink, there'll be no great trouble in finding a good number of Earth-like worlds in this part of the galaxy."

"Maybe that's it. Maybe it's just a natural thing for life forms on worlds so similar to hang together," offered Red.

"Sure," said Mike. "Suppose that was true, and suppose we were their old human-style buddies come back. Then there'd be a reason for a real welcome. But we aren't."

"Maybe they think we're just pretending not to be their old friends," said Red.

"No," Mike shook his head. "They can take one look at our ship here and see what we've got. Their old buddies wouldn't come back in anything as old-fashioned as a spaceship; and they'd hardly be wanted if they did. Besides, welcoming an old friend and inviting him to take over your home and business are two different things."

"Maybe—" said Red, hesitantly, "it's all true, but they've got it in for their old buddies for some reason, and all this is just setting us up for the ax."

Mike slowly lifted his head and exchanged a long glance with his Communications officer.

"That does it," he said. "Now you say it. That, my friends, was the exact conclusion I'd come to myself. Well, that ties it."

"What do you mean, Mike?" cried Penny.

"I mean that's it," said Mike. "If that's the case, I've got to see it through and find out about it. In other words, tomorrow I go to Barzalac. The rest of you stay here; and if I'm not back in two days, blast off for home."

"Mike," said Penny, as the others stared at him, "I'm going with you."

"No," said Mike.

"Yes, I am," said Penny, "I'm not needed here, and—"

"Sorry," said Mike. "But I'm captain. And you stay, Penny."

"Sorry, captain," retorted Penny. "But I'm the biologist. And if we're going to be running into a number of other alien life forms—" She let the sentence hang.

Mike threw up his hands in helplessness.

The trip through the transporter was, so far as Mike and Penny had any way of telling, instantaneous and painless. They stepped through a door-shaped opaqueness and found themselves in a city.

The city was even almost familiar. They had come out on a sort of plaza or court laid out on a little rise, and they were able to look down and around them at a number of low buildings. These glowed in all manners of colors and were remarkable mainly for the fact that they had no roofs as such, but were merely obscured from overhead view by an opaqueness similar to that in the transporter. The streets on which they were set stretched in all directions, and streets and buildings were clear to the horizon.

"The museum," said Moral, diffidently, and the two humans turned about to find themselves facing a low building fronting on the court that stretched wide to the left and right and far before them. Its interior seemed split up into corridors.

They followed Moral in through the arch of an entrance that stood without respect to any walls on either side and down a corridor. They emerged into a central interior area dominated by a single large statue in the area's center. Penny caught her breath, and Mike stared. The statue was, indubitably, that of a human—a man.

The stone figure was dressed only in a sort of kilt. He stood with one hand resting on a low pedestal beside him; gazing downward in such a way that his eyes seemed to meet those of whoever looked up at him from below. The eyes were gentle, and the lean, middle-aged face was a little tired and careworn, with its high brow and the sharp lines drawn around the corners of the thin mouth. Altogether, it most nearly resembled the face of a man who is impatient with the time it is taking to pose for his sculptor.

"Moral! Moral!" cried a voice; and they all turned to see a being with white and woolly fur that gave him a rather polar-bear look, trotting across the polished floor toward them. He approached in upright fashion and was as four-limbed as Moral—and the humans themselves, for that matter.

"You *are* Moral, aren't you?" demanded the newcomer, as he came up to them. His English was impeccable. He bowed to the humans—or at least he inclined the top half of his body toward them. Mike, a little uncertainly, nodded back. "I'm Arrjhanik."

"Oh, yes . . . yes," said Moral. "The Greeter. These are the humans, Mike Wellsbauer and Peony Matsu. May I . . . how do you put it . . . present Arrjhanik a Bin. He is a Siniloid, one of the Confederation's older races."

"So honored," said Arrjhanik.

"We're both very pleased to meet you," said Mike, feeling on firmer ground. There were rules for *this* kind of alien contact.

"Would you . . . could you come right now?" Arrjhanik appealed to the humans. "I'm sorry to prevent you from seeing the rest of the museum at this time"—Mike frowned; and his eyes narrowed a little—"but a rather unhappy situation has come up. One of our Confederate heads—the leader of one of the races that make up our Confederation—is dying. And he would like to see you before . . . you understand."

"Of course," said Mike.

"If we had known in advance—But it comes rather suddenly on the Adrii—" Arrjhanik led them off toward the entrance of the building and they stepped out into sunlight again. He led them back to the transporter from which they had just emerged.

"Wait a minute," said Mike, stopping. "We aren't going back to Tolfi, are we?"

"Oh, no. No," put in Moral from close behind him. "We're going to the Chamber of Deputies." He gave Mike a gentle push; and a moment later they had stepped through into a small and pleasant room half-filled with a dozen or so beings each so different one from the other that Mike had no chance to sort them out and recognize individual characteristics.

Arrjhanik led them directly to the one piece of furniture in the room which appeared to be a sort of small table incredibly supported by a single wire-thin leg at one of the four corners. On the surface of this lay a creature or being not much bigger than a seven-year-old human child and vaguely catlike in form. It lay on its side, its head supported a little above the table's surface by a cube of something transparent but apparently not particularly soft, and large colorless eyes in its head focused on Mike and Penny as they approached.

Mike looked down at the small body. It showed no signs of age, unless the yellowish-white of the thin hair covering its body was a revealing shade. Certainly the hair itself seemed brittle and sparse.

The Adri—or whatever the proper singular was—stirred its head upon its transparent pillow and its pale eyes focused on Mike and Penny. A faint, drawn out rattle of noise came from it.

"He says," said Arrjhanik, at Mike's elbow, "'You cannot refuse. It is not in you.'"

"Refuse what?" demanded Mike, sharply. But the head of the Adri lolled back suddenly on its pillow and the eyes filmed and glazed. There was a little murmur that could have been something reverential from all the beings standing about; and without further explanation the body of the being that had just died thinned suddenly to a ghostly image of itself, and was gone.

"It was the Confederation," said Arrjhanik, "that he knew you could not refuse."

"Now wait a minute," said Mike. He swung about so that he faced them all, his stocky legs truculently apart. "Now, listen—you people are acting under a misapprehension. I can't accept or refuse anything. I haven't the authority. I'm just an explorer, nothing more."

"No, no," said Arrjhanik, "there's no need for you to say that you accept or not, and speak for your whole race. That is a formality. Besides, we know you will not refuse, you humans. How could you?"

"You might be surprised," said Mike. Penny hastily jogged his elbow.

"Temper!" she whispered. Mike swallowed, and when he spoke again, his voice sounded more reasonable.

"You'll have to bear with me," he said. "As I say, I'm an explorer, not a diplomat. Now, what did you all want to see me about?"

"We wanted to see you only for our own pleasure," said Arrjhanik. "Was that wrong of us? Oh, and yes— to tell you that if there is anything you want, anything the Confederation can supply you, of course you need only give the necessary orders—"

"It is so good to have you here," said one of the other beings.

A chorus of voices broke out in English all at once, and the aliens crowded around. One large, rather walruslike alien offered to shake hands with Mike, and actually did so in a clumsy manner.

"Now, wait. Wait!" roared Mike. The room fell silent. The assembled aliens waited, looking at him in an inquiring manner.

"Now, listen to me!" snapped Mike. "And answer one simple question. What is all this you're trying to give to us humans?"

"Why, everything," said Arrjhanik. "Our worlds, our people, are yours. Merely ask for what you want. In fact—please ask. It would make us feel so good to serve you, few though you are at the moment here."

"Yes," said the voice of Moral, from the background. "If you'll forgive me speaking up in this assemblage— they asked for nothing back on Tolfi, and I was forced to exercise my wits for things to supply them with. I'm afraid I may have botched the job."

"I sincerely hope not," said Arrjhanik, turning to look at the Tolfian. Moral ducked his head, embarrassedly.

"Mike," said Arrjhanik, turning back to the human, "something about all this seems to bother you. If you would just tell us what it is—"

"All right," said Mike. "I will." He looked around at all of them. "You people are all being very generous. In fact, you're being so generous it's hard to believe. Now, I accept the fact that you may have had contact with other groups of humans before us. There's been speculation back on our home world that our race might have originated elsewhere in the galaxy, and that would mean there might well be other human groups in existence we don't even know of. But even assuming that you may have reached all possible limits of love and admiration for the humans you once knew, it still doesn't make sense that you would be willing to just make us a gift of all you possess, to bow down to a people who—we're not blind, you know—possess only a science that is childlike compared with your own."

To Mike's surprise, the reaction to this little speech was a murmur of admiration from the group.

"So analytical. So very human!" said the walruslike alien warmly in tones clearly pitched to carry to Mike's ear.

"Indeed," said Arrjhanik, "we understand your doubts. You are concerned about what, in our offer, is . . . you have a term for it—"

"The catch," said Mike grimly and bluntly. "What's the catch?"

"The catch. Yes," said Arrjhanik. "You have to excuse me. I've only been speaking this language of yours for—"

"Just the last day or so, I know," said Mike, sourly.

"Well, no. Just for the last few hours, actually. But—" went on Arrjhanik, "while there's no actual way of putting your doubts to rest, it really doesn't matter. More of your people are bound to come. They will find our Confederation open and free to all of them. In time they will come to believe. It would be presumptuous of us to try to convince you by argument."

"Well, just suppose you try it anyway," said Mike, unaware that his jaw was jutting out in a manner which could not be otherwise than belligerent

"But we'd be only too happy to!" cried Arrjhanik, enthusiastically. "You see"—he placed a hand or paw, depending on how you looked at it, gently on Mike's arm—"all that we have nowadays, we owe to our former humans. This science you make such a point of—they developed it in a few short thousand years. The Confederation was organized by them. Since they've been gone—"

"Oh, yes," interrupted Mike. "Just how did they go? Mind telling me that?"

"The strain—the effort of invention and all, was too much for them," said Arrjhanik, sadly. He shook his head. "Ah," he said, "they were a great people— you *are* a great people, you humans. Always striving, always pushing, never giving up. We others are but pale shadows of your kind. I am afraid, Mike, that your cousins worked themselves to death, and for our sake. So you see, when you think we are giving you something that is ours, we are really just returning what belongs to you, after all."

"Very pretty," said Mike. "I don't believe it. No race could survive who just gave everything away for nothing.

And somewhere behind all this is the catch I spoke of. That's what you're not telling me—what all of you will be getting out of it, by turning your Confederation over to us."

"But . . . now I understand!" cried Arrjhanik. "You *didn't* understand. *We* are the ones who will be getting. You humans will be doing all the giving. Surely you should know that! It's your very nature that ensures that, as our friend who just died, said. You humans can't help yourselves, you can't keep from it!"

"Keep from what?" yelled Mike, throwing up his hands in exasperation."

"Why," said Arrjhanik, "I was sure you understood. Why from assuming all authority and responsibility, from taking over the hard and dirty job of running our Confederation and making it a happy, healthy place for us all to live, safe and protected from any enemies. *That* is what all the rest of us have been saddled with these thousands of years since that other group of your people died; and I can't tell you"— Arrjhanik, his eyes shining, repeated his last words strongly and emphatically—"I can't tell you how badly things have gone to pot, and how very, very glad we are to turn it all over to you humans, once again!"